A LITTLE BIT

Wicked

THE WICKEDS: DARK KNIGHTS AT BAYSIDE

MELISSA FOSTER

ISBN-13: 978-1948868433
ISBN-10: 1-948868-43-1

Cover Design: Elizabeth Mackey Designs
Cover Photography: Michelle Lancaster

WORLD LITERARY PRESS
PRINTED IN THE UNITED STATES OF AMERICA

A Note to Readers

Set on the sandy shores of Cape Cod, the Wickeds feature fiercely protective heroes, strong heroines, and unbreakable family bonds. If you think bikers are all the same, you haven't met the Dark Knights. The Dark Knights are a motorcycle club, not a gang. Their members stick together like family and will stop at nothing to keep their communities safe. Justin came into the Wicked family after a harsh upbringing by a thieving father. He's gone through a lot to become a true Wicked, and he's made them proud. Now he's ready to show the woman he loves exactly what type of man he is. But Chloe Mallery has experienced her own difficult times, and as a result she's sworn off tough guys. When tragedy strikes, will their difficult pasts draw them together, or will Justin's protective nature be too much for Chloe's independent heart to accept?

All Love in Bloom books may be enjoyed as stand-alone novels or as part of the larger series, so dive into this hilarious, deeply emotional, heart-pounding romance.

On the next page you will find a character map of the Wicked world. You can also download a free copy here: www.MelissaFoster.com/Wicked-World-Character-Map.html

The Wickeds are the cousins of the Whiskeys, each of whom have already been given their own stories. You can download the first book in the Whiskey series, TRU BLUE, and a Whiskey/Wicked family tree here:

TRU BLUE
www.MelissaFoster.com/TheWhiskeys

WHISKEY/WICKED Family Tree
www.MelissaFoster.com/Wicked-Whiskey-Family-Tree

Remember to sign up for my newsletter to make sure you don't miss out on future Whiskey releases:
www.MelissaFoster.com/News

For information about more of my sexy romances, all of which can be read as stand-alone novels or as part of the larger series, visit my website:
www.MelissaFoster.com

If you prefer sweet romance with no explicit scenes or graphic language, please try the Sweet with Heat series written under my pen name, Addison Cole. You'll find the same great love stories with toned-down heat levels.

Happy reading!
~ Melissa

THE WICKED WORLD

DARK KNIGHTS AT BAYSIDE

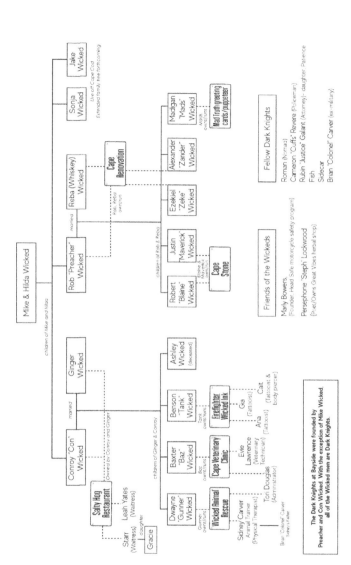

Mike & Hilda Wicked

children of Mike and Hilda

Ginger Wicked — married — **Conroy "Con" Wicked**

Owned by Conroy and Ginger

Salty Hog Restaurant

Leah Yates (Waitress)

daughter

Starr (Waitress)

Gracie

children of Ginger & Conroy

Dwayne "Gunner" Wicked

Gunner owns/runs

Wicked Animal Rescue

Sidney Carver
Animal Trainer

Brian "Colonel" Carver
Sidney's Father

Baxter "Baz" Wicked

Baz owns/runs

Cape Veterinary Clinic

Evie Lawrence (Veterinary Technician)

Tori Douglas (Administrator)

Benson "Tank" Wicked

Tank owns/runs

Firefighter Wicked Ink

Gia (Tattooist)

Aria (Tattooist)

Cait (Tattooist & body piercer)

Ashley Wicked (deceased)

Rob "Preacher" Wicked — married — **Reba (Whiskey) Wicked**

Rob, Reba own/run

Cape Renovation

children of Rob & Reba

Robert "Blaine" Wicked

Justin "Maverick" Wicked

Blaine & Maverick own/run

Cape Stone

Ezekiel "Zeke" Wicked

Alexander "Zander" Wicked

Madigan "Mads" Wicked

Mads owns/runs

Mad Truth greeting cards/puppeteer

Sonja Wicked

Jake Wicked

Live at Cape Cod
Extended family tree forthcoming

Friends of the Wickeds

Marly Bowers
(Founder Head Safe motorcycle safety program)

Persephone "Steph" Lockwood
(P-net/Owns Great Vibes herbal shop)

Fellow Dark Knights

Roman (Nomad)

Cameron "Cuffs" Revere (Policeman)

Rubin "Justice" Galant (Attorney)- daughter Patience

Fish

Sidecar

Brian "Colonel" Carver (ex-military)

The Dark Knights at Bayside were founded by Preacher and Con Wicked. With the exception of Mike Wicked, all of the Wicked men are Dark Knights.

Chapter One

IF ALAN ROGERS had been referred by anyone other than Chloe Mallery—the only woman Justin Wicked wanted in his bed—Justin might have already cut off the long-winded, condescending jerk and been on his way out for a drink with his older brother and business partner, Blaine. They'd spent the hour since closing time listening to the executive director of the Lower Cape Assisted Living Facility (LOCAL) drone on about his expensive home and the elaborate patio he wanted them to install.

"I assume you two will be doing the work?" Alan asked, giving Justin and Blaine a scrutinizing stare.

Justin could feel the pompous prick judging his tattoos, worn jeans, black T-shirt sporting a Dark Knights at Bayside motorcycle club logo, biker boots, and the leather jewelry he wore. The Dark Knights were known in most circles for the work they did to keep the community safe, and for their charitable efforts, like raising awareness about suicide and bullying prevention. Justin doubted this guy, with his fancy suit and patronizing looks, had any idea about the good they did, and he didn't give a rat's ass what the guy thought of them. After spending nearly a third of his life afraid to envision a *tomorrow*, much less a future, not a day passed when Justin didn't thank his lucky stars for the Wickeds and the motorcycle club that his father, Rob "Preacher" Wicked, and his uncle Conroy had founded more than thirty years ago.

The tension on Alan's face eased as he shifted his attention to Blaine, just as Justin had known it would. While Justin carried a *usually* well-hidden chip on his shoulder from the rough life he'd lived prior to being fostered and then adopted by the Wickeds, Blaine was a James Marsden lookalike with an easy smile and clear, unhaunted eyes. Like Justin, Blaine was a member of the club, along with their other two brothers. But Blaine played the games Justin refused to take part in, like wearing button-down shirts or Cape Stone polos and covering most of his tattoos when he was at work. But looks could be deceiving. His badass brother was a fucking *beast* who wouldn't hesitate to unleash his wrath in order to protect others.

No one knew how deceiving looks could be better than Justin. The universe had known exactly where he belonged when he'd been placed in the Wicked household. He and his brothers shared the same tall, broad-shouldered stature, dark hair, and ice-blue eyes as Preacher. Their younger sister also shared their coloring, though she was petite, and her eyes were as clear as the summer sky. No one had ever guessed that Justin was adopted.

"I'll be drawing up the plans," Blaine said, exchanging a knowing glance with Justin.

"But as we explained, our team will be laying the stone." Justin rolled his shoulders back, feeling twitchy from standing still too long, and said, "Our guys are bonded and insured and have worked with us for years. You're in competent hands."

Alan nodded and said, "Chloe has good things to say about

you *boys*."

Justin gritted his teeth against the man's condescending tone. Preacher called them *his boys*, but he said it with respect and pride. Even their sister, Madigan, called them *boys* from time to time, but always with the loving tone of an adoring sibling. But he'd had enough of this guy's attitude. He pushed to his feet and said, "*Boys?* I'm pretty sure Chloe can attest to—"

"That's good to hear," Blaine interrupted, shooting Justin a biting look. "We always appreciate referrals. We'll need to come out and assess the property before giving you an estimate."

They scheduled an appointment to see the property the following Thursday morning. Alan wouldn't be home, but he assured them that his wife could show them around. Justin couldn't imagine what woman would marry his pretentious ass. He bit his tongue until Alan walked out the showroom doors, and then he said, "Fucking prick."

"Maverick, you sure you want to take on this job?" Blaine asked.

Like Preacher, Justin went by his given name in business and by Maverick, his road name, when he was with other Dark Knights, while Blaine and their younger brothers, Zeke and Zander, preferred not to use road names. Before Justin could answer, the showroom doors opened and in walked Zander and their cousin Dwayne aka Gunner. Like Justin's their jeans were worn and their boots scuffed.

Gunner, a stocky Marine-turned-animal-rescuer with closely shorn blond hair and tattoos from neck to wrist, hiked a thumb over his shoulder and said, "Who was that douchebag?"

"He works with Chloe." Justin was as close to Gunner and his brothers, who also went by their road names, Tank and Baz, as he was to his own siblings. He'd also been close to their late sister, Ashley, who had committed suicide by overdosing several years ago, when she was in college.

"Someone needs to take the stick out of his ass," Zander said as he hoisted himself up to sit on the table where Blaine was gathering brochures. Zander's filter was nearly nonexistent. As a kid with a learning disability, he had always been the class clown—anything to keep his nose out of the books. Zeke, who was only a year older, had become his protector and his tutor. Zander was twenty-eight now, and he was still a jokester.

"No kidding." Justin turned to Blaine and said, "And to answer your question, *yes*, I'm sure I want to take on the job. Chloe asked for a favor, and she never asks for a damn thing."

"Then why are you always doing shit for her?" Gunner asked.

"Because we're friends, and that's what friends do."

Zander cocked a grin and said, "He thinks it will get *Uptown Girl* into his bed."

Justin glared at him. They were always teasing him about her being out of his league. He'd met her through his closest female friend, Violet, who owned Summer House Inn in Wellfleet with her sister, Desiree. Chloe had immediately caught his attention, and yeah, at first glance she was a tall, blond, regal beauty. The kind of woman who wouldn't give a biker the time of day. But she sure as hell flirted with him in her own scorching-hot way, though he knew it looked to others an awful lot like she was blowing him off. But he'd learned her little *tells*—the hitching of her breath, the extra second she took before speaking to steel herself against their white-hot chemistry. Her keen hazel eyes and smart-ass banter intrigued him as much as her brilliant mind and gorgeous body. He knew in his gut that there was a lot more to Chloe—and to *them*—than met the eye, and he was determined to peel away those perfectly put together layers even if it took him a lifetime.

"Fuck that," Gunner said. "She's gorgeous, but you've been dicking around with her forever. It's time to find another woman to ride your hog."

"*Jesus*. Do you really do shit expecting sex in return?" Justin shot him a disbelieving look.

"No, man," Gunner said. "I didn't mean it like that."

"But you've got to admit, you're *always* helping her—like she's your *woman*, not just your friend," Zander said.

"I don't keep a tally on friendship, and a woman doesn't have to be *mine* for me to treat her well. Doesn't *love, loyalty, and respect for all* mean anything to you?" He knew they were just giving him shit and that they all lived by the Dark Knights' creed, but Alan Rogers had put him in a crappy mood.

"Of course, man," Gunner said.

"Good. Then shut your mouth about Chloe. I'm not just interested in *screwing* her, and she's not ready for me *yet*," Justin said arrogantly. "She still believes her Prince Charming wears a frigging tie, and that's okay. I get it. She's a classy chick. But trust me, one day she'll get out of her own fucking way and know who her man is meant to be. Some things can't be rushed." That was a lesson Justin had learned long ago. He'd been placed with the Wickeds as a foster child when he was eleven, and it had taken him about a year to open up to them. Twenty-plus years later, he still considered it the best thing he'd ever done.

"I'm going to call Chloe and let her know we met the guy. Be right back." Justin walked out of the showroom and headed toward his office. Chloe answered on the second ring.

"Mr. *Wicked*, my favorite biker boy. To what do I owe this

pleasure?"

Her alluring voice brought a smile to his face. "Hey, heart-breaker. I just met with the guy you referred, Rogers. Can't say I like him much."

"I know he's a little strange, but he's my boss, and his wife is the sweetest woman on earth. When I saw her a few weeks ago, the patio was all she could talk about. She shouldn't pay the price for his being weird. I would really appreciate you helping them out."

"Only for you, princess." He had about a hundred terms of endearment for her because she was too complex and compelling for just one.

"I don't think I've ever worn a tiara," she teased.

"Then I'll have to fix that."

"You realize I said *tiara* and not spiked leather collar, right?"

Man, he dug her. "Does that mean you've worn a leather collar before?"

"Oh my gosh. *No.*" Her embarrassment radiated through the phone.

"I might have to fix that, too."

"In your dreams. Listen, I hate to cut this short," she said apologetically. "But I just got to Undercover. Can we talk later?" Undercover was a bar in Truro owned by their buddy Colton.

"Sure, no worries." Justin ended the call and headed back to the guys, wondering what was going on at Undercover.

"Hey, just a heads-up," Gunner said as Justin joined them. "The cops are closing in on that dogfighting ring." Gunner and his brother Baz, a veterinarian, had uncovered a dogfighting ring a couple of weeks ago and had alerted the police. In situations where animals were at risk, they worked with the authorities to get them to safety at Gunner's rescue. "When they shut it down, I'll need help transporting the dogs back to the rescue. Think either of you can be there to help?"

"Of course," Justin said.

"I'll make time. Any idea when it's going down?" Blaine asked.

"Cuffs will update us at church Wednesday night." Cameron "Cuffs" Revere was a policeman and a Dark Knight, and *church* was what the club called their weekly meetings. Gunner clapped a hand on Justin's shoulder and said, "Want to hit the Hog?" Gunner's parents, Conroy and Ginger, owned a restaurant and bar called the Salty Hog, a favorite haunt for locals, tourists, and of course, the Dark Knights.

"Not tonight," Justin said. "I'm heading up to Undercover."

Blaine pulled his keys from his pocket and said, "Is Chloe going to be there?"

Justin nodded.

"Does she have another date?" Blaine asked.

"Dude, is she still wasting her time using those dating apps?" Gunner asked. "Going out with clean-cut guys who work desk jobs and probably fuck for three-minutes, missionary style, without messing up her hair?"

Justin gritted his teeth against the idea of Chloe fucking anyone but him and said, "I don't know what she's up to tonight, but I want to make sure she's safe."

"If Chloe's there, you can count me in." Zander smirked. "I'll call Zeke and have him meet us there." He was always trying to drag Zeke into his playboy ways, though Zeke preferred to commune with nature rather than hang out at clubs. "Hey, Maverick, may the best Wicked win."

As they left the showroom, Justin said, "I thought you liked your pretty face in one piece, little brother."

"You misheard me, bro. I like my pretty face *on* a *woman's* piece." Zander laughed and high-fived Gunner as they headed for their motorcycles.

"Idiots," Justin said as he locked the showroom doors. "Blaine, you coming?"

"Someone's got to make sure the animals don't get out of hand."

UNDERCOVER WAS THE only nightclub in Truro, a small beach town, and like on most summer nights, it was packed. Justin's eyes swept over the crowded dance floor as he made his way toward the bar. Colored lights rained over scantily clad women and testosterone-laden men, who were bumping and grinding to a seductive beat. He'd seen Chloe dance plenty of times when they were out with friends. She had moves that could make a dead man come. As he wove past the last few tables and joined Blaine and the others at the bar, he was relieved not to have spotted her on the dance floor with another guy.

Blaine ordered a round of beers and motioned across the room. Justin followed his gaze to Chloe, looking sexy as sin in a black sleeveless dress as she entered the room from the hallway that led to the ladies' room. Her hair was like spun gold. It brushed her shoulders and framed her gorgeous face as she moved gracefully through the crowd. She stood out like a diamond in a sea of rocks. Chloe didn't rely on low-cut tops or short skirts like other women did. She was confident and smart, and she had a sharp mouth. A mouth Justin had fantasized about so many times, he was sure he knew exactly how it would taste the first time they kissed, how it would feel the first time she wrapped her luscious lips around his cock, and the way that mouth would look when she cried out his name as his face was buried between her legs.

"Damn, bro," Zander said, tearing Justin from his reverie. "I don't care if you smash my face. She'd be worth every bruise."

Justin shot him a dark stare, then turned his attention back to Chloe as she lowered herself to a chair across from another fucking clean-cut *Ken doll* wearing a button-down shirt and tie.

"Looks like a date to me," Blaine said, handing Justin a beer.

Justin took a swig, his eyes trained on Chloe.

As though she could feel him watching her, she looked over. Their eyes collided with the scorching flames of a blowtorch. Her lips tipped up at the edges, and Justin felt a tug deep in his chest. There it was, the moment that burned past the heat to the *something more* he couldn't name but knew existed.

In pure Chloe fashion, she narrowed her eyes and shifted in her chair, crossing her long legs. He fucking loved her legs and she knew it. She lifted her chin in that defiant way she'd been taunting him with since the day they'd met and turned her beautiful eyes on the geek sitting across from her.

Justin ground out a curse. He tried to focus on the shit his brothers and cousin were saying, but like metal to magnet, his attention was drawn back to Chloe. She looked bored, and her eyes skirted back to him. *That's it, baby, you know you want me.*

Her date pulled out his phone and pressed it to his ear as he stood up. He held up one finger to Chloe and walked away from the table. *Fucking idiot.* Justin took advantage of the opening and headed over to her. She watched him approach. Her poorly stifled smile didn't hide a damn thing.

"Hey, blondie," Justin said as he took the seat across from her. "What kind of douchebag leaves a gorgeous woman alone?"

"The most boring kind on earth," Chloe said, stealing a glance in the direction the guy had gone. She leaned across the table, eyes dancing with mischief, and said, "Any chance you want to pretend to be my jealous ex-boyfriend?"

Justin scoffed. "You've got to be kidding me. Is he being disrespectful? Because if he is—"

"*No.* He's just a total dud, and I don't want to sit here anymore." She sighed and said, "I've ended so many dates before dinner, I'm starting to feel like a bitch."

"Maybe it's time you stop making those dates in the first place."

"I'm not so sure you're wrong about that." She cocked a brow and said, "I'll owe you big-time if you save me the notch in my *bitch belt* and be that jealous ex-boyfriend."

"I'm not into debts. And trust me, babe. I will *never* be your *ex*-boyfriend. But I will be your *last*, because once you realize you're meant to be with me, no other man will ever be enough."

She rolled her eyes. "Never mind. I've got this." She sat up straighter, readying for battle, and looked directly at the soon-to-be-ditched guy, who was now heading back to the table.

Justin knew damn well she could handle herself, but he'd take great pleasure getting rid of that asshole. "What's the dude's name?"

"Jeffrey."

"*Figures.*" He pushed to his feet and strode over to the loser, planting himself between the guy and Chloe. "You Jeffrey?"

"Yes. And you are?" He tried to peer around Justin.

Justin moved with him, blocking his view. "I'm Chloe's friend. She's done with this date. It's time for you to leave."

Confusion riddled his brow. "What…?"

"Sorry, man, but she's not into you. Now turn around and walk out of the bar." Justin had at least twenty pounds of muscle on the guy. But it wouldn't matter if Jeffrey was as big as a house. Justin was fearless, and he backed down for no one.

"But—"

Justin stepped closer.

Jeffrey uttered "bitch" and turned to leave. Justin grabbed his arm and spun him around, getting right in his face, fuming through clenched teeth, "Say one more word about the woman that you *never* should have been allowed near, and it will be your *last*."

A bead of sweat appeared on Jeffrey's forehead.

"Now get out of here." Justin waited until the guy was out the door before returning to Chloe, who was shielding her face in embarrassment. "Come on, dollface. I'll give you a ride home."

"I *told* you I could handle it. You didn't have to go all caveman on him." She reached for her purse and said, "I have my car. I met him here."

"Then I'll walk you to your car."

"I appreciate the offer, but you don't need to."

"No shit. But I'm not the kind of guy who lets a lady leave alone, so let's go, sweet thing. Smile and head for the door."

"You're so pushy," she said as they cut through the crowd.

She'd said it teasingly, but he knew *little Miss Independent* better than that. She was proud of being self-reliant. What he didn't know was *why* she was dead set against letting anyone else take care of her.

"What did you say to him?" she asked.

"I told him the date was over." He held the door open, scanning the lot as he followed her into the warm night. "Do you see his car?"

"No. He was parked over there." She pointed to the far end of the lot. "He's gone," she said.

Justin put his arm protectively around her. As they walked to her car, he slid his hand to her waist and pulled her closer. She lifted her eyes to his and the temperature spiked. Her cheeks flushed, and he knew she felt the same soul-searing impact he did.

She jammed her hand into her purse, moving out of his grasp as she withdrew her keys. "I owe you one," she said a little breathlessly.

"You'll never owe me anything, baby. Why do you waste your time with losers like that?"

She shrugged one shoulder. "On nights like this, I have no idea."

"A woman like you shouldn't be screwing around with dating apps and Ken dolls when you've got a real man standing right in front of you."

"*Justin,*" she said apologetically. "You know I swore off dating bad boys a long time ago."

"That's what you keep saying, but you have no idea how *good* bad can be." He stepped closer, trailing his fingers along her arm, loving the hitch in her breath. "When you realize the error of your ways, you know where to find me." He kissed her cheek and said, "'Night, hot lips. Be safe."

Chapter Two

TUESDAY AFTERNOON, CHLOE was in her office gathering supplies for an orientation meeting while she spoke to her younger sister, Serena, via her Bluetooth earbuds. "What about the grass skirt and coconut top you wore to that Halloween party a few years ago? Do you think you can find it for me?"

"Sure, but let me just remind you how much you teased me for wearing it. I believe you said I shouldn't strut my tatas for every Tom, Dick, and Harry."

"Yeah, well, this is a book club meeting with the girls. I think I'm safe." Chloe ran an online erotic romance book club with her friend Daphne. They were reading a romance novel set in Hawaii, and Chloe had spent weeks planning an island-themed night for their next meeting, which was taking place on Cahoon Hollow Beach a week from Friday.

"What about leis and that kind of thing?" Serena asked. "Do you need any of that stuff? I'm not sure I kept any, but I can look."

"I already bought them and everything else. I even found an awesome drink hut with a grass roof that I can set up over my card table. It came with a grass-skirted tablecloth. I'm going to play tropical music, serve fruity drinks in coconut cups, and grill kebobs over the bonfire. I'm ridiculously excited. I mean, it's a book club meeting, not a banquet."

"It's too bad Harper and Tegan are going to miss it." Harper and Tegan were two of their friends. Tegan owned an amphitheater and she and Harper had recently started their own production company. They were too busy preparing for the opening to join them for the meeting.

"I'll take lots of pictures. They'll feel like they were there."

"Maybe one day I'll become a reader and join your club." Serena sounded serious, but she'd never been one to sit still, and now that she was married to their childhood friend Drake Savage, her downtime was spoken for.

"I won't hold my breath," Chloe said as she opened her file cabinet drawer and fished out the files she needed. "You and Drake could probably *write* the erotic scenes."

"We could write them *better*." Serena laughed. "Hey, Mom called me this morning. Did she call you about going to her house Sunday morning to meet *another* new boyfriend? What is this, like number two *thousand*?"

Their mother introduced them to her new boyfriends several times a year, always with excited whispers about him being *the one*. When Chloe and Serena were growing up, their mother had spent more time hunting for a man to pay her bills than parenting. Sometimes Chloe tried to convince herself that she and Serena were lucky. At least their mother wasn't an alcoholic or a drug abuser. She simply wasn't a very good mother. Or a good girlfriend, apparently, since she'd been serially dating ever since Chloe was eight years old, when her mother had deemed Chloe old enough to babysit Serena.

"Probably two thousand and five. Are you going?" Chloe asked as she entered the conference room. She set the orientation packets for the new program she'd created on the table. It had taken her months to develop the Junior/Senior Program, which would allow high school students to earn community service hours toward graduation by spending time each week with senior citizens at LOCAL. Chloe had worked with high schools in the area and had selected several students to take part in a six-week trial program over the summer. If the trial was beneficial, she would gain the stamp of approval she needed for future funding.

"*Yes*, I'm going," Serena said with great disdain. "Drake is coming with me, and if things get too weird, we're going to say he has a meeting at the music store and leave."

Drake owned a chain of music stores, and he was co-owner of the Bayside Resort in Wellfleet with his brother, Rick, and another childhood friend, Dean Masters. Rick and Dean were married to two of Chloe and Serena's closest friends, Desiree and Emery.

"Your husband is the best."

"I know," Serena said happily.

"You guys are so good together, you give me hope that I'll eventually meet the right guy."

"Speaking of the right guy, I heard Justin got rid of a date for you last night."

Justin's piercing blue eyes and ruggedly handsome face flashed in Chloe's mind. She closed the conference room door and said, "How did you hear that?"

"You always forget that Gavin is Justin's best friend." Gavin Wheeler was Serena's business partner at Mallery and Wheeler Interior Designs. Last month he'd married their friend Harper.

Chloe rolled her eyes. "Right. Sorry. My mind has been on overload lately. I could have gotten rid of the guy myself, but

Justin did me a big favor. I'm kind of sick of making up excuses, but the guy was another dolt. I'm beginning to think it's *me*. Maybe I just attract boring guys."

"Um, *hello*? Justin Wicked is anything but boring. I wish you'd give him a chance. Not all bikers are like the guys Mom goes out with. Look at Gavin. He has a motorcycle."

She glanced at the clock, noting that she still had twenty minutes before her meeting, and said, "Gavin isn't a leather-wearing, tattoo-sporting, badass *biker* and motorcycle club member. He only rides because Justin got him into it."

Serena didn't know about the times their mother's boyfriends had made moves on Chloe or that Chloe had sat guard in her sister's bedroom many nights, watching over her. Even all those years ago, Chloe had been thankful it was her those men had gone after and not Serena. She had always been Serena's protector, emotionally and physically, and that hadn't changed as they'd gotten older. That was why she also hadn't told her sister about the guy she had dated in college who had gotten so physical with her after an evening at the Salty Hog, she'd had to use practically an entire tube of makeup to cover up the bruises. From that moment on, she had sworn off tough guys, or anyone even remotely close, and she'd never returned to the Salty Hog.

Once again Chloe tried to downplay what had gone on without minimizing the realities. She paced and said, "You probably don't remember how many of Mom's boyfriends came over after we were in bed. They'd come around for a few nights, disappear into her bedroom, and then leave her brokenhearted."

"Mom's heart was never broken for long," Serena said casually. "She was always back on the prowl days later."

"I know, but the guys she dated never *stuck*, you know? I've seen enough motorcycle taillights to last me a lifetime. I know

Justin is a great guy, and he's an amazing friend, but we don't know *everything* about him. I mean, we've met his brothers and cousins, but we don't know his parents or what his family is really like. And yes, the Dark Knights do wonderful things for the community, but there's a lot we don't know about that biker world. From what I've seen with Mom's boyfriends, we're not missing much. There are too many unknowns that leave room for trouble where Justin is concerned. And don't forget, he slept with Violet when she first moved back to the Cape, to help her try to *fuck* Andre out of her system."

Their friend Violet was now engaged to Andre. They traveled several months out of the year, setting up medical clinics in newly developed nations, and they were currently in Honduras. When Violet had slept with Justin, she and Andre had been broken up and he'd been overseas. Chloe and their friends had been having breakfast at Summer House Inn when they'd overheard Violet and Andre arguing about her tryst with Justin. She didn't know why it bothered her so much that they'd hooked up with the sole purpose of *fucking* Andre out of her system, but it did.

"Don't you think that's a little questionable?" Chloe asked. "It's not something I would ever do. It's not like they were even dating."

"I think *Long Dong Naked Man* is a *really* good friend."

Chloe felt her cheeks burn over the nickname their friend Emery had given him the summer after Justin and Violet's not-so-secret sex romp, when Emery had been staying with Violet and she'd seen Justin walk out of Violet's bedroom naked. Rumors spread as quickly as weeds around Bayside, and they'd learned that Justin had been posing for a sculpture Violet was making, and he'd stayed over. Violet and Justin had wanted to squash any untrue rumors, and they'd insisted they hadn't had sex since Violet had first come back to the Cape right after she'd broken up with Andre. Justin had simply *slept* naked, which was another thing Chloe would never do with a man who was just a friend.

"You'd probably feel different if Drake had done that with one of *your* friends," Chloe insisted. "But he's loved you since you were kids. Don't you see, Serena? You're lucky. You're with a great, stable guy who has nothing questionable in his background or in his life. I want to be lucky, too. Is that so bad? I'm sure there has to be *one* conservative guy out there who isn't an automaton. Look at Tegan—she'd only *just* moved to town when she met Jett Masters, and he's the love of her life."

"They're so good together. But you know how I feel about your dating decisions. I vote that you stop going after boring, vanilla doughnuts that can only leave you wanting something bigger and better and lose yourself in a thick, creamy éclair, with choco—"

"Stop! You're going to make me gag. Why do you always connect doughnuts to sex?"

"Maybe because my man is as delicious as a cream-filled doughnut. Seriously, though. I bet Justin lives up to his *Wicked* name."

"I'm sure he does, but I want more than hot sex, Serena. Sex is great while it lasts, but if there's nothing more, then I'm left feeling even lonelier than ever. Can we please not talk about this anymore? My Junior/Senior Program starts next week, and I'm holding orientation this afternoon. I have to get ready."

"You must be excited."

"I am. I can't believe it's finally happening. Teenage exuberance is contagious, and these new friendships should go a long way to alleviate loneliness for the residents here. Something as simple as being read to, playing a game, or even taking a walk could brighten their spirits and give them something to look forward to each week."

"You know, those people who live there are lucky to have you. You're always trying to make their lives better."

"Thank you. You should see the collage I made for Louis Flessinger's ninety-second birthday last week. I had taken pictures of him with other residents, his grandchildren, and his daughter and put them on a large board that I decorated with fabric and cute embellishments. He cried when I gave it to him." She loved making keepsakes like picture boards, albums, and cards for her friends, the residents at LOCAL, and for herself and Serena.

"You've always known that the small things make the biggest differences," Serena said.

"Well, I hope this program makes a difference because I've been researching another program I'd like to mention in my meeting with the board next week, just to feel them out. If this one does well and the board doesn't shut down my next idea, I'm going to put together a formal proposal and pitch it to Alan. It can't hurt to strike while the iron's hot."

"You'd know best," Serena said. "What's the other program?"

"Do you remember that puppeteering article I told you about a few weeks ago? The one about the benefits of using puppetry as a form of therapy for dementia patients?"

"Yeah, that sounded really cool. You should talk to Justin's sister, Mads. She's a puppeteer. Remember, we met her at his gallery opening last summer? I really liked her. She's so sweet, it's hard to believe she's got all those tough brothers."

"That's exactly what I was thinking." Although now she was also thinking of one particularly tough and brawny brother of Madigan's. Trickles of heat moved through her. Why did the *thought* of him have that effect on her? She tried to push those thoughts away, but they lingered like the apple in the Garden of Eden. "Mads travels all the time, but I heard she was back in town and looking for work. I thought I'd pick her brain and possibly pitch a test puppetry program. But the Junior/Senior Program really needs to go smoothly if I have any hope of getting another program funded."

The door to the conference room opened, and Alan Rogers walked in. Her boss was an unremarkable middle-aged man of average build who had probably worn his short brown hair in the same boyish style since he was a kid. But he was good at his job, and he held the key to program funding. Luckily, he'd always shown interest in Chloe's ideas, and he usually supported the new programs she pitched. Unfortunately, he was also a close talker who stepped into people's personal space and stared into their eyes as he spoke. He'd never done anything inappropriate, but having *anyone* invade her personal space uninvited was unsettling.

"Serena, I'll call you later. I have to go." Chloe set down her phone and said, "Hi, Alan."

"Getting ready for orientation?" he asked as he walked around the conference table toward her.

"Yes. The kids should be here soon." She began placing the folders around the table, putting distance between them, a strategy she'd developed early on.

"There's an assisted living conference coming up in Boston next month covering a gamut of topics that could help our residents. They're featuring women in management, which I thought you'd enjoy since you're my shining star."

"Well, thank you. That sounds interesting," she said, setting down another packet.

"You know how much I admire you, Chloe. Conferences like this could help us become an even stronger team. I'll email you the information. It's a two-day conference, Friday and Saturday. We can drive together and stay at the hotel where the conference is being held, so we don't miss the morning meetings."

The idea of driving in the same car with the close talker made her want to decline the offer, but she didn't want to miss a conference that might be good for her career and the facility. "I'm pretty busy with new program development, so I'm not sure I can afford two days away, but I'll check it out and let you know."

"Sounds good," he said, following her around the table. "I met the men you referred me to for the work on my patio. They're a little rough around the edges. I thought you said they were friends of yours."

"They are. They're good guys, and they do great work." She set down the last packet, and when she looked up, Alan was *right there*.

"You trust them?" Alan asked.

"Yes, I do."

His expression turned serious. "Are you dating one of them?"

"I don't see how that's relevant, but *no*, I'm not."

"That's good." A slow smile lifted his lips. "A woman like you deserves a man fitting your professionalism. A man who can afford to treat you right."

"I'm sure the Wickeds make fine livings, and you know, not

everyone can be as lucky as your wife." She wasn't above blowing smoke up the guy's ass in hopes of ending the conversation so she wouldn't have to smell his acrid breath anymore.

He held her gaze and said, "There's enough luck to go around. It's all about timing."

Chloe rolled her eyes and took a step back. "Yeah, well, I feel like I've been waiting *forever.*"

"Chloe, you're not one to rush and make mistakes. The right man at the right time is worth waiting for, don't you think?"

"There she is!" Rose Masters exclaimed as she barreled into the room, right past Alan, and embraced Chloe. Rose was Chloe's friends Dean and Jett's grandmother and a longtime resident of LOCAL. As always, she was with her two best friends, Magdeline and Arlin.

"Mr. Rogers, I have been looking for you." Magdeline, a tall, wiry woman who possessed enough gumption for ten people, stepped between Chloe and Alan and said, "My daughter has been trying to reach you to discuss financial matters. Did you get her messages?"

"I, um, *no.* I don't recall getting them," Alan answered as Magdeline and Arlin ushered him toward the door.

"Why don't we go with you to your office," Arlin suggested. She must have just had her hair done, because it was even brighter orange than usual. "We can call her together."

Alan glanced at his watch and said, "I have a meeting now, but I'll look into it as soon as I'm free."

"Perfect!" Magdeline exclaimed, and she closed the conference room door behind him. She and her friends chuckled like they'd just pulled off the greatest scheme.

Rose shuddered, her snow-white hair bouncing with the

movement. "That man gives me the creeps."

Chloe tried to keep a straight face, but laughter spilled out.

"How did he get this job?" Arlin asked.

"I'll tell you how. He's Darren's son," Magdeline said. Darren Rogers was the CEO of LOCAL.

Rose put her hand over her heart and said, "Darren is *dreamy*. I have no idea how he fathered that man, although I have to say that I've heard the board is very happy with the work Alan's doing." She took Chloe's hand and said, "How are you, sweetie?"

"I'm fine, Rose. Really. Alan is harmless." Chloe was careful not to cross any lines with the residents, although she wanted nothing more than to say she was better *now*.

"As harmless as a rattlesnake, if you ask me," Magdeline said. "I wonder what his wife sees in him. She's a lovely woman."

Chloe put on her virtual administrator hat and said, "That's enough, ladies. He's just a close talker. A lot of people are like that."

"Do they all make you feel like you need a shower afterward, the way he does?" Arlin asked.

"Oh, please, Arlin," Rose said. "I'm sure Chloe doesn't waste her time on close talkers. She probably has a gaggle of more appropriate handsome gentlemen vying for her attention. Why, they're probably lining up around the block, and *they're* the ones needing showers after talking with *her*. *Cold* showers."

"Oh my goodness, Rose. No, that's not true." Chloe picked up the folder of presentation materials and began sorting through them.

"What do you mean that's not true?" Rose asked. "You're a beautiful, smart woman."

Chloe met their disbelieving eyes and said, "The dating pool on the Cape is rather slim. I don't have a lot of luck in that department."

"Oh, honey, let us fix that for you. *Sit*." Magdeline nudged Chloe into a chair.

The three of them pulled chairs around Chloe and sat down, like a firing line.

"Okay. Now, Chloe, tell us how you are meeting men," Magdeline said authoritatively.

Chloe knew they'd keep asking unless she gave them an answer, so she made it quick in hopes of returning to her meeting preparations. "I use dating apps, and I go to clubs. Well, *a* club. My friend Colton owns Undercover in Truro, so I hang out there sometimes."

"Clubs are good. Hot guys hang out at clubs," Arlin said.

"My granddaughter uses *Binder*. She said it's the best way to meet guys," Magdeline said. "I swear every time I talk to her, she's going to meet up, or hook up, or whatever *up* it is you kids do these days."

"It's *Tinder*, Mags," Arlin corrected her. "It's a hookup app."

"That's what I said. Kids hook up for dates."

"It's a *sex* app, not a *dating* app," Arlin clarified. "Geez, Mags, you really need to ask more questions before you go spouting off like that. My daughter told me all about Tinder. Kids go on there for sex. Nothing but *sex*." She leaned closer to Rose and lowered her voice to say, "I wish we had that here. It sure would make things a lot easier than all the small talk nonsense we have to go through."

"Okay, ladies, enough about Tinder." Chloe had tried Tinder, but she'd known after the first meet-up that it was *not* the app for her. "And I really don't want to hear about any sexual trysts going on at LOCAL."

Arlin and Mags giggled like schoolgirls.

Rose waggled her finger at them and said, "You're going to get in trouble."

"Hush." Arlin waved her hand dismissively. "Sex is a normal part of life."

"Maybe Chloe *should* be on Tinder." Magdeline looked compassionately at Chloe and said, "Sex is *good*, sweetheart. It can lead to other things."

"I know it can, but I don't think the kind of guy I'm looking for spends time on apps like Tinder. I'm starting to think dating apps aren't the right choice for me anyway."

"What kind of man are you looking for?" Rose asked.

"Someone nice, strong-minded but tenderhearted. The kind of men my sister and friends have found. A man who wants to know me for *me*, not just for sex. Someone who is interesting and funny and maybe holds my hand every once in a while. I can't tell you how long it's been since I held a man's hand."

Rose's gray-blue eyes warmed. "And he should bring you flowers. Flowers fill a woman's soul with happiness." Rose had always been an avid gardener. She helped arrange floral centerpieces for the dining room at LOCAL, and since Dean handled the landscaping for the facility, she gardened with him, as well.

"Flowers are always nice," Chloe agreed. "But you know what I would really like? A man who calls just because he's thinking of me and who doesn't rely only on texts for foreplay. I mean, texts are fun, but hearing a man's voice is much more intimate."

The ladies nodded in agreement.

"Your generation misses out on all the fun," Arlin said. "Phone calls build anticipation, and *nothing* will make your heart race like a good round of foreplay. A girl needs to *want* in order to *enjoy*."

"The digital age has its value, but I'm not sure it's been great for dating," Magdeline said. "When I think of a relationship, I think of two people finding their best friends."

"I like that description." Chloe glanced at the clock. She was enjoying their chat and was glad to see she still had a little time before her meeting. "To me, a relationship is two people who think of each other more than they think of themselves. I'm not a needy person, and I don't want a knight in shining armor to pay my way or give me all of his attention. I want a *partner*. Someone to stand by my side, to be happy for my accomplishments, and not freak out when I need a little emotional support. But some guys are so hung up on themselves these days, *they're* all they talk about."

Rose patted her hand and said, "It's not just these days, honey. Men have always put themselves first. They were the breadwinners for so many years, you can't really blame them. But we've come a long way, and I agree that it needs to continue to change."

"Yes, and you need a man who *doesn't* send pictures of his body parts," Arlin added. "Do you know Jacob Sellers sent Patti Tegrond a picture of his privates? He said he read online that women liked it."

Chloe put on her virtual work hat again and said, "He got in a lot of trouble for that. And yes, *no* body part pictures, please. I'm looking for a professional who does meaningful work and cares about his career."

Rose pursed her lips and waved her index finger. "But

doesn't care *too* much. I was married to a physician for a very long time, and while he was charming to his patients, he was cruel to his family and those he thought were *beneath* him."

Chloe definitely didn't want that type of man in her life. She had heard stories about Dean and Jett's grandfather, and also about their father, who had taken after their grandfather for a long time. Thankfully, their father had changed his ways over the last few years and had become as kind as his sons.

"I didn't meet my true love, Leon, until very late in life, after my husband died," Rose said. "We were together for only a couple of years before he passed away. But they were the best years of my life. You never know when love will show up at your door, Chloe. I wouldn't keep such a black-and-white list of must-haves. The most important things in a relationship are the simple things. Every woman should have a man who makes her tummy tingle as often as he makes her feel safe, valued, and loved."

"Rose is right—feeling safe, valued, and loved has to be constant. But I still say that tummy tingling needs to go further. Not that sex is everything, but *come on*, ladies. Good sex is a *must*," Magdeline said with an emphatic nod.

"Agreed, but sex eventually wanes," Arlin reminded her.

"That's what those little blue pills are for," Rose said with a wink, making them all laugh. "Chloe, honey, when true love hits, you'll know it. You might have to kiss a lot of toads, and your forever love may not fit all of the criteria on your wish list. But you'll know when it's right. When you meet the man who looks at you like you're *so* special, you can *feel* how much he adores you. The one who is there for you in good times and bad, *he's* the man who deserves a chance. Just remember, love is patient and love is kind—"

"And hopefully he has a really hot *behind*," Magdeline added with a snort-laugh.

Rose chuckled.

The intercom beeped, and Shelby, the receptionist, said, "Chloe?"

"Yes?"

"The juniors are here for orientation, and Madigan Wicked returned your call. She said she's tied up until tomorrow but will try you then."

"Great. Thank you, Shelby."

"One more thing," Shelby said. "You got another call for the reference on Janet Kirsh. I put it through to your voicemail." Janet was a single mother who had worked for LOCAL for a couple of years in the accounting department. She'd left a little more than a year ago to move to Florida.

"Okay. Thank you. I forgot. I'll return the call before the end of the day." Chloe and the ladies pushed to their feet.

"Is that about *our* Janny?" Rose asked. "Wasn't she looking for a job last Christmas?"

"Yes. She must be having a hard time finding the right company to settle in with," Chloe explained. Janet had been a stellar employee, but Chloe was contacted every few weeks for references on her.

"That's a shame. She was a doll," Arlin said. "And her little boy is just the cutest."

"He called everyone *Gamma*," Rose said thoughtfully.

What Chloe remembered most about Janet's bright-eyed little boy was the way Janet talked about him like he was the greatest gift she'd ever been given. "Maybe this reference will land her the right job. Thank you for the talk, ladies."

"And for interrupting *you know who*," Arlin said with a wink.

Chloe shook her head at the women who had become like the grandmothers she'd never had, and not for the first time, she felt blessed to have them in her life. "I never said that."

"*All* your secrets are safe with us," Magdeline said as she embraced Chloe.

Chloe embraced Arlin and Rose, too, and after they left the room, she thought about the things they'd said.

Feeling safe, valued, and loved has to be constant…When you meet the man who looks at you like you're so special, you can feel how much he adores you, the one who is there for you in good times and bad, he's the man who deserves a chance.

She remembered the way her date had looked at her last night like she was a business associate and how Justin had looked at her like she was the only woman in the room. Even when she'd first seen Justin standing by the bar, their connection had been *magnetic*. She'd actually had to cross her legs and squeeze her thighs together, because every time he looked at her like that, her pulse revved up and her girlie parts threw a little party. She *was* female, after all. She knew *sexy* when she saw it, and Justin Wicked was sex personified. He was also charming and funny. He didn't just walk; he *swaggered* with confidence and bravado. He was tough and rugged and insanely *hot* with his always-tousled brown hair, intense blue eyes that looked a little haunted, and hard, broad body that Chloe had spent too many sleepless nights thinking about. *And that slightly crooked, cocky smile…*Shocks of heat sparked beneath her skin. The desires he ignited felt dangerous and forbidden, which made him even more enticing, though she knew they shouldn't.

Justin made her feel things no other man had ever come close to, and she definitely felt safe when she was with him, but after the childhood she'd endured, she knew falling for a tough biker wasn't safe for her heart.

Chapter Three

JUSTIN SAT AT a table with his cousins and brothers in the Dark Knights' clubhouse Wednesday evening for church, just as he had every Wednesday evening for nearly thirteen years, since he'd officially been accepted into the Dark Knights. From the outside, the clubhouse was nothing more than an old brick schoolhouse located a few minutes down the road from the Salty Hog. Justin could still remember how desperately he'd wanted to earn the honor of wearing the Dark Knights' patches and attend their meetings when he was a teenager, and the rush of adrenaline and pride he'd felt the first time he'd walked through those doors and into a meeting. That pride had only grown in the years since.

Preacher and Conroy held court at the head table alongside the club secretary and treasurer. Buster, Preacher's golden retriever mixed with who-knew-what, sat at his feet under the table. Preacher and Gunner always brought one or two of their dogs with them to church. As Preacher discussed prospects and club finances, Justin looked around the room at the men he felt like he'd known his entire life. Like the exterior of the club-house, some of the brotherhood had weathered and aged over the years, while others had gotten inked, had families, and beefed up or slimmed down. They had members from all walks of life, from doctors and lawyers to blue-collar workers, and even a stay-at-home father. Beneath the clothes they were all the same fiercely dedicated, upstanding men. Just like the strong, stable structure around them, the hearts of the brotherhood had remained loyal and unyielding.

Justin's thoughts found their way back to Chloe, as they always did. Trying to unravel her refusal to go out with him was an ongoing frustration. He was determined to figure out why and change her mind. He'd been biding his time, letting her get all that other nonsense about her suit-wearing Prince Charming out of her head, but maybe it was time to stop waiting and show her who he really was.

"Wake up, dude," Baz said, jerking Justin from his thoughts. Baz pushed a hand through his longish blond hair and flashed the charming smile that made women lose their minds. He nodded in the direction of Cuffs, who was heading up to the front of the room, and said, "Dogfighting ring update."

Cuffs was clean cut, broad chested, and athletic, with short brown hair and a granitelike jawline. He was a police officer in or out of uniform, but to Justin he'd always be the first guy Blaine had ever stood up to on his behalf. Cuffs had been Blaine's best friend since they were kids. He'd fallen from grace after picking a fight with Justin in middle school. But he'd quickly redeemed himself a few months later when he'd stood by Blaine's and Justin's sides, helping them stop a group of bullies from picking on a hearing-impaired boy.

"As you know, we've been closing in on the dogfighting ring that Baz alerted us to a couple of weeks ago." Cuffs nodded in Baz's direction. "My team was ready to take them down this week, but then we received intel from other sources that they've got another shipment of dogs coming. We want to close down this operation *and* their counterparts, so we're in a holding pattern until next week. We expect to find anywhere from ten to thirty dogs. Gunner's going to be there to collect and transport the dogs to the rescue, and Baz will be handling any medical care they need." Cuffs looked over to their table and said, "Gunner, do you need more hands on deck?"

Gunner was peering into his vest. Granger, one of his dogs, stood between his legs with his chin resting on Gunner's arm, which was belted across the bottom of his vest holding it against his stomach. He pushed one hand into his vest.

"What the hell is he doing?" Tank said under his breath. Tank was the eldest of Justin's local cousins. He was a mountain of a man, covered with tattoos and a few piercings. He owned Wicked Ink, a tattoo shop, and he was a volunteer firefighter. Tank was also the cousin with the most demons, as he'd been the one to find his late sister, Ashley, when she'd committed suicide several years ago.

"*Ow, shit,*" Gunner ground out as he stood up. His vest opened, revealing a fluffy white kitten hanging on to his chest by its claws. "Sorry," Gunner said as he carefully extracted the kitten's nails. Granger wagged his tail, watching Gunner's every move. "I rescued her last night and she needs to be bottle fed. I didn't want to leave her alone."

"You brought your *pussy* to a meeting?" Zander chuckled.

Blaine elbowed Zander and said, "Gives a whole new meaning to *pussy whipped,*" earning a rumble of laughter from around the room.

Gunner nuzzled the kitten against his nose and said, "They don't mean anything, Snowflake. They're just assholes."

"*Snowflake?*" one of the other guys said.

"He's got to sweet-talk her. She's the only pussy he's gonna get tonight," Zeke added.

Zeke was the rare combination of smart-ass and genius, though he typically kept his smart-assery under wraps. Women called Baz *prime husband material*, but Justin thought Zeke would be the first of them to settle down. He'd always seemed more settled than the rest of them. He had a quiet, watchful way about him. Zeke had been a special ed teacher until a guy had made rude comments about "fucking retarded kids" at an event, and Zeke had gone after him. Zeke had lost his job because of the fight, and now he worked with Zander and their father in their family business, Cape Renovations. Zeke also tutored and volunteered at the community center.

"All right, *enough*." Preacher glared at Zander and Zeke, and they held their hands up in surrender. "Gunner, how about you answer Cuff's question? Do you need more help to transport the dogs?"

Gunner stroked the tiny kitten's back and said, "I think we're good. But a few extra hands wouldn't hurt, especially when we get back to the shelter."

A number of members called out, volunteering to help. Conroy held up his hands and said, "I'll put together a sign-up sheet and Gunner can answer questions after the meeting."

Justin's uncle looked more like an aging movie star than a biker. He had a long, straight nose, wavy silver hair that hung to his collar, and an ever-present smile that set off his dimples. His children had inherited many of his traits, including those dimples. Tank not only shared his father's burly stature, but also the jet-black hair of Conroy's youth. Gunner was every bit as cocky as Conroy, and Baz shared his father's ability to remain calm in any situation. Before the tragic loss of their younger sister, Ashley, she had shared their father's zest for life, which had made her death even more devastating. Ashley had been the second person Justin had lost to suicide, the first being his birth mother when he was only seven years old.

As Cuffs returned to his seat, Preacher said, "We're gearing up for the annual Suicide-Awareness Ride and Rally in honor of Ashley Wicked, Conroy and Ginger's beloved daughter. Ginger is looking for volunteers to help with the event."

Sadness moved through Justin and through the room, settling heavily around them. The closeness of the brotherhood included sharing celebrations and heartache. Even those who hadn't known Ashley rallied around their family every year without fail, keeping her spirit alive and helping the family cope with the never-ending sadness of their loss. Preacher had once asked Justin if he'd like them to publicly honor his birth mother at the event, but since he didn't like talking about his mother's death, or the circumstances surrounding it, of which even Preacher wasn't fully aware, he'd passed on the thoughtful offer.

As Preacher went over details for the September event, Justin put a hand on Tank's shoulder and lifted his beer bottle, mouthing, *To Ashley.*

Tank tapped his bottle to Justin's, and they both took a drink.

After the meeting, Gunner and Baz dealt with gathering volunteers for the night of the dogfighting-ring bust, and Zander went across the room to play darts with some of his buddies by the pool tables. Preacher and Conroy made their way over to the table where Justin and the others were sitting.

Preacher gave off an air of authority, exuding the confidence of a man who demanded obedience. He had serious eyes and pitch-black brows and mustache. He wore his salt-and-pepper hair slicked back and kept his silver beard trimmed. Justin hadn't been sure what to make of the tattooed renovations expert when he'd first met him. But as Justin had gotten to know him, he'd found that Preacher was warm and patient. Preacher could joke with the best of them, but when it came to the safety of his family or his community, he didn't mess around. Justin had no idea how Preacher and Reba had put up with his shit and his constant running away when he had first come to live with them, but he was thankful they had. Preacher had been more of a father to him in the first month he'd lived there than his biological father had been in the eleven years they'd lived under the same roof. And Reba? She was a godsend. From what he remembered of his birth mother, he had a feeling the two would have gotten along like sisters. Reba, being the stronger, older sister who would have looked out for his timid biological mother.

If only...

Preacher set his beer bottle on the table beside Justin and put a hand on his shoulder, his eyes moving around the table. "How are our boys doing?"

Tank smirked and looked at Blaine as he said, "This one's thinking about getting a sex change and becoming a chick."

"Did you say *getting into* a chick?" Blaine cocked a grin. "How'd you know I have a date later?"

Tank held his gaze and said, "I didn't. Is Gunner lending you his *pussy*?"

"A'right, boys," Conroy said as he sat down between Tank and Blaine.

Preacher sat beside Justin and said, "Hey, son. Are you still okay to check on Grandpa tomorrow?"

A few months ago, Preacher's father, Mike, had suffered a

fall and had moved in with Preacher and Reba. He'd fallen again a few weeks ago. Since Reba ran the offices of Cape Renovations and wasn't always able to get away, Justin and his siblings took turns checking on their grandfather during the day. Mike was a jokester, like Zander, although he definitely had the grumpy-old-man thing down pat. Mike had grown up with a father who believed in fists as a form of punishment and he had run away at sixteen. He'd met his late wife, Hilda, at seventeen. They'd married at eighteen, had kids a few years later, and together they'd built a life free from abuse. Their new family hadn't had much, but they'd had a safe, loving world in which to thrive. Although Mike wasn't a biker, he respected the hell out of the club and supported their endeavors. After all, he'd raised his sons to be worthy of the Dark Knights' patches.

"Of course. Whatever you need," Justin said. Mike had opened his heart to Justin early on, becoming the grandfather he'd never had. Like Preacher and Conroy, Mike had taken every opportunity to teach Justin right from wrong. He'd once told Justin that the best thing he could do for himself was to be a good man. *Because once you do that, everything else will fall into place.* Justin had taken that advice seriously, and it had yet to fail him.

"Do me a favor," Preacher said. "Lay off bringing him cookies and candy bars, okay? He doesn't need all that sugar."

Justin feigned innocence, pointing at himself and mouthing, *Who me?*

Preacher took a swig of his drink and said, "Seriously, Maverick. He gets all hyped up."

"Is he still giving you and Mom trouble?" Blaine asked.

"If you mean sneaking out and going to Common Grounds, where he flirts shamelessly with Gabe and any other woman who crosses his path, then *yes*." Preacher chuckled and took another drink.

Gabe Appleton was a voluptuous redhead who owned the coffeehouse where they held the suicide-awareness rally each year. Her brother Rod, a guitarist, and Elliott, who had Down syndrome, also worked there. Gabe employed several people with disabilities and fostered an environment where everyone was welcome, which was why, when it had become too emotionally draining for the family to host the rally at the Salty Hog while running the business, they'd chosen to hold it at Common Grounds.

"Your grandfather is worse than you four were," Preacher said.

"I was a prince among thieves." Blaine sat back in his chair, eyeing his brothers as he said, "Always catching shit for what my brothers did."

Justin knew Blaine was only teasing, but he still felt a pang of guilt at that comment. Blaine was only one year older than him, and when Justin had first moved in with the Wickeds, Blaine had rightfully wanted to establish himself as the alpha among the pack. After having a father who rarely remembered to feed him and who used fear as a means for obedience, Justin didn't trust *anyone*. He and Blaine had gone head-to-head often, and Justin had run off dozens of times. But no matter how many times he ran away, Blaine and the rest of his family, along with the Dark Knights, had come after him and brought him home. Justin wasn't *ever* punished for taking flight. He was told how much he was loved and that the family was there for him even when he didn't want them to be. Eventually Justin had learned to trust the strangers who had not only taken him in but had also made him part of a much bigger family.

Though Justin and Blaine had started out on rough ground, often battling at home, Blaine had always had his back in public. Justin would never forget the day in middle school when Blaine had taken down Cuffs, who had been *Cameron* at the time, for giving Justin shit. Afterward, Justin had asked Blaine why he'd taken his side instead of his best friend's, and Blaine had said, *The minute you had a bed in our house, you became family. I'll always have your back, but that doesn't mean I'll take your shit.*

Blaine had become Justin's first real friend, and Justin had never raised a hand to him again.

"Prince among thieves?" Justin laughed. "Our devious deeds were usually *your* idea, like sneaking out to meet Marcy Hurley and her friend by the dunes."

Blaine tipped his face up and smiled. "Ah. Marcy Hurley. She was—"

"Too damn hot for the likes of you," Zeke said.

They all laughed.

"I was going to say she was a nice girl," Blaine said.

"Nice and easy," Tank said under his breath.

Blaine said, "I plead the Fifth."

Preacher shook his head, eyeing Conroy and chuckling as he lifted his bottle to his lips.

"Your Marcy Hurley was our Sally McGee," Conroy said. "Remember her, Preach?"

Preacher lifted his brows, and then his eyes turned serious and he pointed around the table. "You boys cannot say that woman's name around your mamas, got it?"

"Women don't like to hear about the first woman their men slept with." Conroy looked across the table and said, "Seriously, Preach, let's get back to Dad. Are things okay with him? Do you want me and Ging to take him for a couple of months?"

"Nah, we've got him. You have the bar to deal with, and moving is a hassle. Besides, he'd probably take your four-wheeler out for a joyride and get arrested." Preacher and Conroy shared a laugh. "I know the old man misses his freedom, but the years are catching up to him."

"He's stubborn as a mule, like his sons. By the way, I talked to Sonja and Jake the other day. They offered to help, but I told them we've got him covered." Their younger brother and sister had moved away from the Cape right after college. Conroy took a swig of his beer. He looked at Justin and said, "Before I forget, Maverick, Ginger wanted to know if you're still on board to make a sculpture to auction off at the rally."

"Definitely. I've already started designing it." It was true, he had begun. *Several times.* He had been sculpting since he was a teenager, and he had a studio on his property, where he spent many long evenings. Last summer he'd had his first gallery opening, and he'd had a steady flow of clients ever since. But for the first time in his life, he was creatively stuck. Every time he started to conceptualize a piece for the rally, he hit a wall.

"Awesome. I can't wait to see what you come up with." Conroy pushed to his feet and said, "Come on, Preach. I'll beat your ass in a game of pool."

"It's your funeral," Preacher said as he walked away.

"Hey, Mav, you still want to get that tat you mentioned last week?" Tank asked.

"Definitely. As soon as you're free."

"I had a cancellation for next Friday night," Tank said as Gunner and Baz returned with the dogs on their heels.

"Great. I'll take it."

Gunner held the kitten up and kissed her nose. "What are

you *taking?*"

"Booking a tat." Justin reached up and took the kitten from him. He rubbed her soft fur against his cheek and said, "She's pretty damn cute."

"Give me my baby back." Gunner took the kitten from his hands.

"We're heading over to the Hog. Y'all want to come?" Baz looked at Blaine and said, "Marly might be there." Marly Bowers, a gorgeous brunette with olive skin and exotic eyes, was a close friend of their families. She'd lost her brother to a motorcycle accident years ago and had since founded the Head Safe motorcycle helmet safety program.

Buster ambled over to Blaine and licked his hand. Blaine petted him as he rose to his feet and said, "I could definitely use a drink of that hot little cocktail."

"I'm in, too." Zander looked at Zeke and said, "You're not blowing us off again, *teach.* I need my wingman."

Zander dragged Zeke to his feet by the back of his leather vest. Zeke knocked his hand away and said, "You haven't needed a wingman since you were fourteen and you picked up that sixteen-year-old girl on the beach."

Zander grinned. "Yeah, I really don't need one, but I like having you with me, bro." He looked at Justin and Tank and said, "You guys coming?"

"Hell yes." Tank stood up. "Maverick? You coming or are you playing bouncer for Chloe again?"

Justin stood up and said, "How the hell do *you* know about that?"

Zander chuckled.

"Jackass," Justin said, pushing past loose-lipped Zander.

"Did you bring your cape, Captain America?" Zander teased

as they made their way to the door. "You never know when *Uptown Girl* might saunter into the Hog."

Justin glared at him. There wasn't a chance in hell that Chloe would be hanging out at the Salty Hog. She never went there, and he preferred it that way. The last thing he wanted was a bunch of dudes drooling over her—at least until she was on his arm, respected and appreciated as more than a piece of ass. And that day would come soon. He could feel it in his bones.

Chapter Four

CHLOE STORMED INTO Undercover Saturday night, hoping her closest friends were still there. She wove through the crowd, spotting her besties at a table by the dance floor. *Thank frigging God.* She made a beeline for them, feeling better already.

"Chloe made it!" Harper shouted so loud Chloe heard her before she even reached the table. Harper's husband, Gavin, waved from his seat beside her.

Tegan, Daphne, and Steph squealed and jumped off their seats, sweeping Chloe into a group hug.

"The welcoming committee," Jett said.

Tegan exclaimed, "I'm so glad you made it."

Steph, a curvy brunette with red streaks in her hair, touched the frills on the strapless white Bardot top Chloe had paired with wide-legged black slacks and said, "Wow, Chloe, you look amazing. I wish I could wear something like that." Steph was a poet, and she owned an herbal shop in Brewster, a neighboring town.

"What happened with your date?" Daphne asked.

As the girls settled into their seats, Gavin said, "Considering it's only nine o'clock, I'd say it didn't go well."

Chloe set her purse on the table and huffed out a breath.

"I'm *done. Done* looking for a man to spend time with, done wasting my time on losers, and definitely done with dating apps. And I have to pee so bad I might wet my pants. Can you watch my purse?"

"Of course. *Go.*" Harper shooed her away.

Chloe hurried through the crowd toward the hall that led to the ladies' room. She turned the corner and smacked right into a rock-solid chest. "I'm sorr—" She lifted her face, meeting a familiar set of ice-blue eyes. Justin flashed his devastating smile, making her pulse quicken. Damn him. Why couldn't her body react like that to any other guys? Even *one*? *One* other guy!

"Hey there, heartbreaker," he said as his arms circled her. "Where are you rushing off to?"

A group of girls tried to squeeze past, and Justin inched them both out of their way, boxing Chloe in against the wall with his delicious body. His muscular thighs pressed against her pelvis, and his hips brushed her belly, causing her nipples to pebble and burn. She swallowed hard, telling herself not to notice *anything* else, like the wolfish grin spreading his lips. *Oh God, your lips…* She'd been thinking about kissing those lips for a long time, but even more ardently since a few weeks ago, when he'd come over to help her fix her shutters during a storm. They'd been *this close* to kissing, and she'd known they wouldn't have stopped there. She was certain that sex with Justin would rock her world. But she was past that reckless time of her life when flings were fun and friendships with guys were disposable.

She tried to think of something other than the feel of his enticingly *hard* body pressing temptingly against her, but the only other thought she found was based on the very thing she was trying to ignore—Justin Wicked definitely lived up to the nickname Emery had given him: *Long Dong Naked Man.* She told herself not to think about that. She'd never seen Justin with a date, but she'd heard him joking with their friends enough to realize he was still in that reckless phase, and she did not need to be his next conquest. No matter how good he felt.

"Have I rendered you speechless, beautiful?"

He was looking at her like he wanted to devour her, and that did wicked things to all her best parts. "No," she managed.

"What happened, sweetheart? Another Ken doll leave you unsatisfied tonight?" he asked in a low, deep voice.

She couldn't help but wonder how that voice would change in the throes of passion. Would he be demanding? Tender? Romantic? Too lost to speak? She really needed to get a grip. She had so much pent-up sexual frustration she felt like a cat in heat.

She lifted her chin and said, "I left *him* unsatisfied." Just as she'd been leaving men for more than a year.

His eyes drilled into her. "None of those guys are good enough for you."

"I'm not with them, am I?" she countered.

"You sure as hell aren't, and there's a reason. You're your own woman, baby. Smart, confident, *challenging*. But you're wrong in your assumptions, and one day you'll realize that." He leaned in, speaking just above a whisper. "A few weeks ago you were *so* close to finding all the answers you're looking for."

He trailed his rough hands up her arms and rested them on her bare shoulders. His fingers moved lightly along her skin, making her insides turn to liquid heat. He pressed forward, bringing his entire body flush with hers. He touched his cheek to hers. His scruff prickled her skin, and her mind traveled down that dirty path again. What would those whiskers feel like as they kissed?

"Your place, baby. Remember?" He spoke directly into her ear in a gravelly voice that sent pangs of lust darting through her. "The night of the storm."

Geez! Had he read her mind earlier? Heard her thoughts?

That night came rushing back, making her heart thunder and her body *want*. They'd gotten soaked in the storm, and when they'd come inside, Justin had peeled off his shirt, revealing planes of toned, wet flesh and dark ink. She'd wanted to lick the droplets off his glistening skin as he'd tipped his head back and guzzled a glass of water. She could still see those trails dripping down his abs to the waist of his low-slung jeans. When he'd set down his glass and turned, they'd been almost in this exact same position, only she'd been leaning against the counter. She wasn't usually attracted to tattoos, but they looked beautiful and dangerous on Justin. The *good* kind of dangerous. Like the dark fantasies she'd had about him ever since.

"You remember," he whispered in her ear. "You felt it, too."

She'd felt it then as strongly as she did *now*. She pressed her lips together to keep from admitting the truth—her body was on fire. But she couldn't do this. She didn't want a one-night stand *or* a broken heart. She had to regain control before she either combusted or took the kiss she craved.

Steeling herself against the raging inferno between them, she narrowed her eyes and said, "All I remember from that night was you walking out my door."

"Is that so?" he asked in a seductive growl, gazing entrancingly into her eyes. He ran his hand up her outer thigh and hip, squeezing gently as he leaned in again and said, "You don't remember getting *wet*? I know you felt it, sweet thing, just like you feel it pulsing inside you right now, burning through your veins, making you crave more. You feel it in those inescapable vibrations that are making it difficult for you to think. No man on earth can make you feel like I do."

She pressed her thighs together. Lord help her. She was no match for this man.

He brushed his scruff along her cheek and said, "Feel that clench in your belly? The dampness in your panties?" He squeezed her hip again. "The way your pulse just skyrocketed when I talked about your *panties*?"

A strangled, lustful sound escaped before she could stop it. She clenched her mouth shut to keep anything else from coming out.

"You hesitated the night of the storm, sweetheart. That's why I left," he said authoritatively into her ear, then softer, "I'll never force myself on you." He drew back, pinning her in place with another hungry stare. "When you stop running and give in to what you *really* want, you'll feel like this every time we're together. Only better, because you'll know you're *mine*."

He licked his lips, and *holy mother of hotness*, she could barely breathe.

"See you back at the table, sexy girl."

He walked away, and the air rushed from her lungs. Her head fell back against the wall, and she tried to catch her breath. How the hell was she going to make it through the night at the same table with the man who nearly made her come with nothing more than the hard press of his body and a few sinful sentences?

THERE WAS NOTHING cool about having a hard-on for a

woman in public. But watching Chloe get her groove on with the girls on the dance floor was the sexiest thing Justin had ever seen. She was smokin' hot in that clingy top, her slim hips swaying to the beat. Her silky hair whipped around her face as she and the other girls dodged Tegan's flailing arms. Tegan Fine was a cute, confident little blonde, but she was an awful dancer. The way Jett was gazing at her, Justin knew Tegan had found her perfect match. The same way he was sure he'd found his own.

As Chloe gathered the girls on the dance floor to take a selfie, Justin thought about his friends at the table. He'd heard Chloe talking with the girls about Gavin and Jett before they'd coupled off with her friends, and he knew they were the type of guy she saw herself with. Clean-cut professionals. Gavin was an interior designer, and Jett was an investor. But Justin knew it wasn't their careers that made the difference. There was more to whatever was holding her back. Chloe might be classy, but she wasn't a snob.

"Gavin, are you riding with us Sunday?" Justin asked. Gavin had moved into town a couple of years ago to start a business with Serena. He had been single then, and they had quickly become buddies. They spent less time together now that he was married, but he'd turned Gavin on to motorcycles, and they rode together as often as they could.

"Only if I get a road name." Gavin grinned.

Chloe's voice sailed through Justin's mind. *Gavin has a cute boyish grin. He's the ideal mix of professional and fun.* There was nothing *boyish* about Justin. She'd called Jett *handsome as a movie star* and *intriguing*, but she'd never made a move on either of them when they were single. He glanced at the dance floor, where she was bumping and grinding with the girls. He'd seen the restraint in her eyes when they were in the hallway, had practically tasted her desire. He had to hand it to her. She had a will of steel. *One day you'll own up to the fact that I'm the only man you want to be with.*

"They call you Maverick. I can be Goose," Gavin said. "*Top Gun*, bro. Think about it."

Justin sat back and said, "You've got to earn a road name, brother. How long have I been telling you to prospect the Dark Knights?"

"Since you convinced me to ride a motorcycle, but I'm a busy man. I've got my business and my beautiful wife." Gavin glanced over his shoulder at Harper dancing with the girls and said, "Look at that woman. I'm the luckiest guy on the planet."

"No, sir. I've got that slot sewn up. But we won't get in a pissing match over who's woman is hotter." Jett looked at Justin and said, "Looks like you're the odd man out."

"Not for long. That tall, blond bombshell out there will be on my arm soon."

"You'd better stake your claim fast," Gavin warned. "Beckett was asking about Chloe when he called last night. He's thinking about coming up sometime this summer." Beckett was Gavin's younger brother, a wealthy investor who lived in Oak Falls, Virginia.

"I'm not worried, man. Beckett's a good guy, but he's not *me*." Justin took a drink and said, "Before I forget, Dwayne is holding an open adoption in a few weeks. Doesn't every married couple need a dog?"

"Maybe we'll stop by," Gavin said. "Harper loves dogs, but I'm not sure we can adopt until the end of the year. She and Tegan are pretty busy with productions right now."

"Whenever, man. There's never a shortage of dogs, and they

all need loving homes. Jett, my man, save a four-legged friend? I bet Tegan would love a furry buddy."

"I'd love to, but like Gavin said, Teg's busy with the amphitheater and your old man's going to be renovating her house in the fall. But I heard Dean and Emery talking about getting a puppy before their baby is born. I'll mention it to them."

"Thanks, man."

The girls came off the dance floor giggling and whispering. Chloe held out her phone and said, "Will one of you take a picture of us?"

Justin snagged her phone, and as Chloe put one arm around Harper and the other around Daphne, he started taking pictures. Damn she looked good.

Tegan and Steph joined them, and the girls posed for one serious picture, all bright smiles, and then began making silly faces and giving each other bunny ears as Justin clicked away.

"Thank you!" Chloe said, retrieving her phone.

The girls huddled around her as she scrolled through the pictures. They all giggled, and Chloe looked at Justin. "You took a dozen pictures of *me*," she complained, but there was no hiding the spark of intrigue in her eyes. "*Close-ups*."

"What can I say? You stood out."

Chloe put her hand on her hip, eyes narrowing as she struggled to stifle the smile tugging at her lips, and said, "*Justin…*"

"I want copies. Text them to me." He winked, earning more laughs from the others.

Chloe rolled her eyes. "In your dreams."

"*Fantasies*," Harper said, making Chloe blush.

"Oh yeah," Gavin said. "Definitely *fantasies*."

Chloe scowled at him.

"Keep scrolling, hot stuff." Justin motioned toward the

phone and said, "I took group shots, too. I'd never let my girl down."

"I'm not *your* girl," Chloe insisted.

"*Yet*, babydoll. We both know where we're heading."

Daphne's eyes widened. "*Oooh*. Sounds like something's brewing."

"Something hot and delicious," Steph added.

"Yeah, a *witch's brew*," Chloe said.

"Sounds more like a love potion to me," Tegan added.

Chloe swatted her arm. "Don't encourage him."

"Oh my gosh. Listen!" Harper exclaimed, and the girls quieted. "It's 'All to Myself!' Come on, Gav! It's one of our songs." She grabbed Gavin's hand and dragged him toward the dance floor. Chloe, Daphne, and Steph followed them out.

"Come on, Jett!" Tegan urged.

"My pleasure, beautiful." Jett took her hand and led her to the dance floor.

Justin sat back, taking it all in. While most of the girls had moves that could probably lure men from their seats, he was mesmerized by Chloe. Colored lights misted down over her as she moved seductively to the beat, a visual feast of sensuality. Her hips swiveled, and her arms snaked toward the ceiling with fluidity and grace. She tipped her face up and closed her eyes, as if the music lived inside her.

Justin wanted to live inside her.

At a nearby table, two guys were talking about a *hot blonde* and ogling Chloe.

"*Fuck this*." He was done messing around. Justin pushed to his feet and strode onto the dance floor. He swept an arm around Chloe's waist, hauling her against him.

"What the...?" Chloe's eyes focused and turned fierce.

"Sorry, girls, but this dance is *mine*." Justin was speaking to Daphne and Steph, but his eyes remained locked on Chloe as he began moving to the beat. "Right, hot stuff? Or are you afraid to *dance* with a real man, too?"

"I never said I was *afraid* of anything. Think you can keep up, biker boy?" She ran her hands down his chest, her eyes narrowing provocatively as she swung her hips from side to side, brushing against his cock with a challenging grin on her face.

"Baby, I can keep *up* all night long." He slid his hand down her back, spreading it over her ass and holding her tighter against him as he met her move for move. "I'll *never* leave you unsatisfied."

Her eyes darkened, even more alluring *and* defiant. The song changed to a faster beat, with lyrics about busting loose and taking their clothes off. *Perfect.*

Chloe rolled one shoulder back, then the other, moving forward and back in a tempting dance that had him following suit. His hands moved down her torso, and she turned in his arms, rubbing her ass against him. Her arms rose over her head, slithering in the air. He wound his arms around her from behind and ran one hand down her thigh, the other up her belly. His fingertips grazed the underside of her breasts, and he felt her breathing hitch. She turned, facing him again. The *game-on* message in her eyes was received loud and clear. She could try to *outseduce* him, but he didn't play games.

He played for keeps.

Her gorgeous eyes held his, their bodies rocking and grinding erotically. The people, the music, and every other thing in the damn bar faded to black. Chloe was all Justin saw, all he felt, and all he *wanted*. Their hands groped greedily as their bodies moved to a sensual beat all their own. When she danced in a circle in front of him, he tugged her back against his chest and wedged his knee between her legs. Her ass moved enticingly against his cock. He lowered his mouth to her shoulder and dragged his tongue along her hot flesh. He expected her to jerk free, but she must have been as lost in them as he was, because she made a salacious sound, spurring him on. He sealed his mouth over the curve of her neck and, *holy fucking hell*, she ground her ass harder against him.

Her skin was sweet and hot and so damn delicious he trailed kisses up her neck and nipped her earlobe just hard enough to get her attention as he practically growled, "Turn around."

Her eyes met his with the heat of a thousand suns. She was breathless and flushed, and for the first time ever she appeared completely *unguarded*. But as quickly as that sight registered, Chloe lifted her chin with a glimmer of victory in her eyes. How she snapped out of that lust-induced state so fast was beyond him. But he was right there with her, feeling triumphant for achieving that momentary peek at the unguarded beauty. He met every sway of her hips with a celebratory grind of his own.

"*All night long*, sweet thing," he said, earning an extra-sinful grin. The images of her breathless and vulnerable had seared into his mind right beside the one of the victorious glimmer in her eyes. He'd *finally* gotten under her skin, even if only for a moment.

His phone rang with Preacher's ringtone, and for the first time in his adult life, he wanted to ignore it. He wanted to stay right there, with Chloe's sexy body writhing against him, drinking in the incredible I-want-you look in her eyes. It wasn't lost on him that the other night he'd thought her date was an idiot for taking a call and here he was preparing to answer one himself.

But club and family came first.

Always.

Fuck. He pulled the phone from his pocket and put it to his ear. "Yeah?" He continued dancing despite the disapproving look in Chloe's eyes.

"It's Grandpa," Preacher said. "He's in the hospital."

Justin's gut seized. "I'm on my way." He shoved his phone in his pocket, kissed Chloe's cheek, and said, "Sorry, gorgeous. I've got to go," and headed for the table, where Gavin was sitting with Jett.

Gavin turned as he approached. "Hey, man, you two—"

"I've got to take off. Make sure Chloe gets home okay for me?"

"You know I will. Everything okay?" Gavin asked.

"I don't know. I've got to go. Thanks, man." Justin glanced over his shoulder on his way to the door and saw Chloe watching him with a mix of concern and disbelief.

He gritted his teeth. Worry for his grandfather warred with the desire burning through his veins. He pushed through the door, and the cool night air brought reality rushing in. As he climbed on his bike, the fear of losing Mike overshadowed everything else.

Chapter Five

JUSTIN STOOD BESIDE Mike's hospital bed between Preacher and Conroy, holding his grandfather's frail hand. The Dark Knights had shown up en masse, filling Mike's room and spilling into the hallway. Mike had fallen and hit his head on a counter. Seven stitches and several tests later, they were keeping him in the hospital overnight for observation.

"Tell these guys I'm fine and take me home, will you, Maverick?" Mike said in a craggy voice. "I don't need doctors poking at me."

At seventy-nine years old, Mike Wicked was just as ornery as ever. With wispy gray hair, a square jaw, thin lips, and blue-gray eyes, he was a dead ringer for Clint Eastwood in his and Justin's favorite movie, *Gran Torino*. They'd watched it together too many times to count. But the tough old man looked slight and pale in the hospital gown with a bandage on his head.

"No can do, Gramps," Justin said more casually than he felt. His heart had lodged in his throat on his way to the hospital, and it wasn't until he'd seen and spoken to Mike that the oppressive clouds of doom had lifted enough for him to breathe properly again. "You gave us quite a scare and we need to make sure you're okay."

"I just wanted some ice cream," Mike grumbled. "If the damn dog hadn't been in my way, I'd have been fine."

That was Mike's story, that he'd tripped over one of Preacher's dogs. But according to Preacher, the dogs weren't in the kitchen at the time.

Preacher and Conroy exchanged a worried glance.

"We'll have ice cream tomorrow night, Grandpa. I promise." Madigan pushed between Preacher and Justin and said, "Right, Mav? We'll get him his favorite flavor from the Cape Cone."

"Absolutely, Mads." Justin put his arm around her, hugging her against his side. Madigan was seven years younger than Justin. She'd been only four years old when he moved in, and she'd followed him around everywhere. He hadn't known what to do with an adoring little girl with stars in her eyes. But his basal instincts had kicked in, and even when he was a lost little shit, he'd been protective of Madigan.

"You'll be fine," Preacher said. "It's only one night, Pops."

"This is the safest place for you, Gramps. You know that," Baz said.

"You're a doctor. You could have sewn up my head," Mike grumbled.

Baz chuckled. "I could also neuter you to get rid of some of that bullheadedness, but I try not to cross the human-canine lines if I can help it."

"You're no help," Mike grumbled. "I just want to sleep in my own bed." He squinted, eyeing his family members, and then leaned to the side, peering around them. "I thought this was a room full of *men*. Nobody's going to break me out of here?" He swatted the air angrily and said, "Y'all are a bunch of pansies."

"I ain't no pansy," Zander said. "But if I were you, I'd stick around, Gramps. There aren't any hot nurses to take care of you back home."

Zeke nodded in agreement. "He's right, Grandpa. Soak up the attention from the pretty ladies while you can. Like Preach said, it's only one night. You'll walk out of here good as new tomorrow."

"One night is a lot when you have as few left as I've got," Mike complained.

Justin's throat constricted. He'd missed out on knowing this incredible man for the first eleven years of his life. He didn't want to imagine a world without him in it.

"What are you talking about?" Conroy patted his father's leg and said, "You're as strong as a mule and as stubborn as one, too. You're not going anywhere. We're going to be stuck with you for the next decade."

"At least," Preacher added.

"And we're thrilled about it," Ginger said from across the hospital bed, where she stood like a strawberry-blond beacon of light between Tank in his leather vest—arms crossed over his massive chest, dark eyes trained on Mike just as they had been since he'd arrived—and Blaine, a pillar of strength and the calm to everyone's storm.

Blaine placed his hand over Ginger's. She touched the side of her head to his shoulder and nudged her tortoiseshell glasses to the bridge of her nose. Ginger was like a second—*third*—mother to Justin. She helped Conroy run the Salty Hog, and like Reba, she was everything a biker's wife had to be. She took no guff from anyone, and she treated the Dark Knights and their families as just that—*family*. But even with her tough resolve, Justin was always aware of the emptiness Ashley had left behind, in the same way his mother had left a gaping abyss in him. Ginger treated Madigan, Marly, and all of the girls who worked for her as if they were her children, or as she would say, *Gifts from a world that had stolen her only daughter.*

"I'm beginning to think you've all lost your minds, leaving me here overnight," Mike complained. "Old people go into hospitals and they don't come out."

Gunner scoffed as he pushed through the crowd and said, "I'm more worried about those poor nurses than I am about you. The blonde just told me that when they were getting you settled in your room, you asked her for a sponge bath."

Mike snickered. "It was worth a shot. She *is* a cutie." He jiggled Justin's hand and said, "If things don't work out with that pretty little filly you've been chasing, you might think about breaking an arm or something."

A rumble of chuckles rose around them as Reba breezed into the room and said, "Okay, gentlemen, listen up. Apparently the nurses have had enough eye candy for tonight." She patted a few of the guys on their shoulders on her way to the foot of the bed. "We've used up all our favors, and they've given us the boot."

"That's probably for the best. Pop needs his rest," Preacher said.

Mike curled his fingers around Justin's, holding tight as the visiting Dark Knights bade him good night. Mike grumbled goodbyes and said *Get out of here* so many times, the last couple of men to leave said, *We're going, we're going.*

Justin could hear Preacher and Conroy in the hallway thanking the guys for coming.

Mike pulled Justin closer and said, "You remember when your father had those kidney stones? He hated the food here.

You know they won't give me any sugar. Sure you don't want to break me out of here?"

"I'm sure. But I'll be back bright and early tomorrow morning, and I plan on spending the whole day with you. You'll get sick of me fast."

"Thank you, son," Mike said as Conroy and Preacher came back into the room. He pulled Justin closer again and whispered, "Bring cookies, will ya? Or a chocolate chip muffin. *Yeah*, a muffin."

He'd bring Mike whatever he wanted, because the thought of that man lying in a hospital bed tonight slayed him.

When they left the room, Reba wrapped one arm around Justin, the other around Tank. She was only about five three, with shoulder-length mahogany hair, the same shade as Madigan's, and eyes that saw right through just about everyone. She had a knack for knowing who needed a little extra mothering, and Justin wasn't ashamed to be one of the ones to receive it tonight.

"He's okay, sweethearts," Reba said soothingly. "He'll be coming home tomorrow."

Tank grumbled something incoherent.

"Yeah, I know," Justin said, trying to hide his concern.

"Listen, boys. I know how hard it is to see Grandpa like this, but he's not nearly done with us. He comes from good stock. Well, *strong* stock, anyway," she said as they followed the others out of the hospital. "I'm around tonight if either of you wants to come by and talk."

Tank pressed a kiss to the top of her head and said, "Thanks, Aunt Reba. I'm cool." He lumbered off toward his bike.

"I'm good. Thanks, Mom." Justin hugged her.

She held him for an extra moment and said, "I love you, honey."

"I love you, too." It had taken Justin years to say he loved Reba, or anyone else for that matter. She'd been the second person in his life to hear him say those three words. He remembered saying them to his birth mother, but as far as he knew, he'd never once uttered them to his biological father. Calling Reba *Mom* had come years later. But when he'd finally taken those steps, he'd felt like his whole world had changed for the better once again.

"Hey, Ma," Blaine said as he joined them. "Take care of Dad? I don't want to interrupt him and Con."

"Of course, sweets." She hugged him and said, "You boys be safe tonight."

"Always," they said in unison.

After she walked away, Blaine said, "You coming by my place with the guys?"

"Maybe later. I've got something I need to take care of first."

CHLOE AWOKE TO the *ding* of a text. She reached for her phone and sat up on the couch. Given how amped up she'd been earlier in the evening, she couldn't believe she'd dozed off. The lights from the television illuminated her dark living room. She glanced at her phone and saw a message from Justin. Her pulse quickened. She'd been irritated by his abrupt departure, but Gavin had seemed *worried*. She was in such a hazy state of lust when he'd left that she'd noticed he looked a little *some-*

thing, but she hadn't been thinking clearly enough to decipher what that *something* was.

She opened and read his text. *Hey, heartbreaker. You awake?*

It wasn't unusual for her to get a late-night text from Justin. They were usually flirty, or in cases when there was bad weather—like when the storm had hit—protective, asking if she was okay and if she needed anything. She thought about their dirty danceathon and how hot and bothered she'd gotten from his touch, and his *mouth*.

Heat burned through her with the memory.

She curled her legs up on the cushion beside her as she responded. *Yes. What happened tonight?*

She heard the roar of a motorcycle and flew to her feet. He was *here*? Her eyes darted to the light hitting her front window as he pulled into her driveway. *Shit.* She looked down at her silk sleeping shorts and tank top, cursing herself. He probably thought the way she had danced with him had meant she wanted to sleep with him.

Which she *did*, but that was *her* little secret. Her *Wicked* fantasy.

She wasn't going to actually do it!

Her phone dinged with another text, and she clutched it tighter. What had she done? She had been doing such a good job of keeping her distance, or at least she'd tried to keep a virtual wall between them for all this time, and she'd blown it all with *one* dance.

It was *his* fault, unleashing all that raw masculinity on her, like he'd had X-ray vision and had seen her deepest desires. What did she think would happen? That she could put on a show like that for a man like Justin and get away scot-free?

She stood in the middle of her living room clutching her

phone, fully aware that there was no place to hide from what she'd done. He knew she was home.

She lifted her phone and read his text. *Come out front.*

Oh God. She squeezed her eyes shut, knowing what she had to do. Justin was her friend *first*, a flirt *second*. Okay, so he'd started flirting seven seconds after they'd first met, but *still*. She didn't want to mess up their friendship, but more than that, she wasn't going to climb into bed with him just because he knew how to push all her buttons.

She opened her eyes, inhaling deeply, and blew it out slowly, telling herself to *just do it* already. She typed, *I'm not sleeping with you*, and sent it to him. Then she stared at her phone, holding her breath as she awaited his reply.

A knock at her door sent the air rushing from her lungs.

Damn it.

Okay, Chloe. Time to face the music.

He knocked again, making her heart race impossibly faster.

She grabbed her cardigan from the back of the couch and put it on as she stalked to the door. *Fake it until you make it.* She drew her shoulders back, inhaled another calming breath that did nothing to ease her nerves, and pulled the door open. Justin stood in the moonlight wearing the same worn jeans and black T-shirt he'd had on at the bar. His hair had that just-been-fucked look, though she was sure—*or hoped*—it was from his motorcycle helmet and he wasn't actually making a booty call after just having *made* a booty call. She felt a little sick at that thought.

Wait, this was Justin. He wouldn't do that.

Would he?

He was looking at her funny, and she realized she hadn't washed off her makeup before sitting down to watch television.

She probably had bedhead and racoon eyes. She reached up, absently touching her hair.

"Hey, beautiful," he said, but his voice didn't have the same visceral arrogance or flirty vibe as usual. He sounded a little sad. "We have a dance to finish."

She stepped onto the porch, closing the door behind her, and pulled her sweater tight around her, crossing her arms over her middle. "I'm not having sex with you, Justin. I'm sorry if I led you on at Undercover."

The corner of his mouth tipped up, and he said, "Babe, I'm just here for a dance."

He did something on his phone and "Heartbeat" by Carrie Underwood began playing. It was her favorite country song. She couldn't believe her ears.

"Justin...?"

He set his phone on the porch table and said, "You went to see her in concert last fall, and I heard you tell Daphne this was your favorite song."

His arms circled her waist, and he gazed into her eyes, swaying to the beat. She stood rigid, waiting for him to make his move. But then she realized his hands weren't roaming and his hips weren't grinding. His gaze was soft, endearing. They were *just* slow dancing. It was romantic and sweet, and making her melt inside. She didn't know what to say, but as her tension eased, she began swaying with him.

"Did I get the song wrong?" he asked.

"No," she said softly. "I'm just surprised. You really just want to dance?"

"Aw, Chloe. If you need to ask that, you have definitely been going out with the wrong guys." His hand moved up her back, and he played with the ends of her hair. "A gentleman doesn't lie. Especially to a woman he adores."

Adores? Did that word really just come out of Justin's mouth? Everything he was doing was so different from what she knew of him, she couldn't help but say, "Does a gentleman trap a woman outside the ladies' room and make a pass at her?"

"No. Did someone do that?"

She smiled and said, "*You* did."

"That wasn't a pass, sweetheart. If I had made a move on you, you'd know it." He put his lips beside her ear and said, "That was a reminder."

He didn't say anything more, remaining silent long enough for her to realize how much she enjoyed being in his arms and the way their bodies fit together, moving in harmony without the pressure of sex. She couldn't remember the last time she'd simply slow danced with a man.

"You like to pretend you don't feel anything for me," he said, drawing her from her thoughts. "It's about time you stopped doing that."

Maybe it was time, or maybe she was just completely out of sorts, because whenever he was near, he made her feel so many things she never had before. He was dangerous for her heart, wasn't he? She needed to know more about him, about his life, his *world.*

"Why did you leave so fast tonight?" she asked.

"I'm sorry about that. My grandfather, Mike, is in the hospital."

The pain in his voice brought an ache to her chest, and she held him a little tighter. "I'm sorry. Is he okay?"

"Hopefully. They're keeping him overnight."

He'd dropped everything to go see his grandfather. Maybe that shouldn't surprise her, but it did. "Are you close to him?"

"Very. He's a good man. He's taught me a lot."

She realized the song had started over, and she was glad it had. She wasn't ready to stop dancing with him. They fell into comfortable silence, and she found herself hoping the song would repeat a third time. She wanted to ask Justin more questions, but she sensed that maybe he needed this quiet moment, this closeness, as much as she wanted it. It was a strange thought for her to have about the man who took advantage of every chance he got to flirt with her. He probably did the same thing with a lot of other women. She'd seen women ogling him every time they were out with their friends, and just because she'd never seen him bring a date with him or pick up a woman while they were out didn't mean it didn't happen.

Although, now that she was really thinking about it, his eyes were always on *her* when they were out.

Ugh. She was so conflicted. On the one hand, she saw Justin as an impossible flirt without boundaries. But on the other hand, she knew him to be a good, caring, protective friend, a talented artist, and from what she'd seen and heard, an honest, hard worker. She didn't know what to make of everything she felt right then. But she knew one thing for sure. Dancing barefoot beneath the stars on that warm summer night with the man she'd sworn off felt *good* and *right*, and it was the most romantic thing a man had ever done for her.

When the song ended and didn't restart, her heart sank, but neither of them stopped dancing. Justin held her a little tighter, and she gave in to the urge to be closer. She rested her head on his shoulder, enjoying the type of closeness she'd read about in too many romance novels and had never believed could happen in real life.

But it *was* happening. Justin didn't seem to have an ulterior motive for this impromptu completion of their dance, which she found incredibly sexy.

She wasn't sure how long they'd danced to their own silent beat, but when Justin drew back with a soft and compelling gaze, she instantly mourned the loss of their closeness. Those feelings came with a side of confusion, but she didn't try to figure it all out. However long they'd danced, however confused she might be, she wanted to step back into his arms and experience it all over again.

"Thank you for the dance, Chloe. Sorry I came by so late."

"Tha…that's it? That's really all you wanted?"

"For tonight, yes. A gentleman *always* finishes what he starts." He kissed her cheek and said, "But I'm nowhere near done with you, Chloe Mallery." He pocketed his phone and sauntered over to his bike, where he grabbed his helmet and said, "Sleep well, hot lips. Now, get your sweet little ass inside so I know you're safe."

There's the Justin I know…

She went inside, grinning like a fool. When he started his bike, she peeked out the sidelight window, watching him put on his helmet and back out of the driveway.

Maybe it is time I get to know the rest of you.

Chapter Six

MOST OF CHLOE'S friends talked about how wonderful it was to return to their childhood homes and visit their parents. They raved about those visits sparking memories of family dinners, heartfelt moments, and more importantly, the feeling of safety. For Chloe and Serena, family dinners had never been a thing. It was usually just the two of them, and meals were pasta with butter that they'd made themselves, cold cereal, or something else equally easy and cheap. Heartfelt moments were few and far between, and a feeling of safety was something *Chloe* had strived to create for Serena but their mother had never worked very hard at creating for them. As Chloe pulled up to their mother's gray rambler for brunch Sunday morning, the knots in her stomach tightened. Serena's car was parked in the driveway behind their mother's ancient beater. Their mother took care of her car about as well as she had of her daughters and everything else in her life.

Except maybe her boyfriends.

Chloe parked on the street, wondering if her mother's newest boyfriend had already become an ex, didn't have a vehicle, or was simply late, as she was. The kids had been so enthusiastic during orientation for the Junior/Senior Program, she'd gotten even more excited about the potential for other programs she hoped to initiate, and she'd gotten up early this morning to flesh out ideas. But her mind kept tracking back to Justin showing up out of the blue to dance with her last night, and before she'd realized it, she'd daydreamed away the morning and was running late.

She climbed from her car, and as she did every time she visited, she took stock of all the things about herself that were different from her mother and from her upbringing. She drove a car that was only four years old and she took *good* care of it. She always had food in her refrigerator and her pantry, and she'd learned how to cook—*thank you, YouTube*. As she made her way up the walk, she glanced down at her cute cap-sleeved green top, white shorts, and strappy sandals, none of which were secondhand. Not that she had anything against secondhand clothes. She loved shopping at thrift stores. But she didn't *have* to, and that was important to her. She and Serena had lived in ill-fitting secondhand clothes for so many years, *not* wearing them had been a goal of hers when she was young.

She climbed the front steps, and her gaze drifted over the narrow patches of dirt and weeds beneath the windows. She couldn't remember them ever having been planted with flowers or bushes, and she proudly thought about her own bountiful gardens.

Chloe had always thought her mother simply hadn't earned enough money to make a happy home. But eventually she'd learned the truth. She'd lived at home during her first two years at community college in order to watch over Serena. But when Serena went away to school, Chloe left as well, to finish her last two years elsewhere. She'd quickly realized how little it took to make a happy home. The absence of feeling neglected had been enough to allow her to relax and enjoy her surroundings, no matter how unimpressive.

As she stepped onto the porch, the door swung open and Serena exclaimed, "Yay! You're here!"

Chloe had never been bubbly and boisterous like Serena. She didn't know if that was because she'd always had so much responsibility on her shoulders or if it was simply the way she was wired. She had a feeling it was the latter, and she'd always been a little envious of that carefree effervescence and the way it made everything seem lighter and more exciting.

"Sorry I'm late," Chloe said as she hugged her sister. "I lost track of time."

Serena's bracelets jangled as she stepped outside. She looked fashionable and pretty in a flowy white top and blue shorts. When they were young, Serena was always trying to find ways to fit in with the girls in school who wore nicer clothes. As a teenager, she'd decided to start her own trend and had drawn all over her jeans. Sure enough, like everything else her brilliant and creative younger sister put her mind to, Serena's trend-starting dream became reality, and soon all the girls were getting in trouble for writing on their jeans. Except Serena, of course, because their mother never even noticed.

"Daphne said you and Justin were dirty dancing last night," Serena said in a hushed tone. "Did you hook up? Is that why you're late?"

"I swear the gossip at Bayside is ridiculous. No, we did not hook up. I was working." A little white lie to keep from getting interrogated about her daydreams wasn't that bad, was it?

"Bummer." Serena pulled Chloe inside and whispered, "*Tony* hasn't arrived yet, but Mom swears he's coming."

As Chloe put her purse on the table by the door she noticed

a big plastic bag on the floor beneath it. "Is that the luau stuff?"

"Yes. I told you I wouldn't let you down. I found the grass skirt *and* the coconut bra."

"Thank you. I'm *so* excited. I told the girls to dress for a luau. They're probably thinking I'll just hand out leis. I think they'll be surprised at how much I've pulled together." She looked around and said, "Where's Drake?"

"Kitchen—"

"Chloe, sweetheart!" Their mother hustled out of the kitchen wearing skintight cropped jeans, a snug beige tank top with ruffles under her breasts, and sky-high heels. Her blond hair framed her pretty face, and her bangs made her look younger than her fifty-two years.

"I'm sorry I'm late, Mom," Chloe said as her mother hugged her. "I got tied up with work and lost track of time."

Drake walked out of the kitchen looking handsome as ever, pushing his fingers through his wavy dark hair. His eyes moved to Serena, a silent loving message passing between them, before he turned an amused expression to Chloe and said, "Hey, Chloe," then mouthed, *Your mother is wired.*

Their mother had a tendency to get overly dramatic when she was introducing them to a man, as if she could make everything perfect with her bursts of energy. The problem was, Linda Mallery had no concept of how to be a mediocre parent, much less a perfect *anything*. In her eyes, the idea of perfect was catering to a man's wishes, everyone else be damned.

"Let me look at you." Her mother took her by the shoulders, smiling brightly.

Chloe never felt like her mother really *saw* her, no matter how much she pretended to look. Other mothers hung their children's drawings on the refrigerator and kept family pictures in the living room. Their mother hadn't done either. When Chloe and Serena were in grade school, Chloe used to hang up Serena's drawings in her bedroom so Serena would know someone cared. When Chloe was in fifth grade, Drake's parents, who lived around the corner, had given her an inexpensive camera. It was the biggest gift she'd ever gotten, and she'd treasured it for all she was worth. Their mother had claimed not to have enough money to buy their school pictures—probably because she'd spent it on man-seeking clothes. Chloe began taking pictures of Serena, and when her mother would leave money for them to pick up groceries, Chloe had used a little each time to develop her film. She pinned a special picture each year on the wall by the kitchen calendar. Serena had taken pictures of Chloe, too, and at Serena's urging, she'd hung up her picture next to her sister's. That was the year Chloe began making scrapbooks for Serena. When Serena graduated from high school, Chloe had hung a framed picture of her wearing her cap and gown on their mother's wall in the living room. That summer Chloe found a framed picture of herself hanging beside Serena's, and she'd thought their mother had finally taken an interest in them. But then she'd found out that Serena had hung it there, which had meant more to her than if her mother had done it, anyway. Their mother had never once mentioned any of the pinned pictures when they were younger, or the framed pictures of their graduations. But still, when Serena got married, Chloe put up a third, and last, picture on their mother's wall. A picture of her younger sister with her new husband. Maybe it was a passive-aggressive move, but Chloe wanted her mother to see that she hadn't held Serena back.

"You are as gorgeous as ever," their mother exclaimed, pulling Chloe from her thoughts. "Just like your mama! Now, tell me about work. You were doing something the last time we talked, but I can't remember what it was."

Of course you can't. That would take paying attention to something other than your most recent boyfriend. "I was preparing to pitch a trial for the Junior/Senior Program," Chloe reminded her. "I just held the first orientation, and the kids are really excited. I've worked so—"

"That's great!" their mother said as she fluffed the pillows on the couch. "*Wait* until you meet Tony. I know you'll love him. Look." She held out her arm, showing them a cheap silver bracelet. "Isn't it gorgeous? He gave it to me *just because.*"

"Yes, it's beautiful," Chloe said. "Where is he? I thought we were having brunch at ten?"

"Did I say ten? What time is it?" She rushed over to the half-empty bookshelf and pretended to straighten the piles of women's magazines Chloe was sure dated back ten years.

"Ten thirty," Drake said. "And I'm pretty sure you said ten, too."

"Well, he'll be here. He's a busy man. Oh, girls, can you peek into the oven? The food should be just about done." Their mother headed for the stairs and said, "I want to run up and brush my hair real quick."

Chloe followed Serena and Drake into the kitchen, where there was a store-bought Bundt cake sitting on the table still in its packaging with a bright orange sale sticker on the top.

"Sometimes I wonder how she managed to produce us," Serena said.

Drake kissed her neck and said, "I thought we'd covered the birds and the bees pretty extensively."

"Yeah, but you didn't cover the inadequate trapping of a man," Chloe said. "Since Mom doesn't know how to cook, want to make bets about what's in the oven?"

Serena opened the oven door, and they groaned at the sight of something indistinguishable in a disposable tinfoil pan. "What *is* that?"

"The trash can is filled with empty boxes of frozen breakfasts." Drake pointed to the trash can. "Maybe she mixed them together."

"Like I said, how did she give birth to *us*?" Serena said. "Even *I* know how to buy fresh doughnuts."

Drake slung an arm around both of them and said, "I don't care how she managed to do it, but I'm thankful she did. You're two amazing women, and I'm proud to call you family."

"Aw." As Serena hugged him, the roar of a motorcycle sounded out front.

Justin? Chloe's pulse quickened. She barely had time to realize there was no way it could be Justin before the kitchen door flew open and a very large man dressed in head-to-toe black—from the bandanna tied around his head and his dark sunglasses to the studded leather boots on his feet—strode in. He wore a thick silver chain around his neck, and at least two or three days' worth of salt-and-pepper scruff decorated his neck and jaw.

"*Baby!*" he hollered in the husky voice of a smoker as he walked right past the three of them.

Their mother's frantic footsteps thundered down the stairs. She appeared in the doorway, squealed like a teenager, and ran into his arms. He lifted her off her feet, grabbing her ass as he kissed her—*hard*.

Correction.

The black-haired *Dog the Bounty Hunter* practically *ate* their mother's face.

Chloe tried to swallow the bile rising in her throat. She grabbed Serena's hand and whispered, "Please tell me I won't be *her* in twenty years."

As she was set down, their mother said, "Tony, I want you to meet my girls, Chloe and Serena," as beaming and breathless as a new bride.

Chloe had seen that look on her mother too many times to count, and what was Drake? Chopped liver? Why didn't she introduce him?

Tony raked his eyes down Chloe and Serena from their heads to their toes and said, "Baby these aren't *girls*. These are fine-ass women. How's it going? I'm Tony."

Drake stepped in front of Chloe and Serena and crossed his arms. "Drake Savage. That's my *wife* and my sister-in-law you're eyeing."

"Cool name, dude. Hot wife."

Pig. Chloe wondered if he was the type of biker Justin associated with. If he was, she wanted no part of Justin's world, no matter how romantic last night had been. Though she appreciated Drake's efforts, she did not need a man to protect her. She stepped around Drake and said, "Are you a Dark Knight?"

"No way, babe," Tony said. "I don't do any of that group bullshit where you have to attend meetings and do community crap. Ride hard and live free, baby. There ain't no other way."

Relief swept through her, bringing with it a jolt of courage to do what she should have been doing all along. "My name is *Chloe*, not *babe* or *baby*, and my sister, *Serena*, and I would appreciate you *not* looking at us like we're pieces of meat."

Tony chuckled, and as he turned his attention to the cake on the table, he said, "Hey, I meant no offense."

"How about, *I'm sorry if I offended you*?" Chloe said through gritted teeth.

He cut himself a piece of cake and said, "Oh, don't worry, you didn't."

Serena grabbed Chloe's wrist, a warning glare in her eyes as she mouthed, *Let it go.*

Chloe was sure she had smoke coming out of her ears.

Tony looked at their mother and said, "Get your riding boots on, baby. Everyone's driving out to Plymouth for a party at Greg's place."

"*Oh?*" Their mother managed to look a little conflicted as she said, "I thought we'd have brunch."

Tony picked up the hunk of cake he'd cut and handed it to her. "Here's brunch. Eat up and let's go." He cut himself another piece and took an enormous bite.

Their mother's brow knitted, and Chloe felt like a little girl again, hoping her mother would choose her and Serena over a man. Anger boiled inside her. Why did she think her mother would ever change? More importantly, why did she continue to put up with this?

"*Go,*" Chloe seethed. "Serena and I will take care of all this. Just *go.*"

Tony slapped their mother's ass and said, "You heard her. Get a move on, baby."

"I'll make it up to you, girls!" Their mother giggled as she pulled off her heels. Then she ran upstairs, assumedly to get her boots.

Chloe stepped toward Tony and said, "And *you*—"

"Have a good time!" Serena interjected as she grabbed Chloe's hand and yanked her into the living room, scolding her in a hushed tone. "They're not worth it. You'll only feel guilty if you say something."

"Guilty my ass." Chloe shook with anger.

Drake stood between the kitchen and living room like a bodyguard, arms crossed, his back to the girls as Serena said, "You hate saying mean things. Don't do it, Chloe. You know you'll regret it, and not because he doesn't deserve it, but because you're better than him."

Chloe paced, cursing herself for being there and putting herself through that charade for the umpteenth time.

"Bye, girls! We'll do this again soon," their mother said as she ran down the stairs and through the living room. "I love you!" she called over her shoulder on their way out the kitchen door.

"What the *hell* was that?" Drake asked as he strode into the living room.

Chloe put her hands on her hips and said, "Welcome to the freak show at the Mallery house."

"I'm starting to understand why you don't want to date guys who are rough around the edges," Serena said.

Drake pulled her into his arms and said, "That wasn't just around the edges, Supergirl. The guy was a classless asshole. I don't want either one of you anywhere near your mother's boyfriends."

"Don't worry about me. I'm done being part of her dog and pony show," Chloe said. "She'll *always* pick a man over us, and we don't need to feel like shit because she's clingy and pathetic."

Drake looked at Serena expectantly.

"Don't look at *me*. I'm not coming back if you and Chloe aren't."

"Good, because I'd hate to have to forbid you," Drake teased.

Serena scoffed. "That'd go over real well." She wrapped her

arms around him and said, "What happens when you tell me *not* to do something?"

"I know you well, Supergirl. Why do you think I tell you *not* to get frisky on the nights you're tired?" He gave Serena a quick kiss and said, "Why don't I throw that food out and clean up so we can all get out of here."

As he headed into the kitchen, Chloe thought about how lucky Serena was, and her thoughts found their way back to Justin. She remembered how he'd gotten a little aggressive by the ladies' room at the bar and how thrilling it had been. His voice was clear and present in her mind. *That was a reminder. You like to pretend you don't feel anything for me. It's about time you stopped doing that.*

Last night she'd thought maybe it was time she got past her fear of dating tough guys. But Justin's parting words repeated in her head—*Now, get your sweet little ass inside so I know you're safe*—warring with the scenes she'd just witnessed. Were Justin's parting words a tease, like Drake's, underscored with thoughts of her well-being? Or was it just the tip of the iceberg? A warning flag showing her that if she opened that door, Tony-like behavior might come tumbling out?

CHLOE HAD BEEN left so raw and confused after what had happened with her mother's boyfriend, she'd worried that she might be stepping into a lion's den with Justin. She'd fought the urge Sunday night and throughout the day on Monday to text him and ask how his grandfather was doing. On Monday night, Chloe sat on her living room floor sorting pictures for the wedding album she was making for Harper and Gavin, trying to ignore the nagging feeling that she'd let her friend down. She'd taken dozens of photos of Harper and Gavin with their friends in the weeks leading up to the wedding, and last month when they'd gotten married, she'd taken dozens more.

She sifted through a few pictures of Gavin and Harper looking so in love she could feel it. As she set them aside, she spotted a picture of Justin, Gavin, and Beckett standing arm in arm and picked that one up instead. It was taken the night of the wedding. Gavin and his brother looked model perfect with their clean-shaven cheeks and pristine suits. But it was Justin who captured her attention, with his scruffy cheeks and tousled hair. His tie was a little crooked, his clothes slightly rumpled. He had one hand in his pocket, the other around Gavin's shoulder, revealing the leather bracelet he wore. Sometimes he wore other jewelry, but the bracelet was a constant, and she wondered if it was from an ex-girlfriend, or just something he'd picked up for himself. She studied the picture, thinking about that night. Justin had stuck close by her all evening. After most of their friends had turned in for the night, Beckett had invited Chloe to join him at the bar for a drink, and Justin had inserted himself between them for the rest of the night. At the time, he'd said it was because he hadn't wanted her to become a notch on *Beckett's* belt. She'd thought Justin had just been his typical pushy, flirty self, hoping for a one-night stand despite his claim about Beckett. But Justin *hadn't* made a move on her that night, just like he hadn't the night of the storm, when he'd left without so much as a kiss.

You hesitated that night, sweet thing. That's why I left…I'll never force myself on you.

She looked at the picture again, feeling like a heel.

Her worries about Justin didn't even seem fathomable. She had never been a sucky friend to anyone. Why had she let her mother's crazy life change that? Justin wasn't Tony, and he wasn't Drake. He wasn't like any man she'd ever known, and she felt horrible that she hadn't texted to see how his grandfather was doing. Lord knew he'd checked on her for far less important reasons. He was the *only* man who had always been there to help her and to protect her even when she didn't want protecting. He'd held her when he'd found her sitting in her car crying in front of her house after work one night because a resident of LOCAL with whom she'd been friends had passed away. He'd even attended the funeral with her. He might be overly flirtatious and pushy, but he was the very definition of a good friend, and she wanted to be that for him, too.

Her phone dinged with a notification from one of the dating apps she used.

She huffed out a disgusted breath. Using dating apps had been an experiment, one that she had never been very comfortable with, but knew she might have always wondered about if she hadn't tried it. It was time to put that part of her life away. She was *not* a serial dater.

She set down the picture she was holding, picked up her phone, and proceeded to deactivate her accounts on the two dating apps she'd tried.

She felt better.

Sort of.

She looked at the picture of Justin and the guys again. She'd thought Justin was jealous of Beckett that night, and maybe he was. Beckett was definitely worthy of jealousy. He fit all of the *pros* on her dating list. He was professional, clean cut, and *safe*. But he didn't make her pulse race in that dangerous way Justin

A LITTLE BIT WICKED

did. The way that made her feel like she might lose her mind—and her *panties*.

Her belly fluttered at the thought of losing her panties with Justin.

But her fluttery belly twisted uncomfortably, knowing she hadn't been a good friend to the man who she *finally* realized put friendship above all else.

She snagged her phone and texted Justin. *Hey.* She added a smiling emoji. *How's your grandfather?* Her pulse quickened as she waited for him to respond.

The phone vibrated as a message bubble appeared. *He's great. I've been with him all day.*

She sighed with relief and texted, *I'm glad to hear it.*

His response was immediate. *What are you doing?*

She thumbed out, *Making a wedding album for Harper and Gavin. Don't tell Gavin.*

When Justin didn't reply right away, she set her phone down and tried to concentrate on the album, but her eyes kept drifting back to the phone.

A few minutes later his response came through. *Sorry, had to tell Gavin about the album. He's stoked!*

She laughed and texted, *Remind me not to tell you any more secrets.*

He replied, *I'm going to learn them all.*

She typed, *In your dreams.* Her pulse raced, knowing his reply would be fast and dirty—and it was.

They're fantasies, and you star front and center in all of them. Send me the pics from the other night.

God, she loved his brazenness as much as she feared it.

Did that make her like her mother?

The thought soured in her stomach.

79

She texted, *I'm not going to be one of your spank-bank girls.*

His reply was immediate. *You've been my only spank-bank girl since the day we met. I've got pics of you burned into my mind in your sexy bikini, in those fancy outfits you wear, and in the skimpy shorts that make me want to bite your hot little ass.*

She swallowed hard against the tug of desire low in her belly.

Rose's voice trampled through her mind. *Every woman should have a man who makes her tummy tingle as often as he makes her feel safe, valued, and loved.*

Another message appeared with a picture of Justin lying on his side in a black tank top, his muscular, tattooed arms on display. His head was propped up with his hand. His hair was sexily messy, and his eyes were at half-mast, clearly conveying, *Come on, heartbreaker, you know you want me.*

She couldn't take her eyes off him. How could he make her feel hot and bothered with only texts and a picture? And why did she want to *play* so badly when she worried it was the absolute wrong thing to do? Rose was a wise woman. Maybe she was right about not keeping such a black-and-white list of must-haves for the men she went out with. Chloe had come up with that list more than a decade ago, after the awful incident outside the Salty Hog her second year of college. She'd been dating only men who fit that list for so long, she was afraid to live any other way.

Another message bubble appeared. *Dream about me tonight, sexy girl, because I'll be fantasizing about you.*

Good Lord. This was a terrible idea. There was no way she would be able to think of anything *but* him for the rest of the night.

Well played, Wicked. Well played.

Chapter Seven

THE DAYS FLEW by, peppered with a mix of lustful anticipation and anxiety caused by a certain hot biker with a filthy mouth. Justin texted Chloe every night with something flirty and dirty, like *Know what time it is?* When she took the bait, he'd responded with *Chloe o'clock. I'm sifting through my mental images. What are you in the mood for? An ass bite or something more sensual?* Or he'd text something less blatant, like *Busy?* When she said she was working on the wedding album, or anything else, he'd texted, *I can feel you thinking about me. Can you feel me touching you?*

The man knew exactly how to get to her. Not only couldn't she *stop* replying to his messages, but she looked *forward* to them. She'd been wrong about texts and foreplay. It was a very effective method. Thank goodness he hadn't texted her when she was meeting with the board earlier in the day. That would have been embarrassing. She'd have had to lock herself in her office with his picture and finish herself off. *What* was happening to her? She'd never been a *sexter*. She knew she needed to put a stop to the texts, or he'd probably think he could jump her bones the next time he saw her. But it was Thursday afternoon, and she was still at work. With the start of the new

Junior/Senior Program, and the rest of Chloe's administrative duties, she had no time for *hot* or *bothered*. Now was not the time to think about, much less try to disengage from, the dirty talker who was weaseling his way into her every thought.

As she made her rounds that afternoon, talking with residents and checking on the men and women who were taking part in the Junior/Senior Program, her thoughts turned to her mother. Years from now, would she and Serena be making decisions about putting their mother into a facility like LOCAL? Chloe had been hurt and angry enough Sunday to answer that question with a complete and total shun of those responsibilities, but it had been several days, and she'd had time to calm down about the fiasco that had been their morning. The truth was, she knew herself better than that. When and if that time came, she couldn't turn her back on her mother. Just because her mother sucked at parenting didn't mean Chloe had to suck at daughtering.

She stopped by the community room, where Owen Crenshaw, one of the teenagers taking part in the program, was reading to Samuel Warren. Samuel had first arrived at LOCAL five years ago with his wife, Alma. Samuel had suffered an accident as a child that had left him with limited vision. His wife used to read to him, but she'd passed away earlier in the year. Chloe had made a point of reading to him over her lunch breaks as often as she could fit it in.

When she'd first come up with the idea for the Junior/Senior Program, she'd imagined being one of the teenagers given the gift of an elderly friend who could share some of the wisdom that came with age. That was one of the things she enjoyed most about working with the elderly. She had hoped the program would be well received by both the teenagers and the residents, and she was overjoyed to have heard only positive feedback so far. And based on the smiles on Owen's and Samuel's faces, it looked to still be holding true.

On her way back to her office, she made a mental note to stop in and visit Samuel when he was alone, just to make sure her observation was correct.

"Chloe?"

She turned at the sound of Darren Rogers's voice and found the distinguished CEO heading her way. She had a lot of respect for Darren. He was a fair and tactful man who evaluated all sides of situations before making decisions and took the time to get to know residents and staff. "Hi, Darren."

"I'm glad I ran into you," he said kindly. "I wanted to pass along how impressed the board and I were with your ideas this morning."

"Thank you." She had told them about the puppetry program she was looking into. "I've reached out to a local puppeteer to get more information. If all goes well, I'll prepare a formal proposal for Alan."

"Excellent. Your continued commitment to this facility and our residents has not gone unnoticed."

With a friendly nod, he went in the direction of the executive offices. Chloe headed to her office with a little extra pep in her step.

Shelby waved her down as she passed the reception desk. She put a call on hold and said, "It's Madigan Wicked. Do you have time to talk to her?"

"Absolutely, thanks." Chloe hurried into her office and picked up the phone as she walked around the desk. "Mads, hi. I'm sorry for all of the telephone tag we've been playing."

"I'm the one who's sorry," Madigan insisted. "I've been

running all over the place. I've got a conference call in about five minutes, and I've got to prepare for a show I'm doing tonight, but I wanted to try to catch you. I was thinking, since our days are so busy, would you mind trying to get together in the evening?"

"Not at all."

"Great. I know this is short notice, but I'm meeting my friend Marly at the Salty Hog later tonight. Do you want to meet me upstairs in the bar after my show? Around eight thirty? Marly isn't coming until around ten, so we should have plenty of time to talk."

Chloe's nerves prickled. The idea of sitting in that particular biker bar after what had happened that awful night all those years ago made her skin crawl. She knew the Salty Hog was owned by Justin and Madigan's aunt and uncle, and if Madigan was comfortable there, then Chloe should be, too. But it didn't take away those memories. She couldn't tell Madigan she'd rather not go to her relatives' bar, so she agreed to meet her there and hoped for the best.

After ending the call, Chloe pulled up her notes and program ideas and tried to lose herself in those rather than the anxiety prickling up her spine.

LATER THAT EVENING, Chloe changed into skinny jeans and a sleeveless blouse and put on her favorite dragonfly anklet to give herself a little extra courage. Dragonflies symbolized transformations and new beginnings. With a little luck, she and Madigan would have a great meeting and maybe even lessen her bad feelings about the Salty Hog.

She headed out the door with high hopes.

It was a clear night, and as she climbed from her car, she was greeted by music from the bar and the scents of the harbor. All the makings for a nice evening were there, if only the bad memories trying to bully their way in would abate. Chloe decided to avoid the busy restaurant and climbed the steps to the outdoor entrance to the bar, feeling more nervous by the second. She reminded herself that what had happened when she was in college was *not* going to happen tonight, and used all the tricks she'd relied on over the years to give herself courage to push past the bad memories: lifting her chin, breathing deeply, and most importantly, believing in herself.

She stepped into the crowded bar and scanned the room for Madigan. The rustic bar had a rougher vibe than Chloe's usual hangout, with marred wood walls and scuffed floors. The clientele seemed edgier, too, but that might have to do with the dozen or so men, both bearded and clean cut, wearing leather vests with Dark Knights' patches and giving off a tough vibe. There were plenty of other men who weren't bikers and were dressed in button-downs and slacks, shorts, and jeans, and dozens of women decked out in cute summer outfits. Conversation and laughter filled the air, but still a sense of heightened awareness engulfed Chloe.

"Chloe!" Madigan waved from a high-top table. Her mahogany hair fell in soft waves over her shoulders as she stepped off the chair, looking young and beautiful in a short, flowy aqua-and-white sundress. "I'm so happy you made it." She hugged Chloe enthusiastically.

"Thanks for making time to meet." Chloe climbed onto a chair. "I love your dress."

Madigan took her seat across from Chloe and said, "I got this when I was in Spain last spring. I bought it in three colors because I loved it so much."

"You really are a world traveler. The puppeteering business must be booming."

"I have no idea what is going on, but all of a sudden I'm getting all sorts of offers, and not just for puppeteering. I also play guitar and do storytelling gigs, and I write the Mad Truth greeting cards." The Mad Truth About Love line of greeting cards made light of the harder aspects of relationships.

"I had no idea you played guitar *or* created those cards. I love them. How do you come up with so many new ideas?"

"Having your heart crushed to smithereens makes it easy to poke fun at love. Needless to say, I'm firmly rooted in the true-love-doesn't-exist-for-Madigan-Wicked camp."

"Oh, I'm sorry."

Madigan leaned forward and said, "Let's keep the whole *heartbreak* thing between us. That's a long, painful story that my brothers know nothing about. And trust me, I don't need the men in my life getting up in arms."

"Don't worry. I would never say anything." Chloe wondered what *up in arms* really meant. "It must be hard having such overprotective brothers."

"Brothers, father, uncles, cousins." Madigan shrugged and said, "When you're the daughter of the Dark Knights' president, you're considered the club *princess*. Everyone watches out for me."

"Is that why you travel so much? To get away from their eagle eyes?"

Madigan shrugged. "Not really. They might be overprotective, but I miss them like crazy when I'm away. I just love to travel and meet new people. That's why I'm not sure what I'll do about the offers I've been getting. There are some cool storytelling gigs, and of course puppeteering, but I'm also being wooed to expand my Mad Truth line into other areas. The trouble is, most of the offers require pretty heavy travel. My grandfather fell recently and landed in the hospital. He's okay, but it made me realize that I may not have much more time with him. I think I'm going to be sticking around here for a while."

"Justin told me about your grandfather. I'm glad he's all right, and I'm sure your family is happy that you'll be sticking around."

"They are. I've been looking forward to talking with you all afternoon. I can't wait to hear what you have in mind."

"I'm on a fact-seeking mission," Chloe said. "As the director of LOCAL, I'm always on the lookout for new programs for the elderly. I'd like your insight on using puppets to help patients with dementia. Have you ever heard of that, or worked with the elderly?"

"Yes. Puppetry has been used with the elderly for quite some time. Other countries seem to have a better, or more widely recognized, grasp of how beneficial puppetry can be for a host of issues, not just with the elderly. I studied overseas, and I've worked with the elderly in a couple of different countries, but oddly enough, not here in the US." Madigan looked up as a tall strawberry-blonde with tortoiseshell glasses and a warm smile approached the table. "Hi, Aunt Ginger."

"Hi, Mads. I thought I'd see if your friend wanted a drink and if you gals were hungry." Ginger placed her hand on her jeans-clad hip. Her maroon top revealed small tattoos on her upper arms. "I don't think I've seen you around before."

"This is my friend Chloe Mallery. She's the director at LO-CAL. Chloe, this is my aunt Ginger," Madigan said. "She and my uncle Conroy own this place."

"It's nice to meet you," Chloe said.

"So *you're* the infamous *Uptown Girl*." Amusement danced in Ginger's eyes, and she said, "I wondered when I might finally meet you."

"*Uptown Girl?*" Chloe had no idea what she was talking about.

Ginger touched Chloe's shoulder and said, "Oh, honey, it's meant as a compliment. But I just got myself in trouble and let the cat out of the bag, didn't I?" She winced and looked at Madigan.

Madigan's eyes widened. "Hey, don't look at me. I'm as confused as Chloe is."

"Okay, here's the deal." Ginger's face turned serious. "My nephew Maverick—*Justin*—has had one heck of a crush on you for a *very* long time, and his brothers and cousins tease him about you being out of his league. You know how guys joke around."

Chloe had been so swept up in her conversation with Madigan, she hadn't even realized her nervousness had dissipated until now, as her nerves prickled to life and her cheeks burned with embarrassment. "It sounds like they think I'm too stuck-up for him."

"*What?* No. No way," Madigan exclaimed.

Ginger shook her head. "No, honey. I assure you, stuck-up has *never* been mentioned. *Sexy, beautiful, smart*, yes, but *never* stuck-up. The guys think you're hot stuff."

"How come *I've* never heard anyone call her that?" Madigan asked.

"Because *I'm* the bartender and I hear everything." Ginger touched Madigan's shoulder as she'd touched Chloe's and said, "And *you're* the baby sister who the men in our family would like to think knows nothing about the scandalous ways of men and women."

Madigan rolled her eyes. "What*ever*. Well, it's no wonder Justin is into you, Chloe. You're gorgeous. Most of the guys in here were checking you out the second you walked in."

"They were not," Chloe said, looking around quickly, although she was too sidetracked thinking about Justin's brothers and cousins calling her *Uptown Girl* to think about anything else. She'd never felt out of Justin's league. They just had different lifestyles.

"They *were* checking you out, sugar," Ginger said. "And that's a *good* thing. Pretty young women like you two deserve to be checked out." She pointed across the room to a handsome man with longish silver hair and a bright white smile talking with a group of people and said, "Now, if someone like *that guy* checks you out, then you'd better watch yourself. He's a real flirt."

"That silver fox over there? Really? I guess if you're that good-looking, it kind of comes with the territory," Chloe said.

Madigan burst into hysterics. "That's my *uncle* Conroy! He never flirts with anyone but Aunt Ginger."

"Oh my gosh! I'm so sorry for calling your husband a silver fox!" Chloe covered her face.

Ginger laughed and said, "Don't be. Everyone checks him out, as well they should. That man is quite a looker, and he's all *mine*. We tease a lot around here, but it's all in good fun. You should come by more often. And for what it's worth, my sons and my nephews have their heads stuck in their spokes, because

Maverick is one of the finest and most honorable young men I know. Now, what can I get you to drink?"

"After hearing what they call me, a bottle of tequila might be nice," Chloe teased.

"I hear ya on that," Ginger said as her husband headed their way. "Are you driving tonight?"

"Yes, but I was kidding about the tequila. Just an iced tea would be great, thank you," Chloe said as Conroy Wicked stepped beside Madigan's chair and dropped a kiss on her head. He was even more handsome up close, with deep dimples and blue eyes as bright as his smile.

"How're my girls?" Conroy asked.

"Hi, Uncle Con," Madigan said warmly. "This is my friend Chloe. She thinks you're hot."

"*Mads!*" Chloe chided her, causing them to laugh. "I don't think that! I mean, you're a handsome man, but…" She was so screwed, and Conroy was grinning like this was not his first time at this rodeo, so she said, "Okay, she's right. Your wife went fishing, and I took the bait. I'm sorry."

He kissed Ginger's cheek and slid his arm around her waist. "That's my girl, always toying with the customers."

"I was just welcoming her to the Hog," Ginger said sweetly. "Do you have any idea who this gorgeous blonde is?"

"*Chloe.* Mads just told me," Conroy answered.

Chloe stood up and extended her hand. "Hi, I'm Uptown Girl," she said as he shook her hand. "You might have heard of me. Billy Joel wrote a song about me before I was even born." She sat back down and said, "And for the record, I don't think I'm out of *anyone's* league."

Conroy laughed deeply and heartily. "You're the gal who caught Maverick's eye a long, long time ago. Well, this *is* a pleasure, Chloe. You have thrown that boy for a loop. And the nickname is all in good fun. You know, Mav's quite a catch."

"I'm sure Justin has a lot of women tossing him their fishing lines," Chloe said more casually than she felt.

"All our Wicked boys do," Conroy joked. "But Maverick's not a catch-and-return type of guy."

"Do *not* try to set her up, Uncle Con," Madigan said. "Chloe is here to discuss work, not to be on *The Dating Game*."

"Hey, I'm just an uncle bragging about my nephew. No harm in that." Conroy chuckled and turned his attention to Ginger. "Any word from the boys?"

"Not yet," Ginger said. "How is Leah doing shadowing Starr?"

"Is Leah the new waitress? I saw her with Starr when I first came in," Madigan said.

"Yes. She just started," Conroy said. "Leah is fast and capable, and she's friendly *enough*." He gazed across the room at a skinnyish girl with a mass of thick, curly brownish-red hair and a wary look in her eyes. "She's not warm, and the verdict is still out on if she can handle the guys here or not. But it's only her first week, and she's doing a really good job of learning the ropes."

"We're a wild bunch, Con. It takes time to warm up to us," Ginger said. "As long as she can hold her own and she's fast and capable, it sounds like we'll have a great employee. I'll chat with her before she leaves tonight and see if I can help her feel more comfortable." She turned back to Chloe and Madigan and said, "I've kept you girls waiting long enough. What are you hungry for?"

"Nachos would be great." Madigan looked at Chloe and said, "Are you hungry?"

"No, thanks. I ate before I came."

Conroy frowned at Madigan and said, "Nachos aren't dinner, Mads. How about a burger?"

"How about Nachos with extra beef?" Madigan countered.

"I'll see what I can do." Conroy winked, and then he lowered his voice, giving Ginger a smoldering look, and said, "Meet me in the kitchen for a quick make-out sesh?"

"Uncle *Conroy!*" Madigan scolded, but her smile told Chloe she didn't mind his playfulness.

Conroy chuckled as he walked away.

"He's so *bad*," Madigan said.

"That he is, and boy, do I love that man. Even after all these years, he still makes my heart go pitter-patter." Ginger sighed and said, "Everyone should be so lucky. I'll bring your drink in a sec, Chloe."

As she walked away, Madigan called to her, "Stay out of the kitchen!"

"You're no fun," Ginger said over her shoulder.

Madigan flopped back in her chair and said, "I love them so much."

"They seem happy. You're lucky to have so many relatives in the area. I've never met any of mine."

"None?"

Chloe shook her head, but she didn't want to talk about her weird upbringing, so she said, "We're not here to talk about me. I'd love to hear your thoughts on puppetry and the elderly."

"I have *lots* of thoughts on that." Madigan told her about the work she'd done with the elderly and what she'd learned. She explained the benefits of having residents create personal puppets, which would be good for their fine motor skills, and that encouraging the use of the puppets to create their own shows aided with social interaction and stimulated their brains. She told Chloe how the use of puppets could trigger memories and help break down communication barriers that went hand in hand with Alzheimer's and dementia and that it was helpful for people who suffer from depression, too.

They talked for a long time, noshing on nachos and joking as often as they were serious. Chloe explained that she was thinking of putting together a proposal for a trial program involving only a few residents and spanning a four-to-six-week period, just as she was doing with the Junior/Senior Program, and if it proved beneficial, then she would pitch a longer-term program.

"Does that sound like something you'd be interested in?" Chloe asked.

"Yes. Definitely."

"That's great. Would you be willing to help me with the proposal? I want to be sure my terminology is correct and that I don't miss any key elements."

"I'd love to."

They made plans to meet the following Tuesday at Chloe's office, and Chloe explained all of the hoops Madigan would have to jump through in order to work at LOCAL, assuming the proposal was accepted.

"I'm excited about what this program could do for our residents," Chloe said as she gathered her notes and began putting them into her messenger bag.

"Me too." Madigan eyed Chloe's bag and said, "I see a red book cover. Is that *Dirty Island Desires*?"

"Yes. I run a book club and we're reading it. Have you read it? It hit all the bestseller lists."

"My book club is reading it, too! I bet they all are. It's all over social media. I'm almost done with it, and *oh my God*, talk about *hot*!"

"I know. It's *so* good. What book club are you in?"

"It's online, and right now it's just called My Book Club because the founders can't decide on a name."

Chloe laughed and said, "I can't believe this. That's *my* book club. I started it with my friend Daphne. We're still trying to come up with the perfect name."

"Are you ReadingMama or ChapterChick? I'm MadReader!"

"I'm ChapterChick, and Daph is ReadingMama. She has a two-and-a-half-year-old daughter. How did you find the club?"

"My cousin Dixie was visiting last summer and she turned me and my friend Marly on to it."

"Dixie Whiskey?" Chloe asked. When Madigan nodded, she said, "I know her. She and her friends have joined us over video chat a few times. She's a riot."

"Oh my gosh, you have *no* idea. I want to be Dixie when I grow up. I swear she's tougher than half the guys I know." Madigan lowered her voice and said, "And she's married to the hottest guy on the planet, Jace Stone, of Silver-Stone Cycles."

"I don't know anything about motorcycles." *But I think Justin has got that hottest-guy label sewn up.*

"I don't know much about motorcycles, either, but I know Jace's are right up there as some of the best. I drive a pink Vespa, which my brothers *love* teasing me about. Anyway, you should know that I've told *all* my friends about the book club. See that blond waitress? The one with the long kinky hair and tattoos that Leah is shadowing?" She pointed across the room to a pretty girl taking an order from a customer and said, "That's Starr. She's in the book club, too."

"Really? That's awesome. When Daph and I started the club, we never imagined having a whole group of readers in our area. Do you know we have in-person meetings every month at different locations?" Since the club had members all over the world, most of their communication was handled in the online forum, but every month a member was chosen at random to select the book for the following month and to choose the location for the in-person meeting. They had only one rule. The meetings must take place where there was a beach, or at least a body of water. Members who could not make it were always invited to join them via video chat.

"Yes, but I never check out that thread because I'm always traveling. Using the forum is easier."

"I totally get that. But this month's meeting is local. We're meeting at Cahoon Hollow Beach tomorrow night at seven. Do you want to come? You can bring Marly and Starr. It's going to be a lot of fun. I've planned a tropical island luau theme with leis and fruity drinks, island music, the whole nine yards."

"That sounds incredible. I'm sure Marly will want to come, and I'll ask Starr, but she's a single mother and I know she has trouble finding sitters for Gracie. She's an active toddler."

"She can bring her. We're used to little ones. Sometimes Daphne has to bring her daughter, Hadley. I can't wait to meet Marly, and hopefully Starr, too. What are their screen names? I'll hunt them down on the forums."

"Marly's is FlippinPages, and Starr's is RadiantReader. They'll be excited to—"

The doors to the deck flew open and Justin and Tank walked in with Justin's brothers and a handful of other guys wearing black vests with Dark Knights' patches. They stood by the door, a mob of grim scowls, silencing the din of the crowd like a wave of darkness. Their clothes were torn and bloody. There was an angry bruise on Justin's cheek, scratches on his arms, and a tear in his jeans, exposing a bloody thigh. Tank motioned toward a table in the corner where more Dark Knights were sitting, and several of the men headed that way. The crowd parted, wide-eyed, for Tank, Justin, Blaine, Zeke, and Zander as they strode toward the bar shoulder to shoulder, heads down, moving like they carried the weight of the world on their backs.

Justin lowered himself to a barstool, and Conroy set a beer in front of him. He served Tank and the others as Ginger inspected their cuts and bruises. They were too far away for Chloe to hear what they were saying, but Justin was shaking his head. The grave tone of their voices gave Chloe chills. She was riveted to the scene unfolding before her, her worst assumptions appearing to be true—a good reminder of why she dated pretty boys who cared too much about their faces to get in fights.

Justin leaned his elbows on the bar and lowered his forehead to his hands. It was such a strange, unreconcilable sight to see her strong, able-to-handle-anything friend look so defeated. But despite the fears rattling inside her, Chloe ached for him. "They look like they had a rough night."

"Yeah. I guess things didn't go well," Madigan said, watching her brothers.

Chloe saw Leah heading toward the bar, looking down at her order pad. Tank turned just as Leah looked up, and she froze, eyes wide. Tank was intimidating on any given day, but with the scratches on his face and arms and the grim look in his eyes, he was downright *terrifying*. Ginger put a hand on Leah's shoulder and leaned in close to say something. Chloe couldn't imagine what she might say to take away the fear in that girl's eyes, but Leah scurried away like a frightened mouse. Chloe imagined Leah was probably rethinking her new job right about now.

Tank's shoulders sank, and he turned to Blaine, motioning toward the table where other Dark Knights had gathered. Blaine nudged Justin, but Justin shook his head. Blaine and the others headed for the table in the corner, leaving Justin to stare into his untouched beer alone.

"Is it always like this?" Chloe asked, unable to look away from Justin.

"Sometimes," Madigan said. "They do what they have to."

"Since when does anyone *have to* fight?"

"They'd do anything to save another life," Madigan said softly.

Chloe didn't know what that meant, but she was done trying to guess about Justin and his life. It didn't matter how she felt about fighting. She couldn't just sit there and watch him suffer. "Would you mind if I went to check on Justin?"

"Not at all. I want to check on the others, anyway. I'll see you tomorrow night at the book club meeting."

"I'm looking forward to it." Chloe stepped from the chair and grabbed her bag.

With her heart in her throat, and not entirely sure she was doing the right thing, she made her way across the room.

JUSTIN STARED BLANKLY into his drink. He'd had a shit day. Douchebag Alan Rogers had been home when Justin and Blaine had gone to check out his property that morning, and it had taken all of Justin's restraint not to give the guy hell when he'd talked down to them. But that had been nothing compared to the rest of the day. The day's events must have messed him up even more than he'd thought, because his skin prickled the way it did whenever Chloe was nearby. But he knew that was just wishful thinking. She never went to the Salty Hog. He closed his eyes, willing the sensation away, but it only became stronger. He finally lifted his head and looked around, sure he was losing his mind. He scanned the crowd, and when a group of people sat down, his chest constricted. As if he'd conjured her, Chloe came into view across the room—a beacon of hope on the darkest of nights, bringing as much relief as anguish.

Her steps were tentative, her eyes wary. If it were any other night, he'd worry that maybe he'd taken their sexy texts too far these past few days, but he knew that wasn't why she looked a little frightened. He hated the idea of her being scared at all, much less of him, but he knew how strongly she disliked violence, and there was no hiding what he'd done. At least she wasn't walking out the door.

He drew his shoulders back, trying to smile, but sadness and anger gnawed at him. He tried to mask those feelings with humor even though he knew it was a losing battle, and said, "Hey, heartbreaker. What brings you to this side of town?"

"I was talking to Mads about doing some puppeteering at LOCAL." She studied his face, and then her gaze moved down his arms to the bloody gash in his leg. She lifted worried eyes to his and said, "Are you okay?"

That familiar magnetic pull tugged at him, the need to be near her, to let her presence calm him. But he was in too dark of a mood to act casual. He needed to get the hell out of there before he scared her even more. "I'm fine."

"You should probably clean that gash in your leg."

"I'll get around to it." He picked up his beer, wishing he could drink the darkness away, but the thought of the dogs they'd rescued tonight, and the ones they couldn't, turned his stomach. He set the beer back down, swallowing a curse.

"Don't be a pain. You'll get an infection." She dropped an enormous leather bag on the bar and rifled through it. "I'm afraid to ask what the other guys look like."

"Fuck the other guys. They're not the ones who matter."

"*Justin…*" She looked at him with disbelief as she withdrew a first aid kit from her bag and opened it. Turning her attention to the kit, she found a small packet of antiseptic wipes and tore it open. Her eyes shot up to his. "I don't even know who you are right now," she said as she began cleaning the cut on his leg.

"Ow. *Holy hell*, blondie."

"Don't be a baby. If you can fight, you can take a little antiseptic." She continued cleaning his wound and said, "I don't know what you thugs fought about, but *every* life matters, and I don't believe for a second that you think otherwise." She set the dirty wipe on the bar and snagged a new one, then went back to cleaning his cut.

"Why are you doing this?"

"Despite pretending that I don't notice certain things about you, you're always there when I, or anyone else, needs you. The least I can do is be here for you to make sure you don't get an infection. You're all tough now, but you'll probably cry like a baby when your cut gets infected." She glanced at him, and the edges of her lips curved up in a sweet half smile, easing some of his tension. She set down the soiled wipe and used her hand to fan the damp area on his leg dry.

He caught her hand in his and said, "*Pretending*, huh?"

With a roll of her eyes, she pulled her hand free. "How can you flirt at a time like this?" She picked up an individually sealed packet of antibiotic ointment from the first aid kit and tried to rip it open. She tugged and twisted the packet, her eyes narrowing determinedly.

He took the packet from her and tore it open with his teeth. He handed it back to her and said, "Because it's easier than dealing with the shit in my head."

"Then talk to me. Why did you guys get into a fight?"

He clenched his jaw, not wanting to bring something so bleak into her beautiful world.

"Come on, Justin. Whatever it is, it can't be worse than the ideas floating around in my head." She began applying the ointment to his wound, her eyes flicking up to his, and said, "Spill it, Wicked."

He watched her carefully cover the ointment with a bandage. "We went with the police to break up a dogfighting ring, and things got ugly."

"*Dogfighting* ring?" The shock in her eyes was unmistakable. She looked at his arms and said, "Are those scratches from the dogs?"

He nodded. "And from the fencing on the property."

"I hope you have a current tetanus shot. What about your leg? Is that from the dogs or the fence? And that bruise on your face?"

He gritted his teeth, hating to have to admit the rest of the truth, which she wouldn't like, but he wasn't about to hide any part of himself from anyone—*especially* her. "When the police went in the front door, they had the back door covered. But a couple of guys came out the cellar doors on the side of the house, and more from a shed in the back, and we went after them. Like I said, things got a little rough."

Her brow wrinkled, conflicting emotions swimming in her beautiful eyes. "They were the ones running the dogfighting ring?"

He nodded.

"Then they deserve whatever they got." Her voice softened as she said, "And the dogs?"

"We saved the ones we could."

Sadness rose in her eyes, and she put her hand over his. "Some didn't make it?" She looked regretfully at the table where his brothers and cousin were sitting and said, "I thought you guys were just…"

"Being reckless? Troublemakers?" He cocked a brow. "I've heard it all, Chloe. Nothing you say will shock me."

"I'm sorry. I should know you better than to assume something like that. But there's so much that I *don't* know about you, I guess I filled in the blanks based on past experiences."

"No shit, princess." He turned his hand over, holding hers, and said, "I've been trying to fix that."

Her eyes skirted nervously around them. She looked down at their joined hands, and he was sure she'd pull away. But she didn't. She met his gaze again and said, "Do you want to take a walk and talk about it? Get it out of your system?"

"You sure you want to hear about this?" He was thankful for the opening she'd given him but wary about bringing her down. "It's not pretty, Chloe."

"Life rarely is." She put away the first aid kit and shouldered her bag. "I should probably throw away this bloody stuff."

He swept the trash into his hand and went behind the bar to throw it away. Chloe was looking at him so differently, he paused, taking an extra moment to soak in what it felt like to be looked at by her when she wasn't struggling to hide behind her usual armor.

She raised her brows and said, "Are you coming, biker boy? Or do I need to find out the rest of the story from one of your brothers?"

"Like hell you will." He had no idea how she'd done it, but he already felt a little better. He slung an arm over her shoulder as they headed for the door and said, "My road name is *Maverick*, sweet cheeks. Not biker boy."

She flashed a sassy smile. "*Biker boy* is cuter."

As he pushed the door open, he said, "*Maverick* is manlier. And trust me, baby, I'm *all* man."

Chapter Eight

A COLD BREEZE swept across the parking lot as they locked Chloe's bag in her trunk. She wrapped her arms around herself and said, "I should have brought a sweater."

"I've got a sweatshirt." They went to Justin's motorcycle, where he retrieved his black zip-up sweatshirt from the saddlebag. He helped her put it on. It was about three sizes too big on her. "You look adorable."

She rolled her eyes and pushed up the sleeves.

As they walked across the parking lot to the path that led to the beach, the ugliness of what he'd gone through seemed a little farther away. He knew that had more to do with Chloe than the fresh air. "Why do you roll your eyes when I compliment you?"

"I don't know. Habit, I guess."

"It's time to break that habit. Every time you roll your eyes, I'm going to do something to remind you not to."

"Here we go," she said sarcastically. "Like what, smack my ass?"

He grinned. "That's the best idea I've heard all night."

"If you value your hand, you won't try that." She stopped at the edge of the beach to take off her sandals and said, "Aren't

103

you going to take off your boots?"

"No."

"You're going to walk on the beach in leather boots?"

"Yup."

"Don't you want to feel the sand between your toes?"

"You obviously want to get me naked, starting with my boots, so…" He tugged off his boots and socks and set them beside her sandals, and then he popped the button on his jeans.

"*Justin!*" She blushed a red streak and hurried down the path. He caught up to her in three long strides, and she said, "Are you done trying to get naked?"

"For now."

She looked at him out of the corner of her eye, but her smile told him she liked his sense of humor as much as he liked making her blush.

They made their way down to the water, and as they walked along the shore, she said, "Can I ask you about tonight?"

He was hoping she'd let it go. "Yeah," he said tightly.

"Do you do that kind of thing a lot?"

"No. Thankfully there aren't many dogfighting rings around here. This one was about an hour away."

"Why did you guys go? Isn't that what the police are for? Aren't there shelters or groups that deal with that type of thing?"

"Situations like this are *exactly* what Gunner's rescue is for."

"Gunner?"

"*Dwayne*, sorry. Gunner is his road name." Chloe and her friends had met Dwayne around the time they'd met Justin. Since they were outside of the biker community, they knew them by their given names. "Dwayne opened Wicked Animal Rescue *because* of this type of thing and because there are assholes out there who abuse the hell out of animals in other ways, too."

"But aren't there laws about animal abuse?"

"Yeah, and the police do all they can, but they can only go so far. Abusers know that. But the abusers don't know what the hell to expect from a bunch of rough-looking bikers. When Gunner and a bunch of us guys show up at their house, they get scared, and that's okay because their animals are goddamn scared, too. I know you don't like violence, Chloe, but in those cases we usually don't have to do much more than talk to get abusers to give up their animals. Tonight was a whole different ball game." He stopped walking and looked out at the water, trying to calm the ire inside him. "We weren't just dealing with some nutjob leaving his pet chained in the yard twenty-four hours a day, or a hoarder with seventeen cats. Dogfighting is a felony, and a vicious, short life for the animals. A lot of shelters don't have the resources to help dogs that come from those environments. There are security risks involved. Dogfighting is a lucrative business, and the guys who run them have been known to try to steal the dogs back. Dwayne's facilities are gated, with top-of-the-line security systems, and he and Baz live on site. Last year we picked up more than *fifty* dogs from a single ring out in Plymouth, and it took months to get some of them ready for adoption. Most shelters would have no idea how to handle that."

"Fifty? That's terrible."

"Yeah. That's why Dwayne has the rescue, because he fucking *cares*. With the support of the Dark Knights, he and Baz have the resources to not only shelter dogs like the ones we picked up tonight, but to care for them medically and rehabilitate them so they can be adopted into families who will love them and treat them well. And *tonight*?" He scoffed, wishing he could have killed the men he'd rumbled with, and began pacing. "The conditions those dogs lived in makes me sick. They're malnourished, chained to cages, covered in scars and festering wounds. Some had broken bones." He swallowed against the venom eating away at him as he wore a path in the sand. "One of them is going to lose his eye. Half of his ear looked like it had been bitten off, and when I picked him up, I could feel his bones. I swear, Chloe, that dog put his arms on my shoulders like a kid, as if he wanted to stay there forever. We rescued thirteen dogs. One is pregnant, so I guess that's a win if her pups survive. There was a dumpster full of dead dogs. Two of the dogs that were chained in the yard were dead when we got there, and another…" He looked away, clenching his teeth. "Another dog, the one they probably used as bait to train the fighters, died in my arms on the way to the rescue."

"Oh, *Justin*…" She looked as tortured as he felt. "No wonder you guys look like you'd been to war."

She reached for him, but he took a step back. "I can't. I'm too mad, Chloe. I'm sorry. Those dogs know nothing but abuse. They're in pain, and hungry. They should *despise* humans, but they still have *love* toward us. And they're so fucking scared. You should see their eyes. But they're not afraid of *us*. They're taught to kill other dogs. It's just so messed up and so fucking *sad*."

He sank down to the sand and pulled his knees up, crossing his arms over them. He gazed out at the water, trying to focus on the sounds of the waves rolling up the shore, the pounding of blood through his ears, anything to drown out the memories. But nothing could erase the evil side of humanity he'd seen tonight.

Chloe sat down beside him and put her arm around him, resting her head on his shoulder. "Mean people suck," she said softly. "What will happen to the people they arrested?"

"Hopefully the greedy bastards will go to jail for a long time. The cops think they will. Some people are so messed up, Chloe. They treat animals and *people* like throwaways, abusing and neglecting them without a second thought. You've got to be so careful. I know you think if a guy wears a tie, he's got to be safe. But, baby, you just never know."

"I know that." She sat up and moved her arm from around him. "I owe you an apology, Justin. I didn't grow up with normal parents, and because of the way I was raised, I misjudged you. I'm sorry. You've always been good to me, and I'm just scared shitless of making the same mistakes my mother made. *Makes.*" She went silent and pushed her fingers around in the sand.

Justin waited to see if she was going to say more, but she looked so sad, he said, "Hey, beautiful, where'd you go?"

Her eyes flicked up, and she said, "Nowhere."

He turned toward her, though she was still facing the water, and he stretched one leg in front of her, the other behind. He wrapped his arms around her, drawing her side against his chest, and said, "Talk to me, Chloe. What mistakes are you afraid of making? What happened when you were growing up?"

"Let's just say my mother had her sights set on finding a man rather than actually being a parent. I guess Serena and I were *throwaway* kids."

"Aw, *hell*, babe. You were left to fend for yourself a lot?"

"*All* the time, from a very young age. My mother worked as a waitress—sometimes at restaurants, sometimes at bars. When she wasn't working, she was either out hunting for a man or spending time with one. I practically raised Serena, which is why I've always been so protective of her. I made our meals, did our laundry, made sure she got to school on time. It was hard every minute of every day. My mother had me when she was only eighteen, so I get that she felt like she'd missed out on a lot. But she was *never* there. We were lucky that we had friends whose parents were good to us, like Drake Savage's family. They offered us dinners, things like that. But while Serena was best friends with Drake's sister, Mira, I always had my own group of friends. I knew if Serena was with the Savages, she was safe. But I just wanted to get away, you know? Away from the constant reminders of what we didn't have and away from the embarrassment of our friends knowing that our mother sucked."

"I know all about wanting to get away," he said, hating that she'd been brought up that way. "What about your father?"

"I've never met him. My mother claims that me and Serena have the same father, but I don't believe it. I've never seen pictures of my father, and she's vague about what she was doing and where we lived when we were little. And look at me and Serena. Serena is short, curvy, and brunette. We look *nothing* alike. I'm pretty sure my mother got pregnant on purpose to try to keep my father around, and when that didn't work, she probably tried to wrangle another man, Serena's father, into marriage. But I have no proof of that, and it doesn't matter. I'm thankful to have Serena as my sister no matter how we came to be."

"So you've never had a father figure in your house?"

She shook her head. "But don't worry. I'm not looking for a daddy replacement," she said a little sharply.

"I wasn't thinking that, Chloe. I was thinking that you were, as you said, Serena's protector. You were essentially her mother *and* her father."

"Pretty much. That's one of the reasons I was looking for a certain type of man. I crave stability, Justin, and based on the rough guys my mother has always dated, I assumed my father was just like them. So I've looked for the opposite. But again, I don't know anything about my father. The only thing I know for sure is that we lived in the house where my mother still lives by the time I was in kindergarten, because I remember coming off the bus and walking home. I can't even tell you who babysat us back then. It seems like there was a new babysitter every other week, at least until I was eight, when our mother started leaving us alone."

He knew all about being left alone, and it slayed him that she'd gone through that. "Did your mother bring men home with her?" he asked carefully, hoping to hell the answer was no.

"Yes, and we were always supposed to be on our best behavior." Her voice rose an octave and she said, "Have to impress *so-and-so*. He could be *the one*." In her normal voice, she said, "And they were always bikers or construction workers with wandering eyes, and…" Her face clouded with uneasiness.

He held her tighter, sickened by the thought of anyone hurting her. "Did they ever touch you and Serena?"

"Not Serena," she said firmly. "I'd have given my life before allowing that to happen."

His protective urges surged, and he gritted his teeth. "*Christ*, Chloe. What happened?"

She scoffed. "Which time?"

He closed his eyes, teeth clenched, heart hammering against his ribs, and tried to rein in the rage burning through him. But she didn't need to see that rage, so he forced his eyes open and spoke as calmly as he could, which wasn't very calmly at all.

"Fucking hell. No wonder you're afraid to date tough guys."

"Once you've been cornered in a kitchen, on a couch, or you wake up to a stranger's hands on you, it changes your perspective on things."

"Holy *fuck*, baby." He wanted to track down the fuckers who had touched her and rip them to shreds. He rested his forehead on the side of her head, telling himself that the anger he felt was nothing compared to whatever she'd gone through. "How old were you? What did you do?"

"I was about twelve when I was cornered. And let me tell you something—at that age, when a full-grown man is looming over you, it doesn't matter if you know to kick him in the nuts or to scream. At least for me it didn't, because I knew to do both of those things, but my mind went completely blank with fear. Thankfully, my mother came into the room, which enabled me to get away before he did more than paw at me and say crude things. But I made the mistake of running behind her, thinking she might actually protect me. I was crying, and I told her that he was saying things he shouldn't and that he'd trapped me against the counter and touched me. But it was my word against his, and he said he was just talking to me and that I was acting out because I wanted my mother's attention."

"That motherfucker," he ground out through gritted teeth. "What did your mother do?"

"She kind of laughed it off, so I grabbed Serena and locked us in my room." Chloe shifted in his arms. "Justin, you're holding me a little too tight."

"Sorry." He loosened his grip, but his muscles were corded tight, ready for a fight. "I want to kill that guy, and I'm sorry, babe, but I'd like to give your mother a piece of my mind, too."

"Well, get in line. I had always known that she didn't take

care of us, but I never imagined she wouldn't *protect* us. The silver lining on that dark cloud was that I learned from it. From that day on, I made it my mission to never be caught like a deer in the headlights again, or to need someone else to save me."

And there it was, the history behind her independent streak.

"I watched self-defense videos and learned how to become more aware of my surroundings," Chloe said. "I got tougher, and I'm positive that's what kept me out of many bad situations, but not all of them." She looked at him, her face pinched with bad memories, and said, "I haven't told Serena or anyone else about any of this, and I don't want her to know because she'll just feel guilty for not being able to help me. I need to know you won't say anything. Okay?"

"I'd never say a word. You don't have to tell me anything more, but it might help to get it off your chest."

"I want to tell you. It's the only way for you to understand why I have always kept you at arm's length, and it feels good to finally tell someone." She inhaled a deep breath and trained her eyes on the sand as she said, "When I was fourteen, my mother brought a guy home after work. Serena was spending the night at Mira's, and I was sitting on the couch watching television and scrapbooking. My mother went upstairs to change because they were going out, and he tried to make small talk about how old I was and what kinds of things I liked to do. But I knew better than to engage with her men, and I just focused on my project. He sat beside me on the couch, pretending to be interested in what I was making. But I had learned to recognize the look of a guy who thought he could get away with *anything*, and he had that look in his eyes. I tried to get up and leave the room, but he yanked me back down and shoved his hand between my legs."

Justin clenched his jaw tighter to keep his anger from roaring out.

Chloe looked out at the water and said, "I punched that guy harder than I'd ever hit anyone in my life, and it gave me just enough time to get to my feet. But he was right behind me, and he grabbed me." She pressed her hand to her chest and said, "Sorry, my heart is racing."

Justin kept her side against his chest and kissed her temple. "I've got you, Chloe. You're safe with me. You've always been safe with me."

She put her hands over his arm, which was belted around her stomach, and held on tight as she said, "I remember the way my stomach clenched, and for a split second I thought I was going to freeze again, like I had when the guy trapped me in the kitchen, but I didn't. I stomped on his foot and elbowed him in the gut. But I was a scrawny fourteen-year-old, and he was a big man. My mother came downstairs as I was struggling to get free, and he started *laughing*. I'll never forget that sinister sound. He let me go and I went ballistic, yelling at him, telling my mother what he'd done, begging her to call the police. But he told her he was just tickling me, and even though I was screaming and crying, telling her he was lying, it was like she never even heard me. He said they had to leave or they'd be late, and they took off as if it had never happened. On his way out the door, he looked over his shoulder and winked. I tore a lamp right out of the wall and threw it at him. But they were already gone by the time it crashed to the floor."

"I'd like to tear that arrogant fucker to shreds. Do you know who he is?"

"No, but it doesn't matter. Hurting him now wouldn't change what happened then."

He ground out a curse. "Did you ever talk to your mother

about it again?"

"Yes, but like the other times, she just said something about me wanting attention, and she said it didn't matter because she wasn't seeing him anymore—"

"Times, Chloe? There were more?"

She nodded. "I don't want to talk about them. They all pretty much went the same way. Some creep would try to touch me, I'd fight back, and my mother would play it off like no big deal. But that time on the couch was the last time. After that I didn't take any chances. I locked myself and Serena in a room when they were there. But here's the kicker. Not much has changed. My mother still chooses men over us. She did it just last weekend when she asked us to come down and meet one of her boyfriends. Actually, one thing *has* changed. I'm done meeting the men in her life. I always thought I owed it to her for being our mother, but not anymore."

"We don't owe our parents anything for creating us. That was *their* choice."

"I know, and this is pathetic to admit, but while I've made the decision not to go through that again, I know that when the time comes, it'll be hard to silence that hopeful little girl in me that always wonders if maybe *this time* it'll be different."

"Aw, babe," he said softly. He knew all about trying to silence that hopeful child.

Neither one of them said a word for a long time, and when Chloe spoke, her voice was less pained, more thoughtful. "Lately I've been wondering what I'd be like if I hadn't grown up with my mother, if I hadn't been neglected or had those awful experiences. Would I have looked at you differently from the start?" She met his gaze and said, "I think I would have, and I *wish* I would have."

"I CAN'T BELIEVE I told you all that," Chloe said, shocked that she'd dumped her dirty laundry on Justin of all people. "I'm sorry. You must have a zillion red flags waving in your head right now. It's bad enough that I ever thought you could be like the men my mother goes out with, when you've never been anything but good to me, even if you do flirt like crazy."

"I only flirt with you like that, babe. And don't feel bad. You trust me, Chloe, and that's a good thing. You know I would never hurt you."

"I do know that," she said honestly. "But everything I just told you makes me sound like a damsel in distress, and it's embarrassing. Why were we even talking about *me*?"

"You were explaining why you assumed I was bad news, and it all makes sense now. But if anyone should be embarrassed, it's your mother. You were a young girl who never should have been put in those situations. But the guys you call bikers? They're not anything like me, and I assure you, they are *not* members of the Dark Knights."

"I actually asked the guy we met last weekend if he was a member. He was awful."

"I know you think we're all leather-wearing, tattooed roughnecks who probably drink and swear too much and go around looking for trouble. But we're not like that. We do go looking for trouble, but not the type of trouble you assumed. And yes, I'm a leather-wearing tattooed biker, and I definitely swear like a sailor. But I make a habit of *not* drinking too much. Dark Knights are always *on call*, so to speak. We need to be ready to get on our bikes and go if someone needs us at any hour, day or night. Our members are doctors, lawyers, teachers, blue-collar workers, fathers, and grandfathers. It doesn't matter what clothes a person wears or how eloquently they speak. What matters is how they live their life, the moral code they live by. It's easy to say you're a good person or that you'd give your life for another. But *living* that way? Proving it to yourself and everyone around you with everything you do and say? That's not easy, Chloe. And I'm not talking about being perfect, because I'm so far from perfect, it's ridiculous. But I *try* to be the best man I can, whether it's stepping in when I see a guy manhandling a woman or child, or redirecting young kids' negative energy, or even carrying groceries for someone who's struggling. It's about being honest with yourself and with others, being a friend who listens for the sole purpose of offering solace. Those are the things that make a good, consistently trustworthy person. And maybe you think becoming a Dark Knight is easy, but it's not. Ours isn't the type of club where anyone can walk off the street and walk out with patches. It can take *years* to prospect and earn a place among the brotherhood. During that time, every single thing you do is judged and measured in terms of loyalty and respect—to yourself and to others—and not just by Preacher or Con, who founded the club and are the president and vice president, but by every single member. I'm *proud* to have earned the right to be a Dark Knight. We fight to keep our communities *safe*, and we don't put up with, or turn our backs on, the mistreatment of anyone or anything. If you'd told a Dark Knight about any part of what you'd gone through when you were going through it—even being left alone by your mother—it would have been taken care of. *You* would have been taken care of. That's the type of bikers we are, Chloe. That's the type of *man* I am."

Chloe was struck momentarily speechless as she processed everything he'd said. It was all making sense now. His protectiveness, his walking out the night of the storm when she'd hesitated to kiss him, his watching over her with Beckett. When she finally wrapped her head around it all, she said, "I had no idea there was so much to being a Dark Knight, or that it was that much a part of who you are. I had heard about the club doing good things for the community, but everything you just said makes the members sound like an army of *really* good men."

"They are. That's exactly what I'm saying. And that's not to say we're special or anything like that. We're just people who want to help others."

"That makes you special, Justin. I always knew you were a good person, but I didn't give you credit for how good. I didn't have all those pieces to understand why you did the things you did. As I said, my past clouded my clarity."

"Some judgments are harder to let go of than others."

She turned so they were facing each other and sat cross-legged between his legs. "I don't know much about your family, and that leaves room for guessing."

"Then let's take the guesswork out of the equation. You and I have a lot in common, Chloe. I always knew we would, but I never knew why. I just had this feeling the whole time I've known you that we were meant to be together. Now I understand. Your mother was more interested in men than in parenting, and my father was more interested in stealing than in being a father."

"Rob is a *thief?*"

"No. Rob and Reba are my adoptive parents, and they're two of the best people I know. They saved me from myself. My real father is in prison."

"Okay, *whoa*. Way to drop an info bomb on me. I had no idea you were adopted, but that's not important. *Prison?* For how long? Do you ever see him? What about your mother?"

"My mother committed suicide when I was seven." His voice was low and tinged with sadness.

Her heart broke for him. "Oh, Justin. I'm so sorry. That must have been devastating. Do you remember her?"

"Yes," he said softly. "I don't know how much of what I remember is real and how much is what I want to believe she was like. I have a picture of her." He pulled his wallet out of his back pocket and withdrew an old cracked and frayed photograph. He looked at it, and his lips curved into a warm smile. He handed it to her and said, "Her name was Mary."

Chloe looked at the young dark-haired woman. She was pretty, with delicate features, a slightly pointy chin, and an upturned nose. She had the same blue eyes and full lips as Justin, but her eyes brimmed with sadness. Chloe felt like she'd seen her face before, but she had a feeling it was because Justin looked so much like her. She handed him the picture and said, "She was beautiful. You look a lot like her."

"Thanks." He looked at the picture for a long time before finally putting it back in his wallet.

"What was she like?"

"She was sweet, timid, kind. I think she had a pretty voice. I remember her singing to me at night. I know she loved me, but she just wasn't strong enough to deal with our lives."

"Because your father was in prison?"

"No. Because my father knocked her around. I don't have a lot of memories of their relationship, but the one thing I'll never forget was hearing him tell her that if she left him, he'd kill us both. I'm sure that's why she didn't try to run away with me. Or at least that's what I tell myself."

"That's terrible." She scooted closer, tucking her legs under his.

"It was. It *is*. My father didn't go to prison until years after she was gone. He pretty much treated me like your mother treated you. I was lucky if he remembered to buy food for me to eat." His brow wrinkled. "You sure you want to hear this?"

"Yes. I've spent enough time misjudging you and going out with guys who I just ended up comparing to you. I want to know who you are, Justin—the good, the bad, what you've been through. All of you."

He nodded solemnly and said, "After my mother died, I was terrified that my father would kill me since my mother had *chosen* to leave us, or that he'd start knocking me around now that she was gone. And I was just a kid. I missed her like crazy. She was the only person who loved me, so I bawled my eyes out a lot at first. That's when my father got real mean."

"He hit you?" she asked with a lump in her throat.

"Knocked me around a bit, hollered a lot. I learned to hide my emotions, to keep my mouth shut and stay out of his way. I found that picture of my mother in a drawer one night when he was out, and I swear, it made me so happy, you'd think I'd found a million bucks." He sounded choked up, and his jaw clenched as he looked down the beach, out at the water, anywhere but into Chloe's eyes.

Her stomach hurt watching him struggle. She touched his arm, bringing his eyes back to hers, and said, "We don't have to talk about this if it's too hard."

He cleared his throat and stretched his neck to either side the way guys did in movies before they got in fights. "It's okay," he said in a stronger voice. "I hid the picture under my mattress, and every night when I was sure my old man wouldn't come back into my room, I'd take it out and look at it, wishing she'd taken me with her."

"*Justin*" came out strangled. Tears burned Chloe's eyes as she went up on her knees and wrapped her arms around him. "Thank God she didn't," she said against his neck.

His arms circled her. They held each other for a long time, the silence broken by the sounds of the waves rolling up the shore. Even after he loosened his hold on her, Chloe hugged him tighter, holding him for the loss of his mother and for the little boy he'd once been, who must have felt so alone. And then she continued embracing him for the friend—the man—she'd wrongly kept her distance from.

When she finally sat back on her knees, eyes damp for all Justin had gone through, she took his face between her hands and gazed into his eyes, feeling guilty for having read the haunting in them as something that should scare her, rather than realizing it was from wounds that had cut him so deep, he might never heal.

"Are you rethinking getting to know me? Are there alarms going off in your head?" he asked.

"No, and it makes me sad that you'd think that. I know how unfair life can be. I'm thinking about how sorry I am for letting my past cloud my vision of you, how lucky I am that you stuck around, and how much you must have missed your mother. I *can't*…" Tears slipped down her cheeks. "You were so *little*." She leaned forward, hugging him again.

"It was a long time ago, darlin'," he said against her cheek.

She felt him sit up straighter, his back and chest expanding, becoming stronger, as if he realized he'd shown his tender underbelly and was intent on reclaiming his alpha status. Didn't he know that the best and strongest men had soft underbellies? She hadn't met many of them, but her closest friends' significant others *all* had them.

She sat back on the sand between his legs, and he put his arms around her waist, pulling her closer. He flashed that crooked smile that sometimes looked boyish and charming and other times got her so hot she feared she'd melt into a puddle. Tonight that lopsided grin tugged at her heartstrings.

"I'm sorry for getting so emotional."

"Don't be. It's a hard subject. What else would you like to know?"

"God, I don't know. Part of me doesn't want to know more, because it makes me so sad, but a bigger part wants to know all of your *truths*."

"Ask me, sweetheart. Let's do this right."

She sighed. "Okay. Did it ever get easier living with your real father?"

Justin shook his head. "Not really. He didn't knock me around as much once I learned to shut my mouth. But then things got bad in other ways. There were times he'd take me with him in the car when he robbed convenience stores and other places. He'd tell me to get down on the floor of the car and wait for him. I didn't know what he was doing. He made a game out of it the first couple of times, telling me to stay down and not to peek because he was getting me a surprise. When he'd get back in the car, he'd drive real fast, hootin' and hollerin', totally hyped up, and we'd end up in some strange place. Probably in another town. I was too little to know for sure. I'd wait all frigging night to see what my surprise was, but I knew better than to ask. Eventually he'd buy me a burger or pizza."

The anger and disgust in Justin's voice made it even harder to hear.

"During another robbery, he told me if anyone saw me, they'd take me away from him and put him in jail. I knew my life wasn't great, but he was all I had. By the time I was nine or ten, I knew what he was doing. But he'd brainwashed me to believe the world was a shitty place, cops were bad, and we were due the money and other things he stole. I was a badass little prick by then, getting in fights, skipping school. I had no idea what friends were, and I was so broken, I didn't want to know. I had just turned eleven when he finally got arrested. I wasn't with him that night. He said he'd hooked up with some other guys and they were pulling a big job. That we'd be *rich*. I remember sitting at home in a crappy little apartment making plans, thinking of all the things we'd do when we were living like kings." He lowered his gaze and said, "He killed an innocent man that night. Shot him over a few hundred bucks. That was when I went into foster care."

"Did you know he'd killed a man?"

He nodded, his jaw tight, eyes still on the sand. "Eventually. The police and social services showed up at the apartment and said he'd been arrested and I had to go with them. Sometime after that I was told what he'd done."

"Oh God, Justin. Did they let you see him? That's so young to be taken away. Even though things were horrible with him, it must have been so hard for you."

"I was too busy trying to figure out how to live in a new place with people I didn't know or understand to think about him much. My world had been fucked up for so long, I didn't know what normal was. I didn't trust people who tried to be nice. I was awful to my foster families and went through two homes before I ended up with Rob and Reba." He lifted grateful eyes to her and said, "They took me in, and from day one they treated me like I was their kid, while I did everything I could to get the hell away from them. I ran away a hundred times, trying to outrun the hate I had for my life, my father, *myself.* I felt like it was me against the world, like it always had been. But there was no escape. The Wickeds came after me every damn time I ran—so did the Dark Knights. Blaine was *always* there with Rob, which shocked the hell out of me because Blaine and I had knock-down, drag-out fights on a near-daily basis. I didn't trust him, and he sure as hell didn't trust me."

He told her a story about Blaine standing up for him at school and how things had changed between them after that. He went on to talk about the things Blaine had said and taught him about friendship and family. He told her stories about his other siblings, too, but they were much younger than him. They'd never had competitive feelings toward him like Blaine had. They'd followed him around as if he were just another brother.

Chloe would never look at any of them the same way again.

Justin went on to explain how the other foster families had punished him for running away and acting out. "I *wanted* that punishment as a form of penance, but also as a means to keep myself in some kind of warped box so I would remain angry at the world. I thought I was such a badass kid, I could take on the world and win. I never knew how messed up that was until Preacher and Reba came into my life."

"Preacher? The guy who founded your club? Is that Rob, or a real preacher?"

"That's Rob's road name, and it's what I call him. He is the best role model a guy could ask for. He gave me reasons to find my way out of that self-destructive box, and he did it with patience and sometimes with anger, but never aimed at me. His anger was aimed at the life I'd been born into. And even though we call him Preacher, he didn't have to preach to make his point. I remember this time when I was about fourteen—by then I'd learned the errors of my ways and was no longer a dick to everyone—he gave me a pocketknife as a show of trust. I'd whittled a bird one afternoon and tossed it in the trash before going to the beach. When I came home I went into his office to tell him something, and there on his desk was that crappy wooden bird. I asked him why he'd taken it out of the trash, and he told me that I had put time into making it, which, he said, in and of itself made it valuable. I argued, of course, and told him I was just bored and wasting time. He told me to go waste some more time because I was talented."

She laughed softly. "I love the way he encouraged you."

"Yeah. He's a great guy. After that, he'd leave pieces of scrap wood on my bed or on my schoolbooks. Eventually the wood was accompanied by sculpting and art books. He'd mix in tools from time to time, or metals, stone, an enrollment form to an art class. He'd leave books about sculpting around the house, in the bathroom, or on my favorite chair. He was a sneaky bastard. I remember one time I came into the kitchen and he and Reba were looking at an artist's catalog. Reba was gushing over a sculpture of an angel that cost a few thousand bucks. Well, this was the woman who told me how much they wanted me in their home every time they brought me back after I'd run away. She fed me dinners when I didn't deserve them, hugged me when she probably should have slapped me. She tended to my cuts and bruises and treated me the way I think my own mother would have if she'd been strong enough to leave instead of…you know. I *wanted* to give Reba something back, and the one thing I had to offer was the skill that Preacher had been fostering in me."

"You made her the angel?"

"Yeah, and she got so choked up, she cried. She said she'd never seen anything more beautiful. She still has it. She keeps it in the living room. At the time, I didn't know how bad it was," he said with a laugh. "It definitely looks like a kid made it. But I didn't think of that back then. They *believed* in me, Chloe. I didn't trust it at first. It took me nearly a year to believe that the Wickeds and the Dark Knights were who they seemed to be, and it took me even longer to fully trust them. But when that kind of support is there *every day* no matter how much you fight it, you learn the strength of it and the value of being someone who can offer it to others. I wish there had been someone like that in your life when you were growing up."

How could she have ever worried about him hurting her? Even now, when he was pouring out his soul, he was still thinking of her. "I had Serena, and we believed in each other."

"I know, and I'm glad you did. But I wish you'd had an adult to take care of you so you didn't have to do it all yourself."

She shivered against the cool air, and he held her closer, buffering her from the breeze.

"Cold? Do you want to leave?" he asked.

"No. I want to hear the rest of your story, if you don't mind. And I'm warm here in your arms."

"We might never leave if that's the case," he said soft and low, making her belly tingle.

He never missed a chance to flirt, and after they'd bared their souls, she had the urge to kiss him. If they didn't keep talking, she just might do it, so she said, "Did you ever see your father again?"

"Yes. The Wickeds had changed my life, but I was still carrying around a lot of unresolved turmoil. My real father had *killed* a man, and I not only carried my father's name, but also a shitload of guilt because I had known he was going to pull off a big job and I didn't try to stop him."

"You were a little boy, Justin. You couldn't have stopped him."

"I know, but that didn't take away my culpability. When I was fifteen, Preacher helped me track down the family of the man my father had killed, and I apologized to them. They knew I had been just a kid back then, and they forgave me. And *man*, I needed that forgiveness. But I also needed something else that only my father could give me. It didn't matter that by then I felt like a Wicked. I wasn't one. I was a *Brown*, and I hated that so much. It felt like a noose around my neck, a constant reminder of the man I had come from and all that he'd taken from me—my mother, my childhood, hell, even several years of my life following his arrest. But I didn't know what to do about it. Then I saw Violet over the summer, and I told her about my dilemma."

Chloe felt a pang of jealousy. "How long have you known her?"

"I met her out on Wellfleet Pier when I was a long-haired thirteen-year-old punk with an attitude and an unlit cigarette hanging out of my mouth. She was twelve, sitting on the pier dressed in all black, looking like she hated the world. We watched each other from a distance for a while, and at some point she told me to 'sit the fuck down.'"

"Sounds like Vi."

"Yeah, she's awesome. We shot the shit and got to know each other and spent every day together while she was in town, and for many of the summers after that. She'd been ripped away from the only family she'd ever known when she was just a kid, and her crazy mother had dragged her all over creation, never giving her a chance to have friends or a stable home. We both had trust issues, but suddenly we had someone from our own side of the tracks, so to speak, to talk to. We've been best friends ever since. She's the one who suggested that I go see my father in prison and tell him exactly what I thought of him. She said the bastard deserved my wrath. What she knew that I didn't at that time was that *I* needed that closure, too. I needed to tell him how much I hated him for the way he treated my mother, and a whole lot of other shit. Violet's also the one who suggested I ask Preacher and Reba if they'd ever consider adopting me. She said I had a chance at a family, and I should take it."

"I knew you and Violet were close, but I never realized how much you two have been through together or what you really mean to each other." She mustered the courage to tell him what else he deserved to know. "I have something to confess."

He arched a brow.

"Another reason I was keeping you at arm's length was that you...*um*...tried to help Vi forget Andre when she first moved back here by sleeping with her. It wasn't something I would ever do, and I didn't understand it."

"Chloe, Vi and I go way back, and that was a—"

She pressed her lips to his, silencing him. His lips were warm and sweet, and it was just a closed-mouth kiss, but the electricity sparking between them brought a rush of exhilaration. When she pulled back, she was breathless and craving more. Lord help her, because the look in his eyes made her want to take it. She had acted on impulse, and she was afraid she might do it again, so she quickly said, "I don't need you to justify it. I just wanted you to know why else I had held back. So…did you take her suggestion?"

"*Chloe*" came out fast and fierce as he buried his hand in her hair and crushed his mouth to hers.

His lips were soft but insistent as his tongue swept over hers. He kissed her passionately, taking his time, as if he were savoring every moment. His fingers threaded into her hair, and he angled her mouth beneath his, their tongues tangling in an exquisite, toe-curling dance. His arm tightened around her waist, strong and possessive, and he made a low, sensual sound that seared through her like lightning. She'd dreamed of kissing him so many times, she was sure she'd known exactly what it would be like. But boy had she been wrong. She'd never experienced anything close to the divine ecstasy of kissing Justin Wicked. She wanted to stay there in his arms, with the breeze on her cheeks and his lips on hers until the sun came up.

When their lips finally parted, slow and longingly, they were both breathless. Justin kept her close, their foreheads touching, and said, "I've been dying to do that since the first time I set eyes on you."

Her thundering heart drowned out the sounds of the sea, but Justin's confession cut right through both. "Me too." She knew if he kissed her again, she wouldn't want to stop, and she wasn't quite ready for that, so she sat back and said, "You'd better finish your story because kissing you is…"

"Addictive?"

"Uh-huh."

He flashed an arrogant grin and said, "Afraid of attacking

me again?"

Yes. "*No,*" she said unconvincingly. "It's just…I want to hear the rest."

"Yeah, okay. That should be *real* easy when all the blood in my brain has rushed south." He chuckled, and she swatted him. "Hey, it's your fault, sweet lips. I was just sitting here and all of a sudden you were all over me."

She swatted at him again, laughing as he caught her hand midair and tugged her forward, pressing his lips to hers.

"*That* was my fault," he said in a low voice. "And just so we're clear, I'm going to finish my story, but I'm not done with that incredible mouth of yours."

In her head she was doing a happy dance, but outwardly, she lifted her chin and said, "We'll see about that. So, did you take Vi's advice or not?"

"I did. I asked Preacher if he'd ever consider adopting me." Justin's expression turned thoughtful, like he was remembering that very moment. "He said he and Reba had been hoping I might want that one day."

"Yay!" Chloe exclaimed. "I knew they must have agreed, since your last name is Wicked, but hearing it makes me happy."

"It was definitely a *yay* moment. I could have gotten emancipated, and it was probably a prick move on my part not to, but I wanted my father to physically and mentally relinquish his parental rights. I'd hoped that by having him actually sign over his rights, somewhere in his cold heart he'd feel the loss."

"That's understandable. I don't think it was a prick move. Do you think he felt bad?"

"No. But that's okay. In the end, I'd done what I needed to do for my *own* peace of mind, and just having that tie legally severed set me free. The same way that becoming a Wicked felt like I'd finally found my home."

Chloe may not have had a new family when she'd left home to finish college, but she knew what it was like to finally have a place where she felt safe.

They sat on the beach for a long time, each lost in their own thoughts. She felt so close to him. Knowing Justin had overcome so much, understanding the man he truly was and all that he stood for, gave her great admiration for him.

At some point they shifted positions, and Justin tucked her against his side, so they were both facing the water. They talked a little here and there, watching a piece of driftwood moving toward the shore with the force of the waves and then floating back out.

"That driftwood reminds me of how I feel every time I see my mother. It doesn't matter how much I accomplish, or how far I go. When I see her, she still makes me feel like I'm moving backward, drifting, fighting to move forward, to find my island, but never able to stay there." She rested her head on Justin's shoulder and said, "I see your settling in with the Wickeds in that driftwood, too. But instead of being pulled back out to sea, the land was your old life and you were consistently drawn into the welcoming arms of a family as vast and deep as the sea."

Justin rested his head against hers and said, "Two pieces of driftwood looking for their island. That's you and me."

"I think you found yours with Rob and Reba."

"Maybe, but a wise woman just described my family life perfectly as the deep blue sea, so I'm holding out for my island."

The salty air whipped around them, and Chloe shivered again. How long had they been out there? An hour? Two? She didn't know or care. All she knew was that she felt closer to

Justin than she'd ever felt to anyone, and tonight was right up there at the top of her best nights ever list, right along with the night last weekend when they'd danced beneath the stars.

"Is it crazy that I don't want the night to end?" she asked.

"I was just thinking the same thing. It took us what? A year and a half to get here, give or take?"

"Something like that."

He lowered his lips to hers, kissing her softly. "I finally have you all to myself," he said just above a whisper. "Leaving is the *last* thing I want to do, but Baz and Evie, his assistant, are doing surgery on a couple of the dogs tonight, and I promised I'd go back to help."

"Oh my gosh, *Justin*!" She pushed to her feet and said, "Let's go. I'm *so* sorry. I didn't mean to make you late."

He stood up and took her hand, like it was natural. She liked the way they fit together as they walked toward the path. His hand was big, rough, and strong, just like him. If she didn't know better, she'd think Rose had given him CliffsNotes from their conversation.

After stopping to put on their sandals and boots, Justin took her hand again and said, "I want you to know something. Vi and I slept together as teenagers when she was here for a few weeks over the summers. We trusted each other, and we kept each other safe, but it was never a boyfriend-girlfriend thing. Then we didn't mess around at all for about ten years or so, until she was tricked into coming to the Cape by her mother the summer it happened. She'd left Andre overseas in the middle of the night without telling him. She didn't even leave a note, and she and Desiree had barely known each other. She was the saddest I'd ever seen her. She was desperately in love with Andre, and she was really messed up. She honestly thought if she could—not to be crass, but—*fuck* like she used to, with no emotion, just filling a void, she'd get over him. That night was a one-time thing, and it was literally just two friends fucking with the purpose of getting rid of her love for him. She ended up in tears, Chloe. It's not a good memory for either of us. We both knew she'd never move past Andre. She loved him too much. And she hated herself for leaving him the way she did. But I was there to hold her while she cried and to remind her that she was loved and—probably more important—*lovable*. Lovable as a *friend* to me, not in the own-your-heart kind of way. But to the right man, to Andre, she was lovable in the way a life partner should be."

The honesty in his voice, and his need to explain, touched her deeply. "You really didn't have to tell me all of that. What you said on the beach told me how important you are to each other."

"I know, but I want you to know that what happened between us was a moment in time. Just like the time I posed naked for her and spent the night. You already know nothing happened between us then. Those things were moments in time, and they'll *never* happen again. There have never been romantic feelings between us, and there never will be. Even if she and Andre were to break up, which I don't think they ever will, there would never be a *Justin and Violet*. Do you understand what I'm saying? She'll always be one of my closest friends, and I hope you can accept that because I will *always* be there for her, but not in that way ever again."

"Okay," she said, knowing she could trust his word. "She's my friend, too, and I guess I do feel better knowing that."

He exhaled loudly. "Great. Thank you."

They headed up the path, and as the sand turned to gravel,

Chloe felt like she was leaving the chains of her past behind. The Salty Hog came into view, lit up like a celebration against the night sky. Music hung in the air as they crossed the parking lot to her car.

Justin gathered her in his arms. Moonlight reflected in his eyes, and she felt like she was seeing the real Justin Wicked for the first time. Not because he'd never shown her before. The openness, honesty, and appreciation in his eyes had probably always been there, but her armor had been too thick for her to see all of that for what it was.

"Look at us, heartbreaker. What do you think?"

"I think it's new and a little weird to be standing here with you like this. But it also feels good and right, doesn't it?"

"It does, babe. Tell me you're not going to pull away from me tomorrow."

"I'm not. I was actually hoping we could see each other Saturday night," she said coyly.

"You're blushing, sweet cheeks. Does this mean you plan on taking advantage of me this weekend?"

Her pulse quickened from heat flaring between them. "I did enjoy those kisses. But don't get your hopes up for more, biker boy."

"You like our kisses, huh?" His eyes drilled into her. "We can *definitely* enjoy more of those."

He brushed his lips over hers, soft as a feather, and backed her up against her car. She held her breath, readying for a kiss. But his lips passed over hers, across her cheek, leaving her desperate for their touch as he said, "You're busy Friday night?"

"Mm-hm. *Jealous?*"

He pressed his lips to her cheek and whispered in her ear, "Should I be?"

His voice was so sexy and manly, butterflies took flight in her belly. "Of a girls' night with my book club? Maybe if I were into women. I mean Steph and the girls *are* gorgeous."

He kissed the sensitive skin beside her ear, sending ripples of lust slicing through her, and said, "You might turn other guys on with that talk, but not me, blondie." He kissed the edge of her lips. "You're the only woman I want." He brushed his lips over hers and said, "Seeing you—or hearing about you—with another woman would *not* be better than having you all to myself."

Every touch of his lips heightened her anticipation, causing her breathing to shallow.

He trailed kisses along her jaw. "I'm not a twentysomething kid, Chloe. I'm past games and recklessness. I know what I want, and she's standing right in front of me."

Did he know those words were the biggest turn-on of all?

When he brushed his scruff over her cheek, pressing his hard body against her, a lustful sound slipped from her lips. She felt him smiling against her other cheek as he kissed her there. His lips trailed down her neck, and she curled her fingers into his sides, needing stability against her weakening knees. He'd loosened the cork on her resistance, unleashing a burning desire, an aching *need* to kiss him again. She'd held back from him for so long, she felt like she might detonate. Her nerves hummed like live wires as he retraced his path, kissing up her neck, across her jaw and cheek, and dragged his tongue along the shell of her ear.

"*Justin*—" she pleaded unabashedly.

"Something you want, beautiful?"

The heck with waiting. She grabbed his head and crushed her mouth to his. His hands dove into her hair, *fisting*, causing stings of pain and pleasure to ignite inside her. His hips rocked against hers as they devoured each other with reckless abandon. She didn't care that they were standing in a parking lot where anybody could see them making out. They were fully dressed, not naked and groping, and she wasn't about to deny the tantalizing persuasion of his incredibly talented and delicious mouth or the feel of his hard heat pressing against her. Every slide of their tongues, every guttural sound and scratch of his scruff, made her crave more of him. Just when she thought she'd lose her mind, he eased his efforts to intoxicatingly slow, smoldering kisses. She heard a whimpering moan and realized it had come from *her*. She wasn't a *whimperer*. What kind of spell had he cast over her? Whatever it was, she never wanted it to end.

Someone cleared their throat, and Chloe startled, tearing her mouth away, breathless and shaky.

Madigan and Zander were standing beside them grinning, and Tank was closing in on them from a few feet away, his brows knitted with confusion. Justin's hands were still in Chloe's hair, his body pressed temptingly against her. *Oh God.* Justin's kisses had obliterated everything else, even her good sense!

"Hey," Justin said casually, drawing Chloe away from the car and into his protective arms.

Chloe didn't need protection. She wasn't ashamed of her actions. She was just embarrassed about being caught making out in the parking lot like a horny teenager. She lifted her chin and put her arm around Justin, meeting his siblings' curious gazes as his *equal*, not his *charge*.

"We were wondering where you guys had gotten off to," Madigan said.

"Looks like we interrupted them before they had a chance to *get off*," Zander said with an arrogant smirk.

If looks could kill, Zander would be on the ground from the sheer force of Justin's dark stare.

"*Zander!*" Madigan chided.

"That's enough, Zan," Justin warned as Tank joined them. "We were just saying good night."

"Chloe, why didn't you tell me you two were going out?" Madigan asked. "You're so cute together."

"They're *hot*, Mads, not cute," Zander corrected. "I'm surprised the whole parking lot didn't go up in flames."

"Damn right we are," Justin said, grinning proudly as he squeezed Chloe against his side.

"We weren't going out," Chloe said. "I'm not sure what we're doing, actually. This is new between us." She looked at Zander and said, "But I think it's safe to say that *Uptown Girl* finally sees her backstreet guy for who he is."

"About damn time," Tank said.

Madigan cocked her head and said, "Was that a boy-band reference? Because it's Backstreet *Boys*."

The guys chuckled, and Justin said, "It's a Billy Joel reference, Mads. Before your time. Look up the lyrics to *Uptown Girl.*"

"I *know* who Billy Joel is," Madigan said. "Excuse me for not knowing every word to every song ever made. It's late and I've got a children's birthday party to do tomorrow morning, so I'm heading home. I'm glad you two are together, or whatever making out in the parking lot means," she teased. "See you tomorrow night at the book club meeting, Chloe. Starr is going to bring Gracie. She and Marly are excited to meet you."

"Since when are you in Chloe's book club?" Justin asked. "I

don't think I want my little sister reading erotic romance."

"Good thing you aren't the boss of me," Madigan said. "Chloe has a luau planned at Cahoon Hollow, with leis, fruity drinks, and other cool stuff, including lots of *sexy*, *erotic* discussions. I wouldn't miss it for the world." She punctuated her determination with a sassy wiggle of her shoulders.

Justin looked curiously at Chloe and said, "You're doing all of that for a book club meeting? Sounds more like a party."

"I know it's a lot, but I have this thing about special times. When I was younger my mother never threw us birthday parties or celebrated special events, so when it's my turn to host something, I like to do it right."

Zander pointed at Madigan and said, "You're *not* going anywhere to discuss erotic romance, but it sounds like a party *I* need to attend."

"Ha!" Madigan exclaimed. "Dream on."

"Sorry, Zander, but no guys allowed," Chloe said. Justin had crashed her last *three* book club meetings with the sole purpose of hitting on her. The last time he'd even brought a copy of the book they'd read and said he'd reviewed their club rules and there was nothing that stated a man couldn't join. She pointed at Justin now and said, "And *you* are *not* crashing our meeting, either."

"Good luck with *that*." Zander slung an arm over Madigan's shoulder and said, "Come on, Mads. I'll walk you to your Barbie bike and we can discuss this book club party."

"Why can't you just call it a *Vespa*?" Madigan said as they walked away.

Zander called over his shoulder, "See you guys at Gunner's."

"You still going back to the rescue?" Tank asked.

Justin nodded. "Yeah. I'll head over in a sec. I'll meet you there."

"Cool. See you, Chloe."

After Tank walked away, Justin turned Chloe in his arms and said, "At least we weren't caught naked."

"Please tell me you haven't been caught naked in a parking lot. Oh my God, I just realized I don't know your dating history."

"I didn't know I needed a résumé to go out with you."

"That's not what I meant. For all I know, being caught with your pants down is normal for you, and that's something I should probably be aware of."

His expression turned serious. "I kid around a lot, but I'm not that guy, Chloe. After everything I've been through, I don't take anything for granted, including when a woman trusts me enough to get physical." His tone softened, and he said, "I'm sorry I got carried away with you out in the open like this, but I wouldn't have taken it further than kissing. You're just so damn irresistible, and I've waited so long, I couldn't help myself." He leaned closer and said, "The truth is, I haven't been with another woman since we met."

She hadn't been intimate with a man since before she'd met Justin, but she'd always assumed most single guys didn't go more than a week or two without sex. Especially a man as virile as Justin. "You don't mean when we first *met*," she said disbelievingly.

"Yes, I do." A devilish grin curved his lips, and he said, "I wasn't lying about you starring front and center in my spank-bank."

Holy cow. He was brash, but he was honest. She fell a little harder for him right then and there.

"What did they say in that Tom Cruise movie? 'You had me

at hello,' Chloe."

He pressed his lips to hers in a tender kiss. As their lips parted, he grabbed her butt with both hands, sending a thrum of lust skating through her.

"You're so *handsy* all of a sudden." She wasn't used to letting a man grope her, but that spell he'd cast must still be working, because she didn't mind his hands on her. She *craved* them.

"A year and a half, babe," he reminded her. "Let me know if you want me to come over before your meeting to act out some of those erotic scenes."

His lips came coaxingly down over hers, and he kissed her like they had all the time in the world. She was surprised to find herself toying with the idea of taking him up on that pre-book-club-meeting offer. But the longer they kissed, the harder it was to hold on to her thoughts. If she got this hot and bothered by kisses, they'd need *all night* to act out those erotic scenes. As enticing as that was, putting off her friends for a man would make her exactly like her mother, and she was *not* going to be that person.

Not even for the king of mind-blowing kisses.

Chapter Nine

CHLOE CARRIED A pineapple boat full of fruit salad into her living room Friday evening, listening to the rain through the open windows, trying not to let her disappointment bring her down. It had been raining all day, and she'd had to move the book club meeting indoors. A luau wouldn't be the same without sand beneath their toes, but she'd done an admiral job of transforming her cozy cottage into a tropical island. She'd gone to the party store during her lunch break and bought a banner with ALOHA written in letters that looked like sticks, and she'd hung it over the fireplace. She'd bought a grass-fringed tablecloth for her dining room table to match the one that came with the luau hut, which she'd put up around the card table. She'd hung a string of tiki lights from the roof of the hut, and it looked just as cute as she'd hoped it would. The two blow-up palm trees she'd bought on a whim were the perfect addition to the evening. While she was out, she'd also bought a handful of toys for Starr's daughter to play with. They may not have a beach, but they'd have ambience.

She set the fruit salad on the table between the coconut cups with the colorful drink umbrellas and the cheese and cracker spread. The kebabs would be ready shortly after the girls arrived, which should be any minute. She grabbed her phone on her way into her bedroom and gave herself one last look-over in the full-length mirror. The grass skirt and coconut bra were a bit much, but she didn't care. She'd spent too many years wishing for costumes and special parties.

She put on her dragonfly anklet, put two colorful leis around her neck, and took a picture in the mirror to send to Justin. He'd sent her pictures of some of the dogs from the rescue last night. He'd given her fair warning about their appearance, but her heart had broken over the sad shape they were in. Some were so malnourished, their ribs were showing, and they all had cuts and scars all over their bodies. She couldn't get the images out of her head. One dog had to have its leg amputated, and the dog Justin had feared would lose his eye had in fact lost it. In the picture, the one-eyed dog, a brindle pit bull with white fur on his chest, was licking Justin's face. His fur was shaved around the surgical area, and it looked raw around the stitches, but Justin had said the dog was in good spirits. He'd also said the dog had whined when he'd walked away. She could only imagine the rescued animals craving love like she and Justin had as kids. She'd stared at those pictures so often this afternoon, she'd finally printed them out.

It had felt amazing last night allowing herself to feel all of the emotions she'd been holding back for Justin, and when he'd texted later in the night, sending pictures of the dogs he'd rescued, she'd felt all those good feelings again. But when he'd called this morning and said he was doing a sunshine dance for her, hoping her book club meeting wouldn't get rained out, she'd embraced that newfound freedom wholeheartedly.

Her phone vibrated with a message, and Justin's name flashed on the screen. She'd been so lost in thoughts of him, she hadn't sent him the picture she'd just taken.

She read his text on the way into the living room. *Hey, sweet thing. Sorry my sunshine dance didn't work and your luau got rained out.*

How could she ever have thought he wasn't the right guy for her? He was *always* thinking of others. She added the picture she'd just taken to a text, then added two pictures he'd taken with her phone the other night at the bar and sent them to him with the message *I'd like to see that sunshine dance in person*, and added a heart eyes emoji. After sending the text, she queued up Spotify and turned on the tropical music playlist she'd created.

When the doorbell rang, she took one last look around and answered it.

Steph's eyes widened as she set her umbrella on the porch. "Wow! Look at you, hula girl. You look amazing."

"Thanks." Chloe wiggled her hips, making her grass skirt swish. "I borrowed the outfit from Serena." Although Steph never seemed bothered by Chloe mentioning Serena, Chloe always felt a little uneasy because Steph's younger sister, Bethany, had been Ashley's best friend. After Ashley died, Bethany had lost herself in drugs. She'd been in and out of Steph's life ever since.

"I hope you washed it. You know if Drake saw her in that thing, they got down and dirty."

They both laughed, but Chloe was pretty sure the outfit wouldn't have stayed on for more than a few seconds before Drake stripped it off.

She saw headlights coming down the road. Her cottage was tucked away from the rest of the world at the end of a narrow, wooded road. Her home wasn't very big, but it had a beautiful screened-in porch out back, and she loved not having to worry about neighbors.

Two cars pulled up to the curb, and Steph said, "Looks like Starr and Daphne are here."

"You know Starr?"

"Yeah, from the Salty Hog. But I had no idea she was in the book club. Mads told me when she came by my shop earlier today."

Chloe stepped onto the porch and saw Daphne and Starr standing under umbrellas by Starr's car. Daphne took Starr's umbrella and held it over Starr as she leaned into the back seat to pick up Gracie.

"Tag-team mothering," Chloe said as they came up the walk.

Steph called out, "Do you need any help?"

"We're good. I've got Starr's bag," Daphne said. When they stepped onto the porch, she said, "It's nice to have another mom in our group. I was just telling Starr that my mom has Hadley tonight."

"She's lucky to have family nearby." Starr looked at Chloe and said, "Hi. You must be ChapterChick."

"Yes, I'm Chloe. I'm so glad you could make it. And this must be Gracie."

Gracie buried her face in Starr's neck, clutching a stuffed monkey in the crook of her arm. Her wispy blond hair fell over her face.

"She can be shy at first, but she'll warm up. Right, Gracie?" Starr kissed her daughter's cheek and brushed her hair from her face.

Gracie nodded, her tiny brows knitting. Starr set her down, and Gracie rested her cheek on Starr's leg, blinking up at them with the biggest brown eyes Chloe had ever seen.

"Isn't Gracie adorable? She's the same age as Hadley," Daphne said. "We should have a playdate for the girls sometime."

"I would love that," Starr said, pushing her long curly hair over her shoulder.

Chloe crouched so she was eye to eye with Gracie and said, "Hi, Gracie. I'm Chloe, and I'm really glad you and your mommy came to visit tonight."

Gracie buried her face in the side of Starr's leg.

"You and I were on the same wavelength tonight, Chloe," Starr said as she unzipped her daughter's raincoat. Gracie was wearing a grass skirt with flowers around the waist and a cute pink shirt.

Gracie patted her skirt with the monkey in her hand and said, "*Kirt!*"

"I love your pretty skirt," Chloe said. "She is precious. Do you mind if I take pictures tonight for the girls who couldn't make it?"

Two more cars pulled up in front of the cottage as Starr answered. "Of course. Life is so busy, I never take enough."

"Don't worry, she'll take *fifty*," Daphne said. "And if you ask nicely, she'll make you a memory board or a scrapbook, too."

"Starr doesn't have to ask. I make them for everyone. I'll make you one," Chloe offered.

"Thank you. I'd love that." Starr crouched beside Gracie and said, "Do you want to show our new friends your hula dance?"

Gracie nodded, a bright smile forming on her tiny lips. She wiggled her hips, and they all cheered and clapped as Gabe, Madigan, and an exotic-looking brunette Chloe assumed was

Marly joined them on the porch.

"I wish I had that little one's moves, *and* wow, Chloe, look at you!" Gabe exclaimed. "If I could fit my tatas into coconuts and my derriere into a grass skirt, I'd wear them every day." She took off her bright yellow floppy rain hat, and her wild red curls tumbled down her back.

"If I were as voluptuous as you, I'd flaunt it all over creation." Madigan gave Gabe a quick hug and said, "But don't you dare wear a coconut bra around my grandfather. You'd give him a heart attack."

"You can have Gabe's body if I get her hair," the olive-skinned, almond-eyed brunette who'd arrived with them said. "I know everyone except you two." She pointed at Chloe and Daphne and said, "You must be the founders of our book club, Chloe and Daphne. I'm Marly Bowers, FlippinPages on the forum. I *love* the site, by the way, and thanks for letting me tag along tonight. I'm excited to meet you in person."

"We're excited, too. I'm Chloe, ChapterChick on the site. And this is Daphne, my partner in book-club crime. How do you know Mads?"

"I met her through a mutual friend, Jace Stone, who's now married to another book club member, Madigan's cousin Dixie."

"We know her," Chloe said.

"I *love* her," Marly said. "I met Jace at Bikes on the Beach years before he and Dixie became an item, after I lost my brother to a motorcycle accident."

"I'm sorry about your brother," Chloe and Daphne said at once.

"Thank you. It was his first time on a motorcycle, and like a lot of young guys, he thought he was indestructible and rode without a helmet," Marly explained. "It was horrible. I lost my best friend, and I miss him every day. But we're not going down *that* road tonight. Anyway, when I met Jace, I had just started the Head Safe helmet program to try to keep other families from having to face the same thing we did. Jace helped me get started and introduced me to the Dark Knights. That's how I met Mads, and through them I met Gabe, Starr, and Steph."

Madigan put her arm around Marly and said, "And now she's stuck with us."

"I wouldn't want it any other way," Marly said.

"Neither would we," Steph said.

Gracie banged on the screen door, and Starr swooped her into her arms. "No, no, baby. Don't hit the screen."

"Oh my gosh. I'm the *worst* hostess tonight, keeping you on the porch," Chloe exclaimed. "Come inside."

Chloe followed them in, and there was a round of *ooh*s and *ahh*s over the decorations as they took off their rain jackets and hung them in the closet. Chloe was glad everyone had dressed for the occasion in cute Hawaiian-print sundresses and tops.

"This is going to be so fun," Steph said as she walked into the living room. "You really went all out, Chloe. I love the decorations."

"It looks like a certain little lady loves the decorations, too," Daphne said as Starr chased after Gracie, who was making a beeline for the card table's grass skirt.

"Careful, Gracie," Starr said gently. "No pulling on the grass."

Gracie blinked up at her and said, "No *gass*."

"That's right, sweetie." Starr ran a hand down her daughter's back and said to the others, "Thanks for letting me bring my baby girl. If she gets into too much trouble or gets whiney,

I'll take off so she doesn't ruin everyone's night."

"Don't be silly. You've got lots of helping hands tonight," Daphne said.

Chloe pointed to the basket of toys and said, "I bought a few provisions, just in case."

"You didn't have to do that. I brought her toys in my bag," Starr said. "But thank you. That was really nice of you."

Chloe got the kebabs out of the oven and they chatted as she transferred them to a platter. "I set up the dining room table, but it might be more fun if we put a blanket on the living room floor and have a picnic. We can pretend we're on the beach."

"That sounds great," Madigan said, and the others agreed.

Chloe was heading into the other room to get a blanket when the doorbell rang. "Who else said they were coming?" she asked, circling back to answer it. She pulled open the door and found Justin, looking hot and delicious in faded jeans and a white T-shirt. His eyes blazed down her body, leaving goose bumps in their wake.

"Holy hell, gorgeous." He hauled her into his arms and kissed her so thoroughly, she came away dizzy.

"*What* was *that*?" Steph exclaimed, hurrying over to the doorway with the others on her heels.

"The hottest kiss I've ever seen," Daphne said.

"They're together now," Madigan said, jerking Chloe from her lust-filled reverie. "We caught them making out in the parking lot last night."

"Justin, what are you doing here?" Chloe asked as two more trucks pulled into the driveway and three guys piled out. "I told you not to crash the meeting." She had needed that kiss so badly after thinking about him all day—she should probably thank him instead of asking why he was there. She had a fleeting thought wondering whether that kiss made her like her mother, but she quickly nixed it. Justin was nothing like the awful men her mother dated, and *she* was nothing like her mother. She was *allowed* to be happy with a good man.

"Wait a second! Is Chloe *Uptown Girl*?" Starr asked.

"*Yes*," Madigan said with a nod.

Everyone looked surprised and happy, and Chloe was sure she did, too. "I am Uptown Girl, but I'd rather be known as *Justin's* girl."

There was an outpouring of agreement from the girls as Justin pulled her into his arms and said, "My *girl*, Maverick's old lady, Uptown Girl. I don't care as long as you're mine."

Her heart stumbled at the emotions swimming in his eyes.

"I'm not crashing your meeting, babe," he said softly. "I figured my girl would want to put her toes in the sand at her luau, so I brought the beach to you."

Chloe had no idea what he meant, but the idea of him even *wanting* to do something special for her made her all mushy inside. She saw Tank and Blaine coming up the walk in the pouring rain, pushing wheelbarrows piled high with something she couldn't make out. Behind them, Zeke and Zander had their arms full of more indistinguishable items. The girls looked as confused as she was. "I don't understand."

Justin took her hand and said, "We have a lot of years of you *not* having the parties you deserved to make up for, and from now on I'm going to make sure every single event is better than the last. Starting right now. We're going to set up a beach for your luau."

She was speechless.

Daphne nudged Chloe and said, "If you don't marry this

man, I'm going to."

"Daphne, you just climbed to the top of my favorite person list, right beside Chloe," Justin said. He looked at the girls and said, "Okay, ladies, we're moving this party to the screened-in porch out back. If you clear off the tables, we'll take care of the rest."

Chloe helped the girls clear the tables, watching in shock as Zeke and Zander set out tarps on her back porch, and then the four men poured bag after bag of sand on the tarps. Chloe and her friends talked over one another, sharing their disbelief and excitement, as the guys carried the tables, the luau hut, and all the other decorations outside. They restrung the tiki lights around the ceiling of the porch, adding more that Justin had brought with him. He'd even brought a small grated firepit and two sound machines, which played ocean sounds. Her rough and rugged biker had thought of everything. She had no idea he was such a romantic, and she felt herself opening up even more for him.

As the girls gushed over the guys' efforts, Gracie tried to climb Blaine like a ladder. He picked her up, talking to her and tickling her belly. When he tried to put Gracie down, she lifted her knees, clinging to him with all her might.

"Oh God, here we go," Starr said quietly. "She's pulled up her landing gear." The girls huddled around her.

"Too bad big girls can't get away with that." Marly eyed Blaine and said, "He might be the eye of the storm in public, but I'll bet that man is a typhoon in the bedroom. The kind that leaves you limp as a rag doll but craving more because...*well*...just *look* at him."

Madigan crossed her arms, glaring at Marly. "How many times do I have to tell you that I don't want to hear your thoughts involving my brothers in your bedroom?"

"Then I guess I shouldn't tell you about my double-duty dream about Zeke and Zander," Starr teased.

"Don't even get me started." Marly waggled her brows and said, "I've got a book Zeke can study. *The Kama Sutra*. And look at Tank. *Mm-mm*. I'd like to slide down that fireman's pole."

"*Ohmygosh!*" Daphne turned beet red.

Chloe and the girls laughed hysterically.

Madigan scowled at Marly, but her eyes gave her amusement away as she said, "*Girl*, you are all over the place. *Why* did I bring you with me tonight?"

"Because you love me." Marly batted her lashes.

Blaine tried to put Gracie down again, but Gracie cried, "No!" and lifted her legs again.

Starr sighed. "Why does she always do this to me?"

"Seems like you've got the perfect wing-girl," Steph said.

"Right?" Gabe laughed and said, "I might have to borrow her sometime."

"You should see what Hadley does," Daphne said. "She's all over the wrong men. First it was my *boss*, then our friend Jett, and now she's totally into this gorgeous guy named Jock, who, thanks to my daughter, practically runs in the opposite direction every time he sees us."

"Sounds like our girls are going to be trouble when they're older," Starr said, watching Blaine trying to help the guys using only one hand.

"Maybe you should go rescue Blaine," Gabe suggested.

"Can you just leave Gracie with him for a minute longer? He looks *good* with a baby in his arms," Marly said.

"Come on, let's help put the food back on the tables before

you start drooling." Madigan took Marly's hand and dragged her into the house.

Starr went to save Blaine. Steph and Daphne followed, but Zander intercepted them, in full-on-flirt mode. Chloe's gaze was riveted beyond them all to Justin as he and Tank adjusted the position of one of the tables. Justin motioned toward Zander and the girls and said something quietly to Tank. Tank's eyes narrowed, and he strode over to them. Chloe had no idea what Tank did next, because Justin was swaggering toward her with a sinful look in his eyes. He put his arms around her and pressed his lips to hers in a tender kiss.

Was this their new normal? Kisses as greetings? Showing up unannounced for romantic surprises? She could get used to this.

"What do you think, blondie?"

"Who can think when you've done something so wonderful? I'm still in shock that you thought of all this, much less did it. We haven't even gone on a real date yet."

"Real dates are important, but they're just formalities. We've been friends for a long time. We're way past dates. I brought you soup when you were sick, even though you wouldn't let me in the door. Do I need to spell it out for you?"

"I had the stomach flu. I was saving you from catching it."

"Okay, I'll give you that. I took you to the clinic when you twisted your ankle on your mile-high heels—"

"I was going to drive myself," she reminded him.

He gave her a deadpan look. "Which is exactly why I drove you. Take a moment to think about us, Chloe. You were the one who picked out the picture of the stone bench that I made for Harper and Gavin as a wedding present, and it was the perfect gift. You helped me with invitations for my gallery opening."

"That wasn't hard." And she'd had so much fun doing it with him, she'd do it again a hundred times over.

"It's not about how hard the task is; it's about doing things together, helping each other. You were my bra pong partner at Harper's bachelorette party."

"Which you *crashed*," she said with a smile, remembering that night all too well because it was the first night of the storm. *The night before our almost kiss.*

His expression turned serious. "We've had fun, we've been there for each other, and we've even argued. Although I admit I've lost more times than I've won arguing with you. I've given you some of my best come-on lines, and you've spent countless nights stealing glances at me when we were out with our friends and giving me smart-ass retorts that I fucking loved. I've laughed with you, held you when you cried, and now that I know how you feel about parties, I have a sneaking suspicion *you* were behind my birthday dinner at Summer House with Vi and our friends. The motorcycle cake? Cookies frosted to look like artist palettes? Chocolate sculpting tools? Black balloons that said LET'S RIDE? It all makes sense now. I thought it was Gavin who set that up."

"I didn't want you to know," she said softly, remembering the nights last fall when she'd pulled it all together. "Now it seems silly to have kept it a secret."

"Not silly, babe. You were in denial, but I wasn't. Don't you see, Chloe? All of that makes a solid foundation for what will be a great relationship."

She felt a little giddy, which wasn't like her at all. But how could she not be? She knew he was right. "Okay, Mr. Wicked. You've got me. You're pretty amazing, and I must have been walking around with blinders on, because before the night you came over to finish our dance, I thought you were just playing with me."

"I was, but I've always been playing for keeps with you, Chloe. If I'd known that you'd missed out on birthday parties and anything else when you were younger, I'd have been doing things like this for you the whole time I've known you, even if you refused to go out with me."

He paused, as if he wanted his words to sink in, and they sure did.

"I'm going to take these guys and get out of here so you can have your girls' night." He kissed her cheek and said, "Go put your toes in the sand, beautiful. I'll see you tomorrow night for our date."

A COUPLE OF hours and many laughs later, the rain had stopped, Chloe had taken far too many pictures, and Gracie was fast asleep on a blanket, holding her monkey. Chloe and the girls cleaned up the leftovers and reassembled her living room. As they carried the dining room table inside, her mind drifted back to Justin, as it had been doing all night. When she'd first seen him on the porch, she'd thought he'd come to crash the meeting, to flirt and make light of their group as he'd done in the past. She was so thankful that in all the time they'd known each other, he hadn't given up on her. That really told her who he was. She was still thinking about his confession that he hadn't fooled around with anyone else since they'd met. Then again, he was the man she'd compared all other men to. Even over dinner or drinks, none of them had been able to hold a candle to him. Could it really have been the same for him?

"What is that goofy smile for?" Gabe asked as the girls began gathering their things.

"Nothing," Chloe said, but she heard a dreaminess in her voice.

"He's a good egg, Chloe," Gabe reassured her. "I've known Justin for a long time. Everything he does comes from his heart."

"Or his *long dong*," Daphne said in a hushed whisper. Her cheeks flamed, and giggles burst from her lips. She slapped her hand over her mouth, and everyone laughed.

"I can't even tell her *not* to say that about my brother. *Look* at her!" Madigan said. "She's so embarrassed even her ears are red."

"Do I want to know how Daphne knows *that* about Justin?" Starr asked.

"I don't *know* it!" Daphne insisted. "Our friend Emery saw him naked. It's a long story, and she didn't sleep with him, but she swears it's true."

Everyone looked at Chloe expectantly. She couldn't help but make a joke. "It is a *long* story."

They all cracked up.

"On that note, I'm heading out. Come on, Marly, before they get you talking about my brothers' body parts." Madigan hugged Chloe and said, "This has been the funnest night I've had in a long time. Thank you for inviting me."

"I'm so glad everyone came. I'll walk you out," Chloe said as Starr came into the living room carrying Gracie, fast asleep on her shoulder. "Starr, I'll get your bag and umbrella."

"Do you know whose turn it is to choose the next book?" Marly asked as she and the others grabbed their jackets.

"Not yet. Tomorrow morning I'll pull the list of members and use a random number generator to select the member who gets to choose. I'll announce it on the forum." Chloe followed them out to their cars.

"I hope whoever gets chosen lives close so we can all go to the meeting together," Steph said.

"Me too," Daphne said. "This was the best meeting yet. It would have been the best even if the guys hadn't brought the beach to us, although that made it epic."

"That was all Justin, and it was for *Chloe*," Madigan said.

"Did you know he was doing that for her?" Gabe asked.

"No," Madigan said. "I just meant that we shouldn't forget that he did it just for Chloe. All of my brothers have big hearts, but Justin makes extra efforts for the people he cares about. I'll never forget what he did for me when I was in seventh grade."

"Well, don't leave us hanging," Chloe urged.

"There was a school dance, and all of my friends had dates except for me," Madigan explained. "Justin had moved out of the house by then, but when he heard about it, he showed up at the dance. The girls went gaga over him, and the boys thought he was the coolest guy they'd ever seen in his leather jacket and biker boots. He led me out on the dance floor, and I was totally embarrassed because, you know, he's my *brother*. I begged him not to make me dance with him. But you know Justin. He wouldn't take no for an answer. He looked me dead in the eyes and said that dance wasn't for me; it was for *him*. He said he was proud to have me as his sister and that he finally had a chance to let the world know it."

"He said that?" Chloe asked.

"Sure did, and he was nineteen years old, when most guys are jerks." Madigan tossed her purse in her car and said, "But I think the real reason he did it was that he knew once the cool guy danced with me, boys my age would want to."

"I told you everything he did came from his heart," Gabe said to Chloe. "What he did tonight was probably the most romantic thing I've ever seen a guy do in real life."

"I had no idea Justin could even be romantic." *At least not until the night he came over to finish our dance.* Chloe kept that to herself because it felt intimate and special, and she wanted to keep it that way. Thinking about how he'd remembered what she'd said last night about her mother never celebrating special events, she said, "I know better now. But I think a better word for him is *thoughtful.*"

Starr looked up from securing Gracie in her car seat and said, "Whatever he is, I'd like a man who knows how to be that way."

"Wouldn't we all?" Daphne added.

Madigan shook her head. "You girls have at it. I'm perfectly happy with my puppets, where I hold all the power."

"I hold all the power in my life," Chloe said.

"She means the power to break her heart." Marly hugged Chloe and said, "Thanks again. I'm so glad I got to meet all of you. I can't wait until next month so we can all get together again."

Gabe waved and said, "*Hello.* I own a coffeehouse. A girls' night at my place is welcome any night of the week."

"Let's do that. Can we do that?" Madigan asked excitedly.

They agreed to meet a week from Wednesday night at Common Grounds for dinner and said their goodbyes, hugging like they were all old friends. Chloe waited until they'd driven away before heading up the walk. She went around to the back of the house and stood in the grass gazing into the screened porch. The colorful tiki lights lit up the makeshift beach. Tropical music played softly from the living room, and the fire still had a few small flames. She took some pictures for scrapbooks and memory boards, then stood in front of the porch and took a selfie with the lights behind her.

She went onto the porch and sat on a blanket. As she sank her toes into the sand, she thought about Justin. *I figured my girl would want to put her toes in the sand at her luau, so I brought the beach to you.* She took a picture of her toes in the sand and debated sending it to him with a sexy message. *Or an invitation.* Her thumbs hovered over the keyboard, her pulse quickening at the thought of seeing him again.

Chapter Ten

JUSTIN LAY ON his stomach in Wicked Ink tattoo shop. The buzz of Tank's tattoo gun competed with the rock music blaring through the speakers. Tank had just started working on Justin's new tattoo because they had gone out for a beer with the guys after leaving Chloe's house and had stayed for a while. The shop was closed, but two other tattoo artists, Gia and Aria, were talking in the workstation across from Tank's while Aria cleaned up from her last client.

Tank was a talented tattooist, but he wasn't the best conversationalist, and once he got into the *zone*, he tended to stay there. Justin didn't mind. It gave him a chance to think about Chloe and their date tomorrow night. He'd been waiting for a chance to take her out for so long, he should have a list of a dozen out-of-this-world dates at the ready. But out-of-this-world didn't feel right, despite the fact that Chloe was the classiest woman he knew. After their talk on the beach, he knew there was a lot more down-home girl to her than anyone thought. Maybe even more than *she* realized. He wanted to impress her, of course, but not by going all out. He'd rather plan something that would show her he saw who she really was. He'd love to get her on the back of his bike, but he planned to take his truck tomorrow night in case she freaked out about riding on the back of a motorcycle. Baby steps...

Tank turned off the tattoo gun and said, "You riding Sunday?" as he wiped Justin's back.

Summer traffic could be a nightmare on the Cape, so they tried to get together with their brothers and friends on Sundays for long rides off the Cape.

"Absolutely. You?" As he said it, he had visions of Chloe joining them on one of their rides.

Tank nodded and began tattooing again. His cousin looked tired but fierce. He'd looked that way ever since Ashley had died. Between the tattoo shop and the firehouse, Tank worked long hours. Justin had a feeling he was trying to outrun the memories of the night he'd found Ashley. But Tank was locked down tighter than Alcatraz. Justin could never be sure what was going on in his cousin's mind.

"How are things at the firehouse?"

Tank lifted the needle from Justin's back and shrugged. He wiped the area he was tattooing and went back to work.

"Ask him if he's getting any sleep these days," Gia said as she and Aria walked across the aisle.

Gia had worked for Tank for several years. She was all legs, with skin the color of cocoa, colorful tattoos on her arms and legs, and enough sass for an army of women. She towered over petite and shy Aria, who had worked there for about two years and who was also a billboard for body art. Like Tank, she had her nostril pierced.

"You giving Aria a lift home?" Tank asked.

"Actually, I convinced her to go to Undercover with me," Gia said. "It *is* Friday night, you know. You should head over and hang out with us later."

Tank lifted his needle, eyeing Aria. He was protective of all of the people who worked with him, male and female, but Aria had issues with anxiety and social situations, which made him even more protective of her. Zeke had tutored Aria when she was in high school, and when she'd started working with Tank, Zeke had schooled him and their brothers and cousins on ways to help her feel more comfortable.

"You good with that, Aria?" Tank asked.

Aria tucked her long blond hair behind her ear and nodded. "Yeah."

"Is Cait going to be there?" Tank asked.

Cait was another employee of his. She was a sharp, guarded tattooist and body piercer who, though quiet, was acutely aware of everything going on around her. Justin knew exactly what Tank was thinking. If Cait was going to meet them there, she would keep an eye on the girls and make sure nothing bad went down.

"No. She had something going on tonight." Gia put her arm around Aria and said, "I've got her, Tank. I'd never let anything happen to our girl."

"I'll be there as soon as I'm done," Tank said.

"How about you, Maverick? You game for a few drinks?" Gia asked.

The only woman Justin wanted to hang with tonight was Chloe, and since she was busy with the girls, he planned on heading to his studio to try to nail down a design for the piece he promised to make for the suicide-awareness rally. "Not tonight, thanks."

"Okay. Well, you boys have fun." Gia peered at Justin's back and said, "You should let me tattoo you one day. Add some color to that sexy back of yours."

"Thanks, but this guy has had dibs on my tats since I was an obnoxious little shit. I think he'd crush my skull if I strayed."

"Whatevs. Come on, A," Gia said. "Let's go get our groove on."

As the girls walked out, Tank said, "Do me a favor so I don't have to take my gloves off. Dwayne and Baz are tied up at the rescue. Text Blaine and Zeke. Tell them to get up to Undercover to keep an eye on the girls."

"You've got it." Justin texted his brothers, and then he set his phone on the table. As Tank began tattooing again, Justin said, "You getting any sleep these days?"

"No less than usual."

"Then why is Gia worried about you?"

The twitch in Tank's jaw told Justin he was not in the mood to be scrutinized. But that only made Justin worry more, so he said, "Dude, you know you can talk to me."

"I know I can do a lot of shit, but it doesn't mean I'm going to."

Justin's phone vibrated with a text. "That might be Blaine or Zeke." Tank lifted his needle, and Justin reached for his phone. Seeing Chloe's name on the screen made him way too fucking happy. He opened the message, smiling at the picture of Chloe's feet in the sand. Her toenails were painted pink, and a pretty silver chain circled her ankle, a dragonfly charm lying on the top of her foot, reflecting the colored tiki lights. Beneath the picture was the message *Want to come dip your toes in my sand?*

He wanted to dip a hell of a lot more than just his toes in her *sand.*

"Dude, it's my girl. I've got to go. Would you mind if we cut it short and finish up another time?"

"Everything okay?" Tank asked as he set down his tattoo

gun.

"Hell yes. She just wants to see me."

"Give me five minutes to get you cleaned up." He wiped the area clean. As he put clear plastic over it and secured it in place with tape, he said, "I'm happy for you, man. You've waited a long time to go out with Chloe. Don't fuck it up."

Justin climbed off the table and pulled on his shirt. "I'm doing my best. Thanks."

Fifteen minutes later he pulled into Chloe's driveway. As he headed up the walk, Chloe appeared at the edge of the backyard. His body awakened at the sight of his luau goddess basking in the moonlight. She beckoned him toward her with her index finger, reeling him in.

"Good evening, Mr. Wicked," she said huskily.

God, this woman…

"Hello, gorgeous," he said as he wrapped his arms around her.

Her finely manicured brows lifted, and her eyes sparked with heat. She pressed her hands to his chest and said, "I have a bone to pick with you."

"Hold that thought."

He lowered his lips to hers, kissing her slow and deep. But as had happened every other time, sparks ignited, turning slow to urgent, unstoppable passion. She clung to him as their tongues tangled. His hands moved up and down her bare back until he couldn't take another second of not touching her. He lowered his hands, pushing through her grass skirt and palming her ass. The taste of her hot, willing mouth and the feel of her silk panties made him hard as stone. He fucking loved silk. He crushed her to him so she could feel his desire. The hard coconut bra between them should have lessened their arousal, but they were too far gone. She moaned into his mouth, and he lifted her into his arms. Her legs wound around him. They kissed as he carried her onto the porch and sank down to a blanket with her on his lap. He wanted to strip her naked and love every inch of her the way she deserved to be cherished. But somewhere in the back of his mind was a nagging reminder that she had wanted to talk to him.

But her mouth…

He couldn't break away, needed one more glorious minute of kissing her, of her straddling his lap. One more minute of her hands in his hair, holding him like he was *hers*. She made another greedy sound, and his cock twitched, anxious to get into the game. If he didn't stop now, he knew he wouldn't stop at all. He forced himself to break their connection. A rush of air fell from Chloe's lips as her eyes fluttered open.

He was captivated by the raw emotions staring back at him. "Talk to me, baby."

Her cheeks were flushed, her lips pink from their kisses. She held up her index finger as she said, "I need a second to catch my breath."

He touched his lips to hers, loving that she was just as lost in them as he was.

"*Wow*," she said just above a whisper. "My feet are usually planted firmly on the ground, and this is the third or fourth time your kisses have sent me up to the clouds."

"Is that the bone you have to pick with me?"

"Uh-huh," she said softly.

"Well, babe, that sounds like a compliment to me. So feel free to *pick* at my *bone* all night long."

A nearly silent laugh bubbled out of her lips. "You make it hard to be serious."

"You make *me* hard, and to me that *is* serious."

"*Justin*," she said with a hint of embarrassment. Her brows slanted, and she said, "I have to get something off my chest."

"I can help with that. Is there a tie in the back of this coconut bra?"

"*God*. What have I done?" she teased.

"Opened a door that you have no chance of closing. Go ahead, sweet cheeks. Tell me what's got that pretty brow of yours furrowed." He pressed a kiss to the tension lines between her brows, and she sighed dreamily.

"This might sound weird," she said softly but confidently. "So please remember that my background *is* a little weird. When you kissed me at the door tonight in front of all of my friends, I got so swept up in us, everything else disappeared. And when we're close, my heart races and I get butterflies in my stomach. I've never felt this way before, and it's incredible to finally allow myself to feel all the things with you that I've been trying to ignore. But it's like a drug. I want more of us. And that makes me wonder if all these feelings are what my mother is always chasing. That fleeting rush of adrenaline and desire. I've lived my whole life doing everything I can to keep from turning into her, and it's a little scary to suddenly hoist my *lust-for-Justin flag* up the flagpole and let it fly free for everyone to see."

"God, baby, you're so fucking *real*. I dig that about you. But if you're asking me not to kiss you in public—"

"No, that's not it. I just don't want to be *her*, you know? I got completely caught up in our kiss earlier, and I had a house full of friends. And I *wanted* that kiss, Justin. I wanted that kiss more than anything else, which is *why* I got so lost in it. But I don't want to be someone who puts a man ahead of her friends."

"It was one kiss, Chloe. And yeah, it was a damn good one, but, babe, you're not your mother. From what you told me, she chases men and leaves everyone else behind. You could never be that type of woman, and I'm not just spouting shit to make you feel better." He moved a lock of hair from her cheek and said, "What did you say to me after our kiss?"

She rolled her eyes, a smile tugging at her lips. "I can't remember. My head was in the clouds."

He laughed softly. "You reminded me that you'd forbidden me from crashing the meeting. The man-chaser you told me about would *never* have done that." He gazed deeply into her eyes, wanting her to hear every word he said. "Your mother obviously needs a man to fill some void inside her, to make her feel whole because she can't seem to do that for herself. *You* are nothing like that. You said it yourself, Chloe. You've spent your life trying not to become her. You're strong. You've created your own life, with your own friends, and you don't need a damn thing from any man, including me. Everyone who knows you will tell you that you're too caring to ever allow anyone to hurt someone you care about, especially yourself. Just look at Serena. Look at your friends. Drake told me how you gave him hell when Serena was a teenager and he broke her heart."

"He got my wrath that night. I can't believe he told you about it."

"He also said that when they got together as adults, you made no bones about what you'd do to him if he hurt her again."

She whispered, "Also true."

"And Gavin told me about how you stood up to him when he started dating Harper. You might not realize this, but I am one hundred percent positive that the year and a half you kept your distance from me was your way of giving me the don't-break-my-heart speech and making sure I heard you loud and clear."

Her cheeks flushed, and she lowered her gaze.

He put his finger under her chin, lifting her face so her eyes met his. "What we have isn't *fleeting*, sweetheart. It's *real* because you and I are real."

"I've been thinking about what you said earlier about us having a strong foundation built on friendship. I know you're right, but lust doesn't last, Justin, and quite frankly, I'm bursting with it."

"You have a lot of worries in that gorgeous head of yours. I'm glad you trust me enough to tell me about them. You're right about lust, Chloe," he said honestly. "Lust alone doesn't last, and relationships built on it eventually fall apart. But lust *does* have a place in the best relationships. Lust, love, communication, compromise. They go hand in hand. All those things are what make relationships stronger. It took me years to learn what a healthy relationship was, and then it took several more years before I trusted myself enough to know that I was capable of being in a meaningful relationship." He felt her relaxing into him, into *them*, and said, "You and I have lived through perfect examples of what *not* to do. I've watched Preacher and Reba, and Con and Ginger, and you and I have both seen our friends fall in love and create happy lives together. We know it's possible for two people to think of each other before thinking of themselves, and I want to explore those possibilities with you, Chloe."

Her fingers brushed the back of his neck, and she said, "How do you know just what to say to put my mind at ease?"

"Easy, babe. I just tell you the truth. If we weren't meant to be, if you were a woman who was going to chase every dick in town, or if I was a guy who was out to break your heart, we wouldn't be here right now. We're both too smart for games like that."

Her eyes filled with desire, but her brow wrinkled, and she said, "Everything you say tells me who you are, and I *really* like who you are. I want to kiss you so badly right now I could *scream*. But I know if we kiss, I'm not going to want to stop, and there's a fine line between when it's appropriate to do more and when it's not. I don't want to screw us up *or* make you think I'm easy. I haven't had to deal with anything like this in so long, my radar is probably off. But I *really* want to kiss you right now, and I know you want to kiss me. So where is that fine line for us, Justin?"

He ran his hand up her back. Her skin was warm, and she was looking at him like she wanted to eat him alive, and *man*, he wanted that, too. But what he wanted even more was for her to feel safe and in control, so he said, "We've had a year and a half of not crossing lines, and I'll wait however long you want. What matters most is where *you* want that line to be, Chloe."

"I don't want that line at all," she whispered, and reached behind her back. In the next breath her coconut top fell to his lap.

He looked his fill at the woman who had tied him in knots for far too long. Her eyes held the confidence he adored and a secret, unexpected innocence that he knew he'd see in his dreams. "God, you're beautiful, baby." He skimmed his hands up from her waist, light as a feather, and brushed his thumbs over the sides of her breasts.

She inhaled sharply, a small smile lifting her lips.

"I've dreamed of seeing you"—he pressed a kiss to the center of her breastbone—"of touching you, for so long." He ran his finger over a tiny white scar just above the swell of her left breast. "What happened here?"

"I don't remember," she whispered. "Kiss me…"

He kissed the scar, and then the swell of her breast. She inhaled shakily, eyes closed.

"I *need* to feel you against me, sweetheart." He started to take off his shirt, and she opened her eyes, helping him.

"Oh *God*," she said breathily, her hands playing over his chest.

He slid his hand to the nape of her neck, bringing her mouth to his, reminding himself not to get too wild with her. More than a year of pent-up passion mounted inside him as she ground against his hard length and they devoured each other's mouths. The feel of her bare breasts against his chest brought his carnal desires roaring out. His hands were on a mission, touching her everywhere at once—caressing her breasts, moving through her hair, groping her ass. He couldn't get enough of her. Every touch brought a sharp inhalation, an untethered moan, or a rock of her hips. He was going to lose his fucking mind.

He broke their kiss and growled, "I need my mouth on you." He lowered his mouth to her breast, sucking hard.

"Ah, *yes!*" She grabbed his head, arching forward, holding his mouth to her breast, demanding, "*Harder.*"

The need in her voice made his entire body throb. He lowered her to her back on the blanket, and she lifted her hips, brushing against his cock.

"I'll get there, sweet thing," he promised. "But we've both waited a long time for this. There's no way we're going to rush through any of it."

He laced their hands together, pinning them beside her head, and dragged his tongue along her lower lip. When she leaned up for more, he pulled back.

"I told you I *won't* rush this, baby, and I never lie." He ran the tip of his nose along her cheek, breathing her in, and said, "Trust me, Chloe. I'm going to make you feel better than you ever thought possible."

"I'm looking forward to it."

"Not half as much as I am."

He slanted his mouth over hers, kissing her deep and a little rough, *testing the waters*. She craned her neck up, trying to give as much as she took.

Hell. Yes.

He thrust his tongue against hers, exploring, *possessing* her mouth, and then he eased to a series of slower, tender kisses. When she bowed up beneath him, he gave her what she wanted, kissing her harder, *deeper*. She moved with him, her sexy sounds begging him to take them further. They kissed for what felt like forever, and he was lost in those kisses, lost in *her* as they made out fast, then slow, sweet, then rough. When he finally drew back, they were both breathless.

"Your mouth is a piece of art, baby." He traced her upper lip with his tongue, and she made a whimpering sound. "I fucking love your mouth."

She panted out, "I love kissing you."

"What else do you love doing with your mouth, sweetness?" He didn't give her a chance to answer as he slid his tongue into her mouth, stroking over hers without making contact with her lips, leaving her mouth gaping as their tongues teased and taunted.

Her eyes narrowed. "*More.*"

"Oh, you'll get more." She was so demanding, he pushed the boundaries a little further and said, "One day I'm going to see your beautiful lips wrapped around my cock."

Heat flared in her eyes.

"You like that idea, baby?"

"Almost as much as I like the idea of your wicked mouth between my legs," she said haughtily.

Oh yeah, sweetheart. Cut loose with me. "I knew we were a perfect match." He traced his index finger along her lower lip, and she licked it, a challenge boldly appearing in her eyes. He slid his finger into her mouth and said, "*Suck* it, baby. Show me what I have to look forward to."

She didn't suck his finger. She licked along the length of it, teasing him until his cock felt like a steel spike.

"Fuck, sweet thing. We're going to set this world on fire."

CHLOE WAS SURE she'd died and gone to sexual heaven. She'd never been so brazen, but Justin made her feel safe enough to say things she'd never imagined saying out loud. He made her feel so much more than anyone ever had, and she wanted things with him she'd never wanted before. She'd never been with a guy who talked dirty, even though she'd craved it like a drug. Justin's dirty talk drove her as wild as his kisses as he blazed a path down her body, whispering naughty promises between sucks and licks. He was as masterful at turning her on with his mouth as he was at flirting. He teased her with his tongue, circling her nipple until she was writhing and arching, pleading for more. He brushed his scruff along the sensitive skin on her breasts and grazed his teeth over the taut peaks, sending rivers of pleasure slicing through her.

"*Oh God*," she said, fisting her hands in the blanket.

He lifted his eyes to hers. "Too much?"

"*No*. Don't stop."

"Baby, I'm going to give you everything you've ever fantasized about, and then some," he promised.

He covered her breast with his mouth, sucking so deliciously she cried out. She'd never been happier about not having neighbors. He squeezed her other nipple, and she tried to press her thighs together to quell the yearning, but his big body was wedged between them. He ground his erection against her center, making her panties wet with the friction. Heat spread through her like wildfire as he masterfully took her to the brink of orgasm. He shifted onto his side, lying next to her, still loving her breast with his mouth, and stroked her through her panties with his hand. She spread her legs wider, needing more. Thank the heavens above he took the hint and pushed his fingers into her panties, stroking over her wetness. He made a low rumbling sound of appreciation.

"Shaved bare and beautiful," he said hungrily. "I can't wait to get my mouth on you."

She choked out an embarrassingly horny sound, and the edge of his lips tipped up in a sinful grin. "That's right, darlin'. I'm going to make you *so* glad you took the time to do that."

Ohmygod. Justin took *dirty* to a whole new level, and she *loved* it.

He lowered his mouth to her breast again, quickening his efforts between her legs, and rocked his shaft against her thigh. She tried to concentrate on his mouth, but his hand was sending electric currents racing through her. Desire billowed inside her, mounting with every stroke of his tongue, every tease of his fingers. Her emotions reeled as she fought to remain in control. But he was too talented, too determined to bring her pleasure, licking and kissing, squeezing and teasing. Too many sensations rained over her all at once. She moaned and writhed, thrusting and rocking uncontrollably, hanging on to her sanity by a thread.

He put one finger in her mouth and said, "Suck, baby. Suck it like it's my cock as you come."

Just hearing his dirty demands nearly sent her over the edge. She did as he asked, and in return he lowered his mouth to her other breast, sucking so perfectly, her toes curled under. He pushed his fingers inside her, fucking her slowly, and used his thumb on her most sensitive nerves. Her climax crashed over her, stealing the air from her lungs. Her body bucked and pulsed wildly. He covered her mouth with his, still working his magic between her legs as he took her in a punishingly intense kiss. She was soaring, weightless and rapturous, lost in Justin's wicked world of pleasure.

When she finally started the slow descent back to earth, aftershocks throbbing through her, he gazed deeply into her eyes and said, "Stay with me, sweetness."

"I can barely breathe," she panted out.

The pleasure in his eyes was palpable. "Too tired for me to take my first taste of you?"

Oh Lord. Her entire body prickled with anticipation. "Never."

He didn't hesitate. He kissed, tasted, and caressed his way down her body, lighting up every nerve ending. He kissed her thighs as he gently guided them farther apart, sweeping the grass skirt off her legs. He hooked his fingers into her panties at her hips and locked eyes with her as he took them off. Then he lowered his piercing gaze to her sex, creating a tidal wave of heat.

He bit his bottom lip, his eyes predatorial, and said, "*Mm-mm*."

Her stomach went all kinds of crazy at the mix of desire and something much deeper gleaming in his eyes.

"I'd have waited forever for you, sexy girl."

She wanted to say she was glad he'd waited as long as he had, but he pressed a single kiss to the cleft of her sex and her thoughts fragmented. When she opened her mouth to speak, all that came out was a shaky breath. He held her gaze as he squeezed her thighs, kissing a path from her knee to the crease beside her sex. He dragged his tongue along that crease, so close to her sex, her inner muscles clenched. She couldn't look away from his piercing stare as he drove her mad with tender kisses and slicks of his tongue. His eyes were so dark, so hungry, she could feel the restraint in him as he pushed his hands up her thighs, dragging his thumbs over the damp trail his mouth left behind.

She felt his hot breath on her center and closed her eyes. Every inch of her was alive with pins and needles as he lowered his mouth to where she needed it most. The first slide of his tongue brought a long, unstoppable moan. He did it again, slower this time, dragging his tongue all the way up her sex and teasing that magical bundle of nerves with the tip. Her hips rose off the blanket. She was powerless to stop the gasping, wanton noises from tumbling out as he did it again and again, taking her right up to the edge of ecstasy.

"That's it, baby," he urged. "Enjoy every second, because I

sure as hell am."

God, the things he said…

He pushed one hand beneath her bottom, lifting her hips. His mouth covered her sex and his other hand found that mystical spot that made her lose control. Her consciousness ebbed as he feasted on her, expertly playing over all her pleasure points, building her desires to a crescendo that had her thrashing and whimpering. Adrenaline and heat twined together, filling her veins, chest, and limbs. He pushed his fingers inside her, zeroing in on that secret spot like a homing device. When he moved his mouth higher, she nearly detonated. She couldn't think. Couldn't breathe. Could only *feel* as he took her up, up, *up*, and higher still, until she was hanging on the edge of a cliff. He did something out of this world with his mouth, or fingers, or a frigging sorcerer's wand for all she knew, and she shattered into a million glorious pieces.

"*Justin!*" flew from her lips like a demand.

He stayed with her, tasting and touching, heightening every sensation until she collapsed to the blanket, a trembling, boneless mess. He kissed his way up her belly. Every touch of his lips sending tingles skittering over her skin. She'd never been pleasured so thoroughly, and when he gathered her in his strong arms and kissed her, he breathed air into her exhausted lungs.

When their lips finally parted, she felt transformed. He kissed her forehead so tenderly, she rested her cheek on his chest and closed her eyes.

"Feel that, baby?" he said in a low, confident voice. "That closeness? We're anything *but* fleeting."

Knowing he'd taken her worries to heart filled her with happiness. She lay listening to the crackling embers of the fire and the music floating out from the cottage, absently tracing the tattoos on his chest. She opened her eyes, her gaze moving down his stomach to the formidable bulge in his jeans, and she realized that while she was lying in sated glory, he still had a raging hard-on. She had never been into giving oral sex, but everything was different with Justin. She wanted to give him as much pleasure as he'd given her. She moved her hand lower, stroking him through his jeans.

He covered her hand with his, stilling it. "You don't need to do that."

She rose up so she could see his face. He looked as blissed out as she felt. "I can't leave you like that after you made my entire world tilt on its axis."

He pressed his lips to hers and rose onto his elbow beside her so they were face-to-face. "I didn't pleasure you so you'd do it in return. What I did was for me as much as it was for you. I've thought about feasting on you so many times, I could practically taste you in my sleep."

She felt herself blushing and said, "*There's* the Justin Wicked I know."

"That guy never went anywhere, babycakes." He kissed her and said, "Now that you've stopped cockblocking us and realized that I'm your man, we've got all the time in the world."

"God, the way you *talk* is so…"

"Honest?"

She laughed softly. "I was going to say brash. I'm just not used to it."

"Aw, come on. After all the time we've known each other, how can you say you're not used to me?"

"I'm used to *you*. Well, certain aspects of you, like your flirting and pushiness. But I'm not used to hearing you talk dirty to me, or openly *claim* me and mean it."

"I've always meant it." He flashed an arrogant grin and said, "You'll get used to hearing *all* of it. Give yourself a day or two."

"Just don't get all possessive and weird on me. I'm not your property."

"How about *freaky*?" He leaned over her, taking her down on her back, both of them laughing as he smothered her with kisses. "Can I get freaky on you, blondie?"

She squirmed beneath him, grasping at his back as he kissed her neck. She felt something slippery beneath her fingers and said, "What is that?"

"I was getting a new tat from Tank when you texted."

"Can I see it?"

His grin turned wolfish. "Do I get to inspect your body for tats?"

She laughed softly, realizing she'd never enjoyed a man's company in or out of bed as much as she enjoyed Justin's. "I can assure you that I have no tattoos." She pushed playfully at his chest and said, "Let me see your new one."

They sat up, and she covered her breasts, looking for her coconut bra. Justin reached for his shirt. "Here, sweets. Wear my shirt."

"Thank you," she said as he helped her put it on. The fabric held his scent, and as the soft cotton settled against her skin, she felt even closer to him—and a little awkward. "Does this feel weird to you?"

"You asked me that after we kissed last night, and my answer is the same. Not even a little." His brows knitted. "Is it weird for you?"

"To be nearly naked in front of you and wearing your shirt after you just did all those dirty things to me? Yeah, a little. I like it, but it's *new*. I have butterflies again, and I got all tingly just from putting on your shirt. I'm *not* a butterfly, tingly person."

"I hope with me you'll feel, and *do*, a lot of things you're not used to. I'm sure we both will, because what we have is different from anything we've experienced in the past. It's okay to feel all those things, Chloe. They don't make you a weaker person, so enjoy it. Don't overthink it."

Once again, his sensibility calmed her.

"And you look damn hot in my shirt."

She crossed her arms over her belly and said, "Good, because I'm going to sleep in it tonight."

"Don't get me thinking about you lying in your bed or I'll end up carrying your hot little ass in there."

She spotted her panties by their feet and pulled them on, trying *not* to think about Justin in her bed, and said, "We are *not* going there. Let me see that new ink of yours."

"Sure, right after you tell me about this." He touched her anklet. "I noticed you wore it to Gavin and Harper's wedding, and last night at the beach."

"I can't believe you noticed that." And she loved that he did. "Serena gave it to me right before I started college. It's my spirit animal."

"A *dragonfly?*"

"Mm-hm. When we were young, we'd take walks down by a creek near our house and there were always dragonflies flying around us. And not just one or two. We would see like eight or ten. So I looked them up online and found out they symbolized change, hope, and adaptability. They say when you see a dragonfly, it's time to make a change." She touched the anklet and said, "I wear it on special occasions, like the wedding, and tonight with the girls, or when I need strength to make a change, like when I started college or a new job." She didn't say why she'd worn it last night. Now was not the time to talk about something so dark.

"That's fascinating. And you've had the same one all these years?"

"Yes. Now flip over and show me that new ink, biker boy. I'm on a voyage of discoveries tonight."

"And what have you discovered so far?"

"That *you* are a very dirty talker."

"You liked it, pretty girl, and don't try to deny it."

"Hush. You'll embarrass me," she said, nudging him onto his stomach.

He crossed his arms under his head and said, "Tank didn't have much time to work on it before you texted, and you've seen my other tats."

"I know, but I've never really *looked* at them." They'd been to the beach with their friends many times, but when Justin was shirtless, his *ink* was the last thing on her mind.

What she'd felt on his back was a clear film, like Saran wrap, secured in place with tape over the new tattoo. She couldn't tell what the tattoo was, but there was an outline of wings and something that looked like clouds behind them. Her gaze drifted away from the new tattoo to the dark, spiny branches of the meticulously detailed tattoo of a tree spanning from just below his broad shoulders all the way to the waist of his jeans. The branches were nearly bare, and there were several leaves drifting down his back. Each leaf looked so real, she had to touch them. Ribbons were strewn between and over branches, each one with a word or a name printed across it. There were dozens of ribbons, some with names she didn't recognize and others with names she did, like Con, Ginger, Tank, Baz, and

Gunner. An angel was tattooed on a branch, her bare feet dangling beneath her, so detailed and beautiful, her wings looked soft as feathers. *Ashley* was written on a ribbon draped from the branch beside her, below her feet, to the branch on her other side. Steph had told Chloe and their girlfriends about Justin's cousin committing suicide when she was younger. It had made her sad then and even sadder now.

She didn't know what Tank's or Baz's given names were, but she assumed those were their road names. It didn't surprise her that he'd used their road names, given how much the Dark Knights meant to him. What did surprise her were the other names she recognized, like Gavin and Harper, who shared a ribbon, and Violet and Andre, and a few more of their closest friends. Although, now that she understood how important Violet's friendship was to Justin, that surprise turned to admiration.

Etched into the twisted and intricately drawn trunk were several dates and words like *Justice*, *Cuffs*, *Fish*, *Sidecar* and dozens more. Were they more road names? Or did they mean something else to him?

Near the bottom of the trunk was an intricately shaded hollow. The detail was so realistic, it looked as though the cavity existed in Justin's skin. Tucked safely inside, protected by the rest of the sturdy trunk, was his mother's name written in a pretty yellow script. It was the only color on the whole tattoo. Chloe's chest ached anew for his loss.

She followed the long fingerlike roots on his lower back, snaking over and around the Dark Knights' emblem, a skull with dark eyes, sharp brows, and a mouth full of jagged fangs. The scary emblem had never made sense to her. Why would they want something so intimidating to represent a group who fought so hard for the benefit of others? But now it made more sense. They would do whatever it took to keep others safe, and sometimes that meant appearing scary.

Thick roots grew out of the mouth of the skull like serpents, forking off into dozens more, the ends angled like flukes on anchors. The ribbons woven into those roots boasted the names of Mike, Preacher, Reba, Blaine, Zeke, Zander, and Mads.

His family.

His roots.

She touched his back with both hands and closed her eyes, feeling so much for him, it should have scared her. But it felt as right as being intimate with him had. She pressed a kiss to the center of the tree, and then she took in the rest of the tattoo. Some of the roots extended below the waist of his jeans, and she was dying to know if there was more to the elaborate design.

"Chloe?" He tilted his face up, startling her from her thoughts. "You can take off the plastic film. It's been long enough."

As she peeled it off, she said, "What is it going to be?"

"An angel for my mother."

"Like the one for Ashley?"

"A little different, but the same idea."

"I like that. Your tattoos are beautiful. There are so many names and dates. You even have Gavin and Harper."

"I told you that I don't take anything for granted. Those are the names of my closest friends and family. Gavin is like a brother to me, which makes Harper like a sister-in-law. And the dates represent different events in my life, like the date my mother died and when I first met Preacher and Reba. The date I saw my father for the last time, the date my adoption was official, and plenty of others. I'll probably keep adding to it forever."

"And the words in the trunk?" she asked. "Cuffs? Sidecar?"

"Dark Knights I'm close to. Cuffs is a cop. He's the kid I told you about last night. He was Blaine's best friend when we were kids, the one Blaine beat up before saying all that stuff to me about family."

Justin was a much deeper and more emotional person than she'd ever imagined. "I've never thought much about tattoos, but I really like yours. They say a lot about you. The symbolism is intense."

"Life has been pretty intense."

She ran her fingers over the ink on his back, sensing that the symbolism was as vital to him as the blood running through his veins. "Some people wear their hearts on their sleeves. You wear yours on your back."

He sat up and said, "You wear yours in your eyes." He kissed her softly. "When you look at me like you are right now, it makes me want to stay with you all night. But we've got a big date tomorrow, and I think I'd better let you get some sleep."

Stay was on the tip of her tongue, but she held back. There were so many new emotions going on between them, she could practically see them whirling over their heads.

As he helped her to her feet, he said, "I'll come by tomorrow and clean this up for you."

"Can we leave it for a few days? It's a good memory."

"You're not worried about the sand getting on your floors?"

She shook her head. "We live on the Cape. There's always sand on my floors. Besides, these memories are worth it."

He embraced her and said, "You're pretty awesome, sweet cheeks."

"You're not so bad yourself, biker boy. I'll walk you out to your truck."

"That's not how it works, sweets. I'll walk you in and make sure your place is locked up tight."

"Justin, I can handle locking up."

"I know you can, but throw me a bone, will ya? It's my second night as your boyfriend and I want to do boyfriend things."

As they walked inside, she said, "I think you just did some pretty fantastic boyfriend things…"

Chapter Eleven

SATURDAY EVENING JUSTIN climbed from his truck in front of Chloe's house, trying to calm his nerves. He'd been counting down the hours until their date since he left her last night. Chloe had gone into work for much of the day, and he'd worked at Cape Stone in the morning, swung by to check on the dogs, and then spent the afternoon in his studio, so their texts were few and far between. They were just as flirty and fun as always, which was a huge relief. Chloe was an overthinker, and he hoped she didn't regret anything they'd done last night. He also hoped he'd planned a date she'd enjoy. Dinner at a nice restaurant in Provincetown, a romantic moonlight walk, and maybe they'd have a drink on the pier. He wanted time to talk and focus on each other instead of hitting a movie or some club where they'd be distracted from getting to know each other even better.

He grabbed the bouquet of flowers he'd bought and headed up the walk. He'd never bought a woman flowers before, but the gardens in Chloe's yard were gorgeous and well maintained, which meant she appreciated them. Plus, Mike had told him dozens of stories about the times he'd picked flowers for his wife and how much they'd meant to her. Justin wasn't sure Chloe was a picked-flower type of woman, so he'd gone to his friend Lizzie's flower shop. He'd been as drawn to the irises as he was to Chloe. Lizzie had said irises symbolized eloquence, faith, wisdom, and hope, which he thought was perfect for his careful girl who had clung to hope of a better future from the time she was a young girl and who took great care in choosing not just her words and actions, but also the people she surrounded herself with.

As he climbed the porch steps, he looked down at his jeans and the V-neck shirt Madigan had given him for Christmas. Madigan had called the color *distressed sangria*. He didn't know about that, but he hoped Chloe liked it.

He knocked on the door, and when Chloe answered it, there was no faking the happiness in her hazel eyes, waylaying his fears of her overthinking their being close. She looked beautiful in a glittery champagne-colored tank top and cropped black skinny jeans, with a pair of sexy heels with straps that wound around her ankles.

"Hi," she said.

"Hello, sweet darlin'. Damn, you look *fine*. Give me a second to pick up my jaw from the porch."

Her cheeks flushed, and she closed her eyes for a split second. In that moment of bashfulness, it was easy to imagine the innocent teenager she might have been had her mother not fed her to the wolves.

"These are for you." He handed her the flowers and leaned in to kiss her cheek, breathing in her light, summery scent.

"They're beautiful, thank you. Come in while I put them in a vase." As he followed her into the kitchen, she said, "I like your shirt. You look good in red." She grabbed a vase from beneath a cabinet and began filling it with water.

"Thanks. Mads bought it for me." He wrapped his arms around her from behind and kissed her neck. "You look gorgeous in everything."

"Flattery will get you everywhere," she teased. "How did you know that I love irises?"

"I didn't, but once I learned what they represented, I knew they were meant for you." He kissed her shoulder and said, "The blue ones symbolize faith and hope." He kissed her neck. "Yellow symbolizes passion." *Kiss, kiss.* "And purple symbolizes wisdom. If only there was a color for *drives me wild.*"

She laughed. "You have some of the best, and cheesiest, lines."

"Only for you, sweet cheeks." He glanced at the table, which was covered with pictures of older people. "Are one of these pictures of your grandparents?"

"No. I don't know my grandparents, which is one of the reasons I wanted to work with the elderly. Those are residents from LOCAL. I take pictures at our events and put up memory boards in the community room. Sometimes I make albums for them."

"That's nice. You must really enjoy your work."

"More than you can imagine. The people are so grateful for every little thing, it makes me want to do more for them. You'd be surprised at how many families move their loved ones into the facility and promise weekly visits, but then don't come nearly often enough—or at all. I make extra efforts to spend time with the ones who are left behind. And I really enjoy working on their behalf, trying to make their last years the best they can be. I'm always looking into new programs for them."

She told him about her newest endeavor, the Junior/Senior Program, and about the puppetry program she and Madigan were working on. The passion in her voice, and the way her face lit up as she talked about her work, told of her sincerity.

"I had no idea you were so involved with the people there. How did you get into that line of work?"

"I volunteered at LOCAL during my first two years at community college, and a number of the people there suggested I go into the field. I'm glad I did. It fulfills me in so many ways."

His gaze swept over the table and he said, "It sounds like you found the perfect job. I bet the residents really love all your extra touches." He glanced at the counter by the refrigerator, where more pictures were spread out. There were pictures he'd texted to her of him with the dogs they'd rescued, along with a few pictures from his birthday party, Gavin's wedding, and other times.

As she set the vase on the table, he said, "Speaking of all your *touches*." He reached for her hand, enjoying the sparks of heat rising in her eyes, and said, "What's this? Your new midnight fantasy lineup? *Nubbin'-lovin'* material?"

"Ew, *no*!" She swatted him.

He caught her around the waist, hauling her against him. "*Ew* is not the word I think of with the thought of you pleasuring yourself. *Hot, sexy as sin,* and *enticingly erotic* are better descriptors." Her cheeks pinked up and he said, "We could experiment, hit the bedroom and see what words come out of my mouth as I watch you."

"*Ohmygod.*" She twisted out of his grip and grabbed him by the collar, dragging him toward the front door. "Come on, biker boy, before I decide you embarrass me too much to go out with you." She grabbed her purse on the way out the door.

"What *are* you doing with all those pictures?" He opened

the passenger door and helped her into the truck.

"I'm not sure yet. I just can't stop thinking about the dogs."

He put his hands on the top of the doorframe and leaned in. "The dogs, huh? Not the *guy* with the dogs?"

"Well, maybe a tiny bit." Her expression turned serious and she shifted in the seat, facing him. "I really can't stop thinking about them and all they've been through. I know you said they were good with people, but are they really? Do they ever try to bite?"

"The night we picked them up, some of them got a little aggressive with all the chaos, and when we passed by other dogs at the rescue. But they're not aggressive toward people, and Gunner is keeping them away from the other dogs. Some of them are scared of loud noises, and you know, I'm sure certain noises trigger fear and aggression. They need their wounds to heal, and that takes time."

"Emotional wounds, too. The poor things," she said. "Did you see them today?"

"For a little while. They were happy to see me. The one with one eye cries when I leave him."

"Do you think Dwayne would mind if we stopped by?"

The hope in her eyes tugged at him. "Darlin', do you have a soft spot for dogs?"

"For all animals, and I guess people, too. We're not so different. We didn't ask for the parents we were born to, the people at LOCAL whose families don't come see them didn't ask to be forgotten, and those dogs didn't ask to be owned by monsters. My heart goes out to them."

"I dig that big heart of yours. Do you really want to meet the dogs?"

"Yes. Unless you mind? Will it mess up your plans for our

date?"

"Not even a little."

WICKED ANIMAL RESCUE was located on several gated and secure acres in Harwich. Baz's veterinary clinic and the two animal shelters were set far back from the road, and Dwayne's rustic farmhouse was on the west side of the property as they drove in. There were fenced areas with smaller shelters for farm animals like sheep, goats, and pigs, which Dwayne occasionally rescued.

"Dwayne owns all this land?" Chloe said as she stepped from the truck.

"He and Baz do. Dwayne lives in the farmhouse over there." He pointed across the property. "Baz lives above the clinic. Those two long buildings are the shelters. The one on the right is where the rescued dogs are staying. The rescued animals that aren't from the dogfighting ring are kept in the other one." He spotted Sidney Carver, who worked with Dwayne at the shelter, coming across the field toward them with a dog on a leash. He'd know that dog's limping gait anywhere. "That's Sidney and my one-eyed buddy."

"Who is Sidney?"

"She's a canine physical therapist and trainer. She works with Dwayne and rents a room in his house."

"Brave girl," Chloe said.

Justin chuckled. "She's the daughter of a Dark Knight. She's seen the harsh realities of life, and she's not afraid to give Dwayne shit. She's a cool chick, a total tomboy." Sidney was lean all over, with narrow hips and small breasts. Her brown hair was cut just above her shoulders, and she liked to hide behind it. "I doubt there's anything going on between her and Dwayne, but you know, it's Dwayne, so…"

"She's really pretty," Chloe pointed out. "Why is the dog limping?"

"He has a bruised hip." The dog was trying to run to him, barking and whining, pulling against the leash.

"He's so cute!" Chloe exclaimed. "Come on." She grabbed Justin's hand and headed for Sid and the dog, moving like she was wearing sneakers instead of heels.

Sidney said, "Someone's happy to see you. I swear he's been looking for you all evening."

"Hey, buddy." Justin crouched to love him up. The dog went paws-up on Justin's shoulders and licked his face. "I missed you, too, my friend. Sid, this is…" He glanced up at Chloe and couldn't suppress his smile as he said, "My girlfriend, Chloe. Chloe, this is Sid, the best PT and dog trainer on the Cape."

Chloe looked at Justin with a spark of elation in her eyes, and he knew she was reacting to him calling her his girlfriend because he'd felt the same giddiness when he said it.

Chloe looked at Sid and said, "Hi. I hope it's okay that we dropped by."

"Are you kidding? This one thinks Maverick is his daddy." Sidney slipped her fingers into the front pockets of her jeans and said, "I've been with him for the last half hour and he was just lollygagging along, but one look at Mav, and it's like he's had a triple espresso."

"Will he be okay if I pet him?" Chloe asked.

"Yeah, just go slow. He's been great with people."

Chloe crouched beside Justin, letting the dog smell her hand. "Hello, sweet boy." He licked her face, and she stroked his back. "Oh, look at your little ear and all those cuts. Poor thing." The dog pushed forward, pawing at her lap, and she sank down to her butt to pet him.

"He likes you," Sidney said.

"It's mutual," Chloe said. "He's so skinny. Is he going to be okay?"

"He's been through a lot, but he's eating well. He'll put on weight quickly." Sidney reassured her.

The dog pawed at Chloe's shirt.

"Uh-uh, bud. Don't rip her shirt," Justin said gently.

"He's okay." Chloe looked up at Sidney and said, "He's been through so much—it's good for him to be excited about people, right?"

"Yeah, it is," Sidney said. "He'll need to learn manners, but right now he just needs to know he's loved."

The dog climbed into Chloe's lap, and she kissed his head. "He's so sweet."

"You're not worried about getting dog hair on your clothes?" Justin asked.

She kissed the dog's snout and said, "Nope. I can wash them."

"Hey, Mav, Mike and your parents are hanging out at the picnic table by the kennels with Gunner," Sidney said.

"Okay. Are Gunner's dogs outside?"

"No. I put them inside when I work with the dogs from the fighting ring. You can bring your buddy over there to see your family if you'd like. But if you've got him for a bit, I'd like to go clean out his kennel."

Even though Chloe seemed happy playing with the dog,

Justin didn't want her to feel trapped into hanging out there when they were supposed to be on a date. "Are you ready to go, Chloe, or do you want to stick around?"

"Can we stick around? Or are *you* ready to go?"

Justin couldn't believe she was decked out in a glittery top and heels and happy to sit in the grass playing with the dog. "I'm in no rush, babe. I just don't want to rip you off from going on our date."

"We have plenty of time. I'd love to stay and play with him and meet the other dogs, if that's okay."

"Everything's okay. Go ahead, Sid. We've got him."

As Sidney walked away, Chloe said, "I like Sid. She seems nice."

"Yeah, she is," he said, wondering if Chloe would want to meet the rest of his family, or if that would seem like he was pushing her too fast.

They played with the dog for a long time, talking about nothing in particular and laughing at silly things. Chloe took about a dozen pictures. He could have sat there all night and been perfectly content. He loved how easygoing she was. The longer they were there, the more he wanted to introduce her to his family. He decided to throw caution to the wind and said, "What do you think, blondie? Want to meet my family? My grandfather is a bit of a curmudgeon, but he's a good guy."

"I would love to."

"Really? I thought you might hem and haw."

"Why? I want to meet the people who changed your life and helped you become the man you are."

He hooked an arm around her neck, drawing her into a kiss. The dog whined and stretched his paw across Chloe's lap, touching Justin's leg.

Chloe smiled and said, "He wants *all* the attention."

Justin took the dog's face in his hands and kissed him. "It's okay to be a needy pooch, but you need to learn better timing." He rose to his feet, holding the dog's leash, as he reached for Chloe's hand and helped her up.

"Why doesn't he have a name?" she asked, petting the dog again.

"I don't know. They usually pick up names along the way. A few have already been named. The pregnant one is Mama Bear, and the biggest of them all is Rambo. He's solid. He took a beating, but he pulled through."

Justin held her hand as they crossed the yard toward the shelter.

"Shadow," Chloe said softly.

"What?"

"His name should be *Shadow*. On the drive over you said he follows you around when you're here." She crouched beside the dog and said, "What do you think? Do you like the name Shadow?"

The dog licked her face, and she grinned up at Justin.

Justin patted the dog's head and said, "Looks like you've got a name, big guy. Shadow it is."

CHLOE HEARD DWAYNE'S laughter as they came around the side of the building. She was excited to meet Justin's parents and his grandfather. She really did want to meet the people who had loved him through his broken, angry days, had helped him overcome so much, shown him a better way to live, and had given him a better life.

Dwayne was sitting at a picnic table with a cheerful mahogany-haired woman who looked to be in her fifties. The woman was gazing adoringly at Justin. She had a kind smile, and there was a beauty mark near her left eye. She had to be Reba, and the handsome salt-and-pepper-haired man with tattoo sleeves rising to his feet beside her had to be Rob. An older man sat in a lawn chair with a tiny white kitten in his lap. Chloe assumed he was Justin's grandfather. There were three pizza boxes on the table, along with a few beers, sodas, and water bottles.

"Are you using my dogs to win chicks?" Dwayne called out to Justin as they approached.

"Just one dog and one woman." He squeezed Chloe's hand, looking at her with that lopsided grin that made her belly tingle. "And the dog now has a name thanks to that very special woman. His name is Shadow."

"My boy doesn't need a dog to charm a woman, but that's a perfect name for the dog. He follows Justin around like Justin is his proud papa." Reba came around the picnic table with her arms open and said, "Get in here and give me a hug, *charmer*."

Justin hugged her and said, "Mom, Preacher, Gramps, this is Chloe Mallery."

"Formerly known as Uptown Girl," Dwayne chimed in.

Justin glared at him and said, "*Shut it*, Gunner."

"It's okay, Justin. I hear jealous cousins say all sorts of things," Chloe teased.

"Oh my goodness. You *are* fantastic," Reba said. "We've been hearing about you for so long, I feel like you're already part of the family." She hugged Chloe, and in a hushed voice, she said, "He's crazy about you."

"*Mom*, I'm pretty sure she knows that already," Justin said with a shake of his head.

"I do," Chloe said. "Justin makes it hard not to."

Rob clapped a hand on Justin's back. "That's my boy. It's a pleasure to meet you, Chloe." He embraced her firmly, the way a father might hug a daughter. "Let me introduce you to Justin's grandfather, Mike."

"I can introduce myself," Mike grumbled as he rose to his feet, holding the kitten. Rob went to him. Mike handed him the kitten and said, "I can walk ten feet, boy."

Mike ambled over, looking tougher than any grandparent Chloe had ever known in his jeans and a denim shirt.

"You're a pretty woman," Mike said in a serious tone. "What are your intentions with my grandson?"

She wasn't sure what she'd expected, but it wasn't *that*. Justin looked amused. She lifted one shoulder and said, "Well, he's pretty cute, so I'm hoping to get a few kisses."

Reba chuckled.

"Just a *few*?" Mike scoffed.

"The truth is, I was hoping to use him for his body and his money," Chloe teased. "But I figured that wouldn't win me any favors with his family."

Laughter tumbled from Mike's lips. "That's more like it." He gave her a gentle hug and said, "Sit down and have some pizza. You need some meat on those bones."

"Yes, join us," Reba said. "We have plenty."

Chloe looked at Justin, worried about disappointing him if their plans were any further delayed.

"Don't tell me you're one of those gals who only eats salad, or needs a man's approval to put something in her mouth." Mike pointed at Dwayne, who was smirking, and said, "Do *not* say what you're thinking."

"Gramps, you set me up for that one." Dwayne took a swig of his beer.

"You've got a filthy mind, Gunner. A *good* mind, but filthy as can be." Mike looked at Chloe and said, "Come on, now. What's it going to be? Rabbit food or pizza?"

Chloe lifted her chin, and Justin nodded almost imperceptibly, as if he were cheering her on. "Hand over a slice of that pizza," she said as she sat down at the picnic table. "In fact, I'll have *two*, please."

"Do you want to ask Sid if she wants some?" Justin asked.

Dwayne shook his head. "She and Baz ate an entire pizza before he took off to meet Evie."

Justin sat beside Chloe and said, "In addition to being Baz's assistant at the clinic, Evie is his best friend." He lowered his voice and said, "Thanks for hanging with my family."

"Thanks for bringing me. This is fun."

They ate and talked, joking around so much Chloe felt like she'd known his family forever. Shadow slept at Justin's feet, and every once in a while he'd put his chin on Justin's leg for a little love, which Justin was happy to give. Chloe took pictures and explained that she enjoyed making keepsakes of fun times, which Reba seemed happy to hear. Reba asked if she could have copies of the pictures, because she said she was far too lax in the photo department. Dwayne made a few jokes about being careful not to accidentally forward dirty pictures to Reba, earning laughs from everyone, including Chloe, who answered with a sarcastic, *Don't worry. I keep those under lock and key.*

When Rob told her about their annual suicide-awareness rally and mentioned that Justin was making a sculpture to be auctioned off, she realized Justin never talked about his artwork. She was curious about that part of his life and made a mental note to ask him about it later.

Reba asked Chloe about her family, and Chloe told her about Serena and a little bit about their mother. She didn't go into much detail, but the look on Reba's face when Chloe said her mother hadn't always been around much told her that she understood the things Chloe wasn't saying. Reba had a gentle, caring way about her, but her inner strength was apparent. Chloe could envision her herding a pack of wild sons and cousins who had probably run around creating havoc when they were younger, with Madigan and, she assumed, Ashley, trailing after them.

Chloe loved getting to know his family and seeing how they teased each other as much as they built each other up. His family welcomed her into their inner circle so warmly, it was easy to imagine them embracing eleven-year-old Justin and all his troubles. Justin's parents were openly affectionate the whole evening, just as Justin was toward her, and it no longer felt weird to be close to him. It felt right and *wonderful*.

"Seeing you and Justin sitting together like this reminds me of when our kids were little." Reba rested her head on Preacher's shoulder and looked at Justin as she said, "Do you remember the first night you were at our house, sweetheart?" Reba used endearments as often as Justin did, lavishing her son, nephew, and even Chloe with them. It was clear where Justin had picked up that habit. Reba was friendly and compassionate. She listened carefully to every word everyone said.

Chloe would have given anything for a mother like her.

"I remember being pissed off," Justin said. "I was in a new place with an older kid who hated me and a younger boy who looked at me like I was full of secrets he wanted to hear—"

"That's got to be Zan," Dwayne said as he took the kitten

from Rob and sat down to feed it from a bottle.

That was a sweet side of Dwayne Chloe had never seen.

Justin said, "It was Zan. And then there was another boy who was probably thinking I was the perfect specimen to study and evaluate."

"Zeke," Mike said. "That boy has always devoured facts like they were peanuts."

"That's the truth. I've never met a smarter guy than Zeke. Then there was Mads." Justin looked at Chloe and said, "I had no freaking clue what to do with her."

"She had just celebrated her fourth birthday a few weeks before this ornery young man came to live with us," Reba explained. "I'll never forget how she looked at me with those big blue eyes and said, 'Mama, can he be my brother, too?'"

Chloe thought about four-year-old Madigan with three older brothers who doted on her. She probably thought Justin would be the same way. Chloe wondered if he had been. "That's a big question. What did you say to her?"

"We'd fostered kids before, and they always went back to their birth parents," Reba explained. "Justin didn't have that option, so I told her the truth. I said his mama was up in heaven, his father had done some bad things and was going away for a very long time, and that it would be up to Justin if he stayed with us or not." She looked at Justin with the love Chloe had always hoped to see in her own mother's eyes and said, "From the time our kids could understand what it meant to be a friend, they were taught about the strength and loyalty of family and that our family extended to the Dark Knights' families and other close friends. They grew up knowing all about the biker lifestyle, even the hard knocks, and our little Mads was distraught at the thought of Justin not having anyone looking out for him. You need to know a little something before I tell you what our baby girl did about it. Before Justin came to us, she'd spent months asking for a stuffed cow. And not just any cow. A certain brown and white one. Her daddy searched high and low and finally found a woman who made the cows out in Idaho."

"I take full responsibility for that," Mike said. "We had gone to the county fair with the kids, and the boys wanted to go on the rides, but Mads wanted to see the farm animals. She and I spent hours looking at them. She was completely enamored with the cows, and one of the kids there had that particular colored cow. After the fair, Mads wrangled Zeke into reading her just about everything he could find on cows. That's how she learned that unbranded cattle that weren't part of a herd were called Mavericks."

"She named that stuffed cow Maverick and slept with the darn thing every night," Preacher said as he put his arm around Reba. He kissed her head and said, "You tell her the rest, darlin'."

"After I told Mads about Justin's family, she went into her bedroom and got her cow and her favorite blanket. Justin was sitting on the couch stewing about his world being upended yet again, as well he should have been." Reba blinked several times and looked up at the sky. "Sorry. I always get a little choked up when I think of that day."

Preacher pulled her closer, the same way Justin had done to Chloe on the beach the other night.

"Mads climbed up on the couch beside Justin and gave him her cow," Reba explained. "She said—"

"Now you're not alone anymore," Justin said, sounding emotional. "Now there are two Mavericks, you and him."

"Mads curled up with her favorite blanket and her head on Justin's shoulder, and Justin sat stock-still, as if he was afraid if he moved she might break," Reba said warmly. "In that moment I knew he was meant to find us. He might have wanted us to believe he was big trouble, and I think he even believed it himself. But I'd known enough kids to see that on the inside that boy was special. He was pure goodness." She looked up at the sky and fanned her face. "Now I'm going to cry, so don't mind me."

"Special is right," Dwayne mumbled. "A special pain in the ass."

Justin flipped him off, and they both chuckled, but the emotions passing between them were as real as the tears in Reba's eyes.

"That's the sweetest story." Chloe gazed up at Justin and said, "So Mads gave you your road name?"

"I had to earn my road name." Justin looked at Preacher and said, "It was one of the greatest honors of my life."

Preacher gave a manly nod and said, "Madigan coined his nickname. The brotherhood gave him his road name. His road name is Maverick, but not because he wasn't branded. By then Justin was a Wicked. He had a family who loved him. But it turned out that Mads knew what she was doing, because Maverick also means independent minded, which was the perfect description for the angry boy who fought us with everything he had, and became a good, strong man."

Sidney came out of the shelter, breaking the mood, and said, "Are you about ready to let me put your boy to bed?"

"We're calling him *Shadow*," Justin said.

"Can we go with you?" Chloe asked. "Is that okay? I'd love to see the other dogs, but I'd also like to keep visiting with everyone. Will you guys be here when we're done?"

"Yes, honey. Go give them some love," Reba said. "We're not going anywhere."

Chloe and Justin went with Sidney. They gave Shadow an abundance of kisses and pets before she put him in his kennel. He whined as they walked away so Chloe could meet the other dogs, but Chloe couldn't take it and went back to give him more love. Justin ended up sitting with Shadow while Chloe went with Sidney to meet the other dogs. They were in even worse shape than they'd looked in the pictures. They had puncture wounds, areas of missing fur, old wounds that hadn't fully healed. Some were more timid than others, but eventually even the shy ones gave Chloe kisses.

After loving up Shadow one last time, Sidney headed home for the night, and Justin took Chloe into the other building to see the dogs and cats that were available for adoption.

When they finally made their way back outside, she said, "If I had the space, I'd take them all home."

"Now you know why Dwayne has several dogs and cats. It's easy to get attached to them."

"Like Shadow is to you," she said. "Would you ever adopt a dog?"

"Sure, when the time is right. Shadow's not ready to be adopted, and a dog is like a kid. It needs stability, a life where its family is home every night. I was real close to carrying you into your bedroom last night, babe. I can't leave a dog crossing its legs and lonely. That's just not my style."

She loved knowing he didn't take his responsibilities lightly.

They found Reba, Rob, Mike, and Dwayne chatting by a bonfire pit, like a scene right out of her childhood dreams.

"We saved you two the lovers' seat," Dwayne said, nodding

to a glider chair built for two.

"Thanks, man," Justin said as they sat down. He put his arm around Chloe and pulled her closer.

"I want to adopt all of your animals," Chloe said to Dwayne.

Dwayne raised his beer bottle and said, "Hear, hear. I wish you could. I'm holding an adoption event a week from Saturday. You should come by and check it out."

"Do you accept volunteers to help with the event? If so, I'd love to be part of it. Anything to help them find homes."

"Hell yes, I take volunteers. Your boyfriend is one of my best," Dwayne said.

"You're going?" she asked Justin.

"I always do."

"Of course you do." Chloe leaned in for a kiss without thinking.

"You two are just too cute," Reba said.

Chloe realized that was the first time she'd initiated a kiss in public with Justin, and she liked that she'd earned his mother's stamp of approval.

"Damn right we are," Justin said, kissing her again.

"Okay, Casanova, let me talk to your pretty little gal," Mike said with an air of seriousness. "Dwayne was telling us that you work at LOCAL."

"Yes. I'm the director of the assisted living facility. Are you familiar with it?"

"Mildly," Mike answered. "I'm losing my mind living with my son. A man needs his own space, you know what I mean?"

"Pop, come on," Rob said.

"Don't *come on* me. Do you think you'll want your boys running your life when you're my age?" Mike shook his head and said, "I didn't think so. So tell me, Chloe, what's this place got going for it?"

Chloe looked at Rob, not wanting to get in the middle of a family discussion.

"Go ahead, Chloe," Rob said. "He'll just keep asking until you give him what he wants."

"So that's where Justin gets it from," Dwayne said with a snicker.

"Damn right," Mike said. "Let's hear what Chloe has to say."

"Well, let's see. LOCAL has several wings designed to accommodate all levels of care. The Helper's Hand division caters to people who prefer to live alone, and the Live-in Assistance wing is for people who have full-time, live-in care providers. We also offer Nursing Care and Hospice divisions, and of course we have a full medical staff. We have residents who move in as young as sixty-five who are looking for a safe place where they can make friends, and as they advance in age, they won't have to worry about being a burden on their families. Not that they *would be* a burden on their families, but I think it's easy to feel that way when you're used to living on your own and you find yourself in need of assistance."

"What's the environment like? And the food?" Mike asked.

"The environment is very upbeat and positive, and we have an amazing dining hall with top-of-the-line chefs."

"And desserts?" Mike asked.

"Pop, come on. You know the docs don't want you all sugared up," Rob reminded him.

Mike swatted the air in his direction. "You see, Chloe? I'm always under his thumb."

"This dynamic between you two is very normal. In fact, one

of the biggest benefits of having a loved one move into our facility is that it takes this type of responsibility and oversight off their children. We have ways to make sure Mike's sweet tooth is satiated without doing harm to his health." Chloe looked at Mike and said, "But you might find you have less time on your hands to think about sweets. We offer wonderful programs and activities, like exercise classes, swimming, yoga, hiking, and gardening. We have arts and crafts, computer lessons, game and trivia nights, movie nights, group outings and bus tours. And I'm always researching new things for our residents to do. I've just started a program where high school students come in and spend time with our seniors, and everyone seems to be enjoying it."

"What about the ladies? Are there restrictions on *mingling?*" Mike asked.

"Oh boy, here we go," Reba said. "I'm sorry, Chloe."

"No, it's fine. I actually get asked that question quite often. Senior citizens have needs, too, and unfortunately, it seems to be frowned upon by their families. I think even grown children have trouble thinking about their parents' more intimate personal relationships. Facilities like LOCAL are continually grappling with this issue. It's not just the families we worry about, but the health and welfare of our residents and where to draw the line as people begin to lose their cognition. But all the research shows that social relationships are critical to senior citizens, and even more so in assisted living facilities. Intimacy and companionship have positive effects on people's sense of independence, it facilitates good physical and mental health, and helps with loneliness. To answer your question, Mike, there are no hard and fast rules in our facility, but the safety of our residents is always our primary concern."

"If I ever need an advocate, I want you on my side, Chloe," Rob said, reaching for Reba's hand.

"Thank you. I care a great deal about the happiness of our residents. I have friends who have lived there for several years. I join them for lunch or dinners sometimes. Aging is a funny thing. We spend our whole lives raising families, or choosing not to, and working hard to pay the bills. Nowadays many people don't retire until they're in their seventies. They don't want to worry about mowing grass or taking care of a big house, and our facility offers them a chance to spend more time enjoying life and less time worrying about some of the day-to-day responsibilities. For many families, just getting to and from medical appointments can be complicated. Having the offices in our complex makes it easier. The grocery store is a shuttle bus away, and they deliver. Friends are in the same building, dinners are hosted, events are planned, so enjoying life is easier." Chloe realized she'd been going on too long and said, "Sorry. I get carried away when I talk about LOCAL."

Justin pulled her closer and said, "Don't be sorry, babe. Your passion takes my breath away."

"Keep your passion in your pants, Maverick," Mike said, causing everyone to laugh. "I'd like to see the place, Chloe. Can I take a tour?"

"Poppy, are you sure? You know we love having you stay with us," Reba said.

"Darlin', I know you do, and I appreciate you and my boy opening your house to me. But if I don't get my own place, I am going to lose my mind."

Rob and Reba made plans to bring Mike to LOCAL for a tour a week from Thursday, in the afternoon. They talked for a while longer, and by the time everyone got ready to leave, Chloe was walking on air. Justin's family was nothing like she'd thought before their talk on the beach and every bit as loving and welcoming as she'd expected after learning so much about them.

"I'm glad you hung out with us tonight." Dwayne gave Chloe a one-armed hug, cuddling the kitten in his other arm, and said, "Keep this dude in line, will ya?"

"I'll try."

Dwayne and Justin bumped fists. He said goodbye to the rest of the family and headed into the shelter to check on the dogs one last time.

"I really enjoyed getting to know you, Chloe, and I hope we'll see you again soon." Reba embraced her for longer than she had when they'd first arrived.

"Me too. I look forward to seeing you for the tour."

Rob wrapped his arms around Chloe and said, "Be good to my boy."

"I will be. I have months of brushing him off to make up for," she admitted.

Mike winked and said, "The chase is half the fun." He embraced Chloe as Justin said goodbye to his parents.

She and Justin walked to his truck hand in hand, and Justin said, "I'm sorry we spent so much time with my family. I had planned on taking you to P-town tonight."

"I loved every second with them," she said honestly. "You're lucky, Justin. That's what a family should be like, and tonight has already been the best date I've ever been on."

He drew her into his arms and said, "The night's not over. What would you like to do?"

"Provincetown sounds wonderful, but I *like* being in your world, and I'd really like to see more of it. Would it be weird for you to show me your studio where you sculpt?"

"That's a pretty private place." A devilish grin curved his lips, and he said, "No woman I've gone out with has ever seen my studio."

"A *virgin* studio?" She hooked her finger in the waist of his jeans and said, "My, my, Mr. Wicked, that makes it even more intriguing."

Chapter Twelve

REBA HAD ALWAYS said nothing felt as good as coming home, but as Justin pulled up to his secluded pond-front home Saturday night with Chloe by his side, he knew Reba was wrong. Coming home was great, but coming home with Chloe made it a million times better. He was nervous and excited to share this part of his world with her. He'd been honest about having never brought a woman he was dating into his house or his studio before. He knew how it felt to live someplace tainted with negative energy, and that was something he never wanted to do again. His home was his *sanctuary*, where he could kick off his boots and relax in peace, free from bad mojo. He hoped to one day raise his own family there, teach his kids to fish in the pond, to hike the woods, and if they were interested, he'd foster their artistic abilities the same way Preacher had with him.

"Whoa, Justin. Is that your house or your studio?"

He parked next to his motorcycle and said, "That's my house. There's a pond behind it, but it's hard to see in the dark. The studio is down there." He pointed to where the driveway veered off down the hill to the glass greenhouse-type roof of the enormous stone and glass building that never failed to help center him.

"Your house is gorgeous. It looks like that famous house by Frank Lloyd Wright. You know the one with all the cantilevered decks and roof overhangs."

"Fallingwater. That's the property that inspired the architect who built this house." He got out of the truck and came around to help her out.

He put his arm around her as they walked down the hill to the studio, and even though he'd often put an arm around her before she'd agreed to go out with him, it felt damn good to do it as her boyfriend.

"My studio is a mess inside," he said as he unlocked the door. "And however you define *mess*, this is probably about ten times worse."

"I assume messes go hand in hand with being an artist. I'm excited to see where you create and to gain a little insight into how your artistic mind works."

As they stepped inside, the scents of cold stone and shattered ghosts surrounded him. While his home was his sanctuary, free from bad memories, his studio was his *lair*. In his studio he unleashed his anger, wrestled with his demons, celebrated his happiness, and found his way to the peace he carried into his home at night.

He tried to see the studio through Chloe's eyes as she took in the concrete floors, tables, and shelves covered with stone dust and littered with sculpting tools, books, and other paraphernalia. Easels held sketches of future sculptures and ones he'd already finished. There were old pieces of wood and metal and several large slabs of stone placed throughout the studio. Two of his current works in progress were covered with sheets, one in the center of the room and the other to their left on a worktable. Against the far wall were two large stainless-steel sinks, several work areas, and an enormous kiln.

Chloe eyed the worktable to their left and said, "This is kind of a turn-on, like I've been invited into your secret refuge."

"If I'd known that, I would have dragged your pretty little ass here long ago, princess."

She touched the sheet covering his work in progress. "Can I peek?"

"Sure."

She lifted the sheet, revealing an enormous slab of marble, partially carved into a woman, huddled forward. Her shoulders were mostly defined, her head was bowed, her hair spilling toward the ground like a stilled river.

Chloe looked sorrowfully at the piece and said, "Is this what you're making for the rally?"

"No. That's a commissioned piece for a guy in Brewster." He put a hand on her back and said, "I have a long way to go until it's done."

"Do your clients choose what you make?"

"It turns out I don't like to be told what to create, so I guess the answer is no. I made two commissioned pieces where the clients asked for specific designs, and I hated every second of making them. It stifles my creativity and the process becomes frustrating." He shrugged and said, "Now I design what I want to make, and if a client likes it enough to commission it, I'll make it for them."

She ran her fingers over the marble and said, "What will she look like when she's done?"

He reached for the drawing he'd sketched for the piece. "Like this. Her legs will be tucked beneath her, her arms crossed over her face, and she'll be holding her shoulders."

"And what are all these dark lines?"

"Her body will be marred and scratched, with deep pits and angry slashes. The dark lines are representative of the thoughts and fears that bind her. All of that will be polished to a shine, and see that slab that looks like a turtle shell on her back?"

"Yeah."

"That's the weight of those thoughts and fears holding her down. That part will be rough and ugly, not polished."

"Justin, your work is so powerful. That piece might be the saddest thing I've ever seen, if I hadn't seen the ones at the gallery. Did you sell them all?"

He shook his head. "I sold most, but I kept two. They're in my house."

"Which two?"

"Do you remember a piece called *Cornerstone?*"

"Yes, if it's the one I'm thinking of. A woman's face emerging from chipped stone, right?"

He nodded, thinking of the sculpture. He'd defined and polished her lips and nose, but from the apple of her right cheek to the bridge of her nose he'd made it appear as though it had been violently broken off.

Chloe walked a little farther down the table to the sketches he'd drawn for the suicide-awareness auction. Her gaze moved over the image of a woman breaking through a brick wall, a woman with angel wings, and a dozen other sketches of images that just hadn't felt right.

Chloe lifted her eyes to his and said, "Which other sculpture did you keep from the gallery?"

"A naked, armless woman lying on her back on top of what everyone thought were waves. Her head was tilted back, eyes closed."

"I remember her. She was big, right? Her features were intricately carved, and she had wide paths of stone wound around her torso and legs like an enormous flat snake squeezing its prey."

"That's the one. I call her *Beholden*. That thing you think is a snake is *obligation*, and the foundation supporting her that people thought were waves is *love*."

"Justin," she said softly, touching his arm. "When you showed me the picture of your mother, I thought I had seen her before. Now I know why. Is *Beholden* Mary?"

His chest constricted. He turned away and draped the sheet over the sculpture she'd uncovered to give himself time to think. No one had asked him that question before, although he wondered if people who knew about his past had put the pieces together.

"Justin…?"

"They're all her, Chloe," he said, turning to face her. "Every damn one of them, or at least a piece of each of them. And they're me. I'm the obligation that bound her so tight she chose to leave this world instead of risking *my* life by leaving my father."

"That's a lot of guilt on your shoulders, and when you put it together with the guilt you felt about your father's crime, it's a wonder you're still standing. Doesn't all that guilt take a toll on you?"

"No," he said softly, wanting her to understand. "It's not guilt. It's *reality*, and it's how I keep my mother alive in my head. Remembering what she went through, creating her face over and over again, in *all* the ways I've seen it, so I never forget how beautiful she was, all that she went through, and all that she gave up so I could survive. It makes me stronger, and it makes me want to continue being the best man I can be, because she gave me that chance. If anything has taken a toll, it's trying to conceptualize a sculpture for the rally." He waved to the dozens of drawings he'd attempted and said, "Nothing I come up with feels right."

"Can I ask you something? Rob said the rally honors Ashley. Is there a reason they don't also honor your mother?"

"I asked them not to. The rally is important. It offers support for all the people who have been affected by suicide. The people who are left behind. I want to support it, but it's not an easy event for me, and I don't want that kind of attention on me."

"Then why did you agree to make a sculpture for it?"

"Because my aunt Ginger asked me to, and there's no way I'd ever let her down."

"You're such a good person. They're as lucky to have you as you are to have them." She looked at the drawings again. "You said the event is for all the people that have been left behind, right?"

"Yes."

"All these sketches look like you're trying to set your mother free. Maybe that's why it doesn't feel right, because you can't change what she did."

He mulled that over for a moment. "Maybe. I haven't thought of it that way."

"If this event is for everyone who has been left behind, and of course to honor Ashley and all those who were lost, then shouldn't your piece do the same? I'm not an artist, and I don't understand how it works, going from a concept to the beautiful pieces you make. But what if you created something that represented *all* of that? What comes to mind when you think of receiving support from others? People catching you when you fall? Letting you lean on them? Lifting you up?"

He could feel it, the energy of the support she described. "*Hands*," he said, looking down at his own.

"Oh, that's *good*. You can show the hands of people who have helped the ones who have lost loved ones to suicide, lifting and supporting—"

"The faces of the people left behind, not the ones that we've lost," he said excitedly, reaching for a pad and pencil. "That's *brilliant*. That's it, baby. That's exactly what people need. *Hope*."

"Yes. Focus on *survival* rather than on loss or trying to change what can't be undone."

She peered over his shoulder as he sketched faces pointing out in every direction, at different heights, as if they were decorating a pillar. And that was exactly what they should be on. A pillar of support. As he sketched, he said, "They'll all come out of one base, and these whirling lines I'm drawing between and around the faces will be carved like the energy from the support they're giving each other. Sweet cheeks, you are one hell of a muse." Beneath the pillar, he sketched a circle of arms from elbow to wrist, hands bent back, palms up, supporting the pillar. "The elbows will act as the stand for the sculpture, and the hands will hold up the pillar. This piece will give *a world of support* a whole new meaning," he said as he drew the hands around the base, overlapping each other, giving endless support.

"Can you sculpt the hands of people who have been there for Ashley's family? And the people who have been there for you?"

"There's nothing I can't sculpt, baby." It was the perfect

concept to give hope and draw people out of the darkness suicide left in its wake. Even *him*. "I can ask them to come in and model their hands while I work." The more he sketched, the more he felt the hope in the piece and the coming together and love that *he* had felt over the years.

"What if you surprised them?" Chloe asked. "Can you create hands from pictures?"

"Of course. What are you thinking?"

"That Reba, Rob, and the others have done so much for you, this is something you can do to show them how much you appreciate their support. It's a way of calling them out individually, so each person knows how special they are. Not that they don't already know how much they mean to you. But think about it. Rob, Tank, Baz, Zander, and Dwayne have tattoos on the backs of their hands, and Reba and your aunt and uncle have wedding rings that will distinguish them. I don't know about Zeke or Blaine, but maybe they have something unique about their hands, too. We'll have to check it out."

"I love this idea, babe. But how can I get pictures of their hands without them knowing?"

"Leave that to me," she said. "I've got my ways. You'll need to give me a list of the people whose hands should be on the sculpture."

He set down the pad and lifted her onto the table, wedging himself between her legs. She was smiling like a Cheshire cat, and she was the most beautiful thing he'd ever seen.

"What is going on here, Mr. Wicked?" She ran her fingers down his arms and said, "You have me in quite a precarious position."

He brushed her hair over her shoulder and kissed the skin he'd bared. "You haven't seen precarious yet." He slid one hand to the nape of her neck, threading his fingers through her silky hair, and ran a finger down the center of her breastbone. "I love the way you breathe harder when I touch you."

"I had no idea talking about sculptures could get you so hot," she said seductively, running her hands up his arms and into his hair.

"Neither did I." He lowered his lips to hers, earning the hungry sounds he adored.

"I need to talk about art more often," she said breathlessly.

He brushed his lips over hers, whispering as he traced his finger along her skin just above the neckline of her glittery top. "I need to be close to you, baby, as close as two people can get." He slicked his tongue over her lips, and the sound she made was drenched with desire. He guided her hands to the table just behind her hips, so her back arched slightly, and he began kissing the swell of her breasts. Her chest rose with each inhalation as he lifted her pretty top and groaned at the sight of her bare breasts. "God, if I had known you were bare under here…" He licked over one taut peak, and she closed her eyes. "Watch me love you, Chloe."

Her eyes opened, and her cheeks flushed pink as he licked her again, circling the peak with the tip of his tongue. He put one hand on her lower back, keeping her close as he ground against her center and sucked her breast against the roof of his mouth.

"*Ohmygod*" fell from her lips, hot and needy. "*Justin…*"

He rose and fisted his hands in her hair, causing another greedy gasp. "I want you in my *bed*, Chloe, lying naked and wet beneath me. I want your long legs wrapped around me as I drive into you so deep, you'll still feel my cock moving inside you next week. We're going to feel *so* fucking good together, baby, we'll be *all* that you can think about." She made a mewling sound and he fucking loved it. He put his mouth beside her ear and said, "Can you feel it now, baby? The head of my cock rubbing against your wetness?"

"Yes," she panted out.

"Your fingernails digging into my flesh as I enter you?"

Her breath left her lungs and his name sailed out as a plea. "*Justin*—"

"Can you feel your body tightening around me? Craving the next thrust? The feel of my strong hips between your thighs?"

"Yes, *yes*, I can feel it. I want you, Jus—"

He crushed his mouth to hers, more demanding than ever before, and she was right there with him, returning every hungry demand with her own cruel ravishment. She pulled up his shirt, and he tore his mouth away, his eyes blazing into hers.

"As much as I want to bend you over this table and fuck you into next week, the first time we come together is *not* going to be in a dirty studio. I want you in my *bed*, darlin'. *Now*."

CHLOE HAD NO idea how they got up the hill and into Justin's house, much less into his bedroom, one of the many cantilevered rooms with three glass walls looking out into the darkness. His deliciously filthy promises were ringing in her head, and her entire being was on fire as they stripped each other naked in a tangle of gropes and hungry kisses. He pushed his hands into her hair, and his hard body pressed against her, hot and demanding. His forward momentum sent her back against a glass wall as they feasted on each other's mouths. She was all over him, pawing, clawing, and savoring the feel of his muscles pressing her into the glass. He took her hands in his, spreading her arms out to the sides, and pinned them there. His cock ground against her belly so temptingly, she bowed out from the glass and went up on her toes, wanting to feel him inside her.

He broke their kiss, growling, "*Protection?* I'm clean, baby. Are you on something?"

"Yes. *Kiss me*," she commanded.

She felt him smiling into their kisses as his hips drew back and he aligned their bodies. The head of his cock rested against her center. She could feel his girth and desperately tried to sink down onto him. But he was in total control, drawing away with her every effort, then pushing against her again, teasing her until she was so wet and swollen, she ached for him. She put one leg around his, hooking her ankle on the back of his calf, giving him room to move. A deep, guttural sound rumbled up his chest as the broad head of his cock pressed against her. That greedy sound wound through her, igniting flames beneath her skin. He was breathing so hard she knew it took every ounce of his control to keep from giving her what she wanted. This man had the power to take her to her knees, and *oh*, how she wanted that, too! To taste him and tease him the way he taunted her. To make him lose his mind with desire and to pleasure him as exquisitely as he pleasured her.

But right now she needed him inside her more than she needed her next breath. She twisted her mouth away and said, "*Take me*, Justin. Make me yours."

His eyes went volcanic, holding her gaze as he thrust forward, and a sound of shock and delight left her lungs.

"Hold on tight, darlin'. Things are about to get *real*."

She curled her fingers around his, her arms still pinned out to the sides as he lowered his mouth to hers. He kissed her passionately as he pushed in deeper, slowly stretching and filling her so completely, his shaft rested against all her secret pleasure points. Fireworks exploded inside her, sending zaps of pleasure darting through her. Their arms and legs trembled. Her body greedily pulsed around his shaft, soaking in the thrilling tension. She could barely breathe for their toe-curling kisses, the weight of him against her, and the glass at her back. But she was safe in his arms, reveling in their closeness as he breathed air into her tired lungs. She'd never felt anything so all-consuming. She struggled to make sense of the emotions swelling inside her, but her thoughts were swimming in a sea of desire, and *Justin* was the captain of this tsunami.

His mouth slid from hers, and he touched his forehead to the glass beside her head, panting for air. "*Fuck*, sweetness." His voice was rough and raw, as gravelly and powerful as the roar of his motorcycle.

He released her hands and his arms came around her, cradling her against him as his mouth claimed hers again, and they began to move. Every thrust took her higher. Every grind sent electricity arcing through her. She had never felt so *alive*, so in sync with another human being. She clung to him as he pounded into her. His strong hands cupped her ass and he lifted her up, guiding her legs around his waist without missing a beat. She felt his muscles flexing with his efforts. His arms moved up her back, a buffer against the glass, as he grabbed hold of her hair with both hands. Oh, how she *loved* his taking control. He was rough without being hurtful, visceral and somehow also sensual. His tongue swept over hers to the same rapid beat as their bodies coming together. He punctuated every thrust with a gyration of his hips, stroking over the hidden places that made her thoughts fracture. She felt the tug of an orgasm low in her belly. Prickling sensations climbed up her limbs and chest at breakneck speed, burning and tingling at once.

Her emotions whirled and skidded, and she tore her mouth away and cried, "Don't stop!"

He held her tighter, thrust harder.

"Faster...*oh God*...There, there, *the*—"

Her eyes slammed shut as waves of ecstasy throbbed through her, and he thrust and ground perfectly, drawing out her pleasure. Just when she thought she'd hit the peak, he slowed as he withdrew, then thrust in hard and fast, slowing again on withdrawal and repeating the mind-numbing pattern, heightening her pleasure as the broad head of his cock pushed *all* her buttons. She was powerless to silence the sounds she made as she surrendered to their passion. Justin tightened his grip on her hair, guiding her mouth to his, taking her in a deep, sensual kiss, like he wanted to burrow inside her and batten down the hatches.

When she finally drifted back down from the clouds, going boneless in his arms, he kissed her softly and touched his forehead to hers. It was all she could do to try to remember how to breathe. His hands were still fisted in her hair, his body riddled with tension. Her sexy savage was chaining himself down.

"*Bed*, baby," he panted out. "I need you in my bed."

He carried her to the bed and stripped back the covers with one hand. He remained buried deep inside her as he lowered them to the sheets. The emotions pooling in his eyes were like fertilizer to the feelings blooming inside her. She knew she'd always remember every second of tonight, from the look in his eyes and the feel of his body pressing down on hers to the sweetest, most unguarded smile forming on his lips. In that moment, everything changed. The air grew thicker, their bodies moved slower, and their kisses were less urgent and frantic. They were *smoldering* and *potent*, laced with a dreamy intimacy. This wasn't sex as she knew it. This was two people bound together, transported to a higher plane where only *they* existed.

He pushed his hands lower, clutching her bottom, and quickened his efforts. His touch burned her skin. Her nails dug into his arms. She felt him swell impossibly bigger inside her with every thrust. Desire filled her up like smoke from a fire, seeping into every crack and crevice, until it inhabited her entire being. Tingles riddled her from the tips of her scalp all the way to the ends of her fingers and toes. With his next thrust, she bowed up beneath him, an electric shock scorching through her, and she cried out into their kisses. Her hips bucked, and her sex clenched around him like a vise. In the clutches of his own powerful release, Justin tore his mouth away, buried his face in her neck, and *growled* her name with so many emotions, it must have been steeped in them.

When they finally collapsed to the mattress, their bodies glistening from their efforts, Chloe's mind was a whirlwind of lust and desire, and something so much bigger, she couldn't even try to define it. Moonlight streamed through the glass wall as their breathing calmed, their bodies intertwined, hearts beating as one. Justin pressed warm, tender kisses to her cheek, neck, and shoulder, each one sending shivers of heat along her skin.

He rolled them onto their sides, holding her close, and gazed deeply into her eyes as he whispered, "Stay with me tonight."

"There's no place I'd rather be."

Chapter Thirteen

IF HEAVEN WERE a place on earth, Justin found it Sunday morning when he awoke with Chloe sleeping safely in his arms. Her cheek rested on his chest, her arm was draped over his stomach, and her soft curves were nestled against his side. She'd dozed off shortly after they'd made love last night, and he'd lain awake for a long while, riding the high of being with the woman he'd waited so long for. He'd finally fallen asleep, only to wake a couple of hours later, both of them insatiable for each other once again.

Sunlight poured in through the glass wall just like it did every morning, but his room felt different. *He* felt different. Making love to Chloe had been even more incredible than he'd imagined. He hadn't been prepared for the soul-searing emotions that had engulfed him the moment they'd first come together. He'd been certain it was just the build-up of wanting her for so long, but he'd been struck with the same overwhelming sensations when they'd made love again.

He kissed her forehead, hoping she wasn't going to slip back into feeling weird about them, but he sensed they were past that.

Her eyes fluttered open, and she tipped her face up. "Hi,"

she said sleepily.

"Good morning, beautiful." He skimmed his hand down her hip, giving it a gentle squeeze. "Did you sleep okay?"

"Mm-hm. You wore me out," she said sweetly. Her gaze moved around them, and she said, "I've never started my day with a man before, much less in his bed. I can't believe we're *here*."

"*Here* as in my bedroom, or *here* as in together?"

A mischievous look rose in her eyes as she said, "*Both*. I had the best time last night getting to know your family and meeting Sidney. I loved seeing the dogs and playing with Shadow." She rolled onto her back, holding the blanket over her chest as she sat up, scoping out his room.

"*And...?*" He went up on his elbow and kissed just beneath her shoulder.

"The pizza was pretty good, too."

"The *pizza*, huh?" He snuck his hand beneath the sheet and pulled her onto her side against him. "Seems to me you enjoyed more than the pizza, heartbreaker."

"Oh yeah," she said casually. "The orgasms were out of this world. Thanks for those."

He laughed. "Just the orgasms?"

"Maybe the guy, too."

He gave her ass a teasing tap.

Her eyes narrowed. "Did you just slap my ass?"

"Baby, that was a *tap*. The only time I'll slap your ass is when you ask me to."

"Then I'm safe, because there will *never* come a time that I'll ask you to spank me."

He wound the ends of her hair around his finger and said, "If you say so."

"Wipe that smirk off your face." Her gaze locked onto something over his shoulder, and she said, "Is that the cow Madigan gave you?"

Ah, she was looking at his bookshelf. "It is."

"That was a really cute story."

"Yeah, Mads weaseled her way into my heart pretty quickly." He kissed her lips and said, "I don't want to talk about my sister. I want to talk about you. What are your plans today, sexy girl?"

"Well, first I plan on finding out why your bedroom is so orderly. There's no clutter. Do you have a housekeeper?"

"No. I'm just a neat guy, except in my studio. When you grow up taking care of your own stuff, you…I don't have to tell you. I've seen your place. It's just as neat as mine."

"But I'm a *woman*."

"Thank God. Last night would have been a little awkward if you had a dick."

She laughed and swatted him. "You're so crude."

"Just real, baby. Come riding with me today."

"Riding?" She looked skeptical. "Didn't we do that all night long?"

"Hell yes." He kissed her smiling lips and said, "Seriously, we go on long motorcycle rides on Sundays. I want to spend the day with you. Come with me. Get to know the guys. You'll love it."

Her brows knitted.

"Are you scared to ride on my bike? Because I would never let anything happen to you."

"I know you wouldn't, but I've never been on a motorcycle. It's a little intimidating, but I'm not scared of it. I'm just not sure whoever *the guys* are would appreciate me tagging along."

"First of all, I don't care what anyone else thinks. I want you with me, and that's all that matters. Second of all, it's just my brothers, cousins, and Gavin. Nobody's going to mind."

"You sure you want me there? Won't I cramp your style?"

"You are adorable, and sweet cheeks, you *are* my style. I've been waiting a long time to have you on the back of my bike. Come with me. Let me take you for a ride and show you more of my world."

"I think you took me for a couple of long, hard *rides* last night." Heat flared in her eyes. She pushed him onto his back and straddled him. "Maybe it's *my* turn to take *you* for a ride."

"Baby, you can ride me any time, day or night." He put his hands on her waist, grinding beneath her, and said, "Come with me today."

"I do enjoy *coming* with you."

"Those words coming out of *your* sexy mouth are going to get you into big trouble." He palmed her breast, taking her nipple between his finger and thumb, and slipped his other hand between her legs, teasing the spot that made her eyes flutter closed.

She bit her lower lip, and her gorgeous eyes opened. She set a predatory gaze on him, and practically purred, "Maybe I like *big* trouble with you."

She slid along his erection, making his cock wet with her arousal. Her fingers played over his pecs, and then she teased his nipples. Holy hell, he fucking loved that.

"If I come with you, what's in it for me?" she asked.

"Besides the earth-shattering orgasm?"

She smiled and said, "Did you forget we were talking about a *motorcycle* ride?"

"*Fuck me*, dirty girl, and then we can talk about the motorcycle ride."

She lifted up, and he grabbed the base of his cock, holding it up as she sank down, taking in every blessed inch of him. She leaned forward, her hair curtaining their faces as she squeezed her inner muscles around him.

"*Jesus*, baby," he said through gritted teeth. He needed to *move* inside her before he lost his mind. He rocked up and grabbed her hips.

She put her hands over his, refusing to budge, and said, "I want to ride with you today, but if anyone doesn't want me there, you have to promise to take me home and not make a big deal out of it."

"Baby, nobody's going to mind. Harper rides with us."

Her brows slanted. "Why didn't you tell me that? I have her wedding album. I can bring it to her."

He wrapped his arms around her and swept her beneath him. "I wanted you to come with me because you want to be with *me*, because you trust *me* and feel safe with *me*. Not because you assumed if Harper went, it was okay for you to go, too."

"I have news for you, Justin." She wound her arms around his neck, bringing his face close to hers again, and whispered, "If I didn't trust you, I wouldn't be lying beneath you naked or letting you do all sorts of filthy things to me with that giant python of yours." She pressed her lips to his and said, "Now, are we going to *ride*, or what?"

TWO ORGASMS AND one sinfully sexy shower later, Justin

and Chloe grabbed breakfast and he gave her a lesson in motorcycle safety. Then they headed over to her cottage so she could change her clothes and pick up the wedding album for Harper and Gavin. The ride to her place was heaven and hell for Justin. He'd touched and tasted every inch of her body, and that still hadn't prepared him for the feel of her pressed against his back or the pride that swelled within him at finally having his girl on his bike.

When they arrived at her place, he climbed off the bike and took a moment to admire her long legs straddling his bike. She was wearing the glittery top, skinny jeans, and high heels she'd worn last night, and she looked sexy as hell as she took off her helmet and shook her head, her blond hair tumbling around her face.

"Maybe you should take a picture," she said sassily.

He whipped out his phone, and she tucked the helmet under her arm, striking a pose.

"Damn, girl, you are *hot*."

He helped her off the bike, and she thrust out her hip, flashing a sultry smile as he took another picture.

She giggled and said, "That's enough, biker boy."

He pocketed his phone and kissed her. "I'll never get enough. How'd you like the ride?"

"It was fun! I wasn't even that nervous once we got going." She tugged at his hand and said, "Come on. I need to change my clothes so we're not late."

Justin had been in Chloe's house a few times, but he'd never hung out there. While she changed her clothes, he took a moment to look around her living room. Pale green, blue, and yellow accent pillows brought her off-white couches to life. Simple and feminine, but not overly girly. A pastel throw rug picked up on the auburn, orange, and red accents she had scattered around the room. The mantel held framed pictures of Serena as a young girl, at her college graduation, in front of her interior design office, and on her wedding day beaming up at Drake, who was looking at her the way Justin knew he looked at Chloe—like she was the only woman in the world for him. The walls were decorated with pictures of Chloe with their friends. Each frame was decorated with ribbons, fabric, and other embellishments.

He moved to one of the bookshelves flanking the fireplace, where there were romance novels, mysteries, and a few books about working with the elderly. Mixed among them were more framed pictures of Serena and their friends, but not a single picture of Chloe. He glanced at the other bookshelf and noticed several thick binders; some were fabric, others with leather or distressed-looking vinyl. He pulled out a polka-dot fabric binder. Correction—*scrapbook*. On the cover was a picture of Chloe with her arm around Serena when they were young. They were sitting on a log in the grass. Serena was beaming at the camera, and Chloe, who looked to be about nine or ten years old, wore the unmistakable expression of a little girl with heaps of responsibility on her shoulders. Her hair was longer, to the middle of her back. She wore a T-shirt that had PEPSI written across the front, a pair of worn jeans that were frayed on the bottoms, and cheap flip-flops. She was lanky and adorable, all elbows and knees. He opened the album and found pages and pages of pictures of Serena when she was growing up, with a few pictures of Chloe sprinkled in. Every page was meticulously decorated with happy themes, like beaches and butterflies. Dragonflies appeared on nearly every page, and Chloe had written around the pictures, detailing special moments. He couldn't imagine how much time it must have taken to create such beautiful memories on every page. But that was Chloe, wasn't it? Creating memories of a happy life for the little sister she protected from so many harsh realities. Once again he wished he could go back in time and give her the childhood she'd deserved.

He put that album back and pulled out another, and again was met with elaborately decorated pages and happy stories, only these pictures had their friends in them as well. As he flipped through the pages, he found a picture of himself in his bathing suit, sitting on a towel by the water with Gavin, Rick, and Dean. In the distance, more of their friends were throwing a Frisbee. Justin's knees were pulled up, his arms resting on them, and his hair was hanging in his eyes. The page was decorated with stickers of driftwood, starfish, and shells. Chloe's handwriting came down at an angle from the left corner of the page. *Labor Day weekend with the gang. Beach time, sunburn, and s'mores.*

On the next page was a picture of Drake with Serena on his shoulders and Dean with Emery on his shoulders, and in between them was Justin running into the water with Chloe hanging over his back like a sack of potatoes. Her mouth was open like she was yelling, but her eyes were laughing. The page was decorated with a faded tan-and-blue background that looked like wallpaper and had *Beach*, *Sea*, and *Coast* written around images of a dolphin, a seahorse, and shells. Chloe had drawn swirls and pretty designs down the left side of the page. Next to the picture, she'd written *Wicked troublemaker* with an arrow pointing to him. A red heart dotted the *i*. He remembered that afternoon well. They'd had a blast with their friends, and Chloe had driven him crazy in that sexy blue bikini. But what really stood out in his mind was what had come after he'd tossed her into the waves. He'd gone after her and had held her up so she could catch her breath. Her unbridled laughter had stolen his heart. He could count on one hand the number of times he'd heard Chloe cut loose like that, and it was *glorious*. But then their eyes had locked, and as quickly as it had come, her laughter had silenced. She'd been in his arms, her wet body pressed against his, and for the space of a second, they'd both leaned in like two ships colliding, but just as she had during the storm, she'd hesitated. Then she'd wiggled out of his arms and splashed him as she stalked off.

"Hey."

Chloe's voice startled him from the memory. He closed the album, and his body heated at the sight of her wearing a black tank top with a neckline made from a zipper, open just enough to show a hint of cleavage. She wore a pair of tight distressed jeans that had a hole on one thigh and another just above her knee. They were tucked into knee-high black leather boots with silver buckles.

"Wow, babe. You look *smokin'* hot."

"Thank you, and you look *nosy*," she teased as she came to his side.

He was so taken with her, it took a moment for him to realize what she meant. "Sorry. I was just checking out your albums. Did you do all these decorations yourself?"

"Yes." She took the album from him and set it back on the shelf. "You know I make scrapbooks. I told you I made one for Gavin and Harper."

"I know, but I've never seen them. You're really talented."

"Thanks. It's just a hobby. Nothing special. Let me grab their album and then we can go."

She took a step away, and he pulled her into his arms, earning a sweet smile.

"You put your heart into every one of those pages, which makes them all special. I'm sorry I was nosy, but I'm glad I got to see that part of your life." He pressed his lips to hers. "And I saw a very telling little heart used to dot the 'i' in my name. It made me wonder how many more pictures of me you have and what other telling things you drew around them."

She twisted free and headed into the dining room as she said, "It was just a decoration."

"You didn't *just* decorate any of those pages, sweetness. They were *all* very well thought out. Maybe we need to have a scrapbook-reading party one night. Just the two of us looking through all your albums, so I can see *all* your hidden messages about me."

"After the last twelve hours, I'm pretty sure you've discovered all of my secrets."

She turned with the gift-wrapped wedding album in her hand and he closed the distance between them.

"You're a very complex woman." He put his arms around her and said, "It will probably take me a lifetime to discover *all* of your sexy secrets, including your secret fantasies about me."

"I plead the Fifth."

"You can keep your secrets for now. But rest assured, Ms. Mallery, I'll get them out of you one day."

"Mr. Wicked, you are *quite* sure of yourself." A seductive grin lifted her lips and she said, "Instead of expending your energy uncovering the fantasies I had *before* we came together, of which I can assure you there were *many*, maybe you should entice me into coming up with new ones. Who knows what kind of naughty desires you'll uncover."

He kissed her neck and said, "How about if I start right now?" He slipped his hands under the back of her top, holding her against him as he whispered all the dirty things he wanted to do to her.

CHLOE HAD NO idea how she had the strength to drag Justin out of her cottage, but if he'd whispered one more dirty promise, she'd have dragged him into the bedroom and they'd miss the ride. Not that getting on his bike would help to cool her jets. Harper had once told her that riding on the back of Gavin's motorcycle was like foreplay. At the time Chloe had thought her friend had lost her mind. Now she knew better. When she'd climbed off the bike at her cottage, her body still humming with the vibrations of the engine, she'd felt sexy and revved up, and she'd had to fight the urge to tear off Justin's clothes, which was crazy considering she'd had more sex in the last twenty-four hours than she'd had in the last two years. Now, as they drove to Harper and Gavin's house to meet up with the others, the bike revved her up once again. She had a feeling she was going to be hot and bothered all day long.

She clung to Justin, his back muscles flexing against her chest, his abs tight beneath her hands. She wanted to slide her hands to the beast between his legs, but she was afraid of distracting him. How would she survive *hours* plastered against him, with the cool air kissing her skin and the heat of his body seeping through his leather vest? And it was more than Justin and the vibrations of the engine that gave her a rush. Everything looked and felt different from the back of a bike. The air was crisper, the sky was bluer, and the surroundings were more interesting. She thought she'd be scared of falling off or getting hit by another vehicle, but she trusted Justin implicitly to keep her safe on the road just as she trusted him in the bedroom. She knew he would never take a chance of hurting her. With that trust, riding with him brought a deeper sense of closeness and an overwhelming sense of freedom she knew she'd crave like an addict.

They turned down Gavin's driveway. When the other guys' motorcycles came into view, her nerves flared. Hopefully they wouldn't notice that she'd turned into some sort of motorcycle-riding freedom-seeking nymphomaniac.

Tank was on the phone, pacing by the flowerbeds. Zeke and Zander were talking with Gavin and Harper, and Dwayne, Baz, and Blaine were looking at something on Baz's phone. They all glanced over as Justin parked the motorcycle. They looked different in their leathers, rougher and more intimidating. Chloe had a fleeting feeling of discomfort, but as her tough, leather-wearing boyfriend climbed off the bike and took her hand, telling her he was glad she came, that discomfort skated away.

Justin kissed her cheek and said, "Go say hi. I'll get the album."

Harper looked fantastic in blue jeans and knee-high boots. She ran to Chloe, her blond hair flying out behind her. "It's true! I'm so happy!" She hugged Chloe. "I heard you and Justin had gotten together. I guess this explains why you didn't meet me and the girls for breakfast this morning."

Chloe was unable to suppress her smile.

"How did this happen?" Harper asked as Gavin and Justin joined them.

"She finally realized she was missing out on all this." Justin looked seductively at Chloe and waved at his body, like he was presenting himself on a silver platter.

As much as she'd like to devour everything he was offering, she didn't need to get hot and bothered again. She took the gift from him and handed it to Harper to distract herself. "I made you and Gavin a little something for your wedding."

"You didn't have to do that." Harper opened the gift. On the cover of the album was a picture of Gavin gazing into Harper's eyes the night of their wedding. Chloe had taken it after most of the guests had already gone, by the bonfire on the patio at the Silver House on Silver Island, where Gavin and Harper had tied the knot. The picture was cut into the shape of a heart and edged with lace. Above the picture was *Our Love Story* written in white on a gold banner. Two small heart charms, a *G* and an *H*, hung from a ribbon on one side. On the bottom of the cover was a white banner that had their wedding date and *Mr. & Mrs. Gavin Wheeler* written in gold. "Chloe. This is beautiful. Thank you."

"I'm so glad you like it."

Harper leaned against Gavin and opened the album. As they gushed over the pictures, Dwayne and Zander sauntered over. Dwayne bumped fists with Justin and winked at Chloe.

Zander sidled up to her and said, "Chloe, you looked smokin' on the back of the bike. When you're ready for a real man, I'm your guy."

Justin lunged at him, and Zander stumbled backward, laughing, bumping right into Zeke.

"I've got him." Zeke grabbed Zander's arm and said, "Let's go, doofus."

He dragged his brother away, and Chloe noticed Baz jogging over to them and Blaine watching them as he fiddled with his phone.

Dwayne chuckled. "You know he's never going to change, right, bro?"

"No shit," Justin mumbled.

"I'm going to take this inside before we go," Harper said, heading inside.

"That album is amazing, Chloe. Thank you," Gavin said. "I'm glad you're coming on the ride today. It'll be nice for Harp to have another woman around." He patted his back pocket and said, "Shoot. Be back in a sec. I need to grab my keys." He headed for the house, stopping to talk to Baz, who was on his way to Chloe and Justin.

"Don't trap your wife in the bedroom," Dwayne called after him. "We want to leave soon."

Gavin looked over his shoulder and said, "No promises."

"Good to see ya, Mav." Baz slapped Justin on the back. With a jerk of his chin, he flipped his dirty-blond hair out of his eyes and flashed a smile that gave way to killer dimples. He kissed Chloe's cheek and said, "Nice to see you, too, gorgeous."

"Get those dimples away from my girl." Justin gave him a playful shove and put his arm around Chloe.

Chloe laughed and said, "I bet those dimples have women lining up around the block to bring their pets to see you."

Baz winked and said, "You like my dimples, huh?"

"I do, actually, but not as much as I like this ruggedly hand-some face." Chloe kissed Justin's cheek, earning a sexy, appreciative grin. Blaine headed their way, eyeing Baz. Blaine winked at her. She could only imagine the trail of broken hearts these flirty guys left behind.

"Is this fool giving you a hard time?" Blaine asked.

"I can't help it if the ladies like my dimples." Baz's phone rang. "There's a dimple lover now." He walked away to answer the call.

"Hi, Chloe. I'm glad you came." Blaine gave her a quick hug and said, "Did Justin give you the rundown on road safety?"

"Yes, in painful detail," she said teasingly. She'd actually been glad for his detailed lesson in motorcycle safety. It meant Justin took having a passenger as seriously as she took being one.

Blaine's eyes sparked with mischief. He draped an arm over her shoulder and said, "Then you know that we're all going skinny-dipping later, right?"

Justin flicked his arm off her and said, "Go get Tank off the phone, will ya?"

Chloe got the feeling they would all try to get under Justin's skin today, and she liked it. Their playful banter was just what she needed to put her at ease.

Blaine laughed and said, "First I have to settle up with Gunner." He looked at Dwayne motioning to their right. Blaine put his hand out as he and Dwayne stepped away.

Dwayne cursed and took out his wallet, grumbling, "Fucking Maverick."

"*Really*, you two?" Justin said with a hint of annoyance.

"What?" Chloe asked.

"Just a little wager about you and Mav," Dwayne explained as he handed a wad of cash to Blaine. "Nothing to worry about."

"Do I even want to know?" Chloe asked, eyeing Justin.

Justin scowled at Blaine and Dwayne and said, "I'm not sure *I* want to know."

Tank was heading their way, his watchful eyes taking them all in.

"It's nothing bad." Blaine shoved the money in his pocket and said, "We knew you two were going out last night, and we made a bet about today's ride. Gunner said Maverick would ride alone today. But I know how long he's been into you, Chloe, and I knew if things went well, he'd either back out of today's ride to spend the day with you, or he'd show up with you on his bike. One way or the other, I knew he wasn't going to let you go."

Chloe put her arm around Justin and said, "How do you know it wasn't *me* who wouldn't let *him* go?"

"Damn, that's hot." Dwayne whistled. "Chloe, you sure Maverick is *wicked* enough for you?"

"You on the hunt for a ball and chain?" Tank asked.

Dwayne looked at him like he'd lost his mind. "No fucking way."

Blaine leaned closer to her and said, "We're still on for skinny-dipping, right?"

"With Justin? *Absolutely.* With you guys?" She laughed and said, "Not a chance."

Justin swept her into his arms and said, "And *that's* why she's my girl."

Chapter Fourteen

WRANGLING WICKEDS WAS a lot like wrangling puppies. They darted off in every direction, endlessly taunting each other. Dwayne and Zander ended up wrestling on the grass over some woman they'd both gone out with. Zeke and Blaine tried to pry them apart and got yanked into the dogpile. Then Justin and Baz decided to take *them* down as Gavin and Harper came outside. Gavin took one look at the chaos and in the blink of an eye he joined those brawny, tattooed, intimidating bikers who were rolling around in fits of laughter, covered in grass and dirt, like carefree teenagers. Chloe took loads of pictures. When Tank started plucking them out by their collars and tossing them aside, she and Harper doubled over in hysterics. The guys exchanged glances, and in the next second they were chasing Chloe and Harper around the yard. Tank hoisted Chloe over his shoulder and Baz got ahold of Harper. Chloe and Harper squealed and laughed as Justin and Gavin chased after Tank and Baz.

The guys were so different from the friends she usually spent time with, she hadn't been sure she'd fit in, but she'd never laughed so hard or enjoyed herself so much. By the time they got on the road, she felt like one of the pack.

Chloe had always been a planner. She had to be. There was no one else to do it for her and Serena. Because of that, she always knew what was expected of her, where she was going, and how to get there. Keeping on task and remaining in control had kept her safe, made her an excellent student and a valued employee. She rarely allowed herself to feel truly unencumbered, but as she sped down the open highway plastered to Justin's back, with the rumble of the engine echoing through her and Justin's cousins and brothers surrounding them—Tank at the lead, Zeke taking up the rear—that feeling of freedom overtook her again, and her need to remain in control sailed away with the whipping wind. She thought she was past any great metamorphoses in her life, that she was who she would always be. But Justin was helping her shed her old, confining skin, uncovering parts of her that she hadn't even known existed.

After a while they turned off the highway and drove down a long stretch of two-lane road lined with farms and ranch-style homes. They passed under an arched sign above the road that read HARBORSIDE, WHERE HEAVEN MEETS EARTH. A thrill chased through Chloe. She'd lived on the Cape her whole life, and though she'd heard of Harborside, a small beach town with a boardwalk, known for good surfing and the Taproom, a rustic restaurant/bar located on a pier, she'd never been there.

After a few miles, the road widened to four lanes and farms gave way to grass, sand, and gorgeous beach houses. The group turned into town, passing colorful storefronts and cafés. A beautiful beach came into view. The pier shot out over the water, forming a T at the end where the Taproom was located. Chloe was excited to be in Harborside, which she could already see looked remarkably different from the Cape, and equally excited to sneak pictures of the guys' hands for Justin's sculpture.

The group parked at the back of the parking lot by the beach. The sounds of the engines echoed in her ears even after they'd been silenced. As it had earlier, holding Justin, and the ride itself, had left her feeling embarrassingly turned on.

Justin climbed off the bike looking virile and gorgeous as he pulled off his helmet and pushed a hand through his thick hair. Chloe took off her helmet and shook out her hair, and a slow grin spread across Justin's face.

"I love watching you do that," he said as he helped her to her feet. "Almost as much as I dig having your arms around me as we ride."

He lowered his lips to hers, kissing her so deeply, she came away feeling high.

"What do you think, sweet cheeks?"

"I told you I *can't* think when you kiss me like that."

He chuckled and pressed his lips to hers again. "I guess that means the ride was okay, too."

"The kiss *and* the ride were awesome. Riding with the group was nothing like I thought it would be. I wasn't nervous at all. I felt *safe* riding with everyone."

"That's the power of brotherhood, baby."

The guys gathered around, and Chloe learned that they were meeting up with the Dark Knights of Harborside at the Taproom. When Justin heard that Chloe had never been to Harborside, he suggested that they knock around town and meet up with the guys afterward. Gavin and Harper joined them.

They made their way to the center of town, popping in and out of shops and chatting with Gavin and Harper. Every shop was cuter than the last, and the people were warm and friendly.

They passed a diner with a cheerful yellow sign in the window that read GIGI'S, then went into a cool custom-furniture shop called Artsea, where everything was made from driftwood, metal, and glass.

"I think I've died and gone to heaven," Gavin said as they walked through the shop. "My clients would love some of these pieces."

"*I* love them," Harper said, touching a mirror made from driftwood and shells. "Wouldn't this look beautiful in the sunroom?"

"That would look beautiful in any beach house, and Serena would love this chair." Chloe texted Serena a picture of the chair with the message, *I'm in Harborside with Justin and the Dark Knights! Motorcycle road trip! SO FUN! Thought you might like this chair.*

Serena's reply was immediate. *LOVE the chair but OMG I love even more that you're with Justin!*

Chloe had been so wrapped up in Justin, she hadn't realized she hadn't had a chance to tell Serena about what was happening between them. She glanced at Justin, admiring a table at the front of the store. He looked so thoughtful, she had to snap a few pictures while he was unaware. The artist in him was showing. She had never felt strong enough about any man to want to gush about them like she did with Justin. She thumbed out a response to Serena. *Me too! It was weird at first because he knows me so well. I've never dated a friend before. But, Serena...* She had so much she wanted to say, but she didn't want to be glued to answering text messages while she was with Justin, so she added a heart eyes emoji and a celebration emoji and typed, *Can't chat now. Love you!* Her phone vibrated a minute later, and she read Serena's message. *I know. I married my best friend! Friends make the best lovers. Just sayin'. Xox*

Chloe was walking on air as she made her way toward Justin.

She stopped to check out a piece of driftwood with inlaid candles that reminded her of the night on the beach when she and Justin had poured out their hearts. It was a large piece, about four feet in length, and the candles were placed along the high ridges and concave gullies. She ran her fingers over the rough edges and the smooth dips and curves of the wood, which reminded her of her life. Sometimes things were smooth, and other times they were tumultuous, but she could still find the beauty in it. *Even more so now.*

Justin came to her side and said, "The craftsmanship on the furniture is excellent." His gaze moved over the driftwood. "That's a beauty."

"You like it?" she asked. "I was just thinking that it would look nice on the stone table you have by the window overlooking the pond."

He'd given her a tour of his house that morning. Earth-tone decorations and warm hardwood floors made his house feel homey and inviting. His bedroom was one of the cantilevered rooms with glass walls overlooking the pond on one side of the house and woods on the other. His sculptures were prominently placed in two of the cantilevered areas. There were pictures of his family and friends, but not as many as Chloe had at her cottage. Justin displayed the people he loved in an even more important way. Etched into his skin. His house was so artfully done, she'd asked if Gavin had helped him decorate, and she'd been impressed when he'd said he'd done it all himself. Justin was obviously a man who knew what he liked.

As he slipped an arm around her, she thought, *In more ways than one.*

"That would be perfect there." He put his mouth by her ear and said, "We can throw a blanket on the floor and make love by candlelight."

A shiver of heat rippled through her. His eyes flamed, as if he'd felt it, too, and he kissed her.

"I like spending the day with you, sweet thing," he said softly.

"Me too." If anyone had told her two weeks ago that she'd be spending today kissing Justin and out with a group of bikers, she'd have said they were nuts. But now there was no place else she'd rather be.

As they made their way through more shops, Justin held her hand and opened doors for her. He was a gentleman dressed in leather, and she loved being out with him as a couple. He showed her things he thought she might like, and she enjoyed seeing what he was drawn to. She was aware of women checking him out, but even as the green-eyed monster clawed at her, she held her head high, knowing he could have any number of women, but he'd chosen her. Both of those things were also new to her—the jealousy and the realization that out of all the women Justin had known and had met over the past year and a half, he'd chosen her. He'd seen and held on to the very thing she'd been running from—that to the naked eye, they seemed to be opposites.

Now she knew that in the most important ways, they really weren't opposites at all.

She was discovering many things on that sunny afternoon, like how close he and Gavin really were. The two men tried on army jackets and hats in a military surplus store, laughing at inside jokes that Chloe and Harper weren't privy to. But she didn't mind. She and Harper had their own inside jokes. He and Gavin talked about Mike's fall and their upcoming tour of LOCAL. Justin told Gavin and Harper about the dogs they'd rescued and what had happened when they'd gone with the police that night. Gavin put his hand on Justin's shoulder, quietly offering words of comfort. Chloe had known they were close friends, but seeing them in a setting other than a bar when Justin was flirting with her brought the depth of their friendship to life.

When they passed the Endless Summer Surf Shop, Justin said it was owned by Jesse and Brent Steele, two brothers who were also Dark Knights. He said they owned a restaurant in town, too, and that she would meet them at the Taproom, along with Levi, one of their cousins, and a number of other club members.

"It's cool that you know Dark Knights from different areas," Chloe said as they made their way into a music store.

"We're one big family, babe," Justin said.

"I kind of wish Gavin would prospect the club and become a member," Harper said. "But he's worried about having enough time to commit."

"One day," Gavin said as they walked into an eclectic store that had old records, antique furniture, and a hodgepodge of other things. He nudged Justin and said, "Dude, let's check out the vinyl," and dragged him across the store.

Harper took advantage of the men stepping away and said, "Okay, girl, what's the scoop? Daphne told me what Justin did for the book club meeting. Did you guys hook up after, or…?"

Chloe peeked across the store at the guys checking out records and said, "No. Things changed between us the night before the meeting, but we didn't hook up. We talked for a long time, and I realized how wrong I was about him. I don't know how it all happened so fast, but, Harper, I'm *so* happy. I thought he was going to be too rough for me, or his lifestyle would be like the guys my mom goes out with. But he's not like that at all." She saw Justin staring at her with that look in his eyes that turned her insides to mush. "He's pretty wonderful, and I'm kind of bummed that I wasted all that time trying to fight my feelings for him when we could have been together all along."

"I'm so happy for you," Harper said as Justin headed their way. "Things happen for a reason. Maybe you guys needed that time to be sure you were right for each other. Remember, there was a whole year between when I first met Gavin and when I saw him again. And look at us."

Justin reached for Chloe's hand and said, "You girls look like trouble waiting to happen."

"We're the best kind of trouble," Harper said. "You left my hubby alone with records? We'll be in this store forever. I swear he loves shopping even more than I do."

"We're not in a rush." Justin pulled Chloe closer and said, "They have a display by the register of those decorations you put in your albums—stickers, charms, that kind of thing. Want to check them out?"

There was no hiding her joy over his thinking of her scrapbooking.

"Oh boy, Justin. You *are* a goner, aren't you?" As Harper walked away, she looked over her shoulder and mouthed, *He's so cute!*

Forty minutes later, after buying charms and stickers and checking out a few more shops, they stowed their purchases on Justin's bike and made their way down the pier to the Taproom. It was a balmy afternoon, but the breeze coming off the water kept them cool. Justin's cousins and brothers were sitting at tables with a bunch of other guys wearing leather vests with Dark Knights' patches. Chloe had never seen so many bikers in one place. There were other people there, too, couples and families seated around their own tables. A young, lanky guy with pitch-black hair was playing guitar and eyeing Chloe as she followed Justin toward a table where Baz and Tank were sitting with a few men she didn't recognize.

Suddenly Justin stopped walking and put a hand on Chloe's back, setting a dark stare on the guitar player as he said, "*Brandon*, get your eyes off my woman."

Brandon stopped strumming and a devious grin lit up his face. "Dude, I don't want to cause any trouble. You know I'll gladly do *both* of you." He waggled his brows and grabbed his crotch.

A rumble of chuckles rose around them.

"Keep yourself in check, Owens," Justin warned. He moved behind Chloe, keeping a hand on her as they made their way toward his cousins.

As Harper and Gavin sat down at the table with Tank and Baz, Chloe pulled Justin aside. She poked him in the chest, speaking in a hushed voice. "You do *not* need to mark your territory on my behalf."

"I didn't like my buddy Brandon checking you out."

"Well, get over it," she snapped. "That was embarrassing. Open your eyes, Justin. Practically every woman we've seen today has checked you out, and you didn't see me getting green with jealousy."

Justin put his arms around her and said playfully, "I don't mind if you get jealous, baby. I want you to claim me."

How could a man be so cute and so irritating at the same

time? "I don't need to prove my feelings through being a jerk to other women. You know how I feel about you—"

"How *do* you feel about me?" he asked with a knowing smile.

That lopsided grin did her in every time. "I wouldn't be here if I wasn't crazy about you."

"Damn, babe, I love hearing that."

He pulled her closer, the emotions in his eyes softening her resolve.

"I'm crazy about you, Justin. How can I not be? You're charming and funny, and you *know* you're hot. But more importantly, it wouldn't matter how many women checked you out or how beautiful they were, because I know that *I'm* the one you want. Can't you give me the same respect?"

His expression turned serious. "It *is* respectful to keep guys from ogling you."

"No, it's kind of cavemanish. We're a couple, which means we're a team on all fronts. I'm proud of being a strong woman who can take care of myself, and that's not going to change. Can't you meet me halfway on this?" She reached up and stroked the back of his neck the way she knew he liked and said, "Just know I'm yours, and if you feel the need to stake claim in front of other guys, then hold my hand or kiss my cheek. Don't make a scene and embarrass me."

His eyes narrowed, and he said, "And if the guy keeps looking?"

"Then take it as a compliment and know you're the only man I'd go home with."

She went up on her toes and kissed him. He held her tighter as cheers, applause, and whistles rang out around them. Chloe turned to see what all the commotion was about, and her cheeks flamed. The Dark Knights were standing up, applauding *them*.

There was only one thing to do.

She turned back to Justin and said, "I hereby condone two minutes of Neanderthal behavior. Please kiss me until I forget how embarrassed I am."

"Damn, baby. You are one hell of a woman."

"And I'm all yours."

When his lips met hers, more cheers rang out. Justin took the kiss deeper, burying his hand in her hair and turning all the embarrassing nonsense to white noise.

LUNCH WAS DELICIOUS, and Justin introduced Chloe to everyone, including Brandon Owens, the guitar player. It turned out that Harper knew him, too. Brandon was the graphic designer who had created the logo for Harper and Tegan's production company. Chloe knew she'd never keep the names of all the people she'd met straight, but she'd loved meeting them, and they clearly thought the world of Justin.

They were heading back to the table after talking with Jesse and Brent Steele and their cousin Levi, when a chipper little honey-haired girl yelled, "Maverick!" She ran between Tank and Baz and threw her arms around Justin's waist, beaming up at him.

"Hey there, princess." Justin lifted her into his arms, and she hugged him around the neck.

Holy moly. Chloe's heart did a double take. Big and bad, with that sweet little girl in his arms, Justin became ten times hotter.

Justin said, "How's my favorite girl?"

"*Good*," the girl said, basking in his attention. "Did you make my sculpture yet?"

"Peanut, what did I tell you about that?" Levi asked.

"You said not to bug him. But, Daddy, I'm *not* bugging him. I'm just asking."

Justin chuckled and said, "I'm working on it, and you know I won't let you down." He smiled at Chloe and said, "I have someone special I want you to meet. This is my other favorite girl, Chloe. Chloe, this is Levi's daughter, Josephine."

"*Maverick!*" The little girl rolled her eyes, and it was about the cutest thing Chloe had ever seen. "I'm *Joey*. Are you Maverick's girlfriend?"

"Yes," Chloe said, enjoying the grin on Justin's face.

Joey hooked an arm tightly around Justin's neck and said, "Well, I'm going to marry him when I'm older, so don't get your hopes up."

"Josephine Steele, that's not nice." Levi chuckled and said, "Sorry, Chloe."

"It's okay. Your daughter has good taste." Chloe took out her phone and said, "Would you mind if I took a picture of you and Maverick? I'll be sure to print it out and mail you a copy." It was strange using Justin's road name, but in this part of Justin's world, it was probably strange for everyone to hear him called by his given name.

"Nope! Go ahead." Joey rested her head against Justin's. He lifted her hand from his other shoulder and held it as Chloe took the picture.

"Can you text me a copy?" Levi asked.

He gave Chloe his number, and she texted the picture. "I have a photo printer at home. I'll send you a hard copy, too."

"And one for me," Joey reminded her.

"Absolutely. One for each of you."

They visited for a long time with Levi and Joey, and then Levi had to leave to take Joey to a birthday party, but not before Joey said goodbye to all of her Dark Knight *uncles*, which was every member of the Dark Knights, giving Chloe a chance to take more cute pictures. Joey gave Chloe a big hug, too, but not nearly as big as the one she gave Justin, who informed her that Joey had whispered to him, "Don't forget we're getting married."

A little while later, Justin took Chloe, Harper, and Gavin for a stroll down the boardwalk before meeting up with everyone again and getting ready to leave. There was a loud round of goodbyes with manly embraces and many promises from Chloe to come back again sometime with Justin.

Several of the Dark Knights from Harborside joined them as they continued their afternoon motorcycle ride. They drove out of Harborside and through other nearby towns, but her favorite part was cruising along the roads that ran parallel to the water. The group stopped at a roadside café for dinner, taking up every open table and booth.

By the time they arrived back at Chloe's cottage, the sun was starting to set. She felt like she'd lived a month in the past twenty-four hours, and she couldn't wait to do it again.

They walked slowly up to the door arm in arm.

"I had such a good time," she said as they stepped onto the porch. "Everyone is so different than I imagined. I'm glad I got to know them better. Zeke told me that he used to teach special education, and he told me how he lost his job. I had no idea. I thought he'd always worked with your father."

"He's a smart guy, and an excellent teacher. He still tutors kids."

"He told me. I really like him. Did you know that Dwayne called Sid to check on Snowflake while we were at dinner? I never would have imagined him doing that, unless he was really calling because he has a thing for Sid."

"I don't think it's Sid. He called Steph while we were at the Taproom. She was helping Sid at the rescue today. He cares about the animals."

She dug out her keys, and as she unlocked the door she said, "So do you. I heard you asking Baz about Shadow over dinner."

He drew her into his arms with a longing expression. She went eagerly. It was the only place she wanted to be. "I don't want to say goodbye to you, Chloe."

"Then don't," she said softly.

His lips curved up. He touched them to hers and whispered, "What have you done to me?"

"When you figure it out, let me know, because I don't want to say goodbye, either."

"Then come home with me tonight. Grab whatever you need for work tomorrow and stay at my place. We'll go for a walk by the pond, or watch television, or make love in the moonlight. I don't care what we do. I just want to be with you."

A warm glow of happiness flowed through her. "Okay. I need to get my laptop to check the book club forums because I just announced the new book and there will be questions. And I want to bring my photo printer. I got great shots of everyone, and I was able to sneak pictures of their hands. I can't wait for you to see them. Oh, and I got a couple cute shots of Levi and Joey together and of Joey and her *uncles*—Levi's cousins Jesse and Brent, and the other guys, of course—that I want to include when I send her the picture of the two of you. I think I'll make her a little album."

"She'd love that, baby. I like your nervous ramblings." He kissed her again, slow and sweet. "Bring whatever you need. In fact, bring enough clothes for two days."

"Isn't it a little soon for that?" she asked, and immediately regretted it. She'd said what she thought she *should* say, climbing right back into that restrictive, safe skin she'd so happily shed earlier today.

Before she could take it back, he said, "I've waited so long to be with you, darlin', as far as I'm concerned, nothing is too fast."

Chapter Fifteen

CHLOE AWOKE MONDAY morning cocooned by Justin's hard body. *Very hard*, she mused, feeling his erection against her ass as he spooned her. And then it hit her. It was a workday, and she wasn't starting it in her cottage. That was a first, and it was a big deal. A *huge* deal. It was the *mother* of all deals. Her nerves tingled, and she quickly ran through a mental checklist to see if she forgot to bring anything that she needed for work. She closed her eyes, relieved she hadn't forgotten anything, and tried to calm her jitters. She took stock of her emotions, searching for the discomfort of regret or fear, but they were nowhere to be found. There was only happiness. She reminded herself it was okay to feel jittery about staying there on a work night and allowed herself to revel in the moment. Her hand lay over Justin's on her belly, and his breath warmed her shoulder. Her gaze moved to her bag by the bedroom door, where all her belongings had been discarded when they'd come in last night and had fallen into each other's arms. They'd been insatiable for each other, as if taking separate vehicles from her cottage had been too much time apart, and everything else had fallen by the wayside. She glanced at his dresser, where the pictures they'd printed *after* they'd sated their desires were spread out beside her laptop and photo printer.

Justin pressed his lips to her shoulder and said, "I could get used to this."

His voice was low and craggy and so sexy she nestled deeper into the curve of his hips. "Me too," she whispered.

He trailed kisses along her shoulder and neck, moving his hand up her stomach, and fondled her breasts. She closed her eyes, enjoying the feel of him. His tender touch and his openmouthed kisses along her neck and shoulder alighted all of her senses. He spread one hand over her belly, holding her tight as he whispered sweetness in her ears. "Love waking up to you…" His hand moved down her hip and thigh. "So soft and beautiful." His hips rocked slowly and sensually against her. Her insides hummed with desire, and his hand moved between her legs, stroking her so perfectly she could barely breathe.

He made the most appreciative, sexy sound and said, "So wet for me."

"For us," she whispered, rubbing her ass against his hard length. His manly scent wound around her, drawing her into a deeper awareness of the rest of him. His legs curled behind hers, the hair tickling the backs of her legs, his hard length pressed into her flesh, and his rough fingers moving inside her as he thrilled her with his mouth along her neck, nipping and licking, until she was on the verge of coming.

"Yes. *Us*, sweetheart." He slicked his tongue along the shell of her ear and said, "I adore *us*. I want to get *lost* in us."

He guided his cock to her entrance, pushing in unhurriedly. She reached around them, holding his hip as they fell into a slow, sensual rhythm, so different from their lustful devouring of last night. She bent her head back, giving him better access to her neck as he made love to her, using his hand to heighten her pleasure. His cock throbbed inside her like a second heart.

"*God*, Chloe," he said in a hot breath against her neck. "You've gotten under my skin."

The emotions in his voice took her higher, and she moved her hips quicker.

"That's it, baby, you feel it, too. We're so fucking real."

He sealed his mouth over the curve of her neck, sucking exquisitely as he moved inside her, and his fingers hit all the right spots. Her eyes slammed shut as her climax crashed over her, and "*Justin!*" flew desperately from her lips.

"I've got you, sweetheart." He grazed his teeth over her shoulder, sending sparks down her core, catapulting her up to the peak.

She dug her nails into his hip and panted out, "Come…with me."

He withdrew, and in the next breath she was on her back and he was perched over her, burying himself deep with one hard thrust. She cried out in sweet, heavenly agony. He claimed her hands with his, gazing deeply into her eyes, and she tried to keep her eyes open, wanting to hold on to the emotions staring back at her, but the blinding pleasures were too intense. Her eyes fluttered open and closed as ecstasy consumed her. She saw him in flashes, like an old movie, getting glimpses of the tension in his jaw and the lust brimming in his eyes. Then he crushed his mouth to hers in a devastatingly passionate kiss that had her craning up to enjoy every second of it, her whole body craving more. He quickened his efforts, his thick cock burrowing faster, deeper, hitting all of her pleasure points with lethal accuracy. She tore her mouth away, gasping for air, clawing at his back. His every thrust stole her breath anew. He pushed his strong arms beneath her, cradling her like she was precious. Nothing had ever felt so right. There was no separation, no beginning or end to either of them as they moved in perfect harmony, and he ground out, "I'm yours, Chloe. So fucking *yours*," sending them both soaring up to the clouds.

CHLOE FLOATED THROUGH the rest of the morning as they kissed beneath the warm shower spray, washing each other, learning every dip and curve of the other's body. He lovingly dried her with a towel, looking like he wanted to devour her again as she put on her panties and bra, and he stepped into a fresh pair of boxer briefs. Those tingles in her belly turned to full-on fireworks. He eyed her lasciviously as they brushed their teeth, and he was a beautiful sight, leaning against the bathroom doorframe, shirtless and sated, that crooked grin fixed in place, as he watched her put on her makeup and dry her hair.

"I'll be right back, sweet thing."

He kissed her and she watched him tug on a pair of jeans. She enjoyed the view of his low-riding jeans hugging his butt as he made the bed. He moved the rest of her things that they'd left by the door to his dresser, and then he left the bedroom. She went to the closet, unprepared for the thrill of seeing her clothes among his.

Justin sauntered into the bedroom carrying two cups of coffee as she buttoned her blouse, and stopped to watch her slip her feet into her high heels. He whistled and said, "*Mm-mm*, darlin', you are gorgeous," sending those butterflies in her stomach into a frenzy.

"You made coffee?" He'd made her coffee yesterday morning, too, but she'd thought it might be a one-time thing.

"And you look like *breakfast*." He closed the distance between them with a wolfish grin.

Her blood coursed through her veins like an awakened river. "You'd better stop looking at me like that or I'll never get out of here."

"Sick day?" he asked with a lift of his brows.

"I wish I could. The students from the new program will be there today, and I have work to do on the puppeteering proposal before I meet with Mads tomorrow." She glanced at the clock, and her stomach sank. "I hate to say this, but—"

He kissed her cheek and said, "Let me put your coffee in a to-go cup and I'll walk you out to your car."

"You don't have to walk me out."

He cocked a grin and said, "You're my girl—I'm walking you to your car."

Her heart did a happy dance. As he went to swap cups, she straightened her things in the bathroom, feeling another thrill chase through her at the fact that she was *leaving* her things there. Should she put them back in the bag she'd packed? She had no idea what the etiquette was on this type of thing. She grabbed her phone to text Serena, but heard Justin coming into the bedroom, so she slipped her phone into her skirt pocket.

"Here you go, beautiful." His brows slanted. "Why do you look uneasy?"

She glanced at her things on his sink. "Should I put this stuff away? It feels funny to invade your space like this."

He set her cup on the sink and gathered her in his arms. "I *like* you invading my space, and you *know* I want to invade yours."

The honesty in his voice was *everything*. "Okay. Thank you

255

for the coffee."

"Thanks for getting out of your own way and finally giving us a chance."

When he walked her out to her car, she said, "You're very different than I thought you'd be."

"So are you, princess." He opened her car door and drew her into his arms. "We've only scratched the surface, babe. Hold on to all this goodness. It's been a long time coming."

He pressed his lips to hers in a sweet kiss that quickly turned ravishing. She came away breathless, and she knew she'd think of nothing else all day.

"See you tonight, sweet thing."

She turned to get in the car and he gave her ass a quick slap.

She scowled at him. "*Seriously?*" she said as she climbed in and started the car. "I told you not to slap my ass."

He leaned into the car and said, "You also told me you'd never go out with me. You're just lucky I'm not hauling that pretty ass of yours over my shoulder and back to the bedroom."

Her insides flamed. She squeezed her thighs together before she needed to change her panties and tried to stifle a laugh as she said, "*Stop!* I have to go."

"I'll text you later."

He shut her door and she rolled down her windows and said, "Do not *sext* me at work. It makes it hard to concentrate, and I'm already going to have a difficult enough time getting this morning out of my head."

He bent so they were eye to eye and said, "Should I go get you extra panties, just in case?"

She flamed from the inside out. "*Justin!*"

He laughed. As she drove away, her mind raced in a hundred different ridiculously happy directions. "Call Serena," she said through her Bluetooth. Serena answered on the second ring.

"Hey, sis. What's up?"

"Guess where I am?" Chloe said far too giddily.

"Driving…?"

"Yes. To work from *Justin's* house!"

Serena squealed. "On a *school* night? Aren't you a naughty girl."

"Yes, and I promised him I'd stay tonight, too!"

"It's about frigging time. Better watch out, sis. You know what they say—once you bite the forbidden fruit, there's no going back."

"*Hm.* Biting his *fruit.* Now, there's a game I haven't played."

They both laughed, and as Chloe shared her joy and her butterflies with her sister, she realized she hadn't climbed back into the conservative skin she'd once found so perfect and safe. The skin that had become a little too confining since coming together with Justin.

But she hadn't shed it completely.

Justin was helping her develop a new, different layer—a better one that wasn't driven by hiding from the past, but rather looking forward to a future.

Chapter Sixteen

MUSIC BLARED IN Justin's studio late Tuesday afternoon. He was totally in the zone. He brushed his thumb over the stone, wiping dust from the cheekbone of the face he was carving. His mind trickled back to making love with Chloe that morning, when he'd touched her cheek and she'd looked at him like he was everything she could ever want. He'd been spoiled having her in his bed the last few nights. He'd loved every sensual, fun moment of it. But while he wanted her there every night, he had a feeling Chloe needed time to get used to them. As much as he hated it, he was giving her space by not making plans to see her tonight or tomorrow night. His memories of having her in his bed were going to have to hold him over for a few days. He thought about how sexy and adorable she'd looked sitting in the middle of his bed wearing only his T-shirt Sunday night after they'd thoroughly ravaged each other, when they'd gone through pictures she'd taken over the weekend.

He hadn't realized she'd taken so many pictures on Saturday when they'd first gone to the rescue. She'd captured shots of his mother's and Preacher's hands when they were sitting by the bonfire and his grandfather's hands as he'd pet Snowflake—*before* they'd even realized he needed pictures of their hands, as if the decision of what to make for the suicide-awareness rally had been fated to be. She had taken dozens of shots of Justin with Shadow and with his family members. But his favorite was a selfie of him and Chloe with Shadow in her lap. He'd thought he'd romanticized how happy she'd seemed that night, but the pictures had confirmed his memory. She'd taken more beautiful pictures on Sunday at Gavin's house and in Harborside. She had the most amazing eye, capturing people when they were lost in thought and from angles he'd never even think to try. Through her eyes, he'd seen his family and friends differently than ever before. Hell, he saw *himself* differently through her eyes.

He knew *she* was seeing him differently, too, as evident in how comfortable she was in his house and in his arms. She was sharing more of herself with him. While the pictures had printed, she told him about when she'd began scrapbooking and why. And later, as she'd answered posts on her book club forum, she'd told him about how the club had come to be and how much she enjoyed it. She even told him about the book they were reading. He'd enjoyed hearing about all of it. He wanted to know everything there was to know about her.

He took off his goggles, and as he set down his tool, his eyes drifted to the inspiration board Chloe had made for him using the pictures she'd printed. The board itself was a work of art. She'd shown up last night with supplies. She covered a large canvas with burlap. Then she wrapped it with twine, creating crisscrosses. She hung pictures of his family members from the twine, securing them in place with tiny clothespins. Beneath each picture she'd hung another photo of only their hands. She'd added embellishments around each of the photos, like a tiny image of a mother with her arms around several children next to Reba's, and an old man waving a cane beside Mike's, the perfect curmudgeon. Around Preacher's picture she'd put several metal pins with men on motorcycles, and one that said *family*. She'd put tiny animals around Gunner's pictures. The board was covered with dozens of other trinkets, each one perfectly thought out. Most people would have just given him the pictures, but Chloe cherished good memories as much as he did, and that was only one of a million reasons he adored her.

His phone rang, drawing his attention to where it lay on the table. Violet was calling on FaceTime. He turned off the music and answered the call. He was glad to see Violet's face as she appeared on the screen. Her jet-black hair was pulled back with a tie-dyed headband. Her skin glowed with the bronze of a fresh tan, and her narrowed eyes and smirk told Justin that the *Real Housewives of Bayside*, which was what he called Serena, Emery, Desiree, and Daphne, had been gossiping again.

"Now, that's a well-fucked face if I've ever seen one." Violet had never been one to mince words. "It's true, isn't it? You put your snake in Chloe's grass?"

He chuckled and said, "You know I don't kiss and tell."

"I definitely *don't* want all the juicy details about your sex life. But, dude, do you have her *chained* to your bed? Desiree said Chloe hasn't been to breakfast with the girls in days and that you hardly ever stop by to have breakfast with everyone anymore. I told her it's not the same without me there, but I don't know if she's buying it." Violet flashed a cheesy grin.

Violet's sister, Desiree, loved to cook, and Chloe and their friends from Bayside Resort got together pretty often for breakfast with her. Justin tried to join them when he could.

"I can only take the blame for the last three mornings with Chloe, and I've just been swamped, Vi. But now that you've put the idea of chaining Chloe to my bed in my head…"

Violet rolled her eyes. "Maybe you can squeeze in *one* break-fast with Des before she gives birth? She misses you." Desiree was pregnant and due in July.

"We'll get there, Vi, I promise." It felt good to refer to him and Chloe as *we*. "But I'm in no rush to give up my mornings with Chloe."

"I know. I get it. Andre and I have been together for as long as you've been lusting after Chloe, and I *still* hate getting out of bed in the morning. So, Justin Wicked *finally* got his girl."

"She couldn't resist me forever," he said arrogantly.

"No shit. The sexual tension between you two could ignite an iceberg. Just be careful, okay?"

"Careful?"

"*Yeah*. You might be able to hide that big, gooey heart of yours from everyone else, but we both know this isn't just a casual affair for you." Her gaze softened and she said, "I love Chloe. She's a good friend and a really cool chick. But you're a whole lotta man for a conservative woman. I just don't want you to go all in and get hurt because your worlds are so different."

"Hey, *Kettle*, are you really calling me *Black*?" Violet and Andre came from two very different worlds. When they'd met, Violet was a vagabond artist who never wanted to put down roots, and Andre was a highly sought-after pediatrician with a successful practice in Boston and roots that ran to the core of the earth.

"You're right. Sorry. But I'm still worried about you."

"She's a lot more like you and me than you'd think, Vi. I know how you and everyone else sees Chloe. You see a careful, conservative woman who doesn't curse much and is wary of tough guys. And you know I dig those things about her, but she's so much *more* than that." He didn't want to breach Chloe's confidence, so he kept his comments general and said, "What you can't see is that she's had to overcome as much as you and I have, and her refusing to go out with me had nothing to do with *me* and everything to do with the shit she's been through."

"Really?"

"Yeah, you just can't see it because she doesn't throw her past in people's faces like you and I do with our take-us-as-we-are attitudes. And she's not playing the game like Blaine does, either. She has truly risen *above* her past, and she's proud of it, as well she should be. And now that I know what's she's gone through? Everything about her makes sense." Last night he and Chloe had been talking about her childhood, and she'd told him that she and Serena had always worn secondhand clothes and how she'd vowed never to need to do that again. She said she knew that she dressed differently from everyone else and that it had as much to do with rising above her past as it did with trying to stand out, but not in an ostentatious way. She said she'd always felt plain, *invisible*, when she was growing up. Chloe could be dressed in rags and she'd never look plain or fade into the background, but he understood what she meant all too well.

"She's not a fuck-the-world-for-fucking-me type of person, Vi, and she doesn't take *anything* for granted. Friends are at the top of that list. She makes these incredible albums for people. Did you know that? She even makes them for some of the residents at LOCAL."

"Yeah, she made a gorgeous wedding album for Des and Rick."

"Well, I had no idea she was so creative or put so much of her time into doing things for others." He paced the studio as he told Violet about the sculpture he was making and that it had been Chloe's idea to focus on the people left behind rather than those who had been lost. He explained how Chloe had taken pictures of everyone and their hands for him to use while sculpting, and he showed her the inspiration board she'd made.

"It seems like she's just as into you as you are into her."

"I think she is, at least I hope so," he said honestly. "I knew I liked her, but *man*, it's so much bigger than that. She's stayed at my place the last few nights, and last night we went to see these dogs that Dwayne and a bunch of us helped rescue from a dogfighting ring. There's this one dog that Chloe named Shadow. We both hate to leave him, but when I see her loving him up?" He shook his head and said, "I don't know, Vi. Everything she does gets to me."

"Sounds like you're in deep."

"Yeah, and I want to get deeper. *Everything* is better when we're together. We cooked dinner together last night, and even *that* was fun. And don't get me started on what it's like to wake up with her in my arms or watch her get ready for work in the morning, dressing in her fancy clothes with heels that make her legs look miles long. It takes all of my restraint not to sweep her into my arms and haul her gorgeous ass back to bed. And not just for sex. I want to hold her, to be with her, to—"

"To love her?" Violet suggested.

"*Yeah*," he said, surprising himself. "I mean, I don't know. I wouldn't say that and send her running for the hills, but I never thought it could be like this."

"Don't pull that crap with me. Every time she blew you off you told me she was the one for you. Maybe you never thought it could be *this* good, but you definitely knew you two would be good together."

"Whatever. I'm not a wordsmith, but you know what I mean. I literally saw her this morning, and I wish time would move faster so I could see her again."

"Sounds like you've been hit with a cupid's arrow." Violet's eyes filled with compassion. "That's how it happens, Justin. Remember how it was with me and Andre? I fell so hard and fast, it scared the life out of me and I left the *country*. What a mistake that was. I lost two years with him. Don't make the same mistakes I did. Don't get scared because your feelings are so big."

He scoffed. "I'm not scared. I want to spend *more* time with her, to protect her from the assholes in this world and make sure her life is nothing but incredible. My only fear is that I'm *me*, you know? And she's so independent. I'm worried I'll fuck it up. She rode with me and the guys out to Harborside on Sunday, and she enjoyed the hell out of it, but she gave me shit for telling this guy to stop checking her out."

Violet laughed. "You got her on your bike *and* she gave you hell? You do realize that makes her even more awesome, right?"

Justin gave her a deadpan look. "Seriously, Vi. She basically told me not to piss on my territory to keep guys in line."

"I get it, and as I said, it makes me like her even more."

"Yeah, me too. That's weird, right?"

"No, Justin. It's *great*. You would never last with a wallflower. I know you like to take care of people, but you also like a challenge. You need to be with someone who is as smart and as strong as you are, who understands all that goes along with being *you*. But it doesn't mean that she needs to put up with anything she's uncomfortable with. You'd better be careful not to smother her," Violet warned.

"I'm trying not to, but no one has *ever* watched out for her, and I want to be that guy, Vi."

"Hey, I tried to watch out for her. I told you to keep your snake out of her grass the first time you met her," Violet reminded him. "It sounds like Chloe's good for you."

"I think we're good for each other. She gets me, and I don't think she's ever given anyone a chance to know her well enough to really understand who she is, until now."

"I'm sorry she's had a rough go of things, but I'm glad she's letting you in."

"Yeah, me too. I wish I could change all that for her," he said honestly. "And, Vi, you should know Chloe and I talked about us—you and me—because of all that shit that went down when you first got to the Cape and came out when Andre first showed up."

"Oh shit. I was in such a bad place then." Worry rose in Violet's eyes. "I hope that didn't make things more difficult for you two."

"It was definitely one of the reasons she held back for so long, but she understands it now."

"Good. I'm sorry I was so broken back then. I feel bad that you two had to deal with that."

"It's okay. Chloe's tough."

"I know, but tough girls can get hurt, too. If anyone knows that, I do." Violet smiled and said, "You're the best friend I've ever had. You've always been there for me. I can tell you anything without feeling judged, and from what you've said, it sounds like Chloe has never had someone like that in her life. She's lucky to have you, and I'm really happy for you both. But as much as you want to plow into her life and protect her, don't

MELISSA FOSTER

do it, Justin. You waited a long time for her to be ready for you. Don't overwhelm her. As a prideful woman, I can tell you that nothing feels worse than someone you care about acting as though you're not strong enough or capable enough—emotionally or otherwise—to take care of yourself."

Justin thought about that. "I would never want her to feel that way."

"I know. That's why I'm telling you this. I have a feeling if you give Chloe enough space and time, *she'll* show *you* what she needs in a partner."

The studio door flew open, and Chloe rushed in with bags in her hands, talking a mile a minute as she headed for Justin. "Hi! I know we didn't have plans for tonight, but I got off a little early after I met with Mads and I was so excited about getting pictures of her hands, I had to show you! We got lucky. She showed me her new nail polish and let me take pictures of it. I *love* her, by the way. She was so helpful and we had a blast working together. I really think this proposal is going to go over well. Tomorrow is my big pitch day!" She dropped her bags on the table and dug around in one as she said, "I stopped to get tacos for dinner because I thought you might have gotten caught up in sculpting and forgotten to eat, and Mads told me about this T-shirt place, so I stopped and got this on the way here." She spun around, holding up a black T-shirt with white letters across the chest that read MY PRINCE CHARMING DOESN'T RIDE A WHITE HORSE. HE DRIVES A HARLEY.

If she only knew how much her showing up out of the blue, and that silly shirt, meant to him. "I didn't think it was possible for my day to get any better, babycakes, but *damn*. You're *here*, and I fucking *love* that shirt."

"Hi, Chloe!" Violet called out.

Chloe's eyes moved to the phone in Justin's hand, and her eyes widened. "*Violet?* Oh my gosh. *Hi.* I'm so sorry. I had no idea you were on the phone."

"That's okay. I *love* the shirt, too. And you brought tacos for dinner?" Violet smirked and said, "Isn't your *taco* on the menu *every* night?"

"*Ohmygod.*" Chloe's cheeks flamed, and she covered her face.

"Vi, *come on.* That's enough." Justin glared at her.

"I'm sorry," Violet said through her laughter. "I couldn't help myself. I love seeing Chloe blush." She schooled her expression. "Seriously, though. I'm happy for you and Justin. Be good to him, Chloe. He's the best friend a girl can have."

"I know he is." Chloe put her arms around Justin and said, "How's Honduras, Vi? How's Andre?"

"The area is great, and Andre is about to have his clothes torn off." Violet looked to the side and smiled as Andre leaned into the frame to kiss her.

"Hey, Justin. Hi, Chloe," Andre said. "So, you're finally a couple?"

They caught Andre up on their new relationship and talked a few more minutes.

"We have to go if I want time to have my way with my man," Violet said. "But we're coming home in July, so we'll be there when Desiree has the baby. She wants me in the delivery room in case Rick passes out."

After they ended the call, Justin put his phone in his pocket and his arms around Chloe. Her sweet smile cut straight to his heart. "I'm so glad you're here."

"I'm sorry for barging in. I was just so excited about the pictures and—"

"Uh-huh. So you didn't stop by because you missed me?" She didn't need to say a word. The answer was clear as day in her hazel eyes. "I like that you missed me, sweet cheeks." He pressed his lips to hers and said, "Want to know what I like even more? Knowing that you think of me as your Prince Charming."

Her mouth twisted into a sassy smirk, and she said, "I don't really believe in the whole white knight rescuing the girl thing, but they didn't have a shirt that said *boyfriend* instead of Prince Charming."

"Aw, come on, darlin'. Let me be your white knight and slay your dragons."

She wound her arms around his neck and said, "How about I let you be my Dark Knight and eat my *taco* instead?"

"Oh, baby. I'm in the mood for a *feast*." He threw her over his shoulder, and she squealed, giggling as he grabbed her bags and headed out the door.

Chapter Seventeen

CHLOE'S IMPROMPTU TACO dinner with Justin had led to her staying at his place for a fourth consecutive night. She'd gotten up at the crack of dawn to go home and get ready for work, but neither she nor Justin wanted to be apart. What started as a few steamy kisses ended with them tangled up in each other's arms. Chloe had to rush through her morning routine and made it to work in the nick of time for her first meeting. She was swamped all day and had stayed late to pitch the puppeteering trial to Alan. He seemed enthusiastic, and Chloe was keeping her fingers crossed, hoping for his approval. When she finally got home after work, she felt like she'd been gone a month, despite having been there to race through her shower that morning.

She set her things down in the kitchen and looked around at the pictures she'd left spread over the table and the counter. She studied a picture of Justin and Shadow. He'd sent her flirty texts several times that afternoon, and though he hadn't *sexted*, he'd definitely skirted that line. Every time his name had flashed on her phone, her heart had skipped a beat.

There were no two ways about it.

She already missed him.

He was at church tonight, and she had plenty to do. Besides everyday chores like catching up on laundry and mail, she'd totally forgotten about cleaning up the patio from the sand, and she wanted to work on the album for Joey. But even with all she had on her plate, her mind still lingered on Justin. He was never far from her thoughts. She thought of the sweet things he said and did and the way he touched her tenderly one minute and possessively the next. He was so damn sexy she got tingly just thinking about him.

She needed to *stop* daydreaming about him. She refused to become one of those girls who lost her mind over a man, like her mother. She could go *one* night without seeing him.

She slipped off her heels and changed into shorts and a comfy shirt, trying not to think about him. She carried a basket of dirty clothes to the laundry room, and as she separated her laundry, she found Justin's white T-shirt she'd kept the night of the book club meeting. She pressed it to her nose, inhaling his manly scent, bringing all those tingles back to life.

Great. Now she missed him even more.

She debated not washing the shirt so she could sleep with it on her pillow, like a pillowcase, but decided that would make her like a lovesick teenager. *Ugh.* Was this why her sister and her friends all mooned over their men? She took one last sniff and forced herself to throw his shirt in the washer. Before she could change her mind, she threw more whites in, covered his shirt with detergent, and turned the washer on. She grabbed a bucket and broom and padded into the living room, making a plan to get rid of the sand by dumping it in the woods at the edge of her property. It would take a hundred trips, but she could use the exercise. It felt like that enchanting night had taken place yesterday, and at the same time, it felt like a month had passed since she'd opened the door in her hula outfit and been swept into Justin's arms. She queued up one of her upbeat playlists, and Matchbox Twenty's "3 AM" rang out. She bobbed her head to the music as she pulled open the glass doors that led to the porch.

Her jaw dropped at the sight of it. All the sand was gone, and her outdoor furniture had been put in its rightful place. She couldn't believe it. Justin must have cleaned it up one day this week while she was at work. As grateful as she was that he'd gone to all that trouble to clean up, she was a little sad that the remnants of their first intimate evening together were gone.

She set the broom and bucket down and stepped onto the porch. He'd left the tiki lights up. The blanket they'd lain on was folded neatly on the table. Beside the blanket was a mason jar. Her pulse quickened as she picked it up and realized there was sand in it, and a piece of paper. She unscrewed the top, taking out a handwritten note from Justin. She recognized his slanted writing.

Memories of our unforgettable evening. J

The butterflies in her belly took flight again. He sure knew how to stir them up. Heck, he stirred more than butterflies. He'd given her his own brand of a scrapbook. She loved knowing he didn't want to forget that night any more than she did.

She wanted to text him to say thank you, but she didn't want to bug him when he was in a meeting. She put her fingers in the jar, running them through the sand, remembering that night. She'd been so nervous, and all her worries had tumbled out. He'd been so good to her, not pushing her, leaving their path in her hands.

She put the note back in the jar and carried it into her bedroom as she screwed on the top, putting it on the nightstand. Then she went into the kitchen to gather the pictures she'd left out. She brought them into the guest room for safekeeping so she could get started on Joey's album, but instead she sat on the bed and looked through the pictures of Justin and Shadow one last time. When he'd texted earlier, he'd mentioned that he wasn't going to have time to stop by and see Shadow before the meeting. She looked at a picture of Shadow sitting in the grass gazing at the camera, all his pink scars and stitches staring back at her. His stitches weren't quite as angry looking now. Only one more week until he'd have them removed. She wondered if Shadow missed Justin, too.

Of course you do. You get so excited when you see him.

They had that in common.

She and Justin hadn't made plans for the next time they'd see each other, which hadn't struck her as odd until now. Did he miss her, too? Did he need a break from her?

Oh God, I'm becoming one of those girls.

She needed a distraction from her own thoughts, and she'd bet Shadow did, too. A quick visit would probably make Shadow's day, and it would definitely make hers. She knew Dwayne and Baz would be at church with Justin, but maybe she could catch Sid.

She set down the pictures and hurried into her bedroom for a pair of flip-flops.

Twenty minutes later she was stopped by the front gate of the rescue, pushing the button and looking up at the camera, praying Sid would answer.

"Hi, Chloe," Sidney said through the speaker.

Relief swept through her. "Hi. Is it too late for me to visit with Shadow?" She saw the hours posted by the gate and realized they'd closed more than an hour ago. Silently chiding herself, she said, "I should have checked the hours. *Sorry*."

"It's fine. Those hours are for the general public. I'm catching up on some paperwork. I'd love the company."

Sid opened the gate, and Chloe drove through. She parked in front of the veterinary clinic, and Sid came out to greet her. "Hey there."

"Hi. I'm sorry to stop by without calling." Chloe hoisted her bag over her shoulder and said, "I know Justin didn't have time to stop by to see Shadow today, and I thought he could use a little company."

"He'll be thrilled to see you," Sid said as they headed for the shelter.

"Do you work every day?"

"Pretty much. There is so much to do, and some of the animals need daily therapy." Sid opened the door to the shelter, sparking a cacophony of barks, and grabbed a leash from a hook on the wall. She slowed by each kennel so the dogs could sniff their hands and get a few finger pets through the wire.

When they came to Shadow's kennel, he went paws-up on the wire, whining and barking, his stump of a tail wagging.

"Hey, big boy," Chloe said as Sidney unlocked the kennel and hooked the leash to his collar. She petted Shadow, who was sniffing her legs and panting excitedly.

"Let's bring him into the visiting room. I'll stay with you since Justin isn't here. Just in case Shadow gets funky."

She followed Sid down the hall to the visiting room and said, "Has he gotten nasty with people?"

"No, and I don't think he will. But he gets scared sometimes, and that can cause behavioral issues. It's better to be safe than sorry." She closed the door behind them and sat on the floor.

Chloe set her bag down and sat on the floor, too. Shadow climbed in her lap and licked her face as she loved him up. "I missed you, too, Shadow."

"He sure loves you and Maverick. Did you have a dog when you were growing up?"

"No. We barely had enough money to feed ourselves." Shadow sat between them, sniffing first Chloe, then Sid. Chloe stroked his back and said, "What about you?"

"My dad was military, and we moved around a lot. We didn't have pets, but I've always loved animals. I became a dog handler in the military. That's how I met Gunner. We were stationed at the same base, and we ended up in the field together. A few years after we met, my dog, Rosco, and I were clearing a tunnel before Gunner's unit was supposed to go in. Unfortunately, there was a suicide bomber waiting for us. Rosco and I took the hit."

"Oh my gosh, that's awful." A shiver ran down Chloe's back. "Did you get hurt? Did Rosco survive?"

"We both had shrapnel wounds and broken bones. Rosco lost his back leg near his hip, and I had a mild traumatic brain injury. It took a while, but we're both okay. We got lucky."

"That doesn't sound lucky to me. You're so brave."

Sidney shrugged. "Rosco made it easy to be brave."

"Where is he now?" Chloe stroked Shadow's head, and he put his chin down on his front paws and closed his eyes.

"I adopted him. He's in the clinic waiting for me to take him up to the house."

"I don't mean to keep you away from him."

"It's okay. We're together all the time. It's actually nice to have a real person to talk to."

"Justin said you live with Dwayne—I mean *Gunner*. That must be interesting. He's such a flirt."

"I know everyone wonders about us," Sidney said softly. "The truth is, he and Steph are a lot closer than we are. I love Gunner, but once you've seen a guy guzzling milk from a carton and belching the alphabet, attraction goes out the window."

"I'm trying to imagine Justin doing those things, and I gotta say, guzzling milk would not be a deal breaker. Belching the alphabet, on the other hand…" She laughed.

"Those Wicked boys could charm the pants off a nun." Sidney sat back against the wall and said, "But I think they all see me as one of the guys."

"Is there one you'd like not to see you that way?"

Sidney tucked her hair behind her ear and her eyes flicked up to Chloe's. She opened her mouth to speak, and Chloe's phone rang. Shadow lifted his head, and Sidney said, "Saved by the bell."

Chloe pulled out her phone, hoping it was Justin, and tried not to give in to the disappointment when she saw *Madigan Wicked* on the screen. "It's Mads," she said, and answered the call. "Hi, Mads."

"Hi!" Mads yelled into the phone. Chloe could hear music in the background. "Me and Marly are at the Hog, and Starr is working. Since Maverick is at church, do you want to come hang with us?"

"That sounds fun, but I'm with Shadow and Sid at the rescue, and I have a boatload of stuff to get done when I go home. But let me ask"—Chloe looked at Sid, who was waving her hands and shaking her head, mouthing, *No, no, no*—"never mind, I guess Sid can't make it, either."

"Come on, Chloe," Mads urged. "When your man is away, the girls should play!"

Chloe laughed. "Except that I haven't been home in four days, and my mail is piled as high as my laundry. But we're still on for dinner with the book club girls next week at Common Grounds, right?"

"Absolutely," Mads said cheerily. "Tell Sid that Marly is scoping out a man for her."

Chloe told Sidney, who used her fingers like a gun and shot herself in the head. Her head lolled forward, tongue out, eyes closed, and Shadow immediately began licking her face.

"She says that's great," Chloe lied, shrugging. "I promise I'll make it another time."

"Okay, chat soon." Mads ended the call.

As Chloe put her phone in her bag, she said, "What's up with the headshot?"

"Marly and Mads are *always* trying to set me up with guys. The trouble is, once you've lived in the field, you're too tough for regular guys, and the tough guys don't want girls like me." Shadow rolled onto his back, and Sidney scratched his belly. "Finding a guy who's as loyal and unconditionally loving as a dog and can appreciate me for *me* is like finding a needle in a haystack. It's been a long time since anything without three or four legs warmed my bed."

Chloe was pretty sure she'd found her needle in Justin, or rather, *he'd* found *her*. But she'd also been where Sidney was, feeling like the right man may never appear. After Sidney's comment about the Wickeds, she wondered if the right man was right in front of her, too, but instead of feeling her out on the Wicked front, she said, "I know what that's like. Before Justin, all my lovin' came from fictional boyfriends."

"Maybe I need your book list."

"Do you read romance?"

Sidney shrugged again, which seemed to be her go-to mannerism. "I haven't ever read it. I'm mostly a suspense girl."

"Trust me, you are missing out. There are romantic suspense novels. Do you have a Kindle?"

"Doesn't everyone?" She laughed. "I also have a Nook and Apple Books on my phone."

"I'm going to broaden your horizons and loan you some of my romance novels. Trust me, these will tide you over until Mr. Right appears."

"I'll give them a try."

"Great. If you like them, let me know. I run an erotic romance book club, and we're always looking for new members. Marly, Mads, and Steph are in it. Do you know Starr? She works as a waitress at the Salty Hog."

"Yeah, I know everyone there."

"She just joined, too, and some of my other girlfriends are in it. You'd like them. Do you ever go to Common Grounds?"

"Sure."

"Gabe is in the club, too. We're meeting there next week for dinner."

Chloe gave her the details about their dinner, and they exchanged email addresses and phone numbers. Chloe took pictures with Shadow and Sidney, and Sidney updated her on Shadow's progress. She'd been slowly introducing him to other dogs, and he hadn't shown any aggressive tendencies.

"When do you think he'll be ready to be adopted?" Chloe asked.

"It's hard to say, but if he continues to show progress, then I'll start letting him spend more time in the other building and with the other dogs. I still have to see how he is around children and crowds." She petted Shadow's head and said, "If he continues to do well, I'll begin that process over the next few weeks. It'll be a while before he's ready to be adopted. Justin said you're helping with the adoption event."

"I am. I'm looking forward to it. I've been thinking about a few ideas. You know how you have information sheets on each of the animal's kennels? Would it be helpful for the event if I made each of them an introduction board? I could include pictures of them eating, sleeping, playing, to give families an idea of what they'd be like as pets. I have lots of animal stickers and embellishments I could use to decorate the boards."

"Do you have time for all that?"

"I'll make time," Chloe said with a smile. "I was also think-ing that it might be cute to make blue bow ties for the boys and pink bows for the girls and tie them to their collars."

"Oh my gosh. I *love* that idea! It'll make them even cuter."

"Will Dwayne mind?"

"Gunner? No. He's such a sucker for these animals. Have you seen him with Snowflake?"

"Yes, and my ovaries almost exploded."

Sid laughed. "I think he'd love the ideas you mentioned. Do you want help? It sounds like a lot of work. I can help with the bows and bow ties, and I'm sure Evie, Baz's assistant, and Tori, our office administrator, would be happy to help, too. Unless you want to do it all?"

"No, that would be great. I have tons of ribbons. I'll drop some off tomorrow when we come see Shadow. Will Evie and Tori be here? I can show you guys how to make the bow ties. They can be a little tricky."

"I'll ask them to stick around."

Sidney took her to the other building to take pictures of the animals, and they talked about ideas for the introduction boards. When Chloe left, she felt lighter and a little less lonely for Justin. She was glad she'd gone and glad to have gotten to know Sidney better. But when she got home, her cottage was too quiet, and she missed him all over again.

She lifted her chin, refusing to be *that* girl, and she fell back on the habits that had always taken the edge off. She organized, planned, and dove into the work at hand. She put the laundry in the dryer, feeling silly for being happy to see Justin's shirt going into *her* dryer. She weeded through her mail. Then she set herself up in the dining room and began working on an album for Joey.

She relived that incredible afternoon in Harborside while choosing pictures, which only made her miss Justin more. But she pushed through, working diligently and keeping her nose to the grindstone as best she could. When she took a break to fold the laundry, Justin's shirt did her in. She eyed her phone, thinking about texting him. She forced herself *not* to do it and went back to the dining room.

When a text rolled in and Justin's name appeared on her screen, her pulse skyrocketed. She grabbed the phone and read the text. *Hey, sexy girl. Do you have room in your bed for a greedy biker boy?*

"Yes!" she said as she thumbed out a teasing response. *That depends. Which biker boy is this?*

Another message popped up. *The one who will kick the ass of any other man who tries to get into your bed.* He added a devil emoji.

She texted, *Mr. Wicked, is that your territorial side coming out again?*

She sat with the phone in her hand, awaiting his reply, getting more nervous with every passing minute. Five minutes passed in silence. *Ten.* She paced the living room, trying to figure out where that fine line should be drawn. She knew he had a right to be territorial, but the idea of him beating someone up over jealousy turned her stomach.

The roar of a motorcycle sent her darting out the door. She ran to the driveway as he cut the engine and pulled off his helmet. His jaw was tight as he climbed off the bike and strode toward her.

She gulped a breath and said, "Justin, I—"

"Asking me not to be territorial over you is like asking you not to be so protective of your sister." His eyes drilled into her, but his tone softened as he said, "But a pretty dragonfly schooled me on how to do it properly. You see, I wouldn't have to kick a guy's ass. Instead I'd just do this." He grabbed her face and crushed his mouth to hers, kissing her so passionately, her knees weakened. She had to hang on to him just to remain standing. "I think that's within your parameters. Am I right, sweet cheeks?"

"Uh-huh" was all she could manage.

"I missed you tonight." He touched his forehead to hers and said, "When I didn't hear from you, I thought you needed some alone time."

That misconception snapped her out of her drunk-on-Justin stupor. "I wanted to thank you for cleaning off the porch, and for the mason jar, and the romantic note. But I didn't want to bother you at your meeting. I love that you saved some of our sand."

"So we were both worried about smothering each other," he said with a small smile.

"I think so, and I'm glad you didn't hold back."

"Does that mean I have permission to smother you?" he asked coyly as they headed up the walk.

"Smothering is such a negative word, unless you're talking about hot fudge, of course. How about if we agree it's okay to be crazy about each other and go with the flow, texting or seeing each other as often as we feel the urge? If one of us needs space, then we can speak up."

"You're opening a dangerous door, sexy girl," he warned. "You know how I feel about you."

She turned toward him on the porch and wrapped her arms around him, gazing up at his handsome face, and said, "I'll take my chances."

Chapter Eighteen

JUSTIN FELT CHLOE burrowing against his back, trying to hide from the cold, driving rain as he drove the motorcycle into her driveway early Sunday evening. They'd been out riding with the guys when the clouds had opened up, drenching them in minutes. They'd pulled over to wait it out, but it hadn't let up. Chloe had deemed it their *rainy adventure*, and Justin had never driven so carefully in all his life.

Justin whipped off his helmet and helped Chloe from the bike. She hadn't complained once about being soaking wet. She was amazing like that, and she'd been open to even more new things since they'd decided to let go of their worries about smothering each other and let nature take its course.

"*Run!*" she said through her helmet, taking his hand as they sprinted up the sidewalk. She took off her helmet on the porch, her teeth chattering as she said, "*Hold me, hold me, hold me!*" and buried her face in his chest.

He put his arms around her, kissing her head and running his hands up and down her back, trying to warm her, but cold air was whipping around them. "Let's get you inside."

She handed him the keys and he unlocked the door, ushering her inside. They'd been going back and forth between their houses, staying at whichever was more convenient at the time. He didn't care where they were, as long as they were together. He closed the door behind them and took off his wet shirt. Chloe's smile reached her eyes as she grabbed his face with both hands, went up on her toes, and kissed the hell out of him.

"Damn, baby. I ought to take you out in the rain more often."

"I missed out on doing that the night of the storm. I wanted to so badly, but I was scared. I wasn't about to make the same mistake twice."

"Neither am I." He hauled her in for another kiss, and she melted against him. But as soon as their lips parted and she took off her boots, she was shivering again. "Go change into warm clothes, sweets. I'll start a fire."

"*Oh*, that sounds perfect. We can have a picnic by the fire. Want to cook something or order pizza?"

"How about a pizza and a scrapbook party? I want to see how you've changed through the years."

"Yeah, right. You want to see if I have any hidden pictures of you."

"Maybe that, too." He gave her a quick kiss and swatted her butt. "Go change. I'll start the fire and order pizza."

She headed into the bedroom with a bounce in her step. That bounce was new, too, and man, he loved seeing her so happy. He went into the living room and began making the fire. Over the last few days he'd discovered just how organized Chloe was. The clothes in her closet were separated by type and style, her shoes were neatly lined up and separated by type and color. In the kitchen, glasses were on a separate shelf from mugs, and she didn't have a typical junk drawer. All of her kitchen drawers had organizers. The dining room cabinet was full of scrapbooking supplies, labeled and meticulously organized by theme. Although right now the dining room table was covered with animal boards she was making for the adoption event. She'd been working like a fiend to prepare a board for each animal, and they were gorgeous. Of course, Chloe being Chloe, she'd made a checklist of the animals, their personalities, and all of their pertinent information, which would be listed on the boards and also available on flyers.

Her organization didn't stop there. In the living room, there were two closed cabinets in the bottom half of her bookshelves. She'd adhered vinyl to the interior of one, and put a fireplace grate inside. She had wood stacked there, and beneath the grate she'd piled kindling. The other cabinet was stacked with fire starters, newspapers, two lighters, and metal skewers, which she'd said were for roasting marshmallows. For some reason, knowing she was as neat and organized as he was—at least in his house and office—endeared her to him even more.

He made the fire, and Chloe came out of the bedroom a few minutes later looking sexy and cozy in black leggings that hugged her curves, the Prince Charming shirt she'd bought the other day, and blue fuzzy socks. She held up her index finger and disappeared into the laundry room. When she came out, she was carrying the gray sweatpants he'd left there the other night.

"I washed these yesterday. Why don't you give me your wet clothes and I'll throw in a load?"

"You've been trying to get me naked since that first night on the beach," he said as he took off his wet jeans. He stripped off his briefs, and her eyes went dark with desire, but her cheeks flamed pink. He'd never tire of that mix of innocence and temptress.

"Put that thing away right now, you wicked man," she said with a laugh. "We need food and warmth before I let your python in my garden!"

"That's definitely not the reaction I was hoping for." He chuckled and pulled on his sweats. "Your eyes say *yes*. How about they have a chat with that naughty mouth of yours?"

"Leave my traitorous eyes out of this, and maybe *later* you'll have a visit from my naughty mouth." She snagged his clothes and headed into the laundry room.

A LONG WHILE later, they were sitting on the floor in front of the fire, their backs against the couch, surrounded by scrapbooks, their bellies full of pizza. Though Justin hadn't found any hidden pictures of himself, he'd taken a visual tour of Chloe's childhood through her college years. He'd seen a plethora of attendance and honor roll certificates and other awards his academic beauty had earned. There were pictures of her as a teenager when she'd gone through what she called her *badass stage*, dressed in all black, with gothlike makeup. He'd asked her where that wild girl was now, and she'd said she'd been more tough than wild, and he was bringing back the best parts of her. He'd learned that Chloe hadn't gone to her senior prom, choosing instead to stay home in case Serena got caught with one of her mother's boyfriends around. It made him sad that she'd missed so much of her youth, but at the same time, he admired her even more for all she'd overcome. They'd gone through pictures from her middle and high school graduations, each one accompanied by a photo of her and Serena. Serena held a sign in each that read SHE DID IT! They also had pictures of them celebrating with a cake they'd made together. Even though Chloe had lived at home for the first two years of college so she could be with Serena, she'd still applied to four-year colleges, and she'd kept all of her acceptance letters. She said they were proof that one day she'd be free of her mother, of that house, and of that life. She had no pictures of her mother, which was as heartbreaking as it was proof of her strength, even as a young girl.

There were a few pictures of Chloe with Drake's family when they were younger, but not as many as he'd thought he'd find. Those came later, in the albums they were looking through now, when she'd reconnected with them after college. These pages were filled with a different, more confident and less haunted Chloe.

Justin turned the page, revealing a picture of Chloe standing in front of her car, the keys dangling from her finger. Serena stood beside her with a handwritten sign that read IT'S HERS! and had an arrow pointing to Chloe. Neither one could have looked prouder.

"Rick took that picture for us." Chloe snuggled against Justin's side and said, "I'll never forget how it felt to sign the papers and buy that car. I had saved every penny for a down payment, and I was terrified to have that much debt, but at the same time, it was exhilarating to have earned the right to have that loan."

Justin kissed her temple and said, "I know that feeling."

"Serena and I celebrated with huge ice cream sundaes, and that evening we sat in my car listening to the radio, looking out over the dunes at the water. It's one of my best memories. She's been there for all of my big moments."

Chloe turned the page to a picture of her and Serena standing in front of LOCAL. Serena held a sign that read SHE GOT THE JOB! with an arrow pointing at Chloe. Around the picture, Chloe had written information about the dates she'd volunteered at LOCAL, the people she'd interviewed with, the date she was hired, her start date for work.

"Serena's bestie, Mira, took that picture for us the day I was hired. I was so nervous even though I'd been volunteering there. When they called to say I got the job, I cried. I had applied to a few places, just to be safe, but my heart had already belonged to the people there."

"Did that Rogers asshole hire you?" Saying his name was like scratching nails down a chalkboard.

"Yes. I mean, he made the final decision, but I had to pass interviews with everyone—human resources, Alan, Darren Rogers, who is Alan's father and the CEO of LOCAL, the board of directors. Why?"

Justin's jaw clenched.

She touched his cheek and said, "I know he rubs you the wrong way, but you're not going to get all worked up over him right now. Especially when there's more to see." She turned the page, showing him pictures of her, Serena, and Mira huddled together for a selfie at Undercover. "The night I was hired, we celebrated so long we closed down the bar. Rick and Drake had to come drive us home."

"My girl got a little wild, did she?"

"I didn't drink *that* much, but I wasn't going to take any chances in my new car. Not when all my hard work was finally paying off. I was never the kind of girl who partied or got drunk in college. I was always too focused on getting good grades, volunteering, working for spending money. Doing all the things that would help me to achieve a safe, stable future. There were bumps and bruises along the way, a bad decision or two, but I had *made it*. For the first time ever, I allowed myself one night of sheer, unadulterated *fun*. I let everything go that night. I laughed and danced, and we talked to everybody in the bar. I didn't pick up any guys or anything like that. I was just free to have fun, not worrying about what I had to do the next day or anything else. I had a foreseeable future, and it was the future I wanted. It was an amazing feeling. Almost as amazing as this."

Chloe turned the page to a picture of her standing in front of her cottage holding a SOLD sign, smiling brighter than the sun. Serena stood beside her with an enormous bouquet of balloons, holding a sign that read IT'S HERS! with an arrow pointing to Chloe. Justin scanned her notes written around the picture, telling the story of how she'd seen the house listed almost five years ago and had fallen in love with it at first sight. She turned the page, showing him more celebratory pictures with Serena, Mira, Drake, and Rick. "That was our other wild night. I figured I earned it."

"You should cut loose like that more often, make up for all the times you missed."

She wrinkled her nose. "It seems childish now to need to celebrate like that, but I do enjoy going out with the girls when we can find the time."

"It's not childish, babe. I'm not talking about drunk driving and reckless behavior. I'm talking about enjoying life and reaping the rewards of all your hard work. Letting all your responsibilities go for a night. It's good for your soul."

"I never see you cut loose."

"Sure you do."

"When?"

"When I ride. That's the thing that allows me to let all the stress and bad thoughts go." He leaned into her and said, "And riding with you makes it that much better."

"I *love* riding. I never thought I'd enjoy giving up control like that, but it's freeing, and I know I'm safe with you. Maybe scrapbooking *is* my cut-loose thing, because I'm not a partier."

"As much as I like hearing that you love riding and letting me take control—we'll explore that more in the bedroom—"

"Oh, you think you can just drop that there and get away with it?"

"There's no getting away with anything, darlin'." He squeezed her thigh and said, "Want to talk about it? Hit the bedroom and see how much control you'd like to relinquish?"

She laughed.

"You did taunt me with your naughty mouth." He leaned in for a kiss and said, "You're blushing."

"No kidding, you wicked thing. *Stop*. We're having a serious talk here."

"Oh, right. Okay, back to that." He tried to push those delicious ideas aside and said, "As much as you enjoy scrapbooking, that's not how *you* cut loose. You don't have to be a partier to let all your worries go and enjoy the moment. I know how much you love to dance, sweet cheeks, and you know how much I love watching, or dancing, with you. *That's* where you cut loose. We can go out and burn up the dance floor."

She fanned her face and said, "We need a *private* dance floor when we get started."

He brushed his lips over hers and said, "That can be arranged."

THEY RETURNED THE scrapbooks to the shelves, and as they got comfortable on the blankets again, settling in with their backs against the couch and their legs outstretched in front of the fire, Chloe said, "I wish you had more pictures and things from before you went to live with the Wickeds so we could make you a keepsake of the good memories."

"My good memories are so few and far between, they wouldn't fill the smallest of albums."

She laced their hands together and said, "You mentioned that your mom used to sing to you. Do you remember what she sang?"

His eyes softened, and he said, "She loved the Beatles. She couldn't sing when my father was around because it irritated him, but when he wasn't there, she'd sing 'Blackbird,' 'All You Need Is Love,' 'Penny Lane,' 'Lucy in the Sky with Diamonds,' 'With a Little Help from My Friends.' There were so many songs, and always the Beatles, but when she put me to bed every night, she'd sing 'Blackbird' and 'I Want to Hold Your Hand.' After I grew up, I realized that there were probably messages in those songs. When she sang 'Blackbird,' I think she was telling me to take all of my broken parts and fly away, but she could have been saying she was going to take her broken parts and fly away."

She ran her thumb over the back of their joined hands and said, "Maybe she was saying both."

"Maybe. When she sang 'I Want to Hold Your Hand,' she changed 'be your man' to 'be your mom,' and I think she was telling me that I was the thing that made her the happiest." He moved his left arm in front of them and touched his leather bracelet with the fingers on his other hand without letting go of her hand. "This was her necklace. She never took it off. She'd lie next to me at bedtime, and I'd play with her necklace. When she sang 'I Want to Hold Your Hand,' she'd snag my hand and wiggle it, and I'd laugh. I remember the rush of anticipation of waiting for her to do it because when I laughed, *she* laughed, and that was a beautiful thing. Back then it was everything. I'd tug my hand free and play with the necklace again, only to have her recapture it. The image in my head of my father is of a miserable bastard, but I can still see my mom wiggling my hand and smiling…" His voice trailed off, and he gazed into the fire with a thoughtful expression, as if he were lost in the memory.

"I wish I'd known her." She wished she and Justin had known each other when they were younger. Maybe they could have made sense of their awful situations and found a way out.

"She was timid as a baby bird, but I never doubted her love in the same way I never thought my father had an ounce of love for either of us."

"I'm sorry," she whispered. "I didn't mean to make you sad."

"You didn't. Those are my best memories, bedtime with my mom. 'I Want to Hold Your Hand' is all about feeling happy inside when he's holding her hand or when they're touching. My mother's life was so boxed in and awful, I guess I was her only happiness."

"Of course you were. You were her little boy. Her *island*."

The muscles in his jaw bunched, and he shook his head. "No."

"Why would you say that?"

"Because I couldn't save her. She was always drifting at sea.

She never had a chance to find an island."

"I know you feel guilty because you think she committed suicide to give you a chance in life, but you were only a little boy."

"It's so much bigger than that, Chloe."

"I don't understand." She touched his bracelet and said, "Did she give you this before she died?"

He shook his head. "No. Before she died, she said she was going to take a nap, so I lay down with her. I wasn't allowed in their bed, but my father was out, and he wasn't supposed to come home until later that night. So I took a chance. I remember seeing empty pill bottles on her nightstand, and when she was drifting off to sleep, she mumbled something about going to see her father. I thought she was dreaming because she'd told me that my grandparents were dead. When I woke up, I thought she was still sleeping, so I tiptoed into the living room and I guess I watched television or played. I don't really remember what I did. But I remember looking out the window at some point and realizing it was nighttime. I went to wake her up because I was hungry. She was lying on her back, and when I touched her, her head rolled to the side and vomit dripped out."

"Oh my God, *Justin*…" she said in a choked voice as more tragic pieces of his past came together.

"She'd thrown up in her sleep and choked on it. I remember shaking her, and at some point I must have realized she was gone. I don't remember much about what happened next other than thinking my father was going to kill me because I'd let her fall asleep and she'd died. I don't know what else was going through my head, but I took her necklace and hid it under my mattress. And then I hid under my blankets."

Tears slid down Chloe's cheeks as she imagined Justin as a terrified a little boy, having lost his mother and fearing for his own life.

"Other than a therapist I saw when I was a teenager, nobody knows I was there. Not even Preacher and Reba."

"They don't *know*?"

"No, and I want to keep it that way. My father lied and said I was out with him when she died, so it wasn't in my file. I think he was afraid he'd get in trouble if I was there."

"He *lied*? That's awful making a kid keep a secret like that. What did he do when he came home?"

Justin shrugged. "I don't know. Paced, cursed, told me what to say and how to act."

"That sounds scary for a kid. But why would you want to keep that bottled up when Rob and Reba are so good to you? Were you worried they wouldn't want to help you through all of those feelings?"

"No. Of course they'd want to help. But all that went down years before I even met them. I've gone through enough therapy where I did talk about this to know that more talking isn't going to help. It's all in the past now. It happened, and it's over."

She turned toward him and said, "Why did you tell me?"

"Because I don't want secrets between us, and you wanted to know my good memories."

"I'm glad you did, but I think your parents—Rob and Reba—deserve to know."

"Maybe one day."

He inhaled deeply and exhaled a long breath, as if he felt better having gotten it off his chest. She hoped he did.

"What I can't figure out is why she fell for my father in the first place. He was a total tool."

His voice and face were so serious, Chloe knew this was a long-torturing struggle. She had a torturous secret of her own, and while she didn't have anything to offer to ease the guilt and pain of being present when his mother had died, her secret just might help Justin find this answer. Her chest constricted as she mustered all her courage and said, "Sometimes people aren't who they seem. They change over time."

"Not that much."

She held his gaze, willing herself to be strong, and said, "Exactly that much. You know how I said I had some bumps and bruises and had made a few bad decisions?"

He sat up a little straighter, nodding. "Yeah."

"Did I tell you that I had been to the Salty Hog *once* before meeting Mads there?" She swallowed hard, trying to ignore the thundering in her chest.

"No. I don't like the look in your eyes, Chloe. What are you getting at?"

Of course he saw her pain. He noticed everything about her.

"When I was in my last semester of community college, I went out with this guy, a mechanic. He was big, confident, and rough around the edges. We went out for about three weeks. He was a gentleman. Not like Mr. Perfect or anything, but as far as twenty-two-year-old guys go, I guess he was above average. He knew how to treat me right, or so I thought. Until we went to meet his friends at the Salty Hog for dinner one night. I wasn't old enough to drink, but he and his friends were. I thought he'd had a good time, but when we left he started accusing me of flirting with his friends. At first I thought he was kidding. His buddies had their girlfriends with them. But by the time we got to his car, he was fuming. I tried to calm him down and said something about him not seeing clearly because he'd had so much to drink." Her hands were shaking, remembering how he'd changed in the blink of an eye. "I had barely gotten the sentence out when he hit me."

Justin sat up, breathing hard, the ire in his eyes as tangible as the floor they were sitting on. "I'll kill the motherfucker. Who is he?"

Chloe didn't answer. She needed to finish the story before she chickened out. "I stumbled back, and he hit me again. That sent me to the ground. There was broken glass on the pavement. A beer bottle I guess."

Justin pushed to his feet, hands fisting, but she didn't slow down. She had to get it out.

"I got glass in my chest and hands. My face hurt so bad, but he was coming at me, and I was using my heels to push myself backward. A car pulled into the parking lot and the headlights hit us at the same time his friends came out of the bar and saw what was happening. One guy yelled his name and ran over. When the guy who hit me turned to look at him, I got to my feet. The other guy grabbed him and held him back, hollering 'What the fuck, man? You don't hit a woman!' and that kind of stuff. The other guys came to help me, but I was shaking and hurt, off-balance. I was terrified, and I remember being pissed that I hadn't been able to defend myself. One of the girls gave me a ride home. She tried to get me to go to the cops, but I just wanted that guy out of my life. She helped me take out the slivers of glass and lent me makeup to cover the redness and bruising that had started to show on my face in case Serena was home. I didn't want my sister to see me like that. That was the last time I went out with anyone who was tough." She swallowed hard. "Until you."

"Who the *hell* was he, Chloe? I'm not fucking around."

She finally looked up at him. His nostrils were flaring, his muscles flexed, veins swollen. She'd wanted to help Justin understand that people could change on a dime, and instead she'd taken him over the edge. She pushed to her feet and touched his hand. "Don't do this to yourself, Justin. It was forever ago, and I never saw him or his friends again."

"The asshole needs to pay for what he did to you," he seethed, pacing the floor. "If Con had seen it, or *any* of the other Dark Knights, that fucker would have been dealt with and put behind bars where he belongs."

"I'm pretty sure his friends took care of roughing him up. But it doesn't matter one way or the other. Serena doesn't know about it, and I'm *not* going to let you dredge up something from my past. *Look at me*, Justin," she demanded.

He stopped pacing and met her gaze, hurt and anger warring in his eyes.

"You of all people should understand leaving the past in the past."

His shoulders dropped just a fraction, but it was enough for her to know he'd heard her. She went to him and took his hand, feeling inexplicably calm. She led him back to the blankets and pulled him down beside her. Then she straddled his lap to get his undivided attention and caressed his jaw, hoping to soothe the tension there.

"You want to protect me from my past, but that's over with, Justin. The same way we can't change what happened to your mother. I didn't tell you that story to make you mad. I wanted you to see that even when we are looking for all the signs, we can still be blindsided. Even smart people make bad decisions. Your mother was young, and your father may have seemed like a completely different man when they met."

"I hear you, but…" He wrapped his arms around her and touched his forehead to the center of her breastbone. "The thought of that guy hurting you…"

She kissed his head and gently cradled his face in her hands, lifting it so she could look into his tortured eyes. "I know how you feel because I want to go back in time and save you from all the stuff your father did and from being there when your mother died. But we can't do any of those things. All we can do is look harder, listen more carefully, and try to make sure it never happens again." She kissed him softly, again and again, light as a feather, until the tension in his jaw dissipated. "And love the hurt away."

She took off her shirt, and his eyes found the scar on her chest. She saw him putting the pieces of her past together.

"Baby," he said in a pained, craggy voice. He brushed his fingers over the scar, held them there for a moment, then pressed a kiss there. He lifted his gaze to hers and lowered her to the blanket, whispering, "Nobody will *ever* hurt you again."

She wound her arms around him and said, "You can't save me from the world, Justin."

"I'll never stop trying," he promised.

"How about if we make enough happy memories to silence the bad ones?"

He lowered his lips to hers, kissing her tenderly as he undressed her, loving all her newly bared parts as if he were discovering them for the very first time. He kept his eyes on her as he stripped off his clothes and came down over her, muscles taut with remnants of all they'd shared, his beautiful, distraught eyes gazing into hers. They didn't speak, didn't kiss, and didn't move. In the silence she heard whispers of bad memories vying to remain in the forefront. But as she ran her hands up his arms and over his back, his tension slowly dissipated, and she felt her own following suit, seeping out of her pores. She willed all those bad memories to follow the smoke from the fire up the chimney and fly away into the night.

"Chloe," he whispered, a plea and an affirmation in one.

Their bodies came together with the grace of the sunrise and the heat of a storm. He didn't kiss her as their passion built. He sank deeper, holding her gaze. The clarity of emotions in his eyes pushed all those ghosts to the side, telling her all the things his mouth couldn't. She didn't think their lovemaking could feel any better than it had. But this was different, like they'd finally broken the remaining chains that had weighed them down and allowed their hearts to truly beat as one.

Chapter Nineteen

CHLOE GLANCED IN her rearview mirror at Justin following her on his motorcycle as they headed to Summer House to meet their friends for breakfast Thursday morning. It had been four days since they'd confessed their deepest secrets, and Chloe was learning about the freedoms that came with trusting someone so implicitly. She could tell him anything, and that made what they had feel deeper, and truer, than anything she'd ever thought possible.

Over the nearly three weeks since he'd shown up at her house for that midnight dance, his romantic heart had her redefining her thoughts on what romance really meant. There was no doubt that bringing her flowers and creating a beach were romantic. The beach had been *epic*. But it was the little things he did every day that made her feel special, though they might not fit other people's ideas of romance, that were becoming the very definition of it for Chloe. He made coffee for them in the mornings, and he walked her to her car before work. At night they sometimes talked for hours, and they didn't harp on the past, which was nice. She knew she could talk about it if she wanted to, but there was no reason to dwell on ugly memories when their new ones were so beautiful. They talked about their *lives*—simple things like what they did during the day or what they hoped to do next week, next month, or next year. They discussed the complexities of their lives, too, like the programs she was developing and the ways in which Justin and Blaine were thinking about expanding their business. Justin told her about his visits with Mike when he checked in on him in the afternoons, how he feared losing him too soon. They visited Shadow nearly every day, and they both confessed how much they loved the pooch.

As she turned into the driveway toward the old Victorian inn overlooking Cape Cod Bay, she realized this was where it had all started for them.

She drove past the cottage that Desiree and Violet used as an art gallery, which had been damaged in the same storm that had brought Chloe and Justin to a near kiss. The cottage repairs were still under way. She parked in front of Summer House, and before she could open the car door, Justin was there, opening it for her. *Romance at its best.* He was always thinking of her, and she was falling for him, tumbling down that scary hill, and she didn't want to slow down.

"This is where it all started, remember?" she said as she climbed from the car. "I was having breakfast with the girls when you came riding in on your motorcycle to save Violet from big, bad Andre."

He drew her into his arms, just as he did every chance he got, and kissed her. "That was the day we were first introduced, but what I remember most is the first time I showed up to have breakfast with everyone. I'll never forget the hunger in your eyes when you looked across the table and told me that the bagels and muffins I'd brought from the Blue Willow Bakery made me even hotter."

She loved his elephantlike memory. "Is that why you wanted to stop at that bakery this morning for bagels and muffins?"

"My girl thinks bagels and muffins make me hotter. I'd be a fool not to hit that mark every chance I got." He kissed her and said, "I'm thinking about *buying* the frigging bakery."

She laughed and went to retrieve the goodies from the car, bending at the waist as she reached into the back seat. Justin moved behind her and placed his hands on her hips, pressing himself against her ass. She glared at him over her shoulder, unable to hide her smile. "*Stop.*" She grabbed the bakery box, and as she closed the car door with her hip, she said, "They'll know why we're late if you get me hot and bothered again."

"I guarantee they already know why we're late, babe. You can't be around us and *not* feel our fireworks." He took the box from her and put one arm around her waist. He kissed her neck and said, "Speaking of fireworks, you're mine on July Fourth, right?"

"I'm always yours," she said, reveling in how good it felt to say that.

"Good, because I'll never get enough of you, sweet thing. The downside to that is knowing that while you're giving my family the tour of LOCAL this afternoon, all I will be able to think about is bending you over your desk."

Her body flamed at the thought. "*Justin!* Now that's all *I'll* be thinking about, too!"

He chuckled as they walked across the grass toward the inn. It was a warm sunny morning, and their friends' voices carried in the air.

"This is a momentous occasion," he said more seriously. "Our first breakfast as a couple with the *Real Housewives of Bayside*."

They weren't housewives, but they were gossips. "After how much I gushed over you to the girls at dinner last night, I'm sure all of Wellfleet knows we're together." As Chloe and her friends had planned after the last book club meeting, she'd met them at Common Grounds for dinner while Justin was at church.

"You gushed about your man?" he asked with a cocky grin.

"Shut up. You know I did."

"It'd be hard not to since you've got the hottest commodity on the Cape."

She rolled her eyes, and he laughed at her.

"But the gossip girls have never experienced the hottest couple on the Cape *as* a couple," he pointed out. "It's time to blow their minds."

She had to admit that after watching most of her friends fall in love, she was excited to share her happiness with them. Her and Justin's lives were blending together. It wasn't seamless, as they had hiccups to figure out, like which house to stay at and fitting in all the things they each had going on. But she loved figuring those things out with him, seeing his boots by her door, their clothes mingling in the washer, their toiletries in each other's bathrooms. She didn't mind going back and forth between houses, and neither of them wanted to spend evenings apart. She'd spent time in the evenings working on Joey's album and the boards for each of the animals for the adoption day event at Dwayne's rescue and reading her book for the book club in Justin's studio while he sculpted. He was making a special piece for Joey, and the sculpture for the rally was coming along beautifully. She loved watching him pour his heart into the pieces he made. Although the other evening she'd read erotic passages from her book to him while he was working and he didn't get much sculpting done.

As they neared the yard where the table was set for breakfast, Chloe saw Emery and Serena talking by the kitchen door of the inn. Serena was dressed for work in a pretty blue shift, her Rachel McAdams hair flowing in gentle waves over her shoulders. Chloe hadn't seen Emery in a while. She and Dean had recently announced that they were expecting a baby in January. Emery taught early-morning yoga classes. She was still wearing her yoga pants and a sports bra, and there was no hint of a baby belly yet. Chloe wondered what Emery would think of the new *Chloe*, who hung out with bikers and enjoyed it and gave up a modicum of control over her perfectly orchestrated life to fit into Justin's.

Daphne ran past Emery, following Hadley as she chased Desiree's scruffy pooch, Cosmos, and Chloe realized that this time next year, Desiree's and Emery's little ones would be joining them for breakfast. Everyone's life was changing so fast. But this time Chloe wasn't on the outside looking in. Her life was changing, too, in the very best of ways. She glanced at Justin, catching him watching her for the millionth time, and he blew her a kiss. She knew she'd never tire of that.

"Des, they're here!" Emery called through the screen door. She jogged across the grass and said, "It's about time you horndogs showed up," and pushed open the gate to the side yard.

Cosmos sprinted past her, and Justin scooped him up with one hand, balancing the box of treats in the other as the pooch licked his face.

"It's my fault we're late," Justin said with an impish grin. "I had Chloe chained to my bed." He set Cosmos down and Cosmos darted back into the fenced yard.

Emery hugged Chloe and said, "Then by all means, go back home. We don't want to cockblock one of our own."

"I had no idea my sister was so kinky," Serena teased.

Chloe rolled her eyes. "This is *Justin* you're talking to, re-member? He'll say anything. He did *not* have me chained to the bed." Although she kind of liked the idea of doing something so naughty with him.

"Well, that's too bad." Emery's eyes lit up and she said, "I have handcuffs if you want to borrow them."

Justin chuckled and reached for Chloe's hand. He pressed a kiss to the back of it and said, "I'd never use handcuffs on this gorgeous lady. Silk ties are more our style."

Great. Now I'll be thinking about you bending me over my desk and tying me up with silk ties. It was going to be a very long day.

They followed the girls into the yard. Desiree came out of the kitchen door carrying a big bowl of blueberries and strawberries. Her long blond hair had gotten fuller with her pregnancy, and she was all burgeoning baby bump. It was true what they said about pregnant women glowing. Desiree looked radiant.

"Hi, Des. Let me take that." Chloe took the bowl from her and said, "We brought bagels and muffins so you wouldn't have to cook."

"That's sweet, but you know how some women nest by decorating the nursery or babyproofing the house?" Desiree rubbed her belly and said, "Apparently I nest by cooking. I'm convinced our little one is going to be a chef. Or maybe he or she will just be a big eater. Who knows. There are plates of waffles, bacon, and eggs inside."

Justin set the bakery box on the table and said, "I'll get

them. You girls relax."

"Hey, Justin," Emery called after him. "The guys got a late start this morning and just left for their run. I'm not sure if they'll be back in time for you to see them."

"That's okay." He winked at Chloe and said, "I have nothing against eating breakfast with a harem of gorgeous women."

Chloe set the bowl on the table, and the second Justin was inside the house, the girls huddled around her.

"Quick, give us the scoop. Scale of one to ten. How does he treat you?" Emery said.

Chloe's pulse quickened. "Ten."

"How's the sex?" Emery asked.

"*Twenty*, and don't ask for details," Chloe said quickly. Their sex life was beyond incredible, but she wasn't about to share those details with the gossip girls.

"*Go*, Justin," Serena said.

"I'm jealous," Daphne said, keeping an eye on Hadley and Cosmos.

"Well, if she's not sharing sexy details, then that about covers it for me." Emery plucked a strawberry from the bowl and sat down at the table.

"I bet I would have heard all the details if I'd made it to Common Grounds for dinner with the book club girls last night," Daphne complained. "But Hadley was so cranky, I didn't want to leave her."

"You didn't miss any details, Daph," Chloe reassured her. "I didn't share with them, either."

Desiree, the most proper of all her friends, sat beside her and said, "I don't want those kinds of details, but I am wondering what it's like for you after playing cat and mouse with Justin for so long. Are you happy?"

"I'm happier than I ever imagined possible. I always thought I needed certain things in a man," Chloe said as she and Serena sat down at the table. "It turns out, I just needed a certain man. Justin is wonderful. Believe it or not, he's romantic and sweet. He's good to me, you guys. And you know he's funny, charming, *pushy*." She stopped talking as he came outside carrying a tray of food. He looked at her with wanting eyes and lifted his chin. She met the eager eyes of her girlfriends and lowered her voice to say, "He's *everything*."

Justin set the tray on the table and said, "Y'all look guilty. Did I miss something?"

They all said "*No*" at once.

"You all suck at lying." He grabbed a piece of bacon and bit into it. "Des, this spread looks great. Thanks for cooking."

The girls went to work, setting out the plates of food.

"Come on, Had," Daphne called after her daughter. "Time to eat."

Justin scooped up Hadley as she toddled by and said, "You hungry, little princess?"

Hadley clutched her favorite stuffed bird in one hand. The ends of her wispy hair bounced as she nodded, lips pursed in a tiny scowl, brows knitted. She was the most serious child Chloe had ever met. It practically took an act of God to get Hadley to smile, and they all loved her to pieces.

Justin sat with Hadley on his lap and began fixing her a plate. "Berries?" he asked, and the scowling cutie nodded. "Waffles?" She nodded again. "Eggs?" Another nod. He glanced across the table at Daphne, silently seeking approval.

Chloe looked around the table, and it was clear that she wasn't the only one taken with the sight of her bad boy's tender side coming out.

Justin must have misread Daphne's expression, because he said, "What? Is she allergic to something?"

"*No*," Daphne reassured him with a dreamy expression.

"We're used to seeing you *flirt* with Chloe," Emery explained. "But now I'm having visions of you and Chloe with *babies*."

Chloe's eyes just about fell out of her head. *Us? We just started dating.* It was one thing to admire how good Justin was with Hadley, but quite another to think about having babies anytime soon.

"By the look on Chloe's face, I think we're a long way from that," Justin said with another wink.

Chloe breathed a sigh of relief.

"Don't wait too long. Chloe's no spring chicken," Serena teased.

"Hey," Chloe said, putting a waffle and fruit on her plate. "I've got time."

"Don't worry, babe. I'm not in a hurry," Justin said as Hadley plucked a piece of fruit from the plate. "I have a lot of road to cover before I strap a baby seat to my bike. But I do know of a few dogs and cats who need good homes." Justin looked around the table and said, "Who's coming to the Wicked Animal Rescue adoption event this weekend?"

"Harper told us about it," Emery said excitedly. "Dean and I are going to swing by and see if we can find a pup that won't mind living with two crazy cats. But we have to come by early. We're meeting Tegan and Jett at Dean's parents' house for lunch."

"Wait until you see the introduction boards I'm making for the animals." Chloe told them about her newest project and about the bows and bow ties that Tori, Evie, and Sid were making.

"I want to go just to see all that." Desiree patted her baby bump and said, "We'll try to stop by, but between Cosmos and the baby, Rick and I are going to have our hands too full to care for a new pet."

"And I have all I can do to keep up with Hadley," Daphne pointed out. "Sorry, Justin."

Chloe eyed Serena. "You and Drake could use a fur baby while you practice making a real one."

"We'll try to stop by," Serena said. "But I'm not sure if we're ready for a pet just yet. We're still in barely-making-it-through-the-door-before-getting-naked stage."

Justin's gaze collided with Chloe's and a crooked, conspiratorial grin slid into place. They were in that stage, too, and she was in no hurry to leave it.

He winked and turned his attention to Serena. "Even if you can't make it to the event, why don't the four of us grab an early dinner at the Salty Hog Saturday night? You can get to know me and my family better," Justin suggested casually.

The hope in Justin's voice told Chloe it was more than a casual suggestion. The day after she'd told him about that horrible night at the Salty Hog, he'd said they never had to go back. But she'd reminded him that they were making better memories to erase the past. He knew how much Serena meant to her, and the fact that he thought about bringing her along to try to build those better memories, further blending their worlds, made her fall even harder for him.

"We'd love that." Serena raised her brows at Chloe and said, "Meeting the family sounds serious."

"Oh, we're serious." Justin's eyes locked on Chloe and he said, "I've got lots of future plans for me and that beauty over there."

Chloe's heart tumbled in her chest.

"Speaking of future plans, your birthday is coming up in a few weeks, Chloe. *Ticktock*," Serena teased.

"How old are you going to be?" Daphne asked. "Wait, you were twenty-nine last year, right?"

Chloe looked at Serena, and they both said, "Twenty-nine. *Always* twenty-nine."

"When Chloe turned twenty-nine, she decided she would never admit to being any older," Serena explained.

"How long ago was that?" Daphne asked.

"Sorry, sister from another mother, but I cannot reveal that information." Serena looked at Chloe and said, "Are we still on for our annual birthday lunch, or is that tabled now that you have a man in your life?"

"Who am I? *Mom?* I'm not going to ditch my girlfriends because of any man." She looked at Justin and said, "Sorry. I hope that didn't sound mean, but…"

"I have yet to hear you sound mean to anyone, babe," Justin said as he cut a waffle for Hadley. "I knew you had lunch with the girls last year and assumed you would probably do it again. But I'm hoping your schedule is clear for the evening."

"If hers isn't, mine is," Daphne said, looking dreamily at him and Hadley, causing everyone else to laugh.

Hadley wiggled out of Justin's lap and climbed into the empty chair between him and Daphne. She sat up on her knees and continued plucking food off Justin's plate.

Justin set a seductive stare on Chloe and said, "What do you say, sweet cheeks? You and me on your twenty-ninth birthday?"

"For *you*, Mr. Wicked?" Chloe teased with an arch of her brows, thinking about last night when Justin had texted her after his church meeting asking if she was still busy with the girls. His timing had been perfect. She and the girls had enjoyed their time together, and they were in the parking lot saying their goodbyes. She'd responded to his text with, *No, but I'd like to be busy with my biker boy. Race you to your bedroom...* He'd been ready and waiting when she'd arrived, but they never made it to the bedroom.

Justin moved the plate in front of Hadley without taking his eyes off Chloe and said, "That's right, sweetheart. What do you say? Let me spoil my girl for a night?"

"You spoil me every night." She was sure the space between them was going to ignite. She'd watched her girlfriends and their men taunting each other for long enough. It was her turn to be bold. She picked up a strawberry, nervous about trying to seduce him in front of her friends, but maybe that was *why* she wanted to do it so badly. To finally shed her careful, safe skin. Or maybe it was because his animal magnetism was too strong to deny. She had no idea how she had ever held back from him. She didn't know exactly why she wanted to get him hot and bothered so badly, but she wasn't backing down, and that was empowering *and* thrilling. She held his gaze as she slowly licked her lips. His eyes darkened as she placed the berry on her tongue and bit into it as sensually as she was able, hoping she didn't look ridiculous.

Justin bit his bottom lip, as he'd done the first night they were intimate. "*Mm-mm. I could eat your strawberry all day long.*"

Good Lord. That noise he made when he bit his lower lip sent desire pounding through her veins, but the heat in his eyes, and the way he spoke, full of hunger and something much deeper, did her in. She was *toast*.

"Yup. *Twenty* all right," Emery said, and she bit off a piece of bacon.

"More like twenty *thousand*." Desiree fanned her face with her hand. "There's an empty bedroom upstairs if you need it."

Justin's gaze never left Chloe's as he said, "If we hit the bedroom every time we got a little heated up, we'd never come out."

But we'd definitely come.

Holy cow. Her boldness had felt so right, but now she felt a little *exposed*. She lowered her eyes, blushing fiercely.

"Who knew my conservative sister was such a seductress?" Serena said.

"I've always known," Justin said, reaching across the table and taking Chloe's hand, drawing her eyes to his. "Her intimate secrets don't need to be seen to be felt. She needs only to decide who deserves to feel them."

He was no longer looking at her like he wanted to devour her. He looked like he wanted to climb across the table and hold her in his arms, to protect her from her own embarrassment. That look was even more powerful and special than all the others put together.

THE AFTERNOON PASSED in a blur of meetings, phone calls, and ticking off her to-do list, none of which dampened the high Chloe had been on all day. By the time the Wickeds arrived for a tour of the facility, she was nervous *and* excited to show them around. She wasn't surprised that Rob, Reba, Conroy, *and* Ginger had shown up with Mike, and she wasn't even surprised that Justin had come with them. But she was a little surprised that Tank had come along. While Justin stuck by his grandfather's side, Tank took up the rear of the group. He was taller than all of the men, and his watchful eyes took everything in. He didn't say much, though he'd nodded his approval when she'd shown them the separate wings of the facility.

"Let me show you the courtyard," Chloe said as they turned down the hall that led outside.

Agnes Berger's grandson, Kent, was pushing her wheelchair through the doors that led to the patio. Chloe felt bad that she'd already been pulled aside by a few residents who simply wanted to chat while she was giving the Wickeds their tour, but Justin's family seemed to understand, and she'd tried to make their conversations quick. Agnes was in her nineties and Chloe had noticed that she'd become noticeably frailer over the past few months. Chloe didn't know how much time she had left with Agnes, so she took a moment for a brief hello.

"Hi, Agnes, Kent. It's good to see you getting out to enjoy this beautiful weather."

Agnes reached for Chloe's hand, as she always did, and said, "Kent took me to see the gardens earlier. You know, he's still single, and he's staying for dinner if you'd like to join us."

Kent looked at her apologetically.

Chloe received offers like that often from the residents. Luckily, the men who were offered up were kind about their elderly relatives' matchmaking. "Thank you, Agnes. You know how much I like Kent, but actually, this is my boyfriend, Justin, and his family. I'm giving them a tour of the facility." She motioned to Justin.

"It's nice to meet you," Justin said warmly.

"Oh goodness. I'm sorry," Agnes exclaimed. "I hadn't heard the news. I'll be sure to tell my lady friends that you're spoken for." She pointed a shaky finger at Justin and said, "You're a lucky man, Justin. We adore Chloe, so be good to her." She lowered her hand and her gaze moved to the rest of his family. "I have lived here for several years, and there's no place I'd rather be. Chloe is always making sure we have new things to do, and we're well taken care of. We'll let you get back to your tour."

Kent nodded kindly as he pushed her wheelchair past the group.

"I bet that happens a lot," Reba said to Chloe as they continued down the hall. "It's not surprising. It's evident how much you're appreciated here."

"Thank you. I'm lucky to have a job I love, working with people I enjoy. I get to plan new programs all the time. Did Madigan tell you that we worked together to prepare a proposal for a puppetry program?"

"Yes. She is excited about it," Reba said.

"She's been a tremendous help. We're crossing our fingers in hopes of getting funding approved for a trial program." Chloe pushed the button on the wall by the glass doors, and the doors to the courtyard opened. The late-afternoon sun cast shadows over the courtyard, where residents were playing cards and other games. "This is one of my favorite places. As you can see, our residents enjoy it, too. Our yoga instructor, Emery Masters, is a good friend of mine. When the weather is warm enough, she teaches right out there by the big oak tree." She pointed across the lawn.

"I won't be doing any yoga, but I might sit up here and watch the *show*," Mike said with a chuckle.

"*Pops.*" Rob shook his head.

"Not everyone likes to do yoga," Chloe said. "If you enjoy taking walks, we have paved paths throughout the property, and as you can see, there are always games available."

"That sounds great, doesn't it, Poppy?" Reba asked.

"Sure," Mike answered. He said something under his breath to Justin and Tank, who both grinned.

Ginger nudged Chloe and said, "You have to watch Mike around women *and* card tables. My husband's road name is *Con*, and it has got nothing to do with the shortening of his given name and everything to do with the cardsharping his father taught him when he was young."

Mike gave Ginger a sideways glance. "Don't go getting me in trouble when I haven't done anything yet."

"*Yet* is the operative word," Conroy said, crossing his arms and lowering his chin to give Mike a serious stare. "You can't swindle people here, Pops."

Mike said, "*Swindle* is a harsh word, son."

"Not for you it's not," Rob said.

"We have a few shifty card players here that we keep our eyes on." Chloe motioned to a table across the courtyard, where two longtime residents of LOCAL, Nelson Byer and Robert Crumptin, were playing checkers. Nelson winked at Chloe.

"It looks like you have a fan, Chloe," Reba said.

"Nelson is known for flirting *and* for card trickery. He and Mike will get along just fine." She squared her shoulders, looking at Mike as she said, "But I'm sure you'll respect our other residents and play *fairly*. Or you'll have *me* to deal with."

"My girl's tough, Gramps. You'd better listen to her," Justin said.

As Justin and his family looked around the courtyard, Chloe

stopped by Nelson and Robert's table. "Good afternoon, gentlemen. Are you enjoying this lovely weather?"

"I'm enjoying beating my friend in checkers," Nelson said.

Chloe said, "It's good to see you playing something other than cards for a change."

"Figured I'd wrangle a few bucks out of the guys at the card table next and maybe take you to dinner with my winnings." Nelson waggled his brows.

She patted his arm and said, "You have a long enough list of lady friends waiting their turn for a dinner date with you. Enjoy the game, gentlemen."

Chloe wanted to give Justin and his family time to talk among themselves. Reba and Ginger were gazing out at the grounds, and Justin and the men were talking on the other side of the courtyard. She studied the men for a moment. Tank stood with his thick, tattooed arms crossed over his leather vest, chin low, jaw tight, dark eyes as serious as Rob's, who stood next to him in a matching stance. Justin and Conroy appeared far more relaxed as they chatted with Mike. Mike, on the other hand, looked to be hovering someplace between the harsh stances of Tank and Rob and the easygoing natures of Conroy and Justin. Mike's face was serious, but whatever Justin was saying brought hints of happiness. Conroy laughed loudly, and Justin laughed, too, his eyes suddenly catching Chloe's. Justin winked, and a thrill skated through her. She did a quick visual sweep of the courtyard to make sure the residents weren't watching her, and then she discreetly blew him a kiss.

Ginger and Reba sauntered over, following her gaze across the courtyard to the men.

"Rob and Tank are so serious," Chloe said. "Do you think there's something about the facility that they didn't like?"

"No," Reba reassured her. "It's just who they are."

"Tank has always been serious, but he hasn't been the same since we lost his younger sister, Ashley," Ginger explained. "It was a long time ago, but they were close."

"I'm so sorry for your loss."

Ginger said warmly, "Thank you, honey. Losing Ash changed us all, but Tank became even more protective of the people in his life. He joined the firehouse shortly after we lost her, and he's been on a mission to save everyone around him ever since." Ginger nodded toward the men and said, "Like Justin, Tank and Mike have a special bond. I don't want to think about what will happen to those two when we lose Mike."

"Let's hope that doesn't happen anytime soon," Chloe said. "I thought Tank was just broody, but now I see there's much more to it."

"Oh, he is broody," Ginger said, gazing lovingly at Tank.

"I've always said that Tank should have been Rob's son," Reba said, looking at the two men. "And that Zander and Justin should have been Conroy's."

"Not Justin," Chloe said. "I think he's always needed to be exactly where he was with your family. He told me how everyone has been there for him. This might sound a little strange coming from me, but thank you, both of you, for raising Justin to be the man he is. I've never been with someone like him before. I can tell him anything, and I know that if ever I feel overwhelmed, or like I'm standing on the edge of a cliff, he'll be there to soothe my worries or catch me if I fall."

Chapter Twenty

JUSTIN WAS SURE there was some kind of sin in staring at his girlfriend's ass as they followed her back toward the lobby after the tour. And if that was a sin, then thinking about absconding with her so he could have his way with her in any one of the offices they'd passed would definitely get him a ticket straight to hell. But he didn't care. Chloe was always a vision of sexiness, but seeing her in control and taking charge of her professional domain had blown him away—and turned him on. Then again, just about everything she did blew him away and turned him on. Today's tour had given him a whole new level of appreciation and understanding of just how much responsibility Chloe had on her shoulders and how eloquently she handled it.

Tank nudged him, snapping him from his thoughts as they entered the lobby.

"I have to say, Chloe, I'm impressed. I wasn't sold on the idea of Mike moving out of our house," Reba admitted. "But now I can see that he could have a much fuller life here, with people closer to his own age."

"A lot of people have the wrong impression about facilities like ours. They get scared when they hear terms like *assisted living* and think it's the beginning of the end, when really, for many of our residents it's the beginning of a new adventure. I'm glad you enjoyed the tour and had a chance to see for yourselves how wonderful LOCAL is," Chloe said sweetly. "Before I get the information packets I mentioned earlier, do you have any other questions?"

"When can I move in?" Mike asked.

Chloe's gaze softened. "As much as I'd love for you to move in tomorrow, what I'd really like is for you to take some time and think about it. This is a big decision for you and your family. You should probably discuss the pros and cons to be sure it's the right move for everyone. But I'll hold a room with your name on it, don't you worry."

Conroy looked at Preacher, and Preacher gave an almost imperceptible nod. Conroy said, "You've done a wonderful job of covering everything, Chloe, and it was nice to see how much everyone here appreciates you."

"Yes, it was," Reba agreed.

A hint of embarrassment washed over Chloe's face, and just as quickly, she schooled her expression, slipping right back into professional mode, and said, "Thank you. I'll just pop into my office and grab those information packets. I'll only be a minute or two."

As she walked away, Preacher said, "What do you think, Pops?"

"I think Chloe really knows her stuff, and Maverick ought to put a ring on that woman's finger," Mike said.

"Whoa. *What?*" Justin looked at his grandfather. "Since when are you a matchmaker?"

Mike's face pinched with irritation. "Don't look at me like I've lost my mind, Maverick. You know I fell in love with Hilda the day I met her, and I was just a kid."

Preacher laughed. "He said the same thing to me about putting a ring on Reba's finger when I met her. I was in Maryland at the time, and he'd only heard about her over the phone."

"I didn't need to see the woman who had changed my boy's world," Mike said gruffly. "Everything I needed to know was in your voice, son."

"He said the same thing to me when Ginger came into my life." Conroy put his arm around Ginger and kissed her cheek. "And the old man was right."

"Oh, Poppy, you might have a knack for matchmaking, but I don't think Justin and Chloe are in a rush," Reba said. "What did you think of the facilities?"

Justin was thankful she'd taken the conversation in a different direction. The last thing he wanted was for Chloe to catch wind of his grandfather's thoughts and run for the hills. He had no doubt that they were meant to be together, and he was pretty sure she felt the same way, but he wasn't ready to risk it.

Tank cleared his throat, and Justin followed his gaze to Chloe standing outside her office with Alan Rogers. Justin cursed under his breath. He didn't like how close the pompous prick was standing to her. Alan's chest looked like it was touching the back of Chloe's shoulder as they studied a document.

Alan's eyes shifted to Justin, and a smug grin settled across his face.

Fuck this. Justin threw his shoulders back and strode over to them with Tank on his heels.

Chloe looked up as they approached and flashed an effervescent smile. "Justin, sorry, I was just going over something with

Alan. Alan, you know Justin. This is his cousin, Tank."

Alan gave Tank a quick once-over, distaste rising in his eyes as he said, "Are you boys doing work here?"

"Wha…? *No.*" Chloe looked apologetically at Justin and Tank and said, "I just finished giving their families a tour of the facilities. Their grandfather is considering moving here. I'll introduce you to them."

That smug grin rose again as Alan said, "I'd like that." He put a proprietary hand on Chloe's lower back as they returned to Justin's family.

Justin gritted his teeth, his hands curling into fists.

"What the fuck?" Tank said under his breath.

"He's her boss, and a fucking prick," Justin said for Tank's ears only as Chloe introduced Alan to their families.

Alan shook Conroy's hand and said, "I'm sure our Chloe has given you a thorough tour."

Our Chloe my ass. Justin fumed. Earlier that morning, Blaine had delivered the plans for Alan's patio to Alan's wife, and he'd said that Alan definitely wore the pants in that family. Alan's wife had called him *five* times in the hour Blaine was there, running every little thing by him rather than making the decisions herself. Justin didn't like a man that controlling anywhere near Chloe, and he sure as hell hated the prick's hand on her back.

"I'll leave you in Chloe's capable hands." Alan leaned close to Chloe's ear and lowered his voice to say, "Come to my office when you're done and we'll finish our conversation."

Chloe agreed; then she turned her attention back to Justin's family, giving them the packets she'd retrieved from her office. "These cover all of the information we discussed in more detail. Take your time looking them over, and feel free to call me with any questions."

She walked them out, and while she was busy talking with Mike, Con, and Preacher, Reba sidled up to Justin, guiding him away from the others. She kept one hand on his arm as she said, "Breathe, sweet boy. I saw the way that man looked at you and Tank. He looked at Rob the same way. The world is full of judgmental men like Alan Rogers. Do *not* let him get under your skin. We don't hide who we are, and we don't allow ignorant people to make us feel small, so let it go, honey."

"I'm not pissed about that," Justin said angrily. "I deal with douchebags like him all the time. I don't like how close he got to Chloe."

"Oh, honey," she said empathetically. "You are just like your father. You want to protect the woman who crawled beneath your skin and nestled in for the long haul. Chloe is *yours*, baby. We all see it in the way she looks at you."

"I'm not *jealous*, Mom. The guy just rubs me the wrong way."

"This is all so new for you. But, baby, trust me, when we're looking through a cloud of emotions, we don't always see things clearly. Chloe is a smart woman. Confidence practically oozes out of her pores. If she felt uneasy about that man, or anyone else, I'm sure she would stand up for herself. Look at me, sweetheart."

Justin met her gaze.

"Remember what I said. When it comes to matters of the heart, not everything is as it appears. Be careful there, honey."

"I'm being careful, and I know damn well she can protect herself, but she shouldn't have to."

"Those words could have come right out of your father's mouth." Reba touched his hand and said, "Come on, sweetie.

Your girlfriend just gave us a beautiful tour. Let it go now and tell her how spectacular she is."

Justin bided his time as everyone thanked Chloe. When his family headed to their vehicles, he hung back to talk with her, and Tank took up residence a few feet away. He was sure his ever-watchful cousin was making sure he didn't do something stupid like fly off the handle at Alan. As much as Justin would like to give Alan a piece of his mind, Reba's warning had stuck with him. But that didn't mean he wasn't fuming at Alan for getting too touchy-feely with Chloe.

He looked at Tank, and in Tank's eyes he read his silent questions. *Are you going to be cool about this, or do you need backup?* Justin gave him his answer by saying, "I'll meet you at your shop in about an hour."

Tank nodded and said, "See you later, Chloe."

"Bye, Tank." As Tank headed to his bike, Chloe said, "I think that went well, don't you?"

"Yeah. Great. Thank you for taking so much time with us." Justin was in no mood for small talk.

"Are you getting more of your tattoo done this afternoon?" Chloe asked.

"Yeah. Listen, Chloe, I don't like that Rogers guy sticking so close to you."

She rolled her eyes. "I know. He's a close talker. It's just who he is."

"You sure it's not more than that? Blaine went to deliver the patio designs to Alan's wife today, and he got the sense that he was a pretty controlling guy. I don't like him touching you."

"Touching me? He didn't touch me."

"His chest wasn't touching your back when you were look-ing at those papers by your office? He didn't put his hand on your back when you went to introduce him to my family?"

"I don't think so." Her brow furrowed, as if she were thinking about it. "He had some questions about my proposal for the puppeteering trial." Her eyes lit up and she said, "I'm really hoping he's going to approve the funding."

He wondered if Reba might have been right. Was he being overprotective? Not seeing things clearly? He had no fucking clue, because she was right about one thing. When Chloe looked at him with that spark of hope and happiness in her eyes, it clouded his vision. He wanted to see that look every minute of the day.

"Are we still going to see Shadow tonight?" she asked.

There it was again, that spark of light, overtaking his darkness. "Yeah. He's getting his stitches out today."

"Where are you going now?"

"Home to empty a dresser drawer for you."

"*Justin*..." she said softly, looking sweet, sexy, and adorable.

"Babe, you're there half the week. You need space." He reached for her hand, and she touched her fingertips to his, glancing over her shoulder at the entrance of LOCAL. She was so careful not to cross any lines when she was at work, which made him feel a little better about his worries over Alan. She was too aware and confident, and her job was too important to her for her to let *anyone* compromise it.

"Look at you," she said teasingly. "All ready to call the moving trucks."

"Just say the word and consider it done."

He needed to hold her, but he didn't want to do the wrong thing while she was at work, so he stepped closer, keeping his hands to himself. *He* had the right to be a close talker with her, and the hitch in her breath told him she loved it.

"You really kicked ass in there with my family."

"I enjoyed it." She licked her lips and said, "But it was hard to keep from touching you. I almost reached for your hand several times."

"Baby, I know your job is too important for you to risk holding my hand, but when you're not at work, I don't ever want you holding back from touching me. Seeing you take charge was hot as hell. I wanted to haul you into every office we passed, take you against the wall, and make you come so many times your legs would give out." He paused, letting that sink in. Her cheeks flushed, and desire simmered in her eyes. "And just when you caught your breath, when you thought you couldn't take another second of pleasure, I would have bent you over the desk and made good on the fantasies I've been having *all* damn day. Hell, baby, I cannot *wait* until tonight, when I can finally get my hands on you and make love to you six ways to Sunday."

"*Justin*—" rushed out like a plea.

He wanted to bottle that sound and carry it with him forever. "I'll see you tonight, sweet thing."

"*Justin!*" she whispered. "How am I supposed to go back in there with all *that* rattling around in my head?"

He shrugged one shoulder, looked down at the bulge in his jeans, and said, "Guess we're both in a pickle."

"*Geez.* You've ruined me for the rest of the day. Take your *pickle* and get out of here," she said a little breathlessly. She squared her shoulders, challenge rising in her eyes as she said, "Paybacks are hell, Mr. Wicked. Better watch your back."

As she stalked toward the entrance, Justin said, "I'd rather watch yours."

BY THURSDAY EVENING Chloe was so sexually frustrated, she was convinced she was being put to some sort of test. Either that, or she was being punished for having been consumed with such libidinous thoughts all freaking day. She'd had a heck of a time trying to cool off after seeing Justin earlier. She'd been forced to go into the ladies' room and run her hands under cold water for ten minutes before she could even *begin* to focus on anything other than Justin's office fantasies. Every time she'd seen a desk for the rest of the afternoon, his dirty words had seared through her mind and she'd become flushed and flustered. Meeting with Alan had been hell. She'd spent the whole time envisioning Justin bending her over the desk and taking her from behind. She'd had a fleeting thought about what Justin had said about Alan, but all her dirty fantasies had pushed it aside. At least the meeting had gone well, even if it had been difficult to concentrate. Alan had been impressed with the puppeteering proposal and suggested they meet again after July Fourth to finalize a trial period and budget.

She'd spent the rest of the day thinking about how to surprise Justin by being the one to take control in the bedroom. The problem was, the minute he got his hands or mouth on her, her mind always turned to dust. She'd finally come up with the perfect time to make her move, but to pull it off she would have to climb *way* outside her comfort zone.

She was so nervous and excited, she'd barely held it together tonight while they visited with Shadow. She'd tried to concentrate on Shadow, who was stitch-free and doing well, but it didn't help that Justin was looking at her like his naughty thoughts had been brewing all day, too.

After they left Shadow, her pulse sprinted with anticipation as Justin helped her into the truck and she watched him as he walked around the front to the driver's side. It was kind of ridiculous how much she enjoyed looking at him.

Justin climbed into the driver's seat and hauled her across the bench, as he'd been doing every time they'd taken his truck out lately, and took her in a deep, penetrating kiss that made her entire body sizzle and spark. She came away so turned on, for a split second she lost track of her plans. She fastened her seat belt, mentally going over them once again, getting more nervous with every thought. Justin started the engine, and when his piercing blue eyes hit hers, she mustered her courage to give back to the man who had already given her so much.

"Ready to go home, sexy girl? I believe I have a few promises to fulfill."

"*Mm-hm*," she managed.

He drove out to the main road, and she put her hand on his leg. Hoping she could pull this off without causing an accident, she moved her hand between his legs, stroking him through his jeans.

"Mm, *baby*," he said in a gravelly voice as she began kissing his neck.

He put his hand over hers, squeezing it tight around his erection. Lust zinged through her. She loved the feel of his hand on hers and the strength of his grip, but she wanted *control*, and it was too easy to give it up to him.

She pulled her hand out from beneath his and said, "Hands off, big boy. Tonight we play by *my* rules."

"Take *all* you want, sweet thing."

"Oh, I plan to. You just keep your eyes on the road and

your hands on the wheel."

She unbuttoned and unzipped his jeans and slipped her hand beneath his briefs, feeling his hot, hard flesh. He gritted his teeth. His hips rocked up, driving his shaft through her fist. She pressed her thighs together, but there was only one thing that would quell that ache. She unfastened her seat belt, shifting so she was lying on the bench, and lowered her mouth over that magical *thing*.

Justin inhaled sharply and ground out, "*Fuck.*"

The hunger in his voice spurred her on, and she stroked faster, squeezed tighter, and sucked harder. Taking control brought a rush of adrenaline, making her even bolder. "Don't come yet," she demanded. "I want you to come inside me."

"*Jesus,*" he panted out.

He grabbed her hip and held on tight as she teased and taunted him. She felt his thighs and abs flex, and his cock swelled within her hand.

"*Baby,*" he warned. "You're driving me fucking mad."

She withdrew his shaft from her mouth and licked all around the broad head. He gripped her hip tighter, cursing under his breath. She continued her oral assault, and his legs began to shake. He moaned, squeezing her hip so tight, she knew he was on the verge of coming. She had no idea how he was still driving.

"Hang on, baby," he said urgently.

The truck swung to the right. He sped up and made another fast turn. Then he grabbed her by the hair, lifting her mouth off his cock as he slammed the truck into park. It was a good thing he was thinking, because the force of his stop could have caused her to bite that baby off. She didn't know where they were, but she didn't need to because *he* did, and she knew he'd keep her safe. He cut the lights and crushed his mouth to hers as she went up on her knees. He pushed up her skirt and grabbed her bare ass, moaning into her mouth. Knowing Justin would get off when he found out her little secret, she'd taken off her underwear before leaving work. *Oh,* what his greedy sounds did to her! He pushed his seat back and shoved his jeans to his knees. His dark eyes bored into her as she straddled him. She sank down onto his cock, and her entire body cried out with delight. Their mouths came together in a feast of two starving people. They thrust and rocked, their sounds echoing off the windows as he groped her breasts and ass, and she touched him everywhere she could reach. He fisted his hands into her hair, kissing her so deeply her jaw stung. She felt untethered and *wild* as he put a hand between them, zeroing in on the bundle of nerves that had her whimpering into their kisses. She grabbed his shoulders, and her head fell back with a loud, needful moan as she rode him.

Needing to see his rapture, she forced her eyes open and lost herself in the carnal desires staring back at her. "Come with me," she pleaded.

She covered his mouth with hers, unable to stay apart a second longer. His arms circled her. His hips shot up as her inner muscles clamped down, and they abandoned all control, giving into the tidal waves of passion crashing over them.

He tore his mouth away and growled her name like a thunderous prayer, "*Chloe, Chloe, Chloe...*"

Three words hung on the edge of her tongue, vying for release, but she held them back, not wanting to be the first to say them.

He guided her mouth to his, kissing her slowly and tenderly, their frantic hearts slamming against their chests. He kissed her until their breathing calmed, and then he touched his forehead to hers, one arm wrapped protectively around her, his other hand cradling her head, keeping her close as he whispered, "*You...*" His voice trailed off. "I'm falling so hard for you, sweetheart. I never want to let go."

"Then don't" came straight from her heart.

Chapter Twenty-One

THE SOUNDS OF barks and cheery conversations filled the air Saturday afternoon at the Wicked Animal Rescue adoption event. The dogs that were rescued from the dogfighting ring were not up for adoption yet, but there were twenty-six other animals eagerly awaiting forever homes. Most of Justin's and Gunner's families had shown up to help. They'd spent the morning setting up, and now canopies and animal pens dotted the grounds. Balloons bobbed from strings tied to the registration table where Tori and Steph were handling applications. Dozens of people milled about, playing with the animals. The boards Chloe made for the animals were a big hit. She'd gotten along fabulously with Tori and Evie, and thanks to their efforts, the animals sported adorable blue bow ties and pink ribbons.

Justin watched Chloe accompanying another family to the registration desk as he walked a ten-year-old black-and-gray mastiff named Sampson. Chloe had been up at the crack of dawn eager to help, and she'd been going nonstop ever since. She'd even worn her dragonfly anklet for luck. She shook the hands of the people she was talking with, then scanned the property. When she saw Justin, she headed his way with an enthusiastic wave and that gorgeous smile that made him all kinds of happy.

"Come on, Sampson. Let's go see our girl."

The old dog lumbered beside him. Old dogs like Sampson didn't always get adopted, and more often than not, ended up as one of Gunner's pets. People were reluctant to bring an older animal into their home for fear of getting attached to a pet who might not have many years left. Those were the animals Justin had always been most drawn to, and this particular dog was one Chloe had fallen in love with the day he'd landed at the rescue earlier in the week.

"Hi," Chloe said, leaning in for a kiss. She crouched to love up Sampson and her smile faded. "Still no takers for our big boy?"

"Actually, a really cool couple is interested in him. They have another dog at home. After they've gone through the application process and passed a home visit, they'll take Sampson home for a trial run."

"That's wonderful. Do you hear that, Sampson? You're going to get a family *and* a sibling." She stood up, petting Sampson's head as the old dog leaned against her leg. He did that a lot with them, his way of giving hugs. "I'm happy for Sampson and for the family, but I'm going to miss him."

"I know you are, babe." Justin grabbed the belt loop on her pretty blue shorts, gently pulling her in for another kiss.

"Chloe!" Evie called out as she jogged toward them, her long dark hair flowing over her shoulders. "I saw you at the registration table. Did you get another application?"

"Yup. That makes nine," Chloe exclaimed. "They loved Sparky, the chihuahua mix. It's such a good feeling when you see the families and the animals connecting. How many applications does Baz have?" She and Baz were having a friendly competition over who could get the most applications. Chloe was giving him a run for his money.

"Ask him yourself." Evie pointed to Baz and Gunner, who were walking over from the registration table. "*Dr. Dimples* looks pretty sure of himself."

"I have a feeling those dimples open many doors for him," Chloe said. "Did you see those three girls wearing bikini tops and shorts that flocked to him when he was walking around with one of the kittens?"

"Oh, *please*. That's nothing new. Women have been flocking to him since birth." Evie reached down to pet Sampson and said, "And the rotten doctor eats it up."

"Man, you're harsh," Justin teased Evie, as he always did.

Evie had known Baz all his life, and she knew him as well as any of their siblings did. Baz was a good guy with a great personality, and Evie was right, women had always flocked to him. But Baz wasn't a pig. He had his fair share of women, but he also had bigger plans for himself than a lifetime of just getting laid. But he was coy about those plans and had never clued Justin in on any of the details.

"*Harsh?*" Evie put her hands on her hips and said, "He's a bigger flirt than Gunner. He just does it *non*verbally."

"All right, you've got me there," he said as Baz and Gunner joined them. He'd witnessed Baz getting women's phone numbers by doing nothing more than sharing glances across a crowded bar.

"That makes *ten* applications, thank you very much," Baz said, draping an arm around Evie. "Tori said Chloe has nine. Guess that makes me the *master* once again."

"The day is *not* over." Chloe looked around. "Aha! I see a family that looks like they need some help. I wouldn't get used to that *master* title if I were you, *Dimples*." She jogged toward a family looking over the dogs.

Evie grinned and said, "I *really* like her, Maverick."

"That makes two of us," Justin said, watching Chloe dazzle another couple.

"*Three* of us," Gunner chimed in. "Chloe's hired for *every* event from now on. She's killin' it, dude. And those boards she made are getting all sorts of attention."

"I'm sure she'd love to help out again." Justin scratched Sampson's head and said, "Have you guys seen Zan? I need to talk with him about something."

"No, but I'm sure he's coming to the Hog later." Baz crooked his arm tighter around Evie's neck, pulling her closer. "You're coming with me tonight, right, Eves?"

"Yup. Tank will be there, so you *know* I'll be there." Evie loved hanging out with Tank, which drove Baz crazy. She was one of the only people who could get Tank to say more than a few words.

Baz grumbled something that Justin couldn't hear, but whatever it was made Evie roll her eyes.

"Mav, are you and Chloe coming tonight?" Baz asked.

"Yeah. We're having dinner with Serena and Drake, and then we'll meet you guys in the bar." Serena and Drake had stopped by earlier with Emery and Dean. Emery and Dean had filled out an application for one of the dogs, but Serena and Drake had passed this time around. "Gunner, I think your old lady needs you." He nodded toward Steph, who was heading their way with Snowflake.

"Cut the shit. She's not my old lady." Gunner reached a hand toward Steph and said, "What's up, babe?" Gunner and Steph had always been close, but they'd become even closer

since Ashley's suicide.

Steph handed Gunner the kitten and said, "She's missing her daddy."

Gunner nuzzled the kitten's fur and said, "Did Mommy take good care of you?"

Steph rolled her eyes.

"Oh, don't tell me…" Evie said.

Justin followed her gaze to a dozen or so twentysomething females strutting up from the parking lot wearing bathing suits and beach cover-ups.

Evie glared at Gunner. "Did you put your posters up at the beaches again?"

Gunner had made posters for the last event featuring shirt-less pictures of himself holding puppies with WICKED ANIMAL RESCUE ADOPTION EVENT HOSTED BY GUNNER WICKED written across the top and PETTING ENCOURAGED written just above his knees. He'd put them up at several local beaches.

Gunner feigned innocence with a thoughtful expression and said, "Every animal needs a home. The more people that show up, the better." He high-fived Baz and said, "Looks like you're up, bro. Good luck."

"Don't you mean the more *half-naked girls* that show up the better for *you guys*?" Evie crossed her arms and said, "Maybe next time we'll get pictures of Steph, Tori, Sid, and me in bikinis holding kittens with the caption *Come Make Our Pussies Purr* and we'll put them up at beaches, gyms, and the surf shops."

"I'm in!" Steph said, flashing a *take that* look at Gunner and earning a glowering stare in return.

"Over my dead body," Baz said. At the same time, Justin and Gunner said, "No fucking way."

Evie rolled her eyes. "Y'all are ridiculous."

"Just protecting our girls. Wish me luck, Eves." Baz rubbed his hands together and said, "Your woman's going *down*, Justin."

"Only if I'm lucky," Justin said with a smirk. "Either way, she's going to slay your ass in this competition, bro."

"We'll see about that." Baz set his eyes on Evie and said, "Where's my luck, darlin'?"

"I'm rooting for Chloe," Evie said.

Baz walked away, flashing his puppy-dog eyes over his shoulder.

Evie hollered, "That doesn't work on me!"

Baz turned around and lifted his shirt, flexing his abs with an arrogant grin.

Evie scoffed. "In your dreams!"

"Way to break a dude's heart," Justin teased.

"*Please*...those eyes do not do for me what they do for other women," Evie said flatly.

"Baz reeled you in as his best friend using those puppy-dog eyes," Gunner reminded her.

Evie crouched by Sampson and loved him up as she said, "Biggest mistake of my life. That man is nothing but trouble, right, Sampson?" Sampson licked her face. "I should definitely stick to dogs."

LATER THAT EVENING at the Salty Hog, Chloe licked hot fudge from her dessert spoon, hoping Justin had caught her seductive intent—and Drake and Serena *hadn't*. She and Justin had been riding high after their fantastic afternoon, and though they'd gotten frisky in the shower before dinner, it had barely dimmed their desire. They'd been taunting each other through-out dinner, and Chloe was enjoying every second of it. Justin's hand was resting on her thigh. Her pulse quickened as his fingertips found their way to the hot spot between her legs. She stole a glance across the table at Serena and Drake, but they were busy making googly eyes at each other.

Chloe tried to concentrate on finishing her story about the day's events. "I beat Baz by *three* applications, but you know, it was all in good"—Justin applied pressure between her legs, and her thoughts stumbled—"um…"

"*Fun?*" Justin said coyly.

"*Very*" came out before Chloe could stop it. *Shootshootshoot!* She squeezed her legs together and quickly added, "I'm *thrilled* to have found potential homes for so many animals."

Serena laughed and said, "It is *thrilling*, isn't it?"

Gulp! Had Serena known what Justin was doing the whole time? Chloe had never had that type of camaraderie with Serena, and she felt her cheeks heating. Thankfully, before she could stumble any further, Justin removed his hand from between her legs and put his arm around her.

He kissed her temple and said, "Everything is thrilling with Chloe."

"It's that Mallery blood." Drake looked hungrily at Serena and said, "They're thrilling, determined, fiery."

"Damn right," Serena said.

Justin flagged down the waitress and said something to her that Chloe couldn't hear. After she walked away, he said, "I think Baz learned his lesson about going head-to-head with Chloe. My girl doesn't give up."

"Like someone else I know, Mr. Year and a Half." Chloe pressed her lips to his, thanking her lucky stars he'd never given up on them.

"I'd have waited even longer." He slid a hand to the nape of her neck and kissed her.

"I think we'd better get our check before you two light the table on fire," Serena teased.

"The check is already taken care of," Justin said, rising to his feet and bringing Chloe up beside him. He rolled his shoulders back, looking hot in his leather vest.

Chloe knew exactly when that vest with the Dark Knights' patches had gone from being a little scary to something she loved seeing him in. It was that night on the beach when he'd told her the truth of who they were and what they'd done for him. Now she was proud to be a part of that world with him.

Drake reached for Serena's hand and said, "Dude, we were going to treat tonight."

"Guess you'll have to catch it next time," Justin said as they made their way toward the stairs.

Next time. Chloe loved the sound of that.

Justin kept his arm around her as they headed upstairs. He lowered his voice and said, "Are you doing okay? Do you have any bad feelings about being here?"

"I'm better than okay, but thank you for worrying," she said, grateful he remembered that she hadn't wanted Serena to know about what had happened in the parking lot all those years ago. "Did I tell you that I've never gone on a double date with Serena before?"

He flashed a wolfish grin. "You mean I popped your sister-double-date cherry?" He held her close as they stepped into the loud, crowded bar.

"They have a band and dancing!" Serena said over the loud music. "Chloe, why haven't we come here before?"

Justin said, "Because she wasn't with *me*, and she didn't want guys drooling over you two without Colton there to shut things down if they got out of hand."

There he went again, protecting her in a way she truly appreciated.

"You told him about your deal with Colton?" Serena asked.

Chloe had mentioned it during one of their long evening talks. "He has a way of getting all sorts of things out of me."

"And *into* you," Serena said with a laugh.

"No more drinks for you, Supergirl," Drake said, pulling her into his arms.

"Aw, come on. My sister finally has a man in her life she's crazy about. *Look* how happy they are." Serena waved toward them. "When you're that happy, you *need* to be teased. It's a rite of passage."

Chloe couldn't stop smiling and not only because Justin had just whispered something dirty in her ear, but also because she'd never had this with Serena before, and it *did* feel like a rite of passage. One she was proud to endure with Justin.

"There she is. The woman of the hour," Reba said as she and Mads came through the crowd. Reba and Rob had been at the adoption event for most of the afternoon, but Madigan had missed it because of a puppeteering job. Reba hugged Chloe and said, "You're the talk of the Hog tonight, sweetheart."

"Me?" Chloe glanced at Justin, who looked as surprised as she was.

"Yes *you*," Reba said.

Madigan said, "No one has ever gotten more applications than Baz."

"Nobody dangles a challenge in front of my sister and wins," Serena said. "Chloe might look like the poised, professional type, but she's got the fangs of a viper and the claws of a wolverine, and she knows when to use them."

Reba laughed and said, "Your *sister?*"

"Yes," Chloe said, realizing she'd forgotten to introduce them. "Reba this is my younger sister, Serena. Serena, this is Justin's mom, Reba."

"It's nice to meet you," Serena said.

Reba hugged her and said, "Aren't you a sweet one. We're going to have to watch our boys around you."

"I've got that covered." Drake stepped forward and extended his hand. "I'm Drake Savage, Serena's husband. It's a pleasure to meet you."

"You sure do have it covered, you handsome thing. Put that hand away before you get yourself in trouble." Reba embraced him and said, "The pleasure is all mine."

"Stop hogging the hugs. It's so good to see you again, Serena." Madigan hugged her and then said to Drake, "I'm Mads, Maverick's sister, and you're getting a hug, too."

As she hugged Drake, Justin said, "Mads is a little pushy."

"So is my wife. It's all good." Drake clapped a hand on Justin's shoulder and said, "Sounds like I need to get used to hearing your road name around here."

"That and probably a whole lot of other names that are not as nice," Justin said.

"He's *joking.* Why don't you kids go sit down and enjoy yourselves? I need to catch up with Ginger." Reba pointed to a long table by the windows where Steph, Marly, Tori, Sid, Evie, and Justin's cousins and brothers were sitting with Mike—which surprised Chloe—Rob, Conroy, and a handful of other guys wearing vests with Dark Knights' patches. "I'll send one of the girls over to take your drink orders."

They followed Madigan to the table. Rob, Conroy, and Mike pushed to their feet and came around to greet them.

Madigan held her hands up and said, "Eyes over here boys and girls. I'm doing this introduction once and once only. Y'all know Chloe, Maverick's old lady, and I'm sure some of you know her sister. But for those who don't, this is Serena and her husband, Drake Savage."

There was a round of *hellos* and waves. After Rob, Conroy, and Mike had a chance to shake Drake's hand and embrace Serena, they settled back into their seats.

As the rest of them found chairs, Gunner stole a fry off Steph's plate and said, "Chloe, your drinks are on me tonight."

Baz winked at Chloe, then said, "What the hell, dude? I never got free drinks."

"If you were as hot as Chloe, maybe that'd be different." Gunner laughed, along with most of the guys, and he reached for another fry.

Steph smacked his hand and said, "No more fries for you. Baz is every bit as hot as Chloe."

Gunner turned to Sid, sitting on his other side eating a burger and fries. She covered her plate and said, "Sister solidarity, sorry."

Gunner grumbled, "Traitors."

Baz blew kisses to Steph and Sid, and Gunner sneered at him. That started a litany of hilarious remarks. Chloe was laughing along with everyone else as Leah approached the table. Her mass of brownish-red corkscrew curls hung around her heavily freckled face like a lion's mane. Her skin was the color of sweet cream, and she had a slightly flat nose and full lips.

"Can I get y'all something?" Leah asked with a slight Southern drawl. As she moved around the table jotting down orders, her eyes moved warily beneath her thick auburn brows.

When she reached Zander, he flashed a cocky grin and dragged his eyes down her body. "What I want isn't on the menu."

Leah's eyes turned serious and studied Zander's face. Zander sat up straighter, puffing out his chest with an expression that conveyed, *Oh yeah, baby, you know you want me.*

"*Jesus,*" Justin snapped. He reached over and swatted Zander on the back of the head.

Zander ran a hand over the same spot and said, "Dude! Don't touch the hair."

"Don't be an ass," Blaine said. He nudged Marly. "Women don't like asses, right, Mar?"

"Don't get me involved." Marly picked up her drink and said, "I love a good ass in tight jeans."

Blaine shook his head.

"See? Women like my ass." Zander rolled his shoulders back and winked at Leah.

Leah's stoic expression didn't change. She was still studying Zander's face like she was trying to figure him out.

"*Alexander.*" Rob stared Zander down and shook his head.

"Aw, come on, Preach." Zander pushed to his feet and jokingly said, "Tell 'em, Leah. You like my ass, right?" He turned around and slapped his back pocket, grinning over his shoulder.

"It's not bad, but I've seen better," Leah said evenly, brows knitted. "Maybe Zeke can help you study up on better butt exercises."

Everyone laughed, except Zander, whose grin faltered. He eyed Zeke, and Zeke held his palms up, shaking his head.

Leah looked down at her order pad and said, "Who's next?"

Tank said, "I'll take whiskey, neat."

Leah lifted her eyes to his, and the little color she had drained from her face. "I'll go...I'll get...Be right back with those drinks." She scurried off toward the bar.

"Geez, Tank. What'd you do to her?" Madigan asked.

Tank looked offended. "*Me?* I didn't do shit. It was Zander."

"No, that was definitely you," Blaine said. "That poor girl looked scared."

"Yeah, dude. It wasn't me. She totally digs my ass." Zander chuckled.

"You must have done *something* at some point," Steph added.

Tank scoffed. "I ordered a drink. What'd you want me to do? The shit Zan does?" His voice rose an octave as he said, "*Hey, little lady, want to suck my dick?*" Uproarious laughter erupted, and in his normal voice, Tank said, "Sorry, dude, but I'm not an asshole."

"Dude, I'm not an asshole," Zander said. "I'm *playful*."

Rob glowered at Zander. "You just about crossed the line with that little gal, Zan. Watch it next time." His eyes shifted to Zeke, who gave him a confirmatory nod.

"In Tank's defense," Chloe said carefully. "He's a big guy, and with all those piercings and tattoos, he can be intimidating. Tank, maybe you could smile at her sometime."

Justin leaned closer and said, "Babe, that steel don't crack."

"Oh, come on. Tank has a great smile," Evie urged.

Baz gave Evie a sideways look.

"It's *true*," Madigan agreed. "Show 'em, Tanky."

Tank bared his teeth, making a low growl. The guys chuckled, and all the girls spoke at once.

"Oh my *God*," Evie exclaimed.

Madigan pointed at Tank and said, "Don't *ever* do that again. Especially around Leah."

Steph said, "Yeah, save that for the dogfight guys."

"Your bed will be empty forever if that's your come-get-me smile," Serena chimed in.

Serena's comment spurred a ruckus of the other guys showing their come-get-me smiles and loudly debating the pros and cons of each.

Madigan pushed to her feet and said, "Come on, girls! Let's dance!"

All the girls got up, except Sid. Marly and Madigan each took an arm and pulled her up despite her complaints.

"Go get 'em, beautiful," Gunner said to Sid, who rolled her eyes.

Zander and Baz began chanting, "Sidney! Sidney!"

Chloe got up, and Justin pulled her down for a quick kiss. "Show them how it's done, sweet thing." He smacked her butt, and she followed the girls to the dance floor.

The band was great, and they danced to several songs Chloe had never heard before. Reba and Ginger joined them on the dance floor, giving Chloe a chance to introduce Ginger to Serena. She greeted Serena with the same welcoming embrace Reba had. Reba and Ginger knew how to work a dance floor. They had great moves and they weren't afraid to show them off, which made Chloe like them even more. They joked and talked about the guys' banter, finding boyfriends for the single girls, and the adoption event. The list went on, and Chloe enjoyed every second of it. She loved the group of close-knit friends who were starting to feel like family.

Conroy and Rob broke through the crowd and swept their wives into their arms, slow dancing to the fast song. The love in their eyes was tangible, reminding Chloe of the way Justin looked at her. She glanced at Justin, catching him watching her with a protective *and* lascivious look in his eyes. She had no idea how he could show both emotions at once, but she loved it. She turned up the heat on her dance moves, just for him.

Serena followed her gaze, dancing close so her words hit Chloe's ears only. "He's mad about you."

"I know," Chloe said, taking stock in how good it felt to hear her sister say it.

"They all are, Chloe. You *fit* here. I know you love our friends from Bayside, but I've never seen you look so comfortable in a big group like this. I'm seeing parts of you I've never seen before, and I've known you my whole life. It's like you were treading water, and Justin pulled you out and set you free."

Chloe stopped dancing, meeting Serena's gaze. She hadn't been living underwater. She'd been living in the shadows of her past.

Serena leaned closer and said, "I think you found your family."

Family. Chloe choked up. She looked at Justin, who was rising to his feet along with Drake and several of the other guys. They strode toward the dance floor, shoulder to shoulder, with Tank taking up the rear. Justin *felt* like family.

"What a beautiful sight they are," Chloe said, drawing Serena's eyes to her husband, who was walking beside Justin with his eyes locked on Serena.

Serena grabbed Chloe's hand and said, "How many years did we dream of being this happy?"

"I'd say forever, but our forevers have just begun. We

dreamed of it for a very long time, Serena." As the guys began pairing up with the girls, she said, "Now it's our turn to live it."

Justin bowed his head to speak to Tank, their ever-present steady sentry, who stood with his arms crossed, eagle eyes taking everything in from the edge of the dance floor. Madigan ran over and tried to tug Tank onto the dance floor, but he was immovable. Justin said something as he patted Tank's arm; then he headed for Chloe.

"Hello, beautiful." He swept her into his arms, his loving eyes holding her captive as they danced.

"What took you so long, Mr. Wicked?"

"I was savoring the view of my favorite girl, but you were busy checking out *other* views." He kissed her softly and whispered, "The only man you should be looking at is the one holding you in his arms."

She knew he wasn't jealous. He knew she was crazy about him, and he was letting her know he saw *everything*. Chloe was okay with that. She wound her arms around his neck and said, "I disagree."

His brows slanted in confusion.

She leaned closer, never missing a step of the dance as she said, "When you're falling for a man, you fall for his family and friends, too, his *world*. It's perfectly reasonable for me to take pleasure in the happiness of your family and friends."

"In that case, darlin', you can look your fill." He nipped at her lower lip and said, "But are you ever going to stop fucking with me?"

She whispered, "Probably not."

He lowered his lips to hers, taking her in an exquisitely long kiss. When the band stopped playing, everyone else left the dance floor. Chloe moved to follow them, but Justin held her tighter.

"Not yet," he said softly.

An army of Dark Knights surrounded the dance floor, arms crossed. Just beyond them, Serena and the girls were huddled together whispering behind their hands.

"*Justin*, everyone is looking at us," she whispered urgently. "We should go sit down."

"I think that would be a really bad idea. They're about to play our song."

Delight and curiosity bloomed inside her. "We don't have a song."

"We do now."

Justin looked at the stage, where Zander stood at the microphone holding a guitar, and he nodded. Zander began strumming the guitar, singing a slow rendition of "Uptown Girl." Chloe felt her cheeks flame and buried her face in his chest. Her heart was beating so fast, she thought it might break free just to get to him.

"Eyes up here, Uptown Girl."

He kissed her forehead, and she met his elated gaze. "You're crazy!"

"Crazy about *you*, sweet cheeks. I have a feeling we're going to be spending a lot of time here. Take a good hard look at all those men. They will always keep you and Serena safe, even when I'm not around."

She choked up again, and they continued swaying, though she no longer heard the music. The emotions in Justin's eyes drowned out everything else.

"I hope I've found an acceptable way to stake my claim."

Her emotions reeled, and nervous laughter bubbled out with her words. "You definitely did. Now kiss me before I climb you like a tree right here in front of everyone."

His eyes went dark as midnight as he lowered his lips to hers. Cheers, whistles, and whoops rang out. The band started playing the song at normal speed, and friends and family poured onto the dance floor. Chloe added another night to her best nights ever list. With Justin in her life, she had a feeling the list would be never-ending. And there in his arms, with the beat of the music pulsing between them, surrounded by the people they loved most, she gave herself over to the sweetest kiss she'd ever experienced—and to the man she adored.

Chapter Twenty-Two

THE WARM DAYS of June gave way to an even balmier July. It had been eight blissful days and seven sexy nights since that wonderful night at the Salty Hog. Busy days had led to full evenings for Chloe and Justin. They tried to visit with Shadow and Sampson as often as they could. Sampson's adoptive family was working with Sidney to try to acclimate him to their current pet. Justin continued working on the sculpture for the rally, and Chloe made an album of Gracie for Starr, as promised. Chloe was also working with Madigan to flesh out a long-term puppetry program in hopes of the funding for the trial being approved. Chloe and Justin had made time for breakfast with their friends at Summer House one morning, and last night they'd met Serena and Drake at Gavin and Harper's for dinner. She'd enjoyed spending the evening with them. But what she'd enjoyed even more was when they'd gotten back to Justin's house and he'd led her around to the deck, where they'd danced beneath the stars, just as they'd done a month earlier at Chloe's cottage. It was another unforgettable night. It didn't matter how busy or tired they were, they ended each night tangled up in each other's arms.

While Justin was working in his studio the afternoon of July

Fourth, Chloe headed to her cottage to pick up a few things. "Seriously, Serena, life is more beautiful than ever," she said through her Bluetooth. "We spent the *whole* morning in bed."

"No way. You've never slept in. Not even when we were kids."

"I know, and I learned something about myself now that weekends have become our time. I always told myself I liked getting a jump on the day and staying one step ahead. But after spending lazy mornings lying in Justin's arms talking, making love, or just *being*, I think I've always been *running*, afraid to slow down and just enjoy life. I've never felt safe enough to slow down before. Does that make sense to you?"

"*Yes.* You were always taking care of me or planning things for work or making something for someone. I'm glad Justin's got you loosening up and letting yourself relax. He really sees who you are, Chloe, even better than I do. He's bringing out parts of you that you had to shove down deep in order to survive. Not all guys are like that."

"I realize that. I got lucky," Chloe said as she parked in front of her cottage.

"I'm happy for you, but I'm not gonna lie, sis," Serena said. "It feels weird to spend the Fourth without you." Serena was spending the Fourth on Drake's boat with their friends from Bayside, and Chloe could hear them chattering in the background.

Chloe had a fleeting pang of guilt about choosing to spend the evening with Justin instead of their friends, but it disappeared as quickly as it had come. This was a first for her and Justin, and they deserved it. "I know. I'm sorry. It is for me, too. But I'm excited to watch the fireworks alone with Justin tonight. Please don't hate me for it."

"I could never hate you, and I don't blame you one bit. But I *do* have to say this." She began singing, "Chloe and Justin sitting in a tree, K-I-S-S-I-N-G—"

Chloe climbed out of the car, laughing as her sister sang the silly song. She felt like she hadn't been home in a month. She and Justin usually went back and forth between houses. But lately Justin had put in more time sculpting and Chloe had projects set up at his place, so it had been easier to stay there. Although they'd spent Wednesday night at her place since Justin had attended church.

"How many drinks have you had?" Chloe asked as she headed up the walk.

"Only two. It's gorgeous on the water. In all seriousness, are you going to get matching tattoos and start driving a motorcycle?"

"*No.*" Chloe laughed. "But if I were to get a tattoo, I'd have Tank do it. You should see the angel he tattooed on Justin's back to honor his mother. He finished it this week, and it's gorgeous." She unlocked her cottage door and said, "Want to hear something weird?"

"Sure. I love *weird*."

"You know my cottage has always meant *everything* to me."

"Yeah…?"

"I used to feel like being home was my reward at the end of every day. But I just got to my cottage to pick up a few things, and it doesn't feel that special anymore."

"That's not weird. You're spending almost every night having crazy monkey sex in your secluded love nest overlooking a pond with a man who treats you like gold. That love nest has become your home."

Chloe looked around her cottage at the fine furniture and

color-coordinated decorations that had once meant so much to her and she said, "I don't think it's that. I think I'm having an epiphany. I worked *so* hard to buy my cottage, to have nice things, and to create a perfect life. It took years of planning and saving money, being careful with every penny I spent. Then this incredible guy finally breaks down my walls enough for me to let him into that life, and in a *month* he shows me that I hadn't been living a perfect life at all. I'd been stacking things in my favor, trying to prove with material things that I'm not Mom. It's like I was *still* trying to prove that I survived our childhood."

"Wow, you're so much deeper than me," Serena teased.

"Shut up. I'm being serious."

"I know you are. I was, too. You *are* deeper than me. You always have been. You're my responsible big sister. It's your *job* to be more of a thinker and mine to be…*me*. I don't think any of that is bad. What did you go home for anyway? Your mail goes to a post-office box, and you must have half your closet at Justin's by now."

"I do," she said. It was an amazing feeling seeing their lives blending together in so many ways. "I'm making him a present for our one-month anniversary, and I needed some of my crafting supplies."

"Seriously? Your *one-month* anniversary? Chloe Mallery, have you gone all swoony girl on me?" Serena laughed.

"I can't help it," she confessed a little giddily. "I've never allowed myself to be a swoony girl, but with Justin it's not even a *choice* I'm making. It just happens. When he looks at me, or touches me, or just…*God*, Serena, you know what I mean."

"Of course I do. You look at him like he's hung the moon. I love Justin for making you so happy. But I have to tell you a secret." She lowered her voice and said, "I can't see him without hearing *Long Dong Naked Man* in my head."

"Ohmygod! *No!*" Chloe snapped, but she was smiling so hard it hurt. "Do *not* think about my boyfriend that way."

"I'm *trying* not to. But Emery made such a big deal out of how *big* it was when she saw him naked, that…*you know*. I can't just turn that thought off."

"Well, you have to, because he's mine now. And I'll freaking bring in the Men in Black to erase your memory if you don't stop."

Serena laughed hysterically. "It's so *fun* teasing you! I don't really think of that every time I see him. Just *almost* every time."

"I'm hanging up now."

"Wait! How *wicked* is Long Dong?"

"*Goodbye,* Serena." Chloe ended the call and said, "Very wicked, but I'll never tell *you* that, baby sister."

JUSTIN SET DOWN his pneumatic chisel and blew the dust from the stone. The sculpture for the rally was coming along nicely, though it would take another few weeks before it was complete. He checked the time and realized the afternoon had flown by. He put away his tools and headed up to the house to see Chloe. She'd stopped into the studio when she'd come back from her place, and after they shared a few steamy kisses, she'd gone up to the house to work on a project.

His phone rang, and Levi Steele's name appeared on the screen. "Levi, how's it going, man?"

"Really well, thanks. It was great seeing you again and meeting Chloe. Sorry Joey was so mouthy."

Justin squinted against the sun, dragging his forearm across his brow as he walked up the hill and said, "Joey was great. She always is. Did she get the album Chloe sent?"

Chloe had spent hours making sure every page was perfect. She'd used Joey's favorite colors and embellishments that represented all the things Levi had told her his daughter enjoyed. She'd even put pink hearts and written *First Crush* above one of the pictures of Justin holding Joey, and she'd had Justin write a personal note to Joey on that page, something she could treasure forever.

"Yeah. It's really beautiful. I can't believe how much trouble she went to."

"She enjoyed making it."

"That's actually why we're calling. Joey wants to thank her, and I thought I should let you know before calling your better half."

Respect went a long way in the brotherhood.

"Thanks. She's right inside," he said as he climbed the porch steps. "Let me get her for you." He followed the sound of music to the dining room, where Chloe was leaning over the table as she worked, wiggling her butt to the music. "Hey, sweets—"

She gasped and spun around. Her arms flew out to the sides. "Stay there!"

"What?" He laughed, stepping into the room.

"No, no, *no*!" She ran forward and pushed him out of the room. "I'm making you something. You can't go in there."

She was so damn cute he could barely stand it. "Okay, I'll stay out. Levi is on the phone. Joey wants to thank you for her album."

"Oh! She got it?" She took the phone and held it up to her ear. "Hi, Levi."

Justin peeked into the dining room.

Chloe stepped in front of him, pushing him backward as she spoke into the phone. "It was no trouble at all. I had fun making it." She scowled and pointed into the living room without breaking her conversation. "Sure. I'd love to talk to her. Just give me one sec, okay?" She lowered the phone and said, "If you go in there, you're watching the fireworks by yourself tonight."

She was sexy when she was adamant. He couldn't help but egg her on. "Come on, babe. Just a peek?"

"I'll give you a *peek*," she said snarkily. She gave him a gentle shove toward the living room, then put the phone to her ear and said, "Okay, sorry, Levi. I'm back. Yeah, he's a pest, and he's going to ruin his surprise if he's not careful."

Justin held up his hands in surrender and blew her a kiss. He took off his shirt and waggled his brows. "Shower?"

She grinned and mouthed, *I'll be right in.*

More often than not, Chloe joined him in the shower after he got out of the studio.

He took his time washing up, eagerly awaiting her arrival. But a few minutes alone became far too many. He dried off, pulled on a clean pair of jeans, and put on his shirt as he went in search of her.

"Chloe?" He took a quick peek into the dining room, purposefully not looking at the table. Despite how much he loved teasing her, he'd never ruin her surprise. She wasn't there, so he headed for the kitchen and saw her through the glass doors, pacing the deck with the phone pressed to her ear. As he stepped outside, Chloe looked over with damp, angry eyes, and his gut seized. "Baby, what's going on?"

She turned away, speaking angrily into the phone. "*No.* I'm *done* meeting the men in your life. Serena and I are not accessories for you to flaunt around like you had *anything* at all to do with our upbringing!"

Her goddamn mother.

He reached for her, but she twisted away.

"How can you even say that to me?" she fumed, stalking across the deck. "I had to grow up when I was *eight* years old because *you* refused to. You were never there, and even when you were there, it wasn't for us." She fell silent, listening for a few seconds, before saying, "That's bullshit. Where were *you* when Serena fell off her bike and needed stitches? Thank God Mr. Savage was home to take us to the doctor. Who do you think got Serena on the bus every morning? Who made her breakfasts, lunches, and dinners? Who freaking watched over her when the men you brought home wandered out of your bedroom in the middle of the night?" Chloe swiped at her eyes with a shaky hand.

Justin wanted to take the phone and give her damn mother a piece of his mind, but he knew Chloe had to do this once and for all, even if it killed him to stand back and let her.

Chloe tipped her face up toward the sky, groaning with frustration, and said, "Leaving money on the counter is *not* parenting." She paced again and said, "Don't pull that crap with me. The *only* time you call us is when you want to show us off to some new man." Her voice went ice cold and deathly calm. "I'm done being your doormat. I don't want to have *anything* more to do with you, and don't you *dare* try to get Serena to meet your newest jerk. She's finally happy, and if you think Drake or I will let you bring her down *ever* again, you're dead wrong."

She ended the call and faced Justin with tears streaming down her cheeks. He gathered her trembling body in his arms, struggling to suppress the anger eating away at him as her body jerked with sobs.

"It's okay, babe. I've got you," he said, trying to soothe her. "You did the right thing."

She pushed out of his arms. Frustrated groans spilled from her lips as she shook her fists at the sky. "Can you *believe* she wants me to meet another one of her boyfriends? It's like she doesn't even *see* what she does to us," she fumed, stalking across the deck again, swiping at her tears. "I *never* cry. She is the *only* person who can get to me like this, and she's the *one* person I wish wouldn't."

"That's because she's your mother, and you can't help but care about her. That's normal, sweetheart. What's not normal is what she does to you and Serena. What can I do to make this easier?"

She shoved her phone into her back pocket and shook her head. She turned toward the woods and grabbed the railing. Her head fell between her shoulders. Seeing her that hurt and defeated killed him.

He put his arms around her from behind and kissed her shoulder. "Whatever you need, whatever you want, I'll make it happen."

She turned in his arms and said, "I need to call Serena, but then will you take me for a ride on the bike? I always feel good when we're riding."

"Absolutely. But you know it's the Fourth of July. Traffic will be awful. We won't be able to ride fast, but we can still ride."

"I don't care," she said, holding him as tight as he was holding her. She tilted her tear-streaked face up and said, "I just want to be wrapped around you and on the road, away from everything."

He kissed her softly and said, "Put on sunscreen and your hiking boots, babe. I know the perfect place to go."

Chapter Twenty-Three

THE FREEDOM OF the bike and holding Justin brought the relief Chloe so desperately needed. She soaked in his strength as the motorcycle crawled through the charming town of Wellfleet, which was decked out for the holiday. Flower boxes overflowed with colorful blooms beneath storefront windows, and American flags waved from above the entrances. People meandered in and out of shops, children carried ice cream cones and cotton candy, and couples sat on blankets in front of the town hall. Chloe remembered wishing her mother would *want* to bring her and Serena to see the fireworks and parades when they were young, but their mother had always done her own thing on holidays other than Christmas, leaving Chloe and Serena to join the Savages instead.

As she'd done millions of times before, Chloe tried to shove years of hurt down deep, well aware that she couldn't change the past.

If only she could forget it.

Justin turned onto a residential street, and a block later he turned onto another. They picked up speed, and the air cooled as they drove beneath an umbrella of trees. Water appeared briefly between houses and trees, like snapshots in the wind.

Chloe rested against Justin's back, welcoming the serenity of the view and soaking in the safety of him.

They came to a roundabout and drove toward Great Island, a hiker's heaven with miles of trails and water views. The hiking boots suddenly made sense.

Justin parked and helped Chloe off the bike. As he locked the helmets in place, he said, "Have you hiked the Island before?"

"No. I've actually never been hiking."

There was no hiding the shock on his face. "But you have hiking boots."

She wrinkled her nose and said, "Fashion statement."

Justin laughed. "Don't tell Zeke that. He can't imagine a life without trails and hiking in it. He'd give you a lecture about the benefits of losing yourself in nature." He draped his arm over her shoulder and kissed her temple. "Get ready to have your mind blown, baby. If you think the open road is awesome, just wait until you experience this."

They headed down a trail holding hands, surrounded by pitch pine trees and leafy bushes and serenaded by the sounds of birds singing and leaves brushing in the warm breeze. The trail led them out of the woods, down an incline, and along a hard-packed sand surface at the base of the dunes, where it ran along a river. Chloe appreciated that Justin wasn't peppering her with questions about the phone call with her mother or pushing her to talk about her feelings. She just wanted to forget them and explore the new door he'd opened for her.

The sun beat down on them, but Chloe didn't mind the heat. Sweating actually felt like purification, getting rid of all the bad feelings her conversation with her mother had left behind. The sand became deeper, and the trail forked.

"Preacher and Con used to take us here," Justin said as they followed the trail away toward the woods. "I remember thinking hiking was stupid. The other kids had been coming here since they were little. They knew all the trails. Ashley and Madigan would skip ahead of the group. Zander and Dwayne usually ran off, and of course Zeke was always watching over Zander, so he'd take off after them. Preacher or Con would send Tank and Blaine to 'take care of the troops.'" He laughed softly. "I remember wondering why they listened to them. I'd never been exposed to anything having to do with the great outdoors, much less a family in which kids watched after each other as much as the parents did." He looked thoughtfully at Chloe and said, "But it wasn't like your mom, babe. They weren't avoiding parenting. They were teaching us how to *be* watchful and responsible. Dwayne and Zander never ran too far ahead, and I didn't get that, either. I mean, for me, running had always meant running *away*. But I quickly learned that Preacher and Con had also taught them boundaries."

"They care so much about all of you. I can't imagine grow-ing up in a family like that," Chloe said as they followed another fork in the trail up a dune to another woodsy area. The shade cooled her off. "I know you said it took you a long time to trust them, but what did it feel like as things changed and you became part of their family?"

Justin hugged her against his side and said, "I think about that a lot, actually. It felt *so* good and made me *so* happy that it scared me. I had never felt that way before, and I didn't trust it, so every time I made progress, I'd inch back out of fear by doing something bad."

"You were testing them," she said.

"I know that now. It was not a smooth transition, babe.

Sometimes I felt like a bystander watching someone else's life. It didn't seem possible that the life I'd led had brought me *there*. What seemed even more unbelievable was that they *wanted* me there. But eventually it all came together."

As they made their way up a hill, she thought about what it must have felt like to be that wanted. Justin took her hand, and she realized *he* made her feel that way, and he had done so even when she'd been denying her feelings for him.

They came to a dead end in the trail, and he led her into a thickly wooded area.

"There's no path here," she said.

"I know, but you haven't taken any pictures yet, and I know you'll regret it if you don't."

"You think you know me, huh?" she teased, loving that even with everything going on, he still gave importance to the things that she held close to her heart.

"Oh, I *know* you, sweet thing."

He helped her over rocks, brush, and a fallen tree as they made their way up an incline to a clearing. Stunning views of Wellfleet Harbor spilled out before them. The tide was going out, and she gazed down at the shoreline snaking along the beach to a mass of green grasses popping up like islands in shallow marshes. Just beyond the marshes, the beach appeared again, only to disappear around a long stretch of tree-covered dunes.

"This is beautiful." Chloe pulled out her phone and began taking pictures.

"Yeah, it is. That's why this is where you're going to let go of your past."

She lowered her phone, meeting his serious gaze. "What do you mean?"

"The first time Preacher took me on this hike alone, he brought me to this spot. He told me to get all those shitty feelings out of me or they'd gnaw at my gut like cancer. I stood right where you are and let it all out. I yelled at my father for being a shit and at my mother for leaving me. I cursed the foster care system, and I said some pretty horrible things about myself, too, that I didn't even know I had inside me." He took her hand and said, "It's not a cure-all, Chloe, but it helps."

"You want me to stand here and shout about my dirty laundry?" She shook her head. "I can't do that. Someone might hear me."

"We're alone, babe. But even if we weren't, you can't keep that shit inside you. Preacher was right—it will eat you alive. You need to get it out, and who *cares* if someone hears you? *Everyone* has baggage. But if we don't get ours out, it'll come out in other ways, maybe not now, but years from now. You think Reba and Preacher are perfect?" He shook his head and said, "They're not. They have their own troubles, but they don't let them fester." He squeezed her hand and said, "They deal with shit when it happens, and they do it together. That's how they remain strong in a world that has so many reasons to be weak. You've spent a lifetime playing by the rules, Chloe, being who you think you *have* to be for everyone else. I understand that you have to play that game at work, but you don't *ever* have to do that with me."

Her stomach knotted. He was trying so hard to help her, and she wanted his help, but she'd hidden her painful past for so long, it had become a ravenous beast. It had already taken parts of her that she could never get back. And even if she wanted to, she didn't know how to *yell* about those things. "I'm not a yeller, Justin. I can't do it."

"Have you ever tried?"

She shook her head. "I got pretty mad at my mother today, but you heard me. Even then I didn't shout."

"Maybe you should have. Just try it once for me, babe. We both felt better after I told you about finding my mother and you told me about what happened in the parking lot of the Hog. This will feel ten times better than that. It will free you, like when we ride the motorcycle."

"That's different. I don't have to scream my feelings to the world."

"The vehicle is different, but the outcome will be similar. You'll see. It'll ease your pain and bring clarity. You don't have to do it if you don't want to. I'll go first. Then you can decide." He faced the water and shouted, "I fucking hate working on the job for Alan Rogers *and* seeing him near my girl!"

"*Justin!* What if someone hears you? He's my *boss*! You could get me fired."

"Do you see anyone around us? Did we pass *one* person on the trails?"

Her gut knotted tighter. "No, but still."

"Okay, I get it. Don't mess with your work. No problem. Let's try this again." He drew in a deep breath and hollered, "I hate that your mother makes you sad! I hate that my father was an asshole! I fucking despise that suicide is ever an option!" He tapped his fist to his chest and said, "It feels good, baby."

His gaze shifted over her shoulder. She spun around, worried he'd seen someone, but no one was there. "What are you looking at?"

He put his finger over his lips, shushing her, and pointed to a branch as two dragonflies took flight.

"There's your sign, dragonfly girl."

Goose bumps chased up her arms. "I can't believe it."

"Believe it, sweetheart. This is your moment. It's your decision, but I think the universe is giving you a nudge in the right direction. Do you want to give it a try? Let all those bad feelings fly?"

"Sort of. But I'm nervous," she said anxiously.

He held out his hand, and when she took it, he held tight and said, "I'm right here, and nothing bad is going to come from getting out your true feelings. You can do this, Chloe, and I promise you'll feel better afterward."

"Or I'll just be embarrassed."

"You'll never know unless you try. Those bad thoughts are like the stuff in your stomach when you're sick and you can't throw up. They fester and burn, and then when you finally get them out, you're like, *cool, now I can sleep.*"

"That's disgusting. True, but disgusting."

"Get that emotional barf out of you, baby."

"Okay, I'll try." She closed her eyes, mustering her courage. Her heart slammed against her ribs as she opened her eyes and said, a little louder than normal, "I hate that my mother tried to make me feel guilty."

"What was that?" he teased. "I could barely hear you."

She rolled her eyes and said a little louder, "I hate that—"

"*Louder*, Chloe." He squeezed her hand and said, "Let that shit *go.*"

She filled her lungs with the salty sea air and shouted, "I hate that my mother made me feel guilty! I hate that she hurt me and Serena! I hate that she didn't want to *be* our mother! I hate that I never knew my father!" Looking through the blur of tears and panting for air, she couldn't stop the hate from spewing out. "I hate the men who hurt me, and I hate the people who hurt you! And the pigs that hurt Shadow and all those other dogs!"

"That's it, sweetheart, let it *all* out."

She was out of breath and felt a little better, but at the same time, more words vied for release, the secrets she hated most. It took all her confidence and all her trust to set them free.

"I hate that I'm scared I'll turn into my mother and I won't love my kids enough" fell quietly, *mortifyingly*, from her lips, bringing a rush of tears. She knew she and Justin weren't at the talking-about-kids point in their relationship yet, but she'd known the moment she'd seen him with Joey and with Hadley that he was meant to be a father, and he deserved to know her fears.

"Oh, sweetheart," Justin said sadly, gathering her in his arms. "That's why you looked scared when the girls made those comments at breakfast about having babies."

She nodded. "I want kids," she choked out, swiping at what felt like endless tears. "I really do. But I'm scared."

"I get it, and it makes total sense for you to be scared. But you need to know, to truly *believe*, that you could *never* be her. The proof is in your past, baby. Even as a little girl you had better maternal instincts than your mother. You *raised* Serena, and you did it with love and respect. You are the one who taught her to be strong. You made sure she went to school and took care of all the things that helped her become the successful, smart, kind person she is. She wouldn't be all those things if not for you, Chloe."

He brushed away her tears with the pads of his thumbs and said, "And *you*, my beautiful, strong girl, are even more amazing than your sister. You care so much, you hollered about Shadow and the other dogs. That should tell you something about your ability to love."

She pressed her face to his chest, smiling as gratitude swelled inside her. She dried her eyes and gazed up at him, asking, "How do you know just what to say to make me feel better?"

"It takes no thought, babe. It's the truth. I know all too well how hard it is to look in the mirror and see the person we've become and not the one we've spent our lives trying to outrun."

"That's exactly it." She drew in a few cleansing breaths, feeling less ravaged and stronger with each one. "Getting it out helped, too. Thank you. I'm sorry my mother ruined our one-month anniversary."

His lips quirked up and he said, "One month, huh?"

She hooked her finger around his belt loop, feeling a little silly, and said, "I was making you something, but I'll never get it done in time to give it to you tonight."

"Then it becomes our two-month anniversary gift, or one-year, or six-year…" He pressed his lips to hers and said, "*This* right here? You and me on the same page, helping each other be the best we can be? That's all I need."

"I don't know why you chose me when I kept denying us, but I'm so glad you did."

"It wasn't a choice, Chloe. When I saw you, all other women failed to exist."

He kissed her again, longer this time, healing the fissures in her heart. "We're meant to be, babe," he whispered, and came back for more.

When their lips finally parted, she felt better, rejuvenated and freer. She was sure her nose was pink from crying and her hair had probably gone flat and lifeless, but she didn't care because her heart was full, and she wanted to remember this moment forever.

"Will you take a selfie with me?" she asked.

"Always," he said.

As she took pictures, he kissed her cheek, her lips, and her neck, making her giggle.

"You've got to get pictures of *all* of the good stuff. Mind if I take a few?" He reached for her phone, turning the camera on her.

"Justin." She turned away, embarrassed.

"Hey, I want pictures of *you*."

"We took some of us already."

"Of *us*. I want some of *you*, Chloe." He stepped in front of her and said, "Every moment is a new chance to move forward. We'll never get this moment back, and I want to remember it exactly as it is."

"I'm a mess. I've cried more today than I have in ages. When we're both in the picture, you don't notice me as much. It's better that way."

He put his arm around her, drawing her against him as he said, "I *love* your face, baby. It doesn't matter if you've got makeup on or you're fresh out of the shower, if you're teary eyed or sweaty from making love or hiking. *Yours* is the face I see when I close my eyes at night and the one I carry with me during the day." He gazed deeply into her eyes and said, "I love you, Chloe," just above a whisper. "*All* of you. All of your moods and all of your moments. Please let me capture this moment, *your* moment, in a picture."

Tears slid down her cheeks *again*. "*Justin...?*" Had she heard him right?

"I mean it, baby. I started falling for you the second your first snarky comment hit my ears, and I knew that was it for me. *You* were it for me. I love being with you, hearing your voice, holding your hand. I love the way you scowl at me when I'm being a pain and how you look at me like I'm your entire world when we're making love."

"You *are* my world. I love you, too, Justin," she said breathily. "Everything about you."

His mouth came lovingly down over hers and salty tears slipped between their lips.

"I'm yours, baby. Only yours." He rubbed his nose over her cheek, so sweet and intimate, it brought more tears.

Overflowing with love and hope, and everything in between, she said, "*God I love you*," and went up on her toes, kissing him with all she had.

LATER THAT EVENING, Justin and Chloe snuggled beneath blankets in the back of his truck, waiting for the fireworks to start. Justin kissed her temple, thinking about when they'd arrived home after their hike. Chloe had shown him the gift she was making for him. She'd framed a metal grate with distressed wood, and in the upper-left corner of the grate she'd hung glittery stars from black ribbons. Below them she'd clipped a picture of the two of them slow dancing that Serena had taken of them at the Salty Hog. They were gazing into each other's eyes, their emotions seeping off the image. Chloe had burned the edges of two pretty pale-yellow pieces of paper, and on them she'd written some of the lyrics to "Heartbeat" and "Uptown Girl." In the upper middle of the grate, not yet attached, she'd set out pictures of Shadow in Justin's lap, licking his face, and a selfie of the two of them with the adorable one-eyed pooch.

Chloe had made a tiny wooden doghouse and printed SHADOW over the door. A ribbon dangled from the peak of the roof with ONE DAY written across it. The rest of the items weren't yet in position on the grate, but she'd shown him charms and embellishments of miniature sculpting tools and a motorcycle and truck that looked like his. She had pictures of him working in his studio. There was a tiny bottle with sand and shells in it, and a card from the Salty Hog to remind them of their long talk on the beach the night that had changed everything between them. She'd saved a napkin from the Taproom in Harborside and had laid out pictures from their rides. There was a selfie of them in bed taken last Saturday. In the picture, their hair was tousled, he was shirtless, and she was wearing one of his T-shirts. He was holding her from behind, kissing her neck, and she was making a funny face. They'd taken dozens of silly pictures that morning. But of all the moments she'd captured, of all the feelings she'd portrayed, there was one that had stolen his breath—a picture of their intertwined hands, his mother's leather necklace resting on his wrist. Beside it was a picture of Reba's hand in his, and a paper heart that had *I want to hold your hand* printed in Chloe's handwriting.

She'd done him in. She saw the truth in his heart, and instead of running from his past, which represented all that she feared, she'd *embraced* it. He imagined years of memories seen through Chloe's eyes hanging on their walls, framed on their bookshelves, and *rooted* in his heart.

He kissed her temple and said, "I love you," for what was probably the hundredth time. He'd probably say it a hundred more before the night was through, and it still wouldn't be enough to convey how much he adored her.

She snuggled deeper into his side and said, "I can't stop

thinking about Shadow and Sampson."

"Me, either," he said. "Hopefully they'll be all right."

They'd wanted to stop by the rescue before the fireworks, but after admiring Chloe's artwork, they'd had just enough time to shower and get to the beach before all the good parking spots were taken. They'd called Gunner to check on the dogs, and he'd said that he, Steph, and Sidney were staying with the animals in case the noise from the fireworks scared them. The shelter was located around the corner from one of the firework celebrations.

"I keep thinking about Shadow having been chained outdoors during fireworks in the past, and now he's locked inside. I know Dwayne, Steph, and Sid are there, but there are so many animals, and they can't be everywhere. You have such a calming effect on Shadow, and I know Sampson is older and low key, but we don't know how he'll react. Would you be bummed if we went to be with them instead of watching the fireworks?"

"Man, Chloe. We really *are* meant for each other. I think that's a great idea." He kissed her and said, "I'll make it up to you."

"There's nothing to make up for. We'll still be together, and that's all that matters."

They packed their things, and twenty minutes later they were sitting on blankets in the visiting room of the rescue with Shadow lying between them. They'd checked on Sampson, and he'd been fine when the fireworks had started. Gunner was keeping an eye on him, and he'd texted to say Sampson was sleeping soundly. Fireworks rang out, muffled by the thick walls of the building and the soothing sounds of waves from the sound machine Justin had given Chloe the night he'd brought the beach to her back porch. On the way over, they'd stopped at the cottage to pick it up.

Chloe kissed Shadow's head, and he rolled onto his side for belly pets. "We made the right decision," she said as she loved him up. "Thank you."

"I should be thanking you, hot stuff. Not many women would give up a front-row seat to fireworks to spend the evening with a dog."

"A very *special* dog and his ruggedly handsome friend."

Justin scooted closer and put his arm around her, leaving just enough room between them for Shadow. "Is it possible that I love you more now than I did half an hour ago?"

"Mm-hm," she said with a sexy smile. "And in ten minutes, you'll love me even more."

Shadow made a whimpering sound and inched forward on his belly. He rolled onto his side again and put his left front and back paws on Chloe's leg.

"Dude, really?" Justin said. "Scamming on my girl? That's not cool."

Chloe scratched Shadow's belly. "Don't pay him any mind, Shadow. He's just jealous."

They stayed with Shadow until well after the fireworks were over. When they returned to the truck, Chloe sat tucked beneath Justin's arm.

As he drove away, Justin said, "Seems to me we've been here before, beautiful. You cuddled up to me, your hand on my thigh. I believe I ended up buried deep inside you on a back road with the truck still running."

She lifted her face with a seductive glimmer in her eyes and slid her hand between his legs, stroking him through his jeans. A thrum of heat spread through his core, and a greedy sound rumbled up his chest.

"You're playing with fire, baby."

"That sounds *promising*," she said coyly. "Do you have a desk in your office?"

Just the thought of bending her over the desk made his cock throb. "*Fuck*, Chloe, you know I do."

"Since we missed the fireworks, I thought we could make our own."

Best. Idea. Ever.

Ten minutes later they stumbled into his private office at Cape Stone in a tangle of greedy gropes and hungry kisses. Their shirts sailed through the air, and with a quick flick of his fingers, Chloe's bra fell to the floor. Their kisses were messy and wild as he unzipped her shorts and pushed his hand between her legs, sinking his fingers into her tight heat. He was hard as stone, and she was wet and ready. She rode his hand, moaning into his mouth.

"Christ, baby," he said between kisses. "I want to *feast* on you."

She kicked off her sandals and wiggled out of her clothes as he swept everything off his desk with one hand, sending papers and pens flying across the room. Chloe laughed as he lifted her onto the desk and spread her legs. He dropped to his knees and lowered his mouth to her sweet center, turning her giggles to moans of pleasure. She threw her head back, locking her legs around his head, grinding against his mouth, making the most sinful noises he'd ever heard.

He guided her hand between her legs and said, "Touch yourself, baby. Touch yourself while I devour you."

And *devour* he did, using teeth and tongue as she teased that sensitive bundle of nerves. She gasped and moaned, whimpered and begged. He licked over her fingers and she moved her hand away, giving him better access as he pushed two fingers into her slick heat.

"*Yes*," she panted out. "Lick me while you do that."

She'd gotten bolder lately, and he fucking *loved* it. He licked and devoured as she rode his fingers. When he reached up, groping her breast, and squeezed her nipple, she cried out, bucking and writhing against his mouth. He stayed with her until her climax engulfed her. As she came down from the peak, he pulled her up to a sitting position, his fingers still buried deep, and crushed his mouth to hers. She didn't pull away from the taste of her arousal on his tongue, and that intensified his pleasure as he sent her soaring again. He swallowed her sounds of ecstasy, and when she collapsed against him, he brought her mouth back to his, kissing her lighter, more tenderly.

He guided her hand back to her center and said, "Keep touching yourself." Holding her gaze, he stripped bare. Her eyes dropped to his cock, and she licked her lips. He put his hand to her mouth and said, "Lick this, baby. Get my hand nice and wet."

She licked up and down his palm, and he fisted his cock, giving it a few slow strokes. Her eyes were riveted to his actions.

"You like that, dirty girl?"

"I love watching you do that," she said breathlessly.

"How about this?" He took her fingers from between her legs and licked up one side of them and down the other, then sucked them into his mouth and swirled his tongue over and between them.

She panted out, "*Sooo hot.*"

He guided her hand to his balls and said, "Touch me."

She touched and teased as he took her in a fierce and possessive kiss. He pushed his fingers into her tight heat again. He was lost in her touch, in the taste of her mouth, and in the desire raging between them.

"That's it, baby," he ground out, focusing on that magical spot that made her breathing hitch. She made high-pitched, needy noises, and he said, "Now stroke me, baby, nice and tight, all the way to the head while I take you to the edge."

She fisted his cock, brushing her thumb over the bead of wetness at the tip, stroking him so perfectly, he nearly lost it. He worked her with his fingers, using his thumb on that taut bundle of nerves, and lowered his mouth to her breast, sucking and grazing his teeth over the peak. She made more pleading noises, rocking her hips to the rhythm of his efforts, and he knew she was close.

"That's it, baby," he growled. "Now guide my cock into you, and I'll make you come."

She widened her legs, and he pushed the broad head of his shaft inside her. He'd learned that she was super sensitive near her entrance, so he moved in and out of her slowly, using only a few inches.

She grabbed his arms. "*Don'tstopdon'tstopdon'tstop!*"

He drove in deeper, withdrawing slowly, then pushed in deep again, withdrawing slowly once more, and continued the maddening rhythm that had him clenching his teeth to keep from coming. She squeezed her legs tight around his hips, and he slanted his mouth over hers, thrusting faster, harder. Her hips bucked and her fingernails dug into his flesh, her inner muscles clenching tight and heavenly around his cock. It took all of his concentration to stave off his orgasm. When she came down from the peak and tore her mouth away to rest her forehead on his shoulder, her body jerked with aftershocks.

He kissed her neck and said, "Still with me, baby?"

"Yes," she said in one long breath.

"Do you want more?"

She lifted her head and said, "I want *everything*."

His heart thundered at the love and lust swimming in her eyes. "Can you stand? I want to see your beautiful ass as I take you from behind."

She slipped off the desk, still trembling, and held on to him.

"Lie on the couch, sweetheart. You're too shaky. I don't want to hurt you."

Her brows knitted, and in pure Chloe fashion, she lifted her chin and straightened her spine, setting a challenging glare on him. "Don't tell me what I can handle, Mr. Wicked, or I'll have to *punish* you."

Well, fuck him sideways, she was on *fire*.

She turned toward the desk, spread her legs, and bent at the waist, glancing over her shoulder at him. Her hair fell over one eye, sexier than all his fantasies, as she said, "Think you can handle this?"

"There's nothing I can't handle, you gorgeous thing." He licked between her legs, kissed the soft globes of her ass, and sank his teeth into one just hard enough to hear her cry out. Then he kissed the tender spot and said, "The question is, can *you* handle *me*?"

Her eyes hit his with the force of a cyclone. "I like your mouth on me, no matter how you use it."

"Good to know, baby, because I plan to use it on every inch of you."

He ran his hands down her back, over her ass, and down her legs, taking his time as he kissed his way north, up her legs from ankle to ass. He teased her sex with his fingers, then used his mouth on her sweet center, caressing her ass as he took his fill.

He rose to his feet and ran his hands up her torso, kissing along her spine.

"Justin, *please*," she pleaded. "I'm going to lose my mind."

"*Soon*," he promised. "Legs together, sweetness."

He thrust his cock between her thighs without entering her, sliding along her wetness. Her fingers curled around the other side of the desk as he showered her back and shoulder blades with kisses, fondling her breasts. His hips pressed against her ass, and he said, "Up on your toes, baby."

She rose onto her toes, bringing her ass higher. He ran his hands over each cheek, squeezing and earning more delicious sounds. He had to taste her one last time, and dropped to his knees, palming her ass as he spread her cheeks and slicked his tongue over her arousal.

"Oh *God*," she said huskily, pushing her ass farther up in the air as he licked her again.

He rose to his feet, nestling his cock against her entrance. He put one hand on her shoulder, one on her waist, and drove into her with a single deep thrust, burying himself to the root.

"Oh, Justin—"

He stilled. "Did I hurt you?"

She shook her head, and it dropped between her shoulders. "*No*," she panted out. "You just feel so good, I could come again."

Just hearing her say that made his cock ache. "Come, baby. Come all over my cock."

He began moving at a quicker pace. She was so tight, so wet, and she took him so deep, it wasn't long before heat skated down his spine. He put one hand around her middle, using his fingers to send her skyrocketing at the same time as lights exploded behind his closed lids and he lost all control. Their pleasure-filled sounds hung in the air as their bodies slapped together, and his name sailed from her lips. *"Justin—yes! Oh...Justin—"* She clung to the desk, driving her hips back, meeting his every thrust as he pounded into her through the very last pulse of his powerful release.

He collapsed over her back, one arm around her waist, the other holding him up. "God, baby, you fucking own me." He held her there, both of them trembling as he kissed her neck and whispered, "I love you." He lifted his chest off her back, rubbing his hands along her body, massaging her arms, shoulders, hips, and thighs. Then he pressed a kiss to her lower back and said, "I need to see your face, sweetheart."

He helped her up and gathered her in his arms. "I kind of lost my mind at the end. I didn't hurt you, did I?"

"No, and I know you never will."

She wound her arms around his neck, and he felt himself getting lost in the love brimming in her eyes. He brushed his lips over hers and said, "What do think, heartbreaker?"

"Best Fourth *ever.*" She pressed her lips to his and said, "How will we ever top that next year, Mr. Wicked?"

"I don't know, Ms. Mallery, but we'll sure as hell have fun trying."

Chapter Twenty-Four

THE NEXT FEW days passed in a blur of busy days, steamy nights, and *I love yous*. Justin had made plans for Chloe's birthday dinner, and though he wouldn't tell her where they were going, he'd said to plan for something fancy. She'd gone out for dinner and dress shopping with Madigan and Marly last night while Justin was at church, and she'd ended up buying two dresses. One for their dinner date and one for work. She'd also bought new sexy black lingerie made by Leather and Lace, which Marly had informed her was co-designed by Jace Stone and renowned fashion designer Jillian Braden.

Chloe stood by her office window thinking about the weekend. She'd been swamped with guilt and sadness when she'd ended the phone call with her mother, but after the hike with Justin, she knew she'd done the right thing, and in the days since, a great weight had lifted from her shoulders. She could finally move forward without fear of being yanked back to the craziness of her mother's unstable life.

A text rolled in from Serena as she sat down at her desk. *Can we do your birthday lunch at 12:30 instead of 12? Emery's morning sickness has gotten worse. She should be ok by then.*

Chloe's thoughts drifted back to Great Island. Ever since she told Justin how she felt about having children, she hadn't been able to stop thinking about it. The advice she'd given Serena about taking her mother out of the equation when making life decisions had never been more valuable than when it came to her own future, and she finally felt free to heed it. Without her mother in the picture, she felt like the luckiest girl in the world. Her programs were running smoothly, and today Alan was going to give her his decision about funding the puppetry trial.

Another text bubble popped up from Serena, jarring Chloe from her thoughts. *Since you're not seeing Justin until dinner on your birthday, can we steal you for the whole afternoon? Girls' day on the beach?* A girls' day on the beach sounded wonderful.

"Chloe?" Shelby called over the intercom.

Chloe sent a quick reply to Serena agreeing to the time and said, "Yes?"

"Reba Wicked is on line two for you."

Reba had called Tuesday morning with follow-up questions about the facilities. It had sounded as if they were leaning toward moving Mike into the property. Chloe had made a point not to talk with Justin about his family's decision. She didn't want to put any pressure on them.

"Thanks, Shelby." She picked up the phone. "Hi, Reba. How are you?"

"I'm doing great today, thank you. I'm calling to let you know that we've decided to move forward with the facility for Mike. I'll be filling out the paperwork this week."

"That's wonderful. You won't regret it."

"We all feel very good about it. It will be strange not having him in the house, but it's probably best that he has his freedom."

"That seems very important to him."

"I know, and I understand it, although that puts us one step closer to being empty nesters again," Reba said with a sigh. "Mads is staying with us while she's in town, but once she finds a place to live, that'll be it."

"You don't sound like you're looking forward to that."

"Parenting is a funny thing, Chloe. When you raise children, you have days when you're not sure how you'll survive, and as they get older, you wonder how you'll survive without them." Her tone turned solemn and she said, "And then there are parents who survive their children, and you wonder how they manage."

"I can't imagine," Chloe said softly.

"Hopefully you won't ever have to. Lord knows if it were up to my son, he'd build you a perfect world in which hardships didn't exist."

Chloe felt herself smiling. "He is very protective of me, but he seems that way about everyone he's close to."

"Yes, all our children are. I'm not one to meddle in my kids' lives, but I have never seen Justin happier, and I know that's because of you. So I am going to meddle, just this once. He loves you, sweetheart, and the Wicked men are a passionate group. They tend to act first and think about consequences later. If he gets too protective and you feel smothered, I hope you'll find a way to let him know so he can try to fix it. He's got a really good heart, but even big, strong men can be scared of losing the things they love most."

Chloe realized how much Reba must like them as a couple for her to trust Chloe with her motherly advice. "Don't worry, Reba. I'm no pushover. I have no trouble speaking my mind."

"I gathered as much. My boy could never be this happy with a woman who wasn't every bit his equal, and then some.

But as a mother, it doesn't matter how old your kids get, the worrying never ends. I'd better let you go before I get myself in trouble by rambling on about him or how wonderful everyone thinks you are. Thank you again for being so patient with my questions the other day, sweetheart. I know we're doing the right thing for Mike."

Chloe had no sooner taken a breath after she ended the call than Alan walked into her office. She tried to read his expression, hoping he'd approved the funding for her program, but he had a half smile on his face that gave nothing away.

"Hi, Alan. I was just wrapping up a few things before coming to see you."

"I was in your neck of the woods and thought I'd save you the walk down the hall."

He walked around her desk and sat on the corner of it. She shifted in her seat, glad he was sitting and wouldn't be encroaching any further into her personal space. His eyes swept over her desk and then briefly over her. Justin's worries trickled through her mind, and she tucked her legs beneath her desk.

"That's a pretty new dress," Alan said without a hint of innuendo. "It's only appropriate that you're wearing something new to celebrate the news that your trial program has been approved."

"It has?" she exclaimed. "That's fantastic. Thank you, Alan. I know this program will make a difference in the lives of our residents."

He stood up and extended his hand. "Congratulations, Chloe. You're doing great things here." She rose and shook his hand. He put his other hand over hers and said, "With my support, there's no limit to how far you can go."

"Thank you for your vote of confidence," she said as he

released her hand. "It means the world to me."

"I wish you'd consider attending that conference with me this weekend. It could be beneficial to your career."

"I'm sorry, but I can't. It's my birthday this weekend, and Justin has already made plans for us."

"Justin *Wicked*?" he said with an air of distaste.

She held her head high and said, "Yes, Justin Wicked."

His eyes narrowed. "I thought you said you weren't dating him."

"I wasn't when you asked, but things have changed."

"Have they? Or were you keeping the truth from me so I'd hire him to do the work on my patio? Because that would be *very* disappointing. We rely on each other, Chloe, working closely to achieve the things we both want. Trust is everything, don't you agree?"

His accusatory tone made her feel defensive. "Of course. Why would I lie about something like that?"

"I don't know, Chloe. Maybe I'm wrong and you just got tired of waiting. I thought we were on the same page that some things simply cannot be rushed."

"I didn't *rush*, Alan. I've known Justin for a long time, and quite frankly, it's none of your business."

"Chloe?" Shelby's voice came through the intercom.

Glad for the interruption, Chloe said, "Yes, Shelby?"

"Is Alan still in your office? His wife is on the line, and she said it's important."

"Yes, he's right here."

"I'll take it in my office," Alan said sharply, and headed for the door.

"Thanks again for the approval on the project," she called after him. She closed her office door and picked up her phone to call Justin, her happiness about the project pushing aside Alan's bizarre comments.

"How's my girl?"

"Fantastic. I got the funding for the puppetry program!"

"That's awesome, babe. You deserve it. Have you told Mads yet?"

"No. Alan *just* left my office and I wanted to share the news with you first."

"I'm so proud of you. I don't like that Rogers guy, but I'm glad he did the right thing. He didn't get touchy with you, did he?"

"No. I told you he was weird, but not like that. Although he did kind of get under my skin just now."

"What did he do?" he asked with an edge to his voice.

"He brought up a conference in Boston this weekend that I'd opted out of, and when I said you'd made plans for us for my birthday, he basically asked if I'd lied about dating you so he'd hire Cape Stone to do his patio. I thought that was weird."

"*Real* fucking weird," Justin fumed. "Your personal life is none of his business, and you're not a liar, Chloe. I don't like him accusing you like that. I need to have a talk with him."

"*No*, Justin, you don't. I appreciate your support, but I didn't just kowtow to him. I addressed it, and this is the first time he's said anything like that. I can handle myself, and if he brings it up again, I'll let him know in no uncertain terms that I don't appreciate being accused of something I'd never do. Okay?"

"No, it's *not* okay, but I get it, so I'll back off."

"Thank you," she said sweetly. "I know you hate that."

"Like a motherfucker."

She smiled at his vehemence. "Well, we *do* have something

to celebrate tonight since the funding came through, so maybe I can figure out a way to wash away all that irritation. I bought a few pieces of Leather and Lace lingerie while I was out with the girls last night. Maybe a fashion show would help ease your pain."

"The thought of you in leather and lace has just obliterated my ability to think of anything else. The only pain I'll be feeling is driving home with a hard-on."

"I promise to ease *all* your pains and kiss *all* your boo-boos better."

"Just kiss?" His words were laden with lust.

"Kiss, lick, suck…"

"Shit, Chloe, you'd better be in your car in five minutes, or I'm coming over there to christen your desk."

She heated up at that idea.

"I need to call Mads. Then I'll meet you at home." In her most seductive voice, she said, "Race you to the bedroom, Mr. Wicked?"

He chuckled. "We never make it to the bedroom."

"I know…"

CHLOE SURE KNEW how to take Justin's mind off things. She had done such a good job of distracting Justin last night, he'd forgotten about her conversation with Alan until breakfast this morning. When he'd brought it up, she'd brushed it off as no big deal, but it was almost noon and Justin had been at Cape Stone working all morning, and it was still grating on his nerves.

"The guy is fucking with us," Blaine said when he strode

into Justin's office.

Justin looked up from the contract he was reviewing and said, "Rogers again?"

Their guys had been making good headway on his patio, but last week Alan Rogers had called to make a significant design change. Their guys had been forced to rip out the work they'd done and start over.

Blaine nodded and sank into the chair across from Justin.

Justin ground out a curse. "I told you I didn't like the guy. He's a sniveling prick."

"No shit, Maverick. You also said he was Chloe's boss and that we should suck it up and make it happen."

"That still holds true. What does he want now?"

"To change the *stone*. All of it."

"He is definitely fucking with us. He got miffed when he found out Chloe was my old lady."

Blaine leaned forward, elbows on knees, leveling a serious stare on Justin. "Something we need to take care of?"

He shook his head and said, "Chloe handled it."

"You good with that?"

"*No*, I'm not good with that," Justin snapped. "But I'm also not a dick. Rogers hasn't crossed any lines. I can't hang him by his balls for asking her a question or giving me and Tank shitty looks. Chloe says she can handle him. I'll give her the space to do it, but if he crosses a line, I'll kill him."

"Okay. So what do you want to do about our issue?"

Justin narrowed his eyes, thinking about wringing Alan's neck.

Blaine shook his head. "Let me rephrase that. What do you want to do about it that will keep you *out* of jail?"

"He thinks he's got us bent over a barrel because of Chloe.

Let's show the pompous prick that we own his ass. Charge him for the stone we tore out and leave it on his property. Tell him we can't restock it without risking chips and cracks. If he wants us to haul it away, then charge him for that, too. But let him know we can't get to that for another week. Let's let him feel the pain of these changes. If that doesn't put a stop to him jerking our chain, I will."

"I'll take care of it." Blaine looked at his watch and said, "Do you know why Mads wants to have lunch with us?"

"She's been helping me with something for Chloe's birthday. I figured it was about that and didn't think to ask."

"When is she getting here?"

"Right now," their sister said as she breezed into the office wearing a bikini top and cutoffs. She plunked her pink helmet and her beach bag on Justin's desk and said, "What's going on? Are you in a rush for lunch?"

"I just want to get out of here and blow off some steam." Blaine pushed to his feet as Marly came through the doors in her bikini top and shorts.

"Hi, guys. I hope you don't mind that Mads invited me to tag along." Marly set a large purse on the chair and fanned her face. "Boy, it's hot out there."

Blaine raked his eyes down her body and said, "It just got a hell of a lot hotter in here."

Marly smirked. "Thanks, big guy."

"Hi, Marly." Justin glowered at Madigan and said, "Where's your shirt? You shouldn't be riding around topless."

"It's a *bazillion* degrees out there," Madigan said.

"*Shirt*, Mads," Justin said. "*Now.*"

"*God!*" Madigan grabbed her bag from the desk and said, "Why don't you yell at Marly? It's not like guys don't see me on the beach like this."

"Marly doesn't drive something with only two wheels. On the beach you're supposed to be wearing a bathing suit, but you don't need to distract drivers on the road and end up getting hit by some asshole who's paying more attention to your body than to driving."

"I've got my shirt." Marly pulled a shirt from her bag.

Blaine put his hand over hers and said, "No need to put your shirt on, Mar. I'm about to turn up the heat in here even more." He whipped off his shirt, flashing an arrogant grin.

"Real suave, bro," Justin said with a shake of his head.

Marly's eyes were locked on Blaine's abs. "He might not be suave, but the view is *greatly* appreciated."

"This is *not* happening." Madigan stepped between them and put her hands on her hips, glaring at Blaine. "Put your shirt on before you end up in the supply room with Marly."

Blaine looked over Madigan's head at Marly and said, "What do you say? Up for a little inventory?"

"I usually like a guy to buy me a drink first," Marly countered.

Madigan tipped her face up to the ceiling and sighed dramatically. "Please make it *stop*."

"You mean you *didn't* invite Marly to lunch with us so we could hook up?" Blaine teased.

Madigan rolled her eyes. "Like you guys need setting up? You're always disappearing together. Can you stop ogling her for a second? I need to talk with you and Justin about helping me find a place to live. Do you think you can put the word out that I'm looking for a place to rent? Someplace that does *not* belong to a Dark Knight?"

"Why?" Justin asked. "When I was checking on Gramps

yesterday, he said Preacher and Mom were happy that you were going to be sticking around their place for a while."

She gave him a deadpan look. "And you *know* what that's like. I love our parents, but the last two times I came home after midnight, Dad was waiting up for me. He said he was just getting a drink, but the television was on both times, and he gave me the *nothing good happens after midnight* lecture."

"Ouch. I remember that one," Blaine said.

"It's not a fun lecture," Madigan said. "I've traveled across the country without anyone holding my hand. I don't need to be babysat. I love that Mom wants to make family dinners and do my laundry and all the rest of the motherly things she hasn't been able to do since I moved out, but I don't want her touching my thongs."

"And I don't want to know you're wearing thongs," Justin said sharply.

Marly grinned and said, "Then you really don't want to know what's in her nightstand."

"Enough. We're *not* doing this. She's our little sister," Justin said as he scrubbed a hand down his face.

"Hello? I'm also an adult. Will you guys help me?" Madigan asked.

Blaine folded his arms across his chest and said, "You're asking for a lot, *princess*."

Madigan glowered at him.

"I told her she could stay with me, but she refused." Marly sat in a chair and curled the ends of her dark hair around her finger.

"Because I'm afraid *someone* might come creeping out of your bedroom in the morning." She hiked a thumb at Blaine and pretended to gag.

Marly looked at Blaine and said, "Would you please tell her that you've never spent the night at my place and that we're just friends? She doesn't believe me."

"Who am I to debunk the myth? Are we going to eat, or should I drag Marly into the supply room for my next meal?" Blaine winked at Marly.

"Gross! We're going." Madigan grabbed Justin's wrist, tugging him out of his office.

As they walked through the showroom, Justin said, "I might have a line on a place for you. I'll let you know Sunday."

"You're a *god*," Madigan exclaimed.

"I bet that's what Chloe says," Marly teased as she and Blaine fell into step with them.

"Nah, she usually says, 'Is it in yet?'" Blaine cracked up as he put on his shirt.

Justin punched him in the arm. "Asshole."

Marly took Blaine's arm as they left the showroom and said, "A little bird told me that Maverick has been given *quite* a descriptive nickname for his junk. Maybe you're jealous."

Blaine scoffed. "Does an anaconda get jealous of a garden snake? I don't think so. I heard Maverick bought a strap-on just so Chloe wouldn't leave him."

Justin lunged, and Blaine took off, laughing hysterically. "You're about to hear your head crack open when I slam it against the pavement!"

Chapter Twenty-Five

CHLOE'S ARM SLID over cold sheets on Justin's side of the bed Saturday morning. It was her birthday, and the bed might be empty, but her heart was full. Refusing to give in to the morning just yet, she kept her eyes closed and snuggled deeper under the blankets, thinking about last night. She and Justin had cuddled beneath a blanket on a lounge chair on the deck, stargazing and talking. Justin had asked her what her favorite thing about being twenty-nine was, and her answer had come as easily and honestly as the air she breathed. *You*, she'd said.

She rolled onto her back and opened her eyes. The ceiling was *covered* in balloons, their colorful strings dangling above her. One of the strings had a piece of paper hanging from it. She sat up and snagged the note, reading Justin's handwritten message. *Happy 29th, beautiful! Come find me!* She squealed and hopped out of bed, taking in the streamers draped across the top of the curtains, the edges of the dressers, and the closet and bathroom doorframes. She plucked Justin's shirt from the floor and pulled it on.

As she opened the bathroom door, balloons floated out and up to the ceiling, and another happy sound escaped her. She grabbed a few handfuls of ribbons, pulling the balloons out of the bathroom to make room for herself, and when she stepped inside, she saw *Here's to your best year yet!* written in lipstick on the mirror. There was a gift on the counter. She tore open the pretty silver wrapping paper and found a black tank top with pink letters emblazoned across the chest that read BIRTHDAY GIRL and beneath it, also in pink, was 29! She lifted the tank top out of the box, revealing a pair of skimpy black boy shorts that had SWEET CHEEKS printed in pink across the ass.

Her heart went crazy as she undressed, quickly freshened up, and put on the birthday shirt and shorts. She hurried out the bedroom door to look for Justin and found the hallway decorated with more balloons and streamers. A birthday banner was thumbtacked to the wall, and a funky birthday hat with foam candles sat on the floor. She put on the hat and followed the scent of something sweet toward the kitchen, stopping cold when she got to the living room. Last night she'd given Justin the memory board she'd finally finished making for him, and now it was hanging above the mantel like a piece of art. As she walked closer, she noticed a new picture attached with a tiny metal clip. It was a picture of her sleeping on Justin's chest. She had no idea when he might have taken it, but it made her all kinds of happy as she read what he'd written across the top in black marker: *My girl, my future, my life.*

"I'm not as skilled at that as you are."

She turned at the sound of Justin's voice, emotions clogging her throat. He stood at the entrance to the kitchen wearing nothing but his black boxer briefs and holding a lopsided cake with pink icing and so many lit candles it looked like an inferno. It—*he*—brought tears to her eyes.

"I'm also not very adept in the baking department," he said as he carried the cake to her.

"It's the…" Too choked up to get the words out, she cleared her throat to try again. "It's the most perfect cake I've ever seen."

"My singing is not so hot, either, but you're going to have to deal with it, babe, because I'm afraid it's going to be an annual thing."

He sang "Happy Birthday" in his deep, raspy voice. She couldn't stop smiling as he sang it all the way through, each word more beautiful than the last.

"Make a wish, sweet thing."

Nervous laughter bubbled out as she said, "How can I wish for anything when everything I want is standing right in front of me?"

"Everybody's got to make a birthday wish, darlin'." His eyes turned seductive and he said, "Close your eyes and think *long* and *hard*. I'm sure you'll think of something."

She laughed again. "You are a dirty boy." She closed her eyes and wished for a lifetime of birthdays just like this, and then she blew out the candles. "Thank you. I can't believe how much you did for me."

"You only turn twenty-nine once…*a year*." He winked, and she followed him into the kitchen.

A gigantic vase full of irises sat in the center of the table. There were two plates filled with heart-shaped pancakes and strawberries. Beside one plate was a small gift box with a red bow tied around it. Justin handed it to her and said, "For you, baby."

"*Justin…*This is the best birthday I've ever had. You've already done too much."

He put his arms around her and kissed the tip of her nose. "This is only the beginning, and this gift is for me as much as it is for you."

"Now you've piqued my interest." She pulled open the bow and lifted the top off the box. Inside was a key on a key chain with a little house charm dangling from it.

"It's to this house," he said, bringing her eyes up to his. "I know how hard you worked to buy your cottage and how much it means to you, so if you'd rather we—"

She silenced him with a hard press of her lips. "I want the key," she said breathlessly. "Before we got together, I spent my life ticking off boxes, gathering all the things that I thought would make a happy home and a happy life. But I had the pretty cottage and the nice furniture with matching curtains and walls full of family photos. I had all the things I thought I needed, but I was still searching, using those stupid dating apps, trying to find what was missing. And then your sister asked me to meet her at the Salty Hog, the one place I never wanted to go again. But I would have done anything for the residents of LOCAL. And thank goodness I did, because seeing you walk into the bar that night, bloody and forlorn, was enough to open my heart and my eyes. After a year and a half of running from my feelings, I couldn't walk away when you were in so much pain. You laid your heart out to me that night, Justin, and you gave me the courage to do the same. And every day since, you've shown me how to love without fear or reservation. You made me realize that all those things I collected were just buoys helping me remain afloat in a sea of hopes and dreams. But *you* are my safe haven, my happy place. You are my *island*, Justin, and I want to be yours."

He swept her into his arms, kissing her smiling lips, and said, "I love you."

"I love you, too. This is the most amazing birthday. My

head is spinning. Should I rent my cottage? Sell it? When do you want me to move in? Oh my God, *Justin*. I'm *moving in*!" She launched herself into his arms again, and he twirled her around.

They kissed and laughed, and when he set her on her feet again, he said, "It's a good thing you want to move in, because if you didn't, it would make this a little more complicated." He opened the kitchen door and whistled. In trotted Sampson, with a blue bow tie around his neck.

Chloe squealed and dropped to her knees, loving Sampson up. He licked her face, and suddenly she was laughing and crying. "He's ours? What about the cool couple you told me about?"

"That was us, sweet cheeks."

"What about Shadow?"

"Sid's been working with them, and they get along really well. He'll be coming home soon, too."

"Oh my God!" She sprang to her feet, trying to wrap her head around all he'd done. "*Justin*…We have a *family*. Shadow and Sampson have a family. Thank you for the best birthday ever."

"It's not over yet, sweetheart. There's something I want to run by you."

"Oh my gosh, you've done so much alrea—"

He dropped to one knee, and her heart nearly stopped as he took her hand, gazing up at her with so much love in his eyes it nearly took *her* to her knees. Sampson licked Justin's cheek, then sat beside him.

"I don't know if fate or dumb luck brought you into my life, but I knew the first time we met that we were meant to be together, and every day since has proven me right."

"*Justin…?*" she whispered shakily.

"I know this might feel fast, but I waited a year and a half for you to give us a chance, and I meant what I said about that time giving us a solid foundation." He rose to his feet, gazing deeply into her eyes, and said, "I love you, baby, and I want to spend the rest of my life making every day of *yours* the best it can be. I want you in my arms at night, and I want to bring you coffee every morning. I want to celebrate your twenty-ninth birthday for the next sixty years, go on long motorcycle rides, and dance under the stars. I want it all with you, baby, and I hope you want it all with me."

He reached behind the vase and held up the most gorgeous ring she'd ever seen. A canary diamond lay in a setting of gold flowers with a gold dragonfly across the middle of the stone, its wings spread as if it were caught midflight. Tears spilled down Chloe's cheeks.

"My sexy, sweet girl, will you make me the happiest man on earth and marry me?"

"*Yes,*" she said just above a whisper. Then louder, "Yes, yes, *yes!*"

He slid the ring on her finger, and for the third time that morning, she threw herself into his arms. With their fur baby leaning against their legs and their hearts beating as one, they kissed through salty tears, whispering promises of everlasting love.

Chapter Twenty-Six

IT HAD BEEN hours since Justin had proposed, and Chloe still couldn't stop looking at her ring. They'd forgone breakfast and spent the morning making love. After satiating their desire, they'd talked about when Chloe should move in. Neither of them wanted to wait. After getting ready to face the day, Chloe called Serena to share their good news, and Justin called Preacher. One call was all it had taken for Justin's phone to start vibrating like the Energizer Bunny with congratulatory messages from the Dark Knights and offers to help them move Chloe's things next weekend. She and Justin took Sampson for a nice long walk, and though Shadow wasn't home yet, Chloe already felt the unity of family.

When she drove to meet the girls for her birthday lunch, she once again gushed about her birthday and the proposal to Serena via Bluetooth. "I can't stop looking at my ring. Did I tell you Justin designed it and his friend Sterling made it for him?"

"Four times. Not that I'm counting or anything."

"I'm sorry. I'm just so excited! Serena, we're going to have *two* dogs who really need us, and *I'm getting married*!" She yelled that last part, and they both cheered. "I can't wait to tell all the girls."

"Gee, I couldn't tell," Serena teased. "Oh, shoot! I forgot to tell you that Desiree can't make it. She's due next week and really uncomfortable, so I thought we'd stop by after lunch, before we hit the beach."

"Poor thing. Wait! Change of plans! Let's meet at Summer House for lunch. We'll order pizza. Desiree shouldn't miss out just because she's pregnant. Vi and Andre are supposed to come home sometime this morning. It would be great to see them, too."

"I'm sure Des is resting," Serena said.

"No way. She's baking or something—you know how she is. Even if she is resting, she won't mind if we come over." Chloe made a U-turn and said, "I'm going there. I'll call Tegan and Harper and let them know. Will you call Daph and Emery?"

"Wait! We can't do that," Serena insisted. "Desiree and Rick might be going at it. You know how she is with all those hormones running wild."

"That's doubtful with Vi and Andre coming home. She's way too modest to risk being caught. What is up with you, anyway?"

"We have plans to meet at the restaurant, Chloe. You can't change our plans."

"Sure I can. It's *my* birthday. What's wrong? Can't keep up with your spontaneous sister?"

"It's not that! It's...."

"It's *nothing!* I'm going to call Tegan. Meet you there!" She ended the call and quickly got in touch with Tegan and Harper. She was bursting at the seams to tell them her news, but she waited, wanting to tell them in person.

She rolled down her windows and cranked the radio, singing to every song that came on. When she got to Summer House, she stepped from her car feeling like she was walking on air and hurried across the lawn. Serena flew into the driveway as Chloe opened the kitchen door. She waved to Serena and headed inside. The sweet aroma of fresh-baked goods tickled her senses. She'd been right about Desiree baking. The counters were covered with cooling racks full of cookies, cupcakes, and baking paraphernalia. Cosmos scampered into the kitchen, going paws-up on Chloe's leg. She scooped up the fluffy pup and he licked her face. "Hey, there. Where's your mama?"

Cosmos wiggled out of her hands and darted down the hall, barking.

She followed him, calling out, "Des?" She glanced up the stairs, hoping Serena had been wrong and Desiree and Rick weren't going at it. She peered into the dining room and said, "Desiree?" She heard something in the living room, and as she crossed the hall, she heard the kitchen door open.

"Chloe?" Serena hollered.

"In the living room," Chloe called out.

Cosmos was barking and running around the couch. Serena ran into the room and said, "There you are. We should go." She grabbed Chloe's hand, dragging her toward the hallway.

"*Why?* Desiree is probably in the office or out back relaxing," Chloe said over Cosmos's barks.

"Come on. We shouldn't be in here." Serena tugged her toward the hall again.

Chloe yanked her hand free. "*What* is *wrong* with you?"

Cosmos stood between the edge of the couch and the wall, *growling*.

"And *what* is wrong with *him*? Come on, Cosmos," Chloe coaxed as she walked toward him, but he lunged behind the couch in a flurry of barks and growls. "Cosmos!" Chloe ran around the couch just as a sea of red balloons rose to the ceiling, sending Cosmos into a leaping, barking frenzy. And there behind the couch sat Tank, Drake, and Ginger.

Ginger wiggled her fingers. "Hi, sugar."

For a second Chloe thought she was in the wrong house, and her jumbled mind couldn't make sense of seeing those three people sitting on the floor behind Desiree's couch.

As Tank, Drake, and Ginger pushed to their feet, Cosmos barked furiously.

Tank jerked toward Cosmos and said, "Boo!" sending the little dog scurrying away.

Chloe heard the front door open, and footsteps thundered down the hall. "What is going on?" she asked as Harper, Daphne, Emery, and Tegan ran into the room.

"Oh no!" Daphne exclaimed.

The back door flew open and Zeke and Justin walked in. Justin was leading Sampson on a leash.

"The canopy is all set—" Justin stilled, meeting Chloe's confused gaze. Cosmos ran to Justin, and Sampson pushed his big nose against the little barking dog, shoving him halfway across the floor.

Serena ran over and said, "I *tried* to stop her, but you've created a spontaneous *monster*. She wouldn't listen. I'm sorry."

Cosmos sped past Serena as Zander and Dwayne popped up from behind the piano. Preacher appeared from behind a chair, and Madigan stepped out from behind the curtains, sending Cosmos into a zigzagging sprint from one person to the next. Dean and Rick stood up behind the other couch as Gavin and Andre came through the back doors laughing.

A lopsided grin spread across Justin's face as he went to

Chloe and said, "Hey, beautiful. I thought you were having lunch with the girls."

"I was. *Am.* What is going on?" Chloe asked.

Justin looked around and said, "We were all just, uh—"

"I've got the birthday cake and the banners! Sorry I'm late!" Reba's voice sailed through the air.

Cosmos darted down the hall, and Sampson broke free, galloping after him. Reba shrieked, and then there was a loud *thump.*

"Oh shit," the guys said at once, and everyone ran into the hall.

Reba was lying in the middle of the floor with cake all over her. Cosmos was standing on her chest, licking frosting from her face, and Sampson was gobbling cake off the floor. Reba laughed and said, "I think Cosmos and I are going steady now."

Relieved laughter floated around them as everyone went to help her, but Preacher was already by her side, shooing Cosmos away. "Get outta here, pooch. I'm the only one that gets to lick this sexy gal."

"Wow, I had no idea we were playing kinky cake games at this party," Violet said as she and Desiree came down the stairs.

Justin laughed and swept Chloe into his arms, grinning like a Cheshire cat, or rather, like the gorgeous, thoughtful fiancé he was. As the others tried to stop Cosmos and Sampson from tracking cake and frosting all over the house, Chloe wrapped her arms around Justin and said, "Mr. Wicked, what have you done now?"

"Just living up to my promises of making all of your days special."

Violet sauntered over in her cutoffs, black bikini top, and biker boots, and said, "Just don't start talking about your naughty nights or Desiree might go into labor." She kissed Chloe's cheek and said, "Happy birthday *and* congratulations, Chloe. You've got a good man on your hands."

Chloe grinned at Justin and said, "I've got a *wicked* good man on my hands, and I love him that way."

DESPITE CHLOE'S STUMBLING into the setting up of her surprise party and Reba's unfortunate cake spill, the party was a smashing success. They spent a wonderful day with friends and family on the beach celebrating Chloe's birthday and their engagement. Serena made a big SHE SAID YES! sign with an arrow pointing to the side, and they'd taken dozens of pictures for Chloe's memory books. When evening rolled in, they grilled food for dinner and built a bonfire.

Now the moon hung low over the bay, and the lights they'd set up on the beach twinkled against the night sky. Justin stood by the roaring fire talking with Mike, Preacher, Gavin, Tank, and Blaine as Zander and Drake played their guitars and Gunner chimed in with his harmonica. Baz and Zeke were flirting with the book club girls by the dessert table, and Sid and Evie had found new friends in the couples from Bayside Resort and Summer House. Justin looked past them all at Chloe, chatting with Ginger, Serena, Reba, and Madigan. Sampson was leaning against Chloe's legs, and she'd kept her hand on him all evening, as if he were a child. She looked gorgeous wearing the black sweatshirt Serena had given her for her birthday with ~~GIRLFRIEND~~ FIANCÉE written across the front. She'd shown off her ring and told everyone about the morning, recounting every moment from the second she'd seen the balloons to the moment she'd said *yes*.

Justin had thought she'd never looked happier than when she'd seen the cake he'd made, but when he'd given her the key, she'd put that cake smile to shame. And when he'd brought Sampson in and told her about adopting him and Shadow, she'd stepped up her elation once again. But nothing—*nothing*—could top the look of overwhelming love and happiness in her eyes when he'd asked her to marry him. He knew he'd remember every look she'd ever given him, but that one was wrapped up for safekeeping and tucked away next to his heart.

"I take full credit for this engagement." Gavin nudged Justin and said, "Right, dude? I made marriage look good, didn't I."

"You sure did." Gavin and Harper's love was admirable. But it was Preacher and Reba, and Conroy and Ginger, who deserved the credit for Justin's ability to love and be loved and for his desire to nurture a relationship that could not only survive the worst of times, but one in which he and Chloe would continually help each other become the best people they could be. And it was Mike's sharing of his story and how much he'd overcome with the woman he adored that had underscored the importance of being a good man above all else, because after that, everything else had fallen into line.

Justin looked at Preacher and Mike and said, "These guys deserve a little credit, too."

"Hear, hear," Blaine cheered, lifting his beer.

Mike eyed Tank and Blaine and said, "One Wicked man down. Who's next?"

"Next?" Blaine looked at Tank, who shrugged.

Preacher put a hand on Blaine's shoulder and said, "If your Whiskey cousins are any indication, once one good man falls, the rest follow like dominoes."

"Sorry, Preach. I'm not into dominoes." Blaine looked across the way at Marly and said, "But I'd like to get into a certain exotic brunette. I'll catch up with you guys later."

As Blaine walked away, Mike said, "How about you, Tank? You're getting a little long in the tooth."

Tank scoffed. "Don't hold your breath on my account, old man. All that white-picket-fence shit isn't in the cards for me."

"Maybe if you'd stop scaring the ladies away," Justin teased.

Tank's eyes narrowed. "I don't know what's up with that waitress at the Hog, but the only thing chicks are afraid of is the size of my dick."

They all laughed.

Mike smirked. "He gets that from his grandpa."

"On that note, when are you boys going to start using those appendages for making grandchildren?" Preacher looked at Tank and Justin expectantly. "You too, Gavin."

"Don't look at me, Preach. We don't even have a wedding date yet," Justin reminded them.

"Man, my parents are asking us the same thing," Gavin said. "Nothing like a little pressure."

Mike motioned in the direction of Chloe and Reba and said, "Maverick, I bet your mama's already lodging her vote for procreation with Chloe."

"I'd better go nix that. We need time to be a couple before we're parents," Justin said.

"I'll sidetrack them," Mike offered. "I'm heading over to grab another cookie anyway."

Preacher touched Mike's arm and said, "Pops, you've had a

lot of sugar tonight."

"These next six weeks can't pass fast enough," Mike grumbled. His application had been approved at LOCAL, and he was moving in the week before the suicide-awareness rally. He looked at Justin and said, "Your girl is a godsend for getting me into that facility. Think I can pay extra to get the deal expedited?"

Justin shook his head. "Doubt it, Gramps."

"Worth a try," Mike mumbled; then he headed for the dessert table.

"I'll get him," Justin said.

"Nah. You get your girl." Tank clapped a hand on Justin's back and said, "This is your night. I'll get Gramps."

"I think I'll go lock lips with my wife." Gavin headed up the beach with Tank, leaving Preacher and Justin alone.

"Preach, want to take a walk with me to go see our beautiful ladies?"

"You betcha." Preacher put an arm over Justin's shoulders and said, "I'm proud of you, son."

"I still remember the first time you said that to me, my first night at your place. It was after Madigan had fallen asleep on my shoulder."

Preacher's lips curved up and he said, "You hadn't moved an inch for almost two hours."

"I know. My arm went numb." When Madigan had woken up, she'd run off to play, and Justin had pushed to his feet and shaken out his arm, wincing as pins and needles prickled his limb. Preacher had moved his arm this way and that until the feeling came back, and as he was moving it around, he'd told Justin he was proud of him for putting Madigan's well-being above his own. It was the first of so many important lessons. "I wouldn't be half the man I am today without your guidance and love. I probably don't say this enough, but thank you for all you've done for me."

Preacher tapped his head against Justin's and said, "You say it every day by treating others right, your fiancée included."

"*Fiancée.* I like the sounds of that a whole hell of a lot."

Chloe turned as they approached, and their eyes connected with the heat and love Justin knew would last a lifetime. He wondered if it would be rude for them to sneak off down the beach for a few moonlight kisses. Sampson barked and pulled the leash in his direction. Chloe smiled, and Justin nodded, letting her know she could drop the leash. As Sampson trotted over to him, he said, "I never knew I could love anyone as much as I love her, Preach."

"Really? I always knew you had it in you." Preacher winked.

As Preacher went to Reba, Justin loved up Sampson. Then he put an arm around Chloe and said, "Hey, baby." He kissed her softly. Turning his attention to Reba, he said, "Mom, would you mind if I steal my girl for a minute?"

"Don't you mean *our* girl?" Reba asked. "That's my future daughter-in-law you're holding."

The smile on Chloe's face was as enchanting as the one he'd seen when he'd proposed.

"And she's *my* sister-in-law," Madigan said. "I'm so excited to work with Chloe. I'll get to see her as much as you do, Mav. I know we'll get final funding for a long-term project. I'm a kick-ass puppeteer."

"Have I told you how much I love your sister?" Chloe asked. "I was just telling her and Reba that I'm meeting with our clinicians Monday afternoon to choose the residents who will be taking part in the trial program."

Reba gave Justin an approving look and said, "Your fiancée knows her stuff. She's a real go-getter."

"And guess what else she is?" Madigan didn't give Justin time to guess. "My new landlord! Chloe said I can rent her cottage when she moves in with you next weekend. She's leaving a lot of the furniture, too, which makes it even more perfect."

Justin said, "Remember when we had lunch and I said I might have a lead on a place for you?"

"Yeah." Understanding dawned in Madigan's widening eyes. "*Oh*. You meant Chloe's? You could have told me you were proposing. I kept the secret about her party."

"Yes, you did, but the only person who needed to know was Serena, and that was only because I wanted to ask her for Chloe's hand in marriage." Justin saw a look of disbelief in Chloe's eyes and said, "You were hers long before you became mine. It was the right thing to do."

"You never fail to surprise me," Chloe said with awe. "I can't believe Serena hasn't said anything about it."

"I asked her not to. I only meant until you said *yes*, but it's good to know she's so loyal."

"Yeah, good to know," Chloe said sarcastically. "I might have to rethink my matron of honor."

"Have you given any thought to a wedding date?" Reba asked.

"Mom, we *just* got engaged. I'm still trying to wrap my head around the fact that I'm lucky enough to wake up next to this incredible woman every day for the rest of my life."

Chloe leaned into his side and whispered, "I love you."

"Aw," Madigan said. "You guys make me wish I believed in love for *myself*."

"Don't knock it until you've tried it, baby girl." Reba

looked at Chloe and said, "Have you always dreamed of a big white wedding?"

"To be honest, my life was all about survival for so long, I never dreamed of white weddings or a knight in shining armor. It wasn't until after I'd bought my house and my career was settled that I started hoping I'd meet someone who would love me in the ways I always wanted to be loved. But I think in my head, a wedding was just checking off a box, wanting something because everyone else was moving in that direction." She looked at Justin's parents and said, "Then Justin came into my life, and without realizing it, I spent a year and a half comparing men to him and fooling myself into thinking that we weren't right for each other. Thank heavens Justin didn't give up, because he's showed me that if I'd settled for being loved in the way I *thought* I wanted, I would have been shortchanging myself."

She turned those loving hazel eyes on him and said, "I don't care if I get married barefoot on the beach or in glass slippers in a castle, as long as when I say *I do*, I get to say it to you."

Chapter Twenty-Seven

CHLOE LEFT THE meeting with the clinicians Monday afternoon feeling productive. They'd discussed potential candidates for Madigan's trial program and arranged for Madigan to come in and meet with their medical teams to ensure they were all on the same page. The trial program wasn't due to start for several weeks, but everything was coming together nicely—there and in all aspects of Chloe's life. She glanced at her sparkling engagement ring for the millionth time that day as she followed the sounds of laughter and music into the community room.

Rose was sitting beside Tina, one of the juniors in the new program, and her senior partner, Clara. They were looking at Tina's and Clara's phones. In the middle of the room, Kelly, another junior, was teaching her senior partner, Barbara, and Arlin, how to do the floss, a trendy dance move. The three of them were laughing as Kelly tried to guide Arlin's hips in the right direction. It was good to see so much joy coming from the program.

"Chloe!" Rose waved her over. "Tina is *filtering* us."

"Filtering?" Chloe asked.

"Photo filters." Tina, a petite redhead with a sweet demean-

or, held up her phone, showing Chloe a picture of Rose with bunny ears and whiskers.

"She's showing us how to use Snapchat," Clara said. "It's all the rage these days, and Tina makes it easy to understand."

Chloe loved that they were all enjoying their time together. "Very cute, ladies. Maybe now you'll consider signing up for our technology program."

Clara said, "Tina, would you go with me to a technology class?"

"Sure. Let me know when and I'll check my schedule." Tina handed Clara the phone and said, "Why don't you try a filter?"

As Clara navigated the program on Tina's phone, Rose got up and reached for Chloe's hand. "I just have to see this gorgeous ring one more time. Your engagement is all anyone can talk about."

When Chloe had arrived at work that morning, she'd stopped to chat with Shelby, and when she'd told her about the engagement, Shelby had popped to her feet, letting out a loud "Congratulations!" She'd hurried around the desk to hug Chloe just as two more staff members had come through the door. It hadn't taken long for word of her engagement to make its way around the facility. Residents stopped her in the hall to congratulate her and ask about the lucky man who had snagged her heart. She loved telling them about Justin and his family, and about Shadow and Sampson. Justin had taken Sampson to work with him today, and he'd texted earlier to say how good a boy he was.

Tina got up to check out Chloe's ring. "Wow, that's cool. I've never seen a ring like that."

"It's custom. Her fiancé designed it," Rose said. "I hope you two are as happy as Leon and I were, but for many more years."

"Thank you, Rose."

"Tina, look at this one." Clara waved the phone.

As Tina sat beside Clara, Rose lowered her voice and said, "Emery told me *all* about how Justin wooed you and how you played hard to get for a *very* long time."

"I didn't play hard to get. I just had to get out of my own way and let nature take its course."

"Either way, a man who waits is a man worth waiting for." Rose turned toward the women who were learning the floss, and said, "Do you know how to do the floss?"

"Yes. I love to dance, but that's not my dance of choice."

"I miss dancing with Leon." Rose's expression turned thoughtful. "We used to slow dance, and *oh*, how I loved being in his arms."

"Justin and I love to slow dance, too. I think dancing with him is one of my favorite things to do with him," Chloe said, remembering the way Justin had pulled her into his arms earlier that morning after their shower and they'd slow danced in the bathroom. He'd touched his forehead to hers and whispered, *I will always love you.*

Rose squeezed her hand and said, "That's good, Chloe. I hope you two always have that."

"Me too." Chloe checked the time. It was already three thirty. She and Justin were meeting at her cottage right after work to start packing for her move. "Oh gosh, I'd better get back to work."

"I'll get back to my filtering."

Chloe headed down the hall. Shelby was watching her approach. She'd pinned her curly dark hair up and a few pretty tendrils had sprung free, framing her face.

"Are you knocked up?" Shelby asked. "Because you are

absolutely glowing."

"Not pregnant, just happily engaged."

"Some of the residents asked me to find out about your wedding date so they can throw you a bridal shower."

"Really? That's so nice. I'll let you know when we figure it out." She and Justin had started talking about their wedding date last night. Neither one wanted to wait too long, but between work, acclimating to life with two furbabies, and making the sculpture for the suicide-awareness rally, the rest of their summer was going to be busy. The rally was in September, and Chloe knew that was going to be a difficult time for Justin. The last thing he needed was more pressure, so she suggested they put off talking about a wedding date until after the holidays.

Shelby lowered her voice and said, "Maybe you can introduce me to one of Justin's single brothers. That big guy who was here for the tour was a mighty sexy beast."

"That's his cousin Tank. He's a really good guy, although he doesn't talk much."

"I don't mind a man of few words, if you know what I mean. Speaking of men of few words, Alan is back from his meetings. He was looking for you. He's in a finance meeting now, but he should be out any minute. I'll let him know you're in your office."

"Thanks, Shelby."

Chloe went into her office and answered a few emails. Then she began knocking off items from her to-do list. She was knee-deep in reviewing a state regulatory update when Alan walked into her office.

"Hi, Alan. I'm glad you're back," she said as he closed the door.

"Are you?" he asked in a low voice as he walked toward her desk.

"Yes." She dug through her papers for the puppetry folder. "I know we have a few weeks before the puppetry trial begins, but I want to get my ducks in a row to present the program to the families, and..." She looked up to find him standing beside her, a cold stare locked on her engagement ring. The hair on the back of her neck stood on end.

"If this is your way of getting my attention," he said in a cold, even voice, "you've got it."

"I don't understand. What do you—"

Those icy eyes hit hers, setting off all her internal alarms. Before she could make a move, he put his hands on the arms of her chair, his legs on either side of hers, caging her in. Panic flared in her chest. Images of being trapped against her mother's counter and on the couch flew into her head. *Breathe, breathe, breathe.* Disbelief hung in the recesses of her mind, but it was no competition for the fear engulfing her.

She pushed at his chest and said, "Get back, Alan. *Now.*"

"We both know that's not what you want. You said you'd been waiting forever, and I got the message loud and clear, Chloe. There's no more waiting."

His sinister voice sent ice through her veins. Time and space blurred together, and survival mode kicked in. Chloe jammed her knee up and threw her shoulder into his chest. Her knee missed his groin, but he stumbled, and she got to her feet, choking out an indiscernible noise. He slapped a hand over her mouth and slammed her back against the wall, crushing his body to hers. The metallic taste of blood filled her mouth. His nostrils flared as he ground against her body. She could barely breathe, for his hand pressed against her nostrils as she struggled to break free. She tried to scream, but it was muffled behind his hand.

He'd morphed into someone unrecognizable. His evil eyes drilled into her as he tugged up on her skirt. "You little witch, spreading your legs for that dirtbag to get me jealous."

His sharp, cruel voice cut through her fear and he gripped her inner thigh. Bile rose in her throat. Her mind sped through dozens of self-defense moves, finally catching on one. All at once, she stomped her high heel on his foot, grabbed a fistful of his hair, and bit his hand, using all her might to push forward—and *free*. He lunged, snagging the back of her blouse and yanking her backward, but not before she grabbed the stapler from her desk. She whirled around and smacked him in the eye with it. His hands flew to his face, and she grabbed her purse and ran to the door, but he'd locked it. Her shaking hands fumbled. She felt a *click* and yanked it open at the same second he grabbed her by the shirt. She hurled herself through the door, sending the buttons from her blouse flying as she bolted past reception and out the front doors. She didn't slow down when she barreled into someone, sending them to the ground in her sprint to her car.

She couldn't think, could barely breathe, as she sped toward Justin's house, clinging to the steering wheel, trying to see the road through the blur of tears. She tried to turn on voice commands on the dashboard, but her hand was shaking too badly. It took several tries, and when she finally got it, she choked out, "Call...Justin!"

"Hey, sweet chee—"

The sound of his voice brought sobs, and her attempt to say his name came out all bumbled.

"Chloe? What's wrong? Where are you?"

She coughed and sobbed, feeling like she was going to throw up. "Alan…*attacked* me—"

"Motherfucker."

The malice in his voice brought more sobs.

"Are you hurt, Chloe?"

"*No.*" She gasped for breath. "I'm…going home. I'll"—*gasp, sob, gasp*—"report it after"—she coughed—"I calm down."

"I'm going to kill that fucker," Justin growled.

"No. I need yo—"

The line went dead.

CHLOE STUMBLED INTO the house in a daze of fear and disbelief. Just being home among hers and Justin's things brought solace *and* sadness. She sank down to the couch to wait for him, giving in to more tears.

A few minutes later she heard tires on gravel. Justin had taken the truck so he could bring Sampson to work. She heard a vehicle door close, and a modicum of relief swept through her, though it did nothing to stop the tears or the shaking. The rumble of a motorcycle sounded, and she ran to the window. The front door flew open, and Tank, Blaine, and Sampson strode in. Sampson trotted past them to get to her.

"*Aw, sweetheart*," Blaine said full of anguish. He eyed Tank, who looked like he was ready to kill someone, and said, "Get her a shirt."

Panic chased up Chloe's spine as Tank headed into the bedroom. She pulled her shirt closed, crossing her arms over her middle as a rush of tears flowed down her cheeks. "What happened? Where's Justin?"

"He'll be here," Blaine said gently. "Did he…? Do you need to go to the hospital?"

She shook her head, and he folded her in his arms, drawing more tears.

"I've got you," Blaine said.

"I don't know who that man was that attacked me," she cried. "Alan was like Jekyll and Hyde."

"I'm sorry, Chloe. You're safe now."

The front door opened again, and Chloe spun around, expecting Justin. But it was Serena running toward her with open arms. Reba came in right behind her.

Serena threw her arms around Chloe. "Are you okay? Justin called me."

Chloe nodded, clinging to her sister.

Serena drew back with tears in her eyes, searching Chloe's face. She pulled Chloe's shirt closed and said, "Are you sure you're okay?"

She nodded. "He tried…." Her voice was lost in sobs.

"Oh, my sweet girl," Reba said, gathering Chloe—and Serena—in her arms. "Breathe, baby. We'll get through this together, and that man will pay for what he's done."

Tank came out of the bedroom with one of her shirts and strode directly to them, putting his arms around all three of them, and rested his head on Reba's. Blaine's phone rang, and they all looked at him, but he walked into the other room to take the call.

Tank handed Chloe her shirt and said, "I'm real sorry this happened to you."

"Thank you." She put on her shirt over her blouse and said, "Justin went to my work, didn't he?"

Tank gave one curt nod.

Chloe's stomach lurched. "Oh *God*. Tank, you have to go after him. Justin will kill him. It'll ruin Justin's life."

"Preacher went after him, honey," Reba said. "He took the boys and Gunner with him."

"I hope Justin slaughters him," Serena fumed.

Tears tumbled down Chloe's cheeks as she sank down to the couch. "He *can't* do that, Serena. He'll go to prison, and then what? Alan wins, and Justin's life is ruined? I *told* Justin I was going to report it. I just needed to get my head on straight." Sampson rested his chin on her lap, gazing up at her with his big brown eyes, and for some reason that made her cry harder.

Reba sat beside her and held her hand. "Honey, look at me," she said in a firm voice. She waited for Chloe to meet her serious gaze and said, "The second you told Justin that man hurt you, nothing else registered. Do you understand that?"

"I don't understand any of this," she cried, collapsing into Reba's arms.

Chapter Twenty-Eight

JUSTIN WAS SEEING red as he stormed through the entrance of LOCAL, hands fisted, muscles corded tight.

Shelby looked up with troubled eyes. "Justin, what hap—"

"Where's Alan's office?" The ire in his voice was inescapable.

She pointed to a hallway and said, "End of the hall, last door on the left."

He burned a path down the hall, rage growing with every determined step. He threw open Alan's door, locking eyes with the fucker sitting behind his desk. Justin hoped to hell Chloe had given him that shiner. He kicked the door shut, and Alan's face blanched. All-consuming fear shone in his eyes as he pushed to his feet and reached for the phone. Justin lunged for it, tearing the cord from the wall. He tossed the phone to the floor, closing the distance between them. Alan walked backward, saying something about police, but Justin couldn't process the words over Chloe's sobs echoing in his head. He cocked his arm and threw a right hook, connecting with Alan's jaw with an audible *crack*. Alan's head flew back. He stumbled, careening toward the floor. Blinded by rage and fueled by hate and love and everything in between, Justin grabbed the collar of

Alan's shirt and hauled him to his feet, landing another blow to his bloody jaw, sending him crashing back against the wall. Alan slid to the floor, eyes unfocused, jaw agape.

Justin grabbed him by the hair, lifting him to his feet again. "Those were for Chloe, you motherfucker. You don't deserve to breathe the same air as her. These are for every other woman you've ever touched."

He threw a right uppercut to his ribs, followed by one to his left kidney. The air spilled from Alan's lungs with an *oomph*, and he slumped against the wall.

"And this is from *me*, you pathetic piece of shit." Justin pulled his arm back and let it fly, smashing Alan in the side of his head. Alan dropped to the floor in a heap, unconscious. Justin strode out of the office, dripping blood from the cuts on his knuckles. He headed out the front of the building with only one thing on his mind—reaching Chloe.

Preacher, Gunner, Zeke, and Zander were heading toward the entrance. They fell into step beside him as he crossed the parking lot.

"Is he still alive?" Gunner asked.

Preacher said, "Anything we need to clean up?"

"It's all on me," Justin growled. "Call Justice. I gotta get to Chloe." Rubin "Justice" Galant was an attorney and a Dark Knight, and handled the club's legal affairs.

"Blaine already called him." Preacher motioned for the guys to get on their bikes. When they walked away, he put a hand on Justin's shoulder and said, "Sure you're okay to drive?"

Justin nodded and climbed into his truck. He started it up and called Blaine, listening as he sped out of the parking lot, followed by Preacher and Gunner riding side by side, and Zeke and Zander bringing up the rear.

"She's shaken up, torn shirt, scratches on her face, but he didn't..." Blaine's voice trailed off. "Pushed her against the wall, pulled up her skirt. She fought back. She needs you, man. She needs you bad."

Tears burned Justin's eyes. He ended the call, grinding out curses through gritted teeth, white-knuckling the steering wheel with one hand and slamming the dashboard with the other.

When he pulled down his street, he found Baz, Conroy, and two other Dark Knights sitting on their motorcycles, blocking the entrance to the driveway.

They moved aside, and Baz and Conroy came to the window of the truck. Conroy said, "You a'right?"

Justin nodded.

"I got a call. Cuffs is looking for you," Conroy said. "Better get in there and see your girl."

They took a step back, and Justin drove up to the house, followed by Preacher and the other guys. Justin headed up the front steps trying to quell the tsunami in his gut. He knew the second he saw a scratch on Chloe's beautiful face, the rage consuming him would turn to scorching fury, and that was the last thing she needed. He stood on the porch, hands fisted, face angled up toward the sky, struggling—and failing—to shove all that anger down deep, and blew through the door.

Tank and Blaine stood in the living room. They turned as he came through the door, their faces masks of anger and empathy. Reba and Serena flanked Chloe, who was talking on the phone with tears streaming down her cheeks. A long red gash ran across her upper lip, and she was shaking as she lifted tortured eyes to his and said, "Yes, I understand," in a pained voice, then ended the call.

Justin's gut seized. He felt his heart shattering as he closed the distance between them and gathered her in his arms. Sobs burst from her lungs, and he held her tighter, one hand on the back of her head, the other arm belted around her, wishing he could tuck her under his skin to protect her. "I've got you, baby. I'm so sorry." He shifted his gaze to Reba and said, "Give us a minute?"

Reba ushered everyone out of the house, taking Sampson with them.

"I'm here. You're safe now." He kissed her forehead, feeling a crushing weight in his chest. "I love you, baby. I'm sorry, sweetheart. I'm so fucking sorry."

She fisted her hands in his shirt, clinging to him until her sobs eased. "*Justin...*" she said shakily against his chest.

"I've got you, baby. I'm here." She drew back, and her sad eyes slayed him anew. He wiped her tears with the pad of his thumb and said, "Are you okay? Are you hurt?"

She caught his bloodstained hand, her eyes lingering on it, anger and fear joining the sadness in them. She shook her head, stumbling back, her voice escalating. "What did you do? That was my office on the phone. I've been *suspended*. Alan filed sexual harassment allegations against *me*. He said you found out I was hitting on him and beat him up, and now *I'm* suspended from a job I would have given my life for before all this happened, and Blaine said the cops are looking for you, and—" She gasped for air, sobs engulfing her again.

"I should have fucking killed him!" Anger roared through him. "He can't do this, Chloe. We'll fix it. I promise you, this is not the end."

"*Fix it?*" she hollered. "You'll be in *jail*, Justin! I *told* you I would report what he did and that I *needed* you. I just needed to get my head on straight first." Her shoulders rounded forward, heaving with sobs. "Why didn't *I* see what you saw about him? I know the signs," she cried. "I should have seen them. Why did this...? I'm *so*...Our lives are *ruined*."

He drew her into his arms. She tried to twist away, but he held her tighter. "Our lives are *not* ruined, Chloe. You didn't see who he was because he's a fucking snake and didn't want you to see it."

"Why did you go after him?" she said accusingly.

"Because he deserved it. Because I *love* you, and when you love someone, you don't let anyone hurt them. I couldn't protect my mother, and I'll be damned if I'd let that happen to you."

Her face softened—*crumpled.* "Blaine said you could be charged with assault and battery and get serious jail time. That's *my* fault!"

He took her by the shoulders, staring into her eyes, and said, "*None* of this is your fault. That asshole attacked *you!*"

"But you ruined your life because of *me*. You could go to *jail*, Justin. You don't belong in jail. You're *not* your father."

"*Fuck.*" He stepped away, hands fisting. "I don't give a rat's ass about jail, Chloe. He deserved everything he got and more."

"This is all so crazy." She gasped between sobs. "I'll never work with the elderly again with sexual assault charges against me. I told HR what happened, and they're suspending him while they investigate, but it's my word against his. I'm supposed to go in for an interview tomorrow. How am I going to do that? I can't go back in there right now. I don't know if I will ever be able to face everyone again."

Her knees buckled and she reached for the couch, but he caught her around the waist, sweeping her into his arms. The front door opened, and Preacher walked in with Conroy, Reba,

Serena, and Cuffs. Reba held Serena, who was crying.

Cuffs was in uniform, his face dead serious as he stepped forward, the message in his eyes—*I've got to take you in*—clear.

Chloe made a mewling sound, holding Justin tighter, and his gut plummeted. He'd known this moment would come, but that didn't make it any easier.

"Look at me, baby," he said firmly. Chloe lifted her eyes to his, and the devastation in them brought tears to his. "I promise you I'm going to fix this."

Tears tumbled down her cheeks as she nodded.

"I love you, baby. He will *not* get away with this." He pressed his lips to hers, vowing to live up to that promise. He looked at Reba, a silent affirmation of her agreement to take care of Chloe passing between them.

Preacher and Conroy stepped beside him, and Reba and Serena moved closer to Chloe, causing her to cry harder. Despite knowing Chloe was in safe, loving hands, letting go of her and taking a step back was the hardest thing he'd ever done.

Until he walked out the front door, leaving his heart, his *love*, behind.

CHLOE FELT LIKE she'd been ravaged by the sea, and she wasn't drifting—she was drowning. Even in Reba's and Serena's arms, the waves crashed over her, sucking her under. In her devastation, she couldn't catch her breath. She loved Justin for standing up for her, but at the same time, she hated that he'd put himself—and *them*—in an even worse situation. Her anguish didn't stop there. She hated *herself* for not giving more weight to Justin's instincts about Alan, and she *despised* Alan Rogers.

She was *not* going to let that man ruin their lives.

I can do this. I have to do this. She willed her strength back into her legs, inhaling deeply, filling her lungs with determination as she stepped out of their arms and said, "I need to change my clothes; then I need to go to the police station to file a report."

"I know you want to get those clothes off and feel more like yourself," Reba said caringly, "but it's important that the police see what he did to you. You don't have to go to the station. Cuffs arranged for an officer to come here. We were just waiting for you to be ready."

Chloe swallowed hard, wiping her eyes. "Thank you."

"I'm staying here tonight," Serena said. "Drake is outside, along with about twenty Dark Knights. Tank and Blaine are going to stay until Justin gets back."

"*If* he gets back," Chloe said, tears welling in her eyes again.

"Our attorney is waiting at the station, and he'll be with Justin at the arraignment in the morning," Reba explained. "Justin should be out on bail and home by midday tomorrow."

Arraignment. How did their lives go so wrong? "I should be there, too."

"No, sweetheart. You've been through enough," Reba said. "Talking with the police and relaying what you've gone through is going to take everything out of you. You're going to need to rest so you're strong enough to fight this."

"But Justin—"

"No buts, baby. I promise you, there is nothing he can't handle. Justin's *only* worry is that you and Serena are safe, and seeing you in that courtroom will not help him in the way you think it will. He knows you support him. He knows you love him. But he will be stronger and better able to focus if you're here, *safe*. I think you should give him that peace of mind."

Guilt and worry strangled Chloe, but she managed to nod.

"If you don't mind, I'd like to stay here tonight, too," Reba said. "Just in case you girls need anything."

Chloe and Serena exchanged grateful glances, but there was no holding back the rush of tears for Justin's family's love and support. "You've already done so much."

"You girls are family now, and family doesn't put limits on taking care of one another." Reba took hold of Chloe's hand, then reached for Serena's and said, "We're all going to get through this. It's going to be hard, and heart-wrenching, and there might be times when you think you can't go on. But when your legs give out, I'll stand for you, and when mine need a break—"

"I'll stand for you," Serena said through tears, drawing more sobs from Chloe.

Reba pulled them both into her loving arms and said, "And all those men out there? They've got some mighty strong legs for us, too."

Chapter Twenty-Nine

JUSTIN SQUINTED AGAINST the bright sun Tuesday morning as he pushed through the courthouse doors after the arraignment. Preacher and Justice, a tall, sharply dressed black man with serious eyes, a baritone voice, and a no-bullshit attitude, followed him out. Preacher posted bail, and the trial date was set for five weeks from tomorrow. Justin hated being away from Chloe for even one night during this shit storm, and he was thankful Justice had taken on her case.

"Thank you, brother," Justin said to Justice. "I really appreciate you handling all of this for us."

"Not a problem. Chloe held up well last night when she filed the police report. She's strong, and she has a lot of support," Justice reassured him. "They got Rogers in custody, and we've already checked him out. He's got no priors. The bastard looks squeaky clean."

"No fucking way," Justin insisted. "He knew *exactly* how to handle her, and the looks he gave me? The vibes he gave off? There's no way this was his first time."

Preacher crossed his arms and said, "*Agreed.* She's worked there a long time, and from what Chloe said, your engagement set him off. He snapped. He might be able to keep that shit under wraps, but my bet is he's got a well-hidden trail of victims."

"I said he *looks* squeaky clean," Justice clarified. "We are continuing to check him out, and the police are investigating on all fronts. They'll talk to people at LOCAL to see if anyone there noticed any inappropriate behavior or saw or heard anything the day of the attack. They'll talk to the person she ran into on her way out of the building, too. I've told Chloe that if she has any thoughts on that, she should let me and the police know." He glanced at Preacher, and Justin recognized the look of a man who already knew what was about to be said. Justice shifted his attention back to Justin and said, "Chloe's been through a great deal of trauma. Not just the attack, but all this with you. Don't be surprised if her moods swing."

"Yeah, I get it." Justin knew how much worse he'd made the situation for Chloe, and he was determined to take care of her and make this right. He only hoped she could forgive him. "What about that interview with her HR department today? Does she have to go?"

"In light of his arrest, I would imagine HR will have a very different view of the situation," Justice said confidently. "I'm hoping to arrange a virtual meeting and will call you later this morning with details."

"What does all of this mean for Chloe? That job is her life, man. What can I do to fix the shit I caused?"

"Alan didn't file formal charges with the police against Chloe, which tells them, and us, that he doesn't have a leg to stand on. As far as what you can do? If Chloe were my daughter, I'd want you to be there for *her*, focused on what *she* needs." Justice was a single father to an adorable three-year-old girl, Patience. "I know you're angry at the shit that guy pulled, but she doesn't need to see or feel that anger. It's just a cruel reminder of all that's happened. She needs you to be her rock, to help her realize none of this is her fault and to get her back on her feet."

"Okay. Thanks, man."

Justice held Justin's stare and said, "Maverick, I need you to keep your nose clean these next few weeks. I don't want so much as a speeding ticket on your record. Got it?"

"Yes, sir. Nothing like spending a night behind bars to give a man time to think about his actions."

Justice shook his hand and tugged him in for a manly slap on the back. "I've got your back, brother. Always." He looked at Preacher and said, "That goes to you, too, old man."

"Appreciate that." Preacher gave him the same hand-shake/pat on the back.

Justice walked away, and Justin and Preacher headed for Preacher's truck.

"The guys have been calling all morning checking on you."

Justin stopped by the tailgate of the truck and said, "I know I fucked up, Dad, and I'm sorry."

"You didn't fuck up. You did what we taught you to do. You protected the woman you love, no matter what the price." He cocked a half smile and said, "Should you have done it with one punch instead of several? Probably. But love is a powerful force, son. Much too powerful to be outdone by reason."

"I hate that I disappointed you and Mom."

Preacher shook his head and said, "We didn't raise pansies, Maverick, and we didn't raise assholes. You didn't attack a man unprovoked. He provoked you with those smug looks you told us about last night, and with the attack on the woman you love. Remember, son, this isn't our first time here at the courthouse.

Zeke beat you to it. We weren't disappointed in him, and we sure as hell aren't disappointed in you."

"Thank you. I appreciate that. I'm not sure Chloe will be as forgiving. I really screwed up with her. She hates violence, and she needed *me*. But I was seeing red, Dad. Something inside me snapped, and I couldn't breathe until he was dealt with." His chest constricted and he said, "The part that worries me most is that if I had it to do over, I honestly don't know if I would do it any differently. The thought of anyone hurting her…" He bit back the acrid taste rising in his throat. "Have you been in this position with Mom? How do you find that balance? How do you turn off the rage?"

Preacher looked him dead in the eyes and said, "I've been there many times in protection of others, and twice with regard to people in our family. When we lost Ashley, I wanted to get my hands on the person who gave her the drugs and slaughter them. And when you came into our lives and I learned all that you'd been through, let's just say your father was lucky he was already in prison. We're just as lucky that I haven't had to go there in protection of your mother, because in that situation I'm not sure I would have stopped when you did." He put a hand on Justin's shoulder and said, "You're a good, honest man, son. You've got a big heart and a solid head on your shoulders. Chloe knows that or she wouldn't be with you. She's right not to condone violence, but you're also right to have protected her." His lips curved up and he said, "You're discovering how complicated love can be. This is just the first of many things you two will have to figure out. It won't be easy, but when you go home today and look into your future wife's eyes, I have a feeling it won't matter how much sage advice you've received. You'll know exactly what to say, because it'll come from here."

He patted Justin's chest, over his heart.

Justin embraced him and said, "Thank you, Dad. I love you."

"I love you, too, son. It's good that you worry about doing the right thing by Chloe. But give yourself a little grace, because you are a *man*, and that means you're going to fuck up. We all do. Everyone knows women are the wiser sex when it comes to relationships. Ask your mother how often she has to set me straight." Preacher winked and said, "Now, how about we get you home to your girl and put my theory to the test?"

CHLOE LAY ON the bed with one arm around Sampson, watching the minutes change on the digital clock, trying to figure out how to survive the anger and devastation consuming her. Tank had given her news of Justin's arraignment, bail, and the future court date. She still couldn't believe what had happened with Alan or with Justin. How had her life been turned upside down so quickly? She had been such a mess after rehashing the day's events with the police, she hadn't been able to take her friends' calls. Serena had spoken to them for her, reassuring their friends that she was okay and apologizing that she had not wanted more company. She'd had all the company she could handle. Madigan and Ginger had shown up with bags of chocolate, macaroni and cheese, and a bottle of tequila, and several of the club members' wives had brought by food. They'd left the fridge packed to the hilt, but she hadn't been able to eat a thing. Chloe had never seen so many people come together so fast and remain resolute in standing vigil. When she'd asked

Reba why they were there, Reba had said, *This is what we do, honey. When you're hurting, we're hurting. Nobody goes through hard times alone in this family.* Chloe had been overwhelmed by the outpouring of support.

Blaine, Serena, and most of the Dark Knights who had stood guard outside the house last night had left a couple of hours ago, and Chloe was glad for the breathing space. Although she'd had to force her stubborn sister to leave, and Serena only agreed because Chloe promised to try to take a nap. Reba and Tank had made sure she stuck to the deal, forcing her to lie down. Sampson had stuck by her side like glue through it all, as if he felt her sadness and was trying to fill the void Justin had left behind. Her big, loving pooch helped, but nothing could fill that void.

"Knock, knock," Reba said as she came through the door carrying a tray of food. She set the tray on the nightstand and sat beside Chloe on the bed. "You didn't sleep a wink, did you?"

Chloe sat up and shook her head. Sampson scooched over, resting his head beside her. "I tried."

She'd stayed up half the night with Reba, Serena, and Madigan. They had done most of the talking. Despite their efforts to sidetrack her with humor and other topics, Chloe had been too upset to say much. When they'd gone to bed, Chloe had been too restless to sleep and had gone down to Justin's studio with her Wicked bodyguards in tow. She'd hoped being there might help her feel closer to him. But as she'd admired the pieces Justin was pouring his heart and soul into, she'd remembered all of the struggles and losses he'd overcome to get there, and that had driven the reality of their situation home— Justin could go to prison and lose everything he'd worked so hard for, including the upstanding reputation he'd earned.

Blaine and Tank had been there to catch her when she'd collapsed to the studio floor in tears.

"Oh, sweetheart, you must be dead on your feet." Reba stroked Sampson's back and said, "But I understand. I didn't get much more than a couple of hours' sleep myself. I don't think Mads did, either. She's asleep on the couch with her head in Tank's lap." She patted Chloe's hand and said, "You'll feel better once Justin gets home."

She hoped so. "Did Tank get any sleep?"

"No, but he's used to it with the hours at the firehouse and, well, he's not much of a sleeper anyway. He's worried about you, honey. We all are."

Chloe's eyes filled with tears, and she turned away to wipe them.

"Come here, sweet girl." Reba put her arms around her, and Chloe cried on her shoulder.

"I'm sorry. I'm not usually a crier."

"Your world isn't usually in chaos. You can cry, scream, punch a hole in the wall. Do whatever you need to do because holding it in will only make things worse." She took Chloe's face between her hands, the way Justin did, and said, "Listen to me, honey, because Justin is going to be here any minute and you need to hear this. Whatever you're holding in, you *need* to let it out. You can do that with me, Justin, Serena, Tank, or Sampson. Just please, baby, you have to tell someone what's going on in your head."

"I can't," she said shakily. "I'm angry at everything, even *Justin*, and he doesn't deserve it. He was just protecting me, but I can't stop the anger, and I can't tell him that. I'm embarrassed to admit it to *you*. It's *so* wrong."

Reba took both of Chloe's hands in hers and said, "There is

no right or wrong way to feel in situations like this. You *can*, and you *must*, tell him the truth. Your feelings matter, Chloe." Reba paused at the sound of the front door opening.

The sound of Justin's voice made Chloe's heart race.

"I need you to promise me something, sweetheart," Reba said quickly. "Promise me that you will not ever—*ever*—disregard your feelings for Justin or any other man, because if you don't respect and honor them, no one else ever will."

She couldn't believe Reba was telling her to put her own feelings above Justin's. "He's your son. Why are you telling me this?"

"Because from what you've told me about your mother, she never did, and no matter how many times you tell yourself your feelings matter, sometimes you need to hear it from a mother. I love Justin, and I know he'll do the right thing, but he can't do that if you hide the truth. Can you promise me?"

"I promise," she said, choking back more tears.

"Good, now listen, sweetheart. I'm going to ask you something, and you can be honest with me. There is *no* judgment here. Did all of this change your love for Justin?"

"*What? No,*" she said honestly. "It's just a lot to deal with, and I'm so angry at everything, it's confusing."

A smile lifted Reba's lips. "Love is much stronger than anger and confusion, sweetheart. Honesty and love can conquer anything."

As she pressed a kiss to Chloe's forehead, the sound of footsteps approaching sent Sampson leaping off the bed and trotting out of the bedroom. Reba rose to her feet, holding tightly to Chloe's hand. Chloe stood on shaky legs as Justin came through the open door. His hair was tousled, his clothing rumpled, and the uneasy and apologetic look in his eyes told her that he was just as lost as she was, which made it all that much harder. They stood in awkward silence, looking at each other from opposite sides of the bed. A nest of bees erupted in Chloe's stomach, and she hated that. She missed her butterflies.

Reba hugged her and said, "I'm going to send everyone home so you two can have some privacy. We're only a phone call away."

"Thank you for everything," Chloe said, trying to calm her racing heart.

Reba walked around the bed and embraced Justin.

"I love you, Mom. I'm sorry."

Reba caressed his cheek and said, "You save your *sorrys* for the people who need them. I love you, sweet boy. Nothing will ever change that."

Reba left the room, and Justin came around the bed with Sampson on his heels. She fought the urge to run to him, to tell him how much she missed him and forget all the rest. He'd been in jail because of her. *Jail.* She couldn't fathom the idea of Justin in a jail cell. It burned inside her, making her feel weak and shaky. Justin stopped inches away. His chest expanded with his ragged breaths. The pain in his eyes was inescapable as he touched his fingers to hers. Emotions clogged her throat, stopping her words from forming. He took her hand and hauled her into his arms, holding her so tight, it was hard to breathe. She clung to him, inhaling his familiar scent, feeling safe and loved and able to breathe for the first time in twenty-four hours. Emotions swamped her, bringing an onslaught of unstoppable tears.

"I'm sorry, baby. I'm so damn sorry." His words were drenched in sorrow.

He kissed her head, whispering apologies and affirmations

of his love as she wept. Her well of tears felt endless, and she gave in to their anguish, and to their relief. He didn't ask questions or hurry her along. He simply held her, soothing her with his words, his strength, and his love. She didn't know how long they stood there, but it was long enough that when he pushed his hands into her hair and pressed a tender kiss to her lips, she had no more tears to cry.

He gazed into her eyes and said, "You needed me, and I fucked up. I am so sorry, baby."

"You didn't *fuck up*, but I did need you. I know you did it because you were protecting me, but I hate that you turned to violence, and at the same time, I understand and appreciate it." She took a step back and said, "It's all confusing. You risked your future because of *me*. No one has ever stood up for me, or loved me, like you do. I don't know how to feel. This is such a *mess*, Justin, and it's *Alan's* fault." Her fingers curled into fists and her nails dug into her skin as her voice escalated. "I trusted him*, and he* did this to us. And I messed up, too, Justin. I disregarded your warnings, and I *hate* myself for that. I swore I'd never allow anyone to make me feel helpless again, and because I didn't see him for who he was, I put myself *right back* in that position." She was shouting, but she was powerless to stop. "And what about *Mike*? Your parents will never let him move there after this. Alan's ruined that, too! I feel like I'm *drowning*. I have to go into work to meet with human resources, and I don't know how I'll face anyone there. I've lost *everything*—my job, *you*, my self-respect—"

"*Stop*, baby." He took her by the arms, his eyes drilling into hers. "You have *nothing* to be embarrassed about," he said with unwavering confidence. "You didn't do anything wrong. Your self-respect should be not only intact, but miles high. You cannot blame yourself for *any* of this, and for the love of God, turn your heart *off* for one fucking day. Give yourself a break and *stop* thinking of everyone else. Mike moving in has *nothing* to do with this. Take that, and any blame you're feeling about what I did, *off* your plate. You saw what that monster *wanted* you to see. That's not on you, babe. That's on him. That prick's allegations don't hold water, and the truth is going to come out. People are not going to think differently about you because he tried to hurt you or because I flipped a shit and knocked him out."

Her thoughts came to a screeching halt. "You *knocked* him *out?*"

His jaw clenched. "Don't get lost in the details. Listen to me, Chloe. You are a brilliant, strong woman who worked her ass off to make something of herself. Do *not* let that pathetic excuse of a man destroy your confidence and all that you've achieved. You were *not* helpless. You got out of there in one piece, and he had a pretty bad shiner that I have a feeling came from you."

"I hit him with a stapler." The panic she'd felt came rushing back, making her dizzy. "I think I need to sit down."

He led her to the bed and sat beside her, running his hand soothingly down her back. Sampson ambled over and rested his chin on Chloe's lap.

"Justin," she said, absently petting Sampson. "I'm scared."

"I know you are. We're going to get through this together, babe. I promise." He touched her chin, bringing her eyes to his, and said, "And you have to know that you will *never* lose me."

"But you could go to *prison.*" The word felt like a death sentence.

"Believe me, I'm fully aware of that. I'll do whatever time I have to, because he deserved it. But even behind bars, Chloe, I'll still be *yours*. I'll *always* be yours."

"And our life together? Our *future*?" She shook her head.

"Nobody's going to take that away. It might be delayed a little, but we'll get it."

"This whole thing scares me. It affects so many people. What if they pull the funding for Madigan's trial? Then her plans are ruined, too, and anyone she might have helped will lose out. And what about the Junior/Senior Program? I wish this had never happened." She rested her head on his shoulder.

He put his arm around her and said, "Me too."

"You and I are supposed to be a team. *Partners*. Part of me feels like if I say I need you and that I'm going to do something like report the attack, I should be able to count on you to be there for me and help me do what I need to do. On the other hand, I get why you went after him, and you made sure I was taken care of by an army of men and women, and you even called my sister. I don't know *why* I feel so lost, conflicted."

"Because you've been traumatized, and it's not in your nature to condone violence." He hugged her to him and kissed her temple. "I'll always take care of you, sweetheart. *Always*. But I don't have the answer about how to handle this type of situation differently. I made a promise that I'd never let anyone hurt you, and that fucker got to you. I *snapped*. I take full responsibility for that. I wish I could say I'd never do it again, but the truth is, I would, baby. I can't lie to you about that."

"I know you would, and I can't be mad at you for saying that, either, because you're being honest."

"We *are* a team, baby. I will walk *beside* you, and I will let you lead when you need to, like honoring your request not to claim you in public in certain ways. But I can't give you this. I can't promise you that I won't go after someone who hurts you. I love you too much."

"I know," she said softly. "I love you, too."

"Can we find a compromise? A middle ground we're both comfortable with?"

She lifted her head, meeting his hopeful gaze, and said, "I think we just did."

He slid his hand to the nape of her neck and touched his forehead to hers. "I love you, baby," he said in the most relieved voice she'd ever heard, and pressed his lips to hers.

"I'm so tired," she whispered. "I can't wait to sleep in your arms again."

"Why don't you get comfortable and I'll join you after I shower."

She took his hand, leading him toward the bathroom, and said, "I'll wash jail off you if you'll wash yesterday off me."

He lowered his lips to hers, and in that slow, sweet promise of a kiss, she felt the shattered pieces of herself healing, the love in her heart growing, and the strength in *them* becoming more powerful than ever before.

Chapter Thirty

THURSDAY MORNING AS the sun spilled over Sampson, asleep on his doggy bed by the glass wall, Justin lay awake worrying about Chloe. The last two days had passed in cycles of distress and disbelief with intermittent moments of relief, but at the end of those difficult hours they found their way back into each other's arms. Chloe was nestled against him now, sleeping soundly. He didn't dare move and tried not to breathe too hard. She'd been having nightmares since the attack, jerking in her sleep and calling out. He wished he could wipe her memory clean and take away all of her doubts and fears.

It hadn't taken long for LOCAL's human resources team to conclude their internal investigation. Chloe had been cleared of Alan's allegations yesterday afternoon and given approval to return to work with one caveat. She was not allowed to discuss the incident or have any contact with Darren Rogers because of the familial conflict of interest and ongoing police investigation. They'd given her two weeks to decide if she was going to return to work. Justin knew her indecision was a big part of what was making her feel lost. Chloe thrived on being prepared, knowing what she was doing from one day to the next. Justin was pretty sure she also needed to accomplish more than just *being* on a daily basis. She'd built a life on her accomplishments, whether they were simple, like making albums for friends, or complex, like creating new programs for the residents of LOCAL. Those accomplishments were hers to *own*. They were validations of how far she'd come. There were no two ways about it. Chloe was floundering. Despite family and friends stopping by, and a visit with Shadow yesterday to try to bring a little light into Chloe's day, she still seemed to exist on autopilot. Justin knew she needed more than friends or dogs to get through this. She needed her work and the residents she'd come to love the way other people needed oxygen, and Justin vowed to do everything he could to help her find her way back to them.

She twitched in his arms, and he held her tighter, whispering, "I've got you, sweetheart. You're okay."

"Sorry," she said as she turned in his arms, bringing them nose to nose. Sadness hung in the dark crescents beneath her eyes.

He kissed her softly and said, "Don't be sorry, babe. Maybe we should talk to a therapist and see if they can help."

"Maybe. I'm just…" She sighed, burrowing closer.

"Talk to me, sweets. What were you dreaming about?"

"They were taking you to prison," she said just above a whisper.

Her worries were his fault, and that gutted him. "You know Justice is trying to get the charges dropped. He's pushing Alan's lawyer now that the allegations he made against you have been disproven. LOCAL's HR team interviewed almost *thirty* people, and several said they were uncomfortable with Alan. His allegations did more harm than good for him. That'll bite him in the ass."

"But nobody said he did anything inappropriate. And that

was just the internal investigation at LOCAL. As far as the police are concerned, nothing has been proven."

"Not *yet*, but Justice said Alan dug himself a hole that will be hard to climb out of by placing those false allegations. The police will follow up with the people who claimed to be uncomfortable with him. They'll dig deeper. They're liable to find dirt on him. Justice thinks there's a good chance the charges against me will be dropped."

"I know, but I'm still worried. I *just* got you. I don't want to lose you."

"You *won't*. Let's give the police and Justice's private investigator time to do their jobs." He kissed her again and said, "Have you given any more thought to going back to work?"

"That and you going to prison are *all* I think about. One of my colleagues is handling a meeting with the teenagers who are taking part in the Junior/Senior Program this afternoon. What if those kids find out what's going on?"

Word traveled fast through the small Cape Cod towns. There was a good chance those kids had already heard about the attack, so he focused on the things that mattered. "You were *cleared* of his false allegations. You're the victim in all of this, and I'm sure everyone who knows you has figured that out."

"But still, it feels like my reputation has been tainted. It's basically my word against his as far as the police are concerned."

"And your word is golden. Everyone knows that. Have faith in who you are, sweetheart. I sure as hell do."

She was quiet for a second, before saying, "I miss the people there already. They were like family." Tears slipped from her eyes. "And I have no idea how I can ever face Darren again. He must hate me."

"He can't hate you for being his son's victim. The truth

about Alan *will* come out, Chloe. Have faith in that." He brushed her tears away and said, "Do you think there's any chance Darren knew what Alan was like? Do you think he'd cover up for him?"

"No. No way," she said in a stronger voice. "Darren's old-school, a gentleman. He treats women with the utmost respect. I don't believe he'd look the other way if he knew. But *I* didn't see what Alan was doing, and I was in the thick of it. Darren was probably as blindsided as I was."

"You put a lot of faith in this Darren guy."

"I do, and I know you probably doubt my ability to judge right now, but he's always been fair and stood up for all the right things." She sighed heavily. "This is so hard. Maybe it's best if I just quit and move on."

He wasn't going to let that happen. "First of all, I don't doubt your ability to judge people. Chloe, what happened was an anomaly. You have excellent judgment." Vying for a smile, he said, "You chose me, right?" His words finally earned the smile he missed. "Seriously, sweet cheeks, you've worked too hard to get where you are, and for the people who live there, to give Rogers the power to take them from you."

She rolled onto her back and gazed up at the ceiling. "Can we go back in time to my birthday, when I woke up to balloons and life was blissfully happy?"

"I'll fill the bedroom with balloons every day if it would make you happy." He kissed her shoulder, then trailed his fingers up her belly. Goose bumps rose beneath his touch. Her smile finally reached her eyes.

"I don't need balloons. I love my work, and I wish I felt okay going back, but I could *survive* working someplace else."

"You've spent enough of your lifetime just surviving. Hopefully you'll find a way to feel at peace going back to the people and the work you love." He kissed the swell of her breast and said, "Let's give it a few days and see how you feel. We should get out of here and take a walk, clear our heads."

"That would be nice, *after* you kiss me some more," she whispered.

The longing in her voice made him ache to help her become whole again. He lavished her breasts with sensual kisses, and soon her desires took over and she was moaning and bowing up off the mattress. He lowered his mouth over one taut peak, and she pushed her hands into his hair, holding him there. She writhed beside him, brushing her softness against his hard length.

He rained kisses up her neck, moving over her, and said, "You okay, baby?"

"Yes." Lust and love intertwined in her needful eyes, and she said, "There's only one thing I can't live without."

"What's that, darlin'?" He skimmed his hand down her hip, and as their bodies came together, he saw their love pushing all of those unsettled thoughts away.

She gazed up at him with clearer, loving eyes and whispered, "*You.*"

A DOUBLE DOSE of Justin and fresh air was exactly what Chloe needed. After loving each other senseless, they'd eaten breakfast and taken Sampson for a long walk in the woods. They held hands and talked about their future, which had seemed a painful subject about an unattainable dream just a few hours earlier. But Justin had a way of clearing the clouds and helping her see things more clearly. By the time they came through the woods on the back side of the property, she felt a lot better. The late-morning sun shimmered off the inky pond water. Sampson slowed to sniff something on the ground, and Justin leaned in for a kiss.

They walked along the side yard, making their way toward the front of the house. "You've been home with me for days," Chloe said. "I appreciate it, but I'm sure Blaine needs you. You can go into work. I'll be fine."

"Blaine's got it covered." He lifted their joined hands and kissed the back of hers. "I'm right where I want, and need, to be, babe."

As they came around the side of the house, they noticed Emery's car in the driveway. Sampson gave a lazy *woof* as Emery stepped out of the car and waved.

"I wonder what Emery's doing here. She didn't mention stopping by when I talked to her last night."

He stepped up their pace and said, "Let's go find out."

The passenger doors opened, and Rose climbed out of the front seat holding a large basket, looking stylish in a linen pantsuit.

Magdeline unfolded her long, lean body from the back seat of Emery's compact car and said, "Next time I ride up front."

"Hush up and get the cookies," Arlin directed as she followed her out holding a tote bag in one hand and patted her orange hair with the other.

Happiness bubbled up inside Chloe. "What are they...?" She looked at Justin, knowing this had to be his doing.

"I figured you needed to see a few friendly faces."

"*Justin...*" She threw her arms around his neck, her eyes

tearing up again. She'd been such an emotional mess all week. At least this time they were happy tears. "Thank you!" She ran to her friends, earning a more energetic bark from Sampson as he trotted after her.

Emery hugged her and said, "I had to fight off about a dozen other people who wanted to tag along. You have quite a fan club."

"Yes, she does," Rose exclaimed. "Now get over here and give me a hug."

"I can't believe you're all here!" Chloe walked eagerly into Rose's open arms, laughing as Arlin and Magdeline squished her in a group hug.

Rose smiled at Justin and said, "Believe it, Chloe, and it's all your beau's doing."

"We heard what happened, honey," Magdeline said carefully.

Embarrassment heated Chloe's cheeks. "I'm not allowed to talk about it."

"We heard that, too," Arlin said. "You don't have to talk, but you can listen."

"Everyone is worried sick about you, Chloe." Rose handed her the basket and lifted the lid. It was full of envelopes. "These are letters from people whose lives you've touched."

Chloe was stunned, and tears sprang to her eyes again. "There are so many."

"You're a special gal. There are more letters in here." Arlin handed her the bag she was holding.

Tears slipped down Chloe's cheeks.

"Those better be happy tears," Rose said.

"They are! I can't believe it."

"There's a big investigation going on, and not just by the

police," Magdeline informed her. "We're doing our own sleuthing, asking around to see who's seen what."

"Oh, no, you can't do that. You might get in trouble," Chloe warned as Sampson leaned against her leg. She reached down and petted his head.

"I already told them that," Emery informed her. "It's like talking to three brick walls."

Rose waved her hand dismissively. "We're not getting into trouble, but people have seen things, Chloe. A hand on your back, leering at you from across the room when you were unaware."

"I'm *so* embarrassed," Chloe confessed. "I thought he was just a close talk—" She pressed her mouth shut, silencing herself for a moment, then said, "I can't do this. I can't talk about it or I'll compromise the investigation."

"Do *not* talk about it. Do not do anything to jeopardize putting that monster in a cage," Emery said.

"I agree, but you'd better get over the embarrassment and get your heinie back to work, Chloe," Magdeline said. "We need you."

"It's not quite that easy," Chloe said. "There are other complications making it difficult for me to be there."

Rose said, "Ah, yes. The complication of his father. He's made himself scarce, coming in only late at night. That poor man."

Chloe was dying to ask Rose if she thought Darren believed his son was innocent, but she bit her tongue.

"This is the last thing we'll say on the subject," Rose announced. "We hope you won't let that evil man steal you from us, because we all adore you. You're like our granddaughter, and we need you, honey."

"You're going to make me cry again," Chloe said, willing her tears not to fall.

"No more tears, baby," Justin said as he took the basket from her arms and held her hand. "How about we move this party to the back deck, turn on a little music, and sample some of those cookies Magdeline is hoarding?"

"I like the way you think," Magdeline said.

As they headed inside, Chloe felt happier and stronger than she had in days.

AFTER A LONG and wonderful visit, during which all their troubles felt miles away, Chloe said goodbye to the women who were more a part of her life than her own mother had ever been.

As the others climbed into Emery's car, Rose said, "My Leon used to say that dirt couldn't hide in the wash. Believe that, Chloe. The truth will come out." Her warm gray-blue eyes moved between her and Justin. "You two have something very special. Don't let what happened steal a second of your happiness."

"We're trying not to," Chloe said.

"Good, and for what it's worth, if Justin hadn't knocked that creep out, I would have brought my grandsons in to do the job." Rose hugged Chloe and said, "We love you, honey. Come back to us when you're ready." Then she embraced Justin. "Thank you for inviting us over. We all needed it."

Chloe joined Justin and waved as they drove away. "I can do this," Chloe said, feeling stronger and more confident. "With you by my side, and those ladies behind me, I can fight this battle."

"I always knew you could, baby. I'm glad a visit with the *Golden Girls* helped you to get out of your own way and remember how much you're loved and how strong you are." He wrapped his arms around her, flashing that crooked grin she loved, and said, "I need to tell you something. That call I walked inside to answer while you were visiting with them was from Justice. Do you know someone named Janet Kirsh?"

"Yes. She worked in our accounting department. Why?"

"Well, I guess Alan's wife has left him. She took her kids to her parents' house in Connecticut—"

"Oh my gosh, his *wife*. In all of this mess, I hadn't even thought about her. That poor woman, and her girls…"

"It's a nightmare for sure. But they're better off away from him, and it sounds like she knew, or had suspicions, about what he was like. When she got to Connecticut, she called the police and gave them Janet's number, told them to check her out."

"What does that mean?" Chloe's stomach sank as understanding dawned on her. "Oh no. Do you think he did this to Janet, too? We've been getting calls every few weeks for references. That poor woman. She's a single mom. No wonder she took off so abruptly. That's horrible."

"It is, but if he did this to her, and if she comes forward, it will validate your allegations."

"Talk about a double-edged sword. I wouldn't wish this on anyone."

"Don't wish it on her, babe." He embraced her and said, "Just hope the truth comes out, whatever it is."

"I am, but that still doesn't help the charges against you."

"You're right, but we can't lose ourselves in what might happen five weeks from now. I say we hold on to this thread of hope that the truth will put that guy behind bars, and we focus on the here and now." He pressed his lips to hers and lowered his voice to say, "You have a move on the horizon, unless you've changed your mind."

"You're not getting out of me moving in that easily." She breathed a little easier and said, "How do you always know just what to do and say to help me see past my worries?"

"I love you. That makes it easy."

"Nothing feels easy these days."

"I could make a few great jokes about how good *hard* things can be, but I have a feeling you'd smack me."

She laughed, and it felt so good to finally feel free enough to laugh, she held on to those good feelings and said, "Trust me, Mr. Wicked, I know just how good *your* hard thing can be."

"Careful, heartbreaker, or we'll never make it to your cottage."

She sauntered up the porch steps, gazed over her shoulder with a seductive wink, and said, "It's still early…"

Chapter Thirty-One

CHLOE PULLED A cupcake pan from a kitchen cabinet Saturday afternoon, listening to Marly and Madigan chat as they sorted through the kitchen in Chloe's cottage. She reveled in the sound of Justin's laughter coming from the bedroom, where he and some of the guys were getting another load to take out to the moving truck. Zeke was upstairs clearing out the second floor, and Dwayne and Tank had just gone outside with more boxes from the guest room, where Serena and Drake were probably making out, though they claimed to be marking boxes.

Focusing on the here and now had been exactly what Chloe needed to put a little distance between the troubles she and Justin were facing and the life they were supposed to be living. They'd gotten most of the packing done themselves over the last two days, but their families and friends had rallied today to help them finish packing and move her things to Justin's house. To *their* house.

Chloe warmed at the thought. She held up the cupcake pan and said, "How about this, Mads? Do you want me to leave it?"

"One sec," Madigan said with her nose practically glued to the kitchen window. "Roman is out front talking to Gunner and Tank."

"Who is Roman?" Chloe set the pan down and pulled a few more from the cabinet.

"One of Gunner's hot military buddies," Madigan said. "He's as mysterious as a two-dollar bill. I wonder what he's doing here."

Marly stepped beside Madigan and peered out the window. "Whoa. Who cares why he's here. *Look* at those arms on Mr. Hot and Beasty."

"Damn it, Tank, you're blocking my view," Madigan complained. "Come on, Gunner. *Really?* Great. Now I can't see Roman at all. I swear it's like they know when I'm checking out a guy. I might as well call them the Hoover boys. They totally suck."

"Maybe I should check out that sucking action," Marly teased.

Madigan swatted at Marly, but she dodged the hit and ran behind Chloe. Chloe laughed, loving being part of their close-knit group. It was like having more sisters around.

"Those guys are such dorks," Serena said as she came into the kitchen and Drake walked outside carrying another box. "What's Mads looking at?"

Marly ran back to the window and said, "Three hot guys, two of whom Mads claims really know how to *suck*." A motorcycle roared to life and she added, "Make that *two*, Roman's leaving. Oh wait. *Three!* Gotta include *Drakey* on that list."

"My man deserves the top slot of *any* hot list," Serena said proudly.

"*Woo-hoo!*" Zander hollered as he bolted out of the bedroom, swinging something over his head, and ran out the front door.

Justin barreled out after him, yelling, "You're dead!"

The girls ran outside just in time to see Justin charge Zander, taking him down to the ground. Zander was laughing hysterically as they wrestled for dominance.

"*What* is going on?" Chloe hollered as Blaine walked casually out of the house carrying a dresser drawer.

"Zan has a pocketful of your underwear," Blaine said as he headed down the walkway unfazed by the brawl going on in the middle of the front lawn.

"Prison clause, man!" Zander hollered as Justin pinned his arms to the ground with his knees. "I'll keep her satisfied while you're in the joint!"

"I will fuck you up," Justin growled.

Zeke ran out of the cottage, reaching Justin and Zander at the same time as Tank, Drake, and Dwayne jogged up from the truck. Zeke ground out, "Shit," and hauled Justin off Zander, who was still cracking up.

"Hey, Z, did you forget Zan's leash?" Dwayne teased.

Zander pushed to his feet and said, "Someone's got to satisfy Mav's girl when he gets put away."

Justin twisted free from Zeke's grasp and lunged for Zander, but Tank stepped between them, taking the full hit of Justin's body. They both went down, taking Zander with them. Blaine, Dwayne, and Zeke dove in, wrestling and laughing as they peeled Justin off Zander.

"All of this because of underwear?" Chloe asked as a motorcycle rumbled down the road and parked at the end of the driveway.

A large man with Dark Knights' patches on his vest climbed off the bike. He took off his helmet, and Chloe realized it was Justice. He strode determinedly up the driveway, looking vastly different in his jeans and T-shirt with his tattoos on display than he had in his suit.

"Who's that?" Serena asked.

"Justice. Isn't he gorgeous?" Madigan said, clearly trying to add levity to the situation, and earning scowls from her brothers, who were brushing themselves off.

Chloe studied Justice's serious eyes and tight jaw, and her stomach sank. Justin took her hand, looking as worried as she felt.

"Come on, baby," he said. "Whatever happens, we'll get through it."

Her rampant heartbeat and the fear rattling her nerves left her unable to speak.

"We've got you, bro," Tank said as the guys fell into step beside them.

They met Justice in the middle of the driveway.

Justice nodded and said, "Chloe. Brothers," in a voice as deep and distinct as James Earl Jones's.

"Hey, man," several of them said.

"You have news?" Justin asked, tightening his grip on Chloe's hand.

Justice's dark eyes turned sorrowful. "Yes. Unfortunately, Janet Kirsh suffered greatly at the hands of Alan Rogers."

"Oh *no*." Chloe's heart hurt for Janet. Justin put his arm around her, holding her closer. "Is she okay?"

Justice shook his head. "Not really. He paid her off to keep her quiet, but he also threatened the life of her child. She's been suffering, having trouble holding down jobs, moving around because she thought he might come after her. She didn't want to talk at first, as you can imagine. But she came through and filed a formal statement and charges against him. It looks like

Rogers will go away for a very long time."

Tears spilled from Chloe's eyes as Justin pulled her into his arms and said, "Thank God."

Words of relief and cheers rang out around them, but all Chloe could hear was Justin speaking into her ear as he said, "We got him, baby. We got him."

"There's more," Justice said, drawing all of their attention. "Our investigator has been talking to previous employees of LOCAL, and a third woman came forward yesterday. She's a former nurse who worked at LOCAL prior to Chloe's employment. We have a feeling there will be more, which will help Chloe's case. Darren Rogers has stepped up and intervened on Maverick's behalf. He convinced Alan to drop the charges."

"He did?" Chloe said at the same time Justin said, "Really?"

"Yes, but a victim can't *stop* the process. That can only be done by the prosecutor or a judge," Justice explained. "The prosecutor has a bug up his ass, so I had no choice but to cut a deal."

Chloe held her breath, clinging to Justin as he said, "What kind of deal?"

"I had to pull the Dark Knights card and use the good we do for the community as leverage. You've got to complete an anger management course," Justice explained.

"That's *bullshit*," Tank snapped.

"The prick deserved everything he got and more," Zeke added.

Dwayne said, "No shit."

Justin held his hands up and said, "Hold on, guys. That's fine, Justice. I'll take the course—"

"Are you shittin' me?" Tank growled. "Can't we fight this?"

Justin shook his head. "Dude, risk going to prison or take a fucking class? That's a no-brainer, regardless of if the dickhead deserved it or not." He looked at Justice and said, "I appreciate you having my back on this. Is there anything else? Do I still have to go to court, or will this make me free and clear of all charges?"

"Free and clear once you take the class," Justice said.

Justin hauled Chloe into his arms, hugging her tight. "Free and clear, baby. Free and clear."

"I need you to sign off on the agreement," Justice said. "Can you swing by my office later?"

"Absolutely." Justin shook his hand and pulled him into a manly embrace. "Thank you, brother."

"Thank you so much," Chloe said, hugging Justice.

"I think this calls for a celebration," Madigan exclaimed. "I'll call Mom and have her set it up with Aunt Ginger at the Hog. Let's get this stuff over to Justin and Chloe's and then go crack open some champagne!"

There was a round of cheers and hugs.

Madigan flashed a flirty smile at Justice and said, "You'd better join us tonight."

"I wouldn't miss it for the world. See you then." Justice held her gaze for a beat before heading to his bike.

There was no missing the disapproving looks on the guys' faces, but they only lasted a second, as everyone was excited about the news.

Except Tank, who grumbled, "I still think we could have fought it. It ain't right, the good guy being punished."

Justin drew Chloe into his arms and said, "But, bro, this good guy gets to stay home with his girl, and that's all kinds of *right*." He lowered his lips to Chloe's, earning hoots and hollers from the others. He touched his forehead to hers and said, "I love you, baby."

Zander sidled up to them and said, "And *I* love your silk underwear."

Justin's eyes narrowed, and his entire body tensed.

"You must have a death wish, Zan," Tank said.

"Excuse me, sweet cheeks." Justin gave her a chaste kiss and said, "I have to go strangle my brother."

"Oh *shit!*" Zander took off running.

As Justin chased Zander around the yard, Serena, Marly, and Madigan joined Chloe and told her how happy they were for her and Justin.

"Now you can go back to work," Serena said.

"I'm not so sure about that," Chloe said honestly. "Just because Darren convinced Alan to drop the charges doesn't mean he'll be okay with me, since I'm the one who reported it. This might have made things worse."

"You know what, sis? Today's too fantastic and emotional a day to make that big of a decision," Serena suggested. "Give yourself a day or two to celebrate with your future husband, and maybe you'll feel differently."

"Maybe you're right."

Dwayne tripped Zander, Zeke jumped on Dwayne, and then all the guys were on the ground wrestling again—including Drake.

"I'm so glad I'm not a guy," Serena said. "I told you they were dorks. Mine included."

"I'd like to be in the middle of that dogpile," Marly said, earning another swat from Madigan. This one hit its mark on Marly's arm. "I prefer my smacks where they count, girlie." Marly turned around and wiggled her butt.

Laughter filled the air as the guys rolled around on the grass.

Justin popped his head out of the dogpile and blew Chloe a kiss, only to be slammed down to his back by Blaine. Justin popped up and Zander jumped in front of him, throwing Chloe a kiss with his hand. Justin took him down, making all the girls laugh.

"You sure you want to be part of this crazy family?" Madigan asked.

"More than anything in the world." Chloe didn't care what Justin was—bad boy, biker, sculptor, or dork—as long as he was *hers*.

Chapter Thirty-Two

GINGER AND REBA had put out Justin and Chloe's good news through the Dark Knights' grapevine, and Serena told their friends at Bayside. Conroy had closed the bar to the public, and it was packed with friends and family and more good vibes than Justin could ask for. They'd feasted, toasted, laughed, and danced. And now Chloe was dancing with the girls, and Justin stood by a table with Tank and Preacher, soaking it all in.

"You and Chloe look about ten years younger than you did on Monday night," Preacher said.

"I think we've lived a lifetime in the last few days. We both feel pretty good now, but Chloe has been having nightmares. I'm worried about her, Preach. I'm thinking of hooking her up with Cuffs's sister." Tasha Revere was a therapist who had recently returned to the area.

"I'm sorry to hear she's struggling like that," Preacher said compassionately. "She's been through a lot. I think connecting with Tasha's a good idea."

"Before we found out that Darren convinced Alan to drop the charges, Chloe seemed ready to get back to work. She needs to be there with the people she cares about. But now she's got hesitations again. It's really weighing on her. I'm hoping Tasha can help with that, too."

Preacher took a swig of his beer and said, "It's understandable that she's conflicted after everything that's gone down."

"She may not ever be the same person she was," Tank said in a grave tone. "She might come out stronger, but you should be prepared in case that doesn't happen. She might be skittish for a while."

"I know. I'll take care of her. I'm planning on talking to Tasha to figure out how I can help Chloe. It pisses me off that the pompous prick might have ruined what she's worked so hard for. I thought part of her hesitation might have been that she was embarrassed to face Darren and everyone else at that place because of what I did, so I offered to go with her to try to clear the air with him. I'm not above apologizing to Darren or anyone else in that organization. It's not their fault the guy is a scumbag."

"That's not a bad idea. How does Chloe feel about it?" Preacher asked.

Justin shrugged. "She said she'd think about it."

"That's probably a good idea. Let the dust settle." Tank took a pull of his beer, his gaze following Leah across the floor as he said, "How long does Chloe have before she needs to give her office an answer one way or the other?"

"A little less than two weeks."

"She'll probably need it," Preacher said, glancing at Reba, who was sitting at the table with Baz and Evie, deep in conversation with Violet and Andre. "Well, boys, I'd better go sit with my old lady so I don't end up in the doghouse."

Justin watched Preacher sit down and pull Reba closer. Her expression warmed and she kissed his cheek. Preacher had stuck to Justin like glue tonight, and Reba had hugged him and Chloe so many times, Justin couldn't imagine what it would have been like for them if he'd landed behind bars for any length of time.

"Come on!" Marly said as she dragged Blaine toward the dance floor.

"Bro! Save me!" Blaine called out to them.

Justin and Tank laughed.

"Dude's got to be tappin' her," Tank said. "I'll kill him if he hurts her."

Justin knew Tank wasn't kidding. He looked past Blaine and Marly at Chloe dancing with her girlfriends. Relief washed over him, as it had every time he'd looked at her, touched her, and thought about her since Justice had given them the good news.

When they'd been moving her things into the house, Justin had felt the same overwhelming sensation of knowing he was finally in the right place, with the right person, as when he'd truly become part of the Wicked family. He looked around at his friends and family. Steph was rolling her eyes at Dwayne. Zander was flirting with three daughters of Dark Knights members by a high-top table, and as usual, Zeke was standing nearby, keeping a watchful eye on him.

Some things never changed.

Justin took comfort in that. He knew he'd dodged a bullet today, and it killed him knowing he could have gone to prison and missed out on all this. He was grateful for his good fortune, but he'd trade it all to give Chloe her confidence and her life back.

Tank stood up a little taller. Justin followed his gaze to Leah, who was carrying a tray of drinks to a table where Cuffs was sitting with Justice and a couple of other members. Leah had lowered her eyes every time she'd walked by Tank tonight, and Tank had been watching her all night.

"What're you thinking?" Justin asked.

Tank's gaze never left the waitress as he said, "Wondering why she's so freaked out by me."

"You're a freaky guy."

Tank slid him a sideways look. "The chick's mysterious. I'm just wondering if she's a loner or running from trouble."

"Just because she's leery of a guy who could crush a man's skull with his bare hands doesn't mean she needs saving, Tank. Relax. She probably feels you watching her, and that's not going to make her any less wary of you."

Across the room, Ginger put her arm around Leah's shoulder and said something in her ear. Leah nodded and headed over to another table.

"Ginger keeps a close eye on her girls," Justin reminded him. "I'm pretty sure she'd know if there were trouble brewing under this roof."

Tank nodded and finished his beer.

Mike came through the crowd and said, "I thought your father would never leave your side. You got the goods?"

Justin chuckled and pulled a Twix bar from his pocket. "Don't I always hook you up?"

"I was worried about you getting put in the slammer," Mike said as he tore open the candy wrapper. "You're my best supplier."

"Gramps, what do you think I'm running here? A rinky-dink operation?" Justin teased. "It wouldn't matter if I was in the big house or not. I've got connections. I'd never leave you high and dry and make you go cold turkey."

Tank set his empty beer bottle on the table and said, "He

would have had Chloe hook you up. And if she couldn't, you know I would, old man."

"I'll remember to put you back in the will," Mike teased, and took a bite of the candy. "Now, that's good stuff. Almost as sweet as your little gal, Maverick. How's she doing?"

Justin glanced at Chloe, who was heading his way, and said, "She's got some healing to do, but we'll get there."

The sound of metal tapping glass drew their attention to Preacher standing at the head of the table. "If I could have your attention for a moment."

Justin reached for Chloe's hand and pulled her closer. He wrapped his arms around her from behind so she could see Preacher and said, "Missed you, baby," into her ear.

"Me too," she said over her shoulder, and Justin kissed her.

"I'd like to thank you all for your support during this trying time," Preacher said loudly, drawing their attention. "And for joining us tonight as we celebrate Maverick's name being cleared and his and Chloe's bright future."

Cheers and applause filled the room.

Preacher held his hands up, silencing the crowd, and said, "But with that good news came the discovery of other women who, like our dear, sweet Chloe, have suffered at the hands of a monster. These women all have difficult times ahead of them. They will have to face their attacker in court, and with that will come grief, and hopefully closure and healing. But thanks to all of you, I know they won't have to do it alone. We will be there with them, offering strength in the courtroom and support every step of the way." Preacher looked across the room at Justin and Chloe and held up his glass. "Here's to supporting these incredibly strong women and doing our best to ensure something like this doesn't happen again."

The crowd cheered "Hear, hear!" and *whoop*ed.

Chloe turned in Justin's arms and said, "I love your family so much."

"They love you, too, baby." He pressed his lips to hers as Preacher made an announcement reminding everyone to continue spreading the word about the suicide-awareness rally.

"Okay, enough kissy face," Madigan said, prying Justin and Chloe apart.

Behind Madigan, an army of females stared back at them, bringing a smile to Chloe's beautiful face.

Serena grabbed Chloe's hand and said, "We need to borrow her."

"You just had her," Justin teased.

Evie put her arm around Chloe's shoulder and said, "You're going to have her forever. What's another half hour?"

As the girls dragged Chloe toward the dance floor, Justin turned to Tank and Mike and said, "Guess it's just the three of us."

"Two of you," Mike said. "See that pretty lady at the end of the bar? I'm hoping she has something sweet to share."

Justin and Tank looked over and saw Sidney eating an ice cream sundae. Tank laughed. As Mike walked away, Justin said, "Dirty old man."

Justin and Tank joined their brothers at the table and got caught up in a conversation with Conroy. When Justin glanced at the dance floor to check on Chloe, she wasn't there. He pushed to his feet, scanning the room as he made his way to the dance floor. "Where's Chloe?" he asked the girls who were still dancing.

"She went to the ladies' room," Evie said.

Justin headed there and found Chloe at the end of the hall,

standing with her back to him and her phone pressed to her ear. She turned, and his gut pitched at the tears glistening in her eyes. "What's wrong?" he said as he closed the distance between them.

Chloe held up a shaky finger and said, "Okay, thank you again. I'll see you a week from Monday."

As she ended the call, Justin said, "What happened?"

"That was Darren."

"*Shit.*" He gritted his teeth, hands fisted. If he was trying to get Chloe to back off the charges, Justin would kill him.

"No, it's okay." She touched his arm and said, "He wanted to apologize."

"Apologize?" he asked warily.

"Yes. I was floored, too. He said he would have liked to do it in person but that nobody knew if I was coming back to work or not. Justin, he didn't have *any* idea about what Alan had been doing. He said he's horrified that his son would do the things he's accused of and that he was truly sorry for all I'd gone through. You should have heard him. He was sincere, and he sounded as broken as I've been feeling. He said he would understand if I never wanted to come back to LOCAL, but he hoped I would because the company and the residents would suffer greatly if I didn't."

Justin released a breath he hadn't realized he'd been holding. "Thank God. When I saw your tears..." He drew her into his arms, overwhelmed with relief. "I love you, babe."

"I love you, too."

"I'll still apologize to him. Don't worry."

"You don't have to." She drew back, her eyes clearer than they were just moments before. "Darren said if he were you, he would have done the same thing."

"Wow, that's unexpected."

"I know. I told you he was a gentleman."

"You did. This is great news, babe. How do you feel about it?"

"I feel good." She lifted her chin, and in a voice far more confident than he'd heard all week, she said, "I'm getting out of my own way, Justin. I'm going back to work. You were right. Alan shouldn't have the power to take away all the things I worked so hard for."

"Aw, baby. That makes me so happy." He lifted her into his arms and kissed her as he twirled her around.

Two of the Dark Knights' wives came out of the ladies' room and said, "Excuse us."

Justin set Chloe down, keeping his arms around her, and inched them forward until her back met the wall, making room for the women to walk by.

Desire rose in Chloe's eyes. "This feels like déjà vu."

"It sure does, sweet cheeks. I will never forget the last time I propositioned you by a bathroom in a bar. It was the night I decided I was done letting you stand in your own way."

"The night I should have done this." She grabbed him by the collar and crushed her mouth to his, kissing him with all the passion, and all the *greed*, of a woman in love.

His woman in love.

The music from the bar filtered in, and "Heartbeat" was playing. Justin took Chloe's hand and said, "They're playing your song. May I have this dance, heartbreaker?"

She stepped into his arms and said, "You can have this dance and every future dance for the rest of my life."

As they swayed to the music, she sighed contentedly and whispered, "We have no stars."

"No moonlight kisses," he whispered, holding her tighter.

"Guess those will have to come later," she said seductively. "What do you think, biker boy?"

He nuzzled against her neck, kissing her there. She made an appreciative sound and he whispered in her ear, "I think I've got the woman I adore"—he kissed her cheek—"the star of *all* my dirty fantasies"—he slid his tongue along the shell of her ear— "and the love of my life safe and happy in my arms." He brushed his lips overs hers, whispering, "And I can't wait to make you my wife."

Chapter Thirty-Three

AS THE SUN peeked over the horizon, Justin climbed off his bike in front of Preacher and Reba's house and headed around the side to the kitchen door. The last time Justin had walked into their house with a burden this heavy had been the first day he'd met them. So much had changed since then. Hell, so much had changed in the past few months. July had been a roller coaster, providing lessons in survival, hope, and love, and he and Chloe had come through it stronger than ever. August was a month of blessings. Chloe had received warm welcomes when she'd returned to work, and she'd since settled back in nicely. The Junior/Senior Program had become permanent, and the puppetry program was well under way. More of Alan's victims had come forward, and his attorney had convinced him to take a plea bargain, which kept his victims from having to appear in court. Alan Rogers was sentenced to twenty years behind bars, eligible for parole after sixteen. No punishment would be enough, in Justin's eyes, but he had a feeling Rogers would get his due in the slammer. Shadow had come home a few weeks ago, and he and Sampson rarely left each other's sides. The four of them had become the family Chloe had always dreamed of. They'd rolled happily into September with warm, full days and brisk, loving nights—and for Justin, a need to finally unburden the last of his chains to his past.

As he reached for the doorknob, it was Chloe's love that gave him the strength to walk through the door, though she wasn't aware of his plans or that he'd even left the house. She had been sleeping soundly with their furry boys when he'd snuck out at the crack of dawn to take care of business.

Preacher's dogs, Buster and Milo, greeted Justin with tails wagging. Reba stood beside the counter fixing coffee in her bathrobe. Preacher was dressed in jeans and a Dark Knights T-shirt, sitting at the table sipping a cup of coffee. It was strange not seeing Mike at that table. He'd moved into LOCAL a couple of weeks ago, and he was loving life there. He and Chloe had a standing dinner date on Wednesday evenings, and according to Mike, there was already a long line of women hoping for that seat. But even with all his grandfather's talk, Justin knew no woman would ever get close to his heart. How could they, when Hilda had taken so much of it with her?

"Morning, sweet boy," Reba said, smiling warmly as he loved up the dogs.

The curiosity and worry in her eyes tugged at Justin's heartstrings. He'd woken them up with his call before the sun had breached the horizon, and he'd asked if he could come over to talk. He kissed her cheek and said, "Hi, Mom. Sorry to get you up so early."

"It's okay, baby. You know we don't mind."

Preacher pushed to his feet, studying Justin's face. "Son," he said, embracing Justin. "I'm guessing you're not here to tell us Chloe's knocked up."

Justin chuckled. "She's not, but we're sure having fun practicing."

"Attaboy." Preacher clapped him on the back, and as they sat down at the table, he looked at Reba and said, "You owe me a back rub, babe."

"You made *bets*?" Justin shook his head.

"It was a win-win for me." Reba covered Preacher's hand with hers and said, "I'd either get a grandchild or my hands on this sexy man."

Preacher leaned over and kissed her, then whispered, "Love you, baby."

Justin looked at the man and woman who had taught him to love, to trust, and not to be afraid to speak the truth and knew he was finally ready to set himself free. "No babies just yet, although every time Chloe gets her hands on Desiree's little boy, she gets this look in her eyes..." Desiree had given birth to adorable Aaron the same night they'd celebrated the charges being dropped for Justin and Chloe's decision to go back to work at LOCAL.

"Ah, *the look*," Preacher said, eyeing Reba, a secret message passing between them. "I always loved that look."

"I'm fond of it, too, Preach," Justin said honestly. He looked forward to raising feisty, independent little ones with Chloe, but he was in no hurry to add to their crew just yet. Their four-legged boys were keeping them busy, and he and Chloe both loved the freedom of long Sunday rides and nights when the only thing keeping them awake was their insatiable desire.

"Is this about the rally, son?" Preacher held his gaze and said, "We know how hard this event is for you."

Emotions thickened Justin's throat. "It's about everything. The rally, who I am, what I've become, and who I want to be."

Reba put her other hand over Justin's, her eyes moving

between him and Preacher, finally landing on Justin as she said, "Whatever is weighing on you, sweetheart, we'll get through it together."

He turned his hand over and held hers. "I know, Mom. That's why I'm here. From the day I understood what it means to be a Wicked, I've always been honest with you. But there's one thing I've kept from you. I've never lied about it, but it feels like I did." Tears burned his eyes over that lie of omission as much as from the painful memories he was fighting to keep at bay. "My father lied to the police about my mother's death. I was home with her when she took those pills. I didn't know she was ending her life, but I was the one who found her." He told them everything he'd told Chloe, and when tears slid down his cheeks, Reba's fell, too. "I'm sorry I didn't tell you sooner. I kept telling myself it was in the past and I was over it. But with Chloe I realized I was only fooling myself, running from the thing that hurt me most." He told them about how Chloe had come up with the idea for the sculpture, focusing on the people who had been left behind and the support of those around them, rather than trying to change what could never be undone. "Chloe and I have been talking with Tasha Revere, and she's helped us see many things more clearly." Therapy had helped Chloe to tell Serena about the horrible ways she'd suffered as a young girl at the hands of their mother's boyfriends and the hands of the guy in the parking lot of the Salty Hog. Seeing how much weight that had lifted off Chloe's shoulders had helped Justin get to where he was today. "These past few weeks, as I was finishing the sculpture for the rally, I realized what I'd done wasn't fair to you, to Chloe, who knows the truth and has been keeping my secret, or to myself. I hope you can forgive me."

Reba looked at Preacher with tear-streaked cheeks; then he looked at Justin with sorrow and love in his eyes and said, "We hope you can forgive us, son. We've known about this since a month after you first came to us."

"You've known?" Justin sank back in the chair and dried his eyes, trying to process what he'd said. "How?"

Preacher's gaze never wavered from Justin's. "When you love someone, you want to know *all* of them, about the things, people, and events that made them who they are. The good, the bad, and everything in between. I went to see your father half a dozen times that first month after you moved in. I loved you, son. We loved you, and we needed to know what you'd gone through so we could be there for you. Your father told me what happened. I didn't know all of the details that you just shared with us, but I knew you were alone with her when it happened and that he'd lied about it to the authorities."

Justin couldn't believe they'd known, but he understood what Preacher had done because if he'd had the opportunity to face each of Chloe's attackers, he would have done it. "Why didn't you say something to me?"

"Because we didn't know if *you* remembered, and we were afraid that if you didn't, we'd cause more trauma for you," Reba said.

"We talked to a child psychologist," Preacher explained. "You had so much to overcome, we didn't want to unearth more ghosts. We felt confident that if you remembered, you would let us know in your own time. Remember, we had you talking with a therapist, and we relied on her to let us know if we should do anything differently."

"I talked to her about this. Did she tell you?" Justin asked.

Reba said, "No, honey. We weren't privy to anything you

said in those sessions. She just assured us that if she felt we should intervene, she would let us know."

"I don't know if we did the right thing or not, son, but we did the best we could by you." Preacher glanced at Reba with a sorrowful expression. Then he said, "And we'd understand if this changes things between us."

"You once told me that love was a powerful force. Too powerful to be outdone by reason. This changes everything," Justin said honestly. "For the better."

Reba's breath rushed from her lungs, carrying sounds of relief, and more tears sprang from her eyes as she went to him. He rose to his feet, taking her in his arms. Her tears wet his cheeks as she said, "We love you, sweetheart."

Preacher's strong arms circled them both, and Justin was swamped with love, gratitude, and relief.

"I have to come clean with you about something, son." Preacher put his arm around Reba as he said, "Your mom and I aren't perfect."

They laughed, and Justin said, "Maybe not for some folks, but you're perfect enough for me."

CHLOE AWOKE TO the dogs bounding off the blankets as Justin came through the front door. Sun shone through the glass walls of the cantilevered room overlooking the pond where they'd fallen asleep last night. Her gaze moved to the large piece of driftwood with inlaid candles from Artsea, the cute shop in Harborside. Justin had surprised her with it when she'd come home from her first day back at work. The piece was perfect for the room, and making love by candlelight had become one of her favorite things, right up there with dancing in the moonlight with her favorite person—the rugged bad boy who was closing the distance between them with a to-go coffee cup and a Blue Willow Bakery bag in his hands, and their four-legged boys by his side.

Justin crouched beside her and kissed her cheek. "Morning, beautiful."

"Hi," she said sleepily. "What time is it?"

"Early." The dogs nosed the bakery bag. "I brought you muffins and bagels."

"*Mm*. Special occasion?"

He kissed her neck and said, "Just stockpiling nooky points." He took her hand and said, "Come with me to my studio? I want to show you something."

"Do I *finally* get to see the sculpture, Mr. Mysterious?" Giddy excitement bubbled up inside her, and she popped up to her feet. He'd been working long hours in the studio, and the last couple of weeks, he hadn't allowed her to see the sculpture.

He led her to the front door, and with a coy smile, he said, "If you play your cards right."

"I kept you up *playing* all night long. That should count for something."

As she slipped her feet into a pair of flip-flops, he reached into the coat closet. He pulled out one of his zip-up sweatshirts and helped her put it on over her sleeping shorts and top. His eyes darkened as he said, "Your smart mouth does me in every time."

He took her in a toe-curling kiss.

Every time he talked about her mouth like that, she got as hot and bothered as if he'd touched her all over. Last night he'd said it as she was doing all sorts of delicious things to him. She'd amped up her efforts, and they'd both gone a little wild.

She heated with the memory as they headed down to the studio with Sampson and Shadow. The dogs ran around the studio sniffing everything. The sculpture for the rally sat on the floor in the middle of the room, covered with a sheet.

Chloe bounced on her toes. "I'm so excited to see it."

"As excited as you were when I had your name tattooed on a ribbon on my back?"

"*Yes!*" He'd added more than just her name. Tank had tattooed three dragonflies buzzing around the tree and one perched on the ribbon with her name on it.

"I couldn't have done this without you, babe. I hope you like it."

He whipped off the sheet, and the impact of the lifelike faces looking back at her took her breath away. Unlike his other artwork, there was nothing sad or broken about the piece. The faces were intricately carved and instantly recognizable. She walked around the gorgeous sculpture, taking in the nuances of his family's eyes, smiles, dimples, beards, and so many other small details, like the beauty mark beside Reba's left eye and Zeke's furrowed brow. He'd even captured Zander's playfulness in the laugh lines around his mouth. She ran her fingers along the deep, winding grooves he'd carved between and around the faces. She could feel the energy he'd hoped to convey.

"Justin, this is magnificent." Her gaze dropped to the base of hands cradling the pillar from which all of the faces and energy bloomed. The hands were just as recognizable as the faces—defined by tattoos, thick or narrow fingers, aging knuckles, the shape of their fingernails, rings, and the bracelets Madigan so often wore. Chloe walked slowly around it, admiring every detail. Her eyes caught on a familiar hand, one with a dragonfly engagement ring. She moved closer, unable to believe her eyes.

"*Justin…?* Why am I on here?"

He went to her, his gaze soft and loving. "This is the first year I've been able to face this event without feeling like I'm that lost little boy walking into my mother's bedroom again." He put his arms around her and said, "That's because of you, baby. You helped me realize that I can't change what she did, and I can't keep carrying the guilt of not saving her. Your idea of focusing on the people who helped pull me through was exactly what I needed to find closure. I went to see Preacher and Reba this morning, and I told them everything."

He told her that Preacher and Reba had already known because Preacher had gone to see his father in the first few weeks he'd moved in with them. Today Justin had filled in the blanks for them.

She knew that couldn't have been easy. "I would have gone with you."

"I know you would have, but I woke up before dawn with you cuddled against me and the pups sleeping near us, and I knew I had to get the last of my secrets out if I was going to give us everything I had moving forward. I needed to do it alone."

"I understand. But, Justin, you always give us everything you have, and then some."

"No, babe. I try to, but I've felt her ghost chaining me down. But now, because of you, this event will no longer throw me back to that awful morning. It will carry me forward, reminding me of all the good in the world and the strength love can bring."

"I don't know what to say. I love you so much. I'm just so

happy for you."

"You freed me, baby."

"We freed each other."

He kissed her softly and said, "Yeah, but now I'm ready for a ball and chain, sweet cheeks. How would you feel about a Christmas wedding?"

Her heart leapt. "The same way I'd feel if you said let's go to the courthouse on Monday and get married. I want to be your wife no matter when, where, or how we do it."

"There'll be no courthouse wedding for you, Ms. Mallery. I promised my girl that all her big days would be celebrations. You, my beautiful future wife, are going to get the white wedding you never dreamed of."

Tears dampened her eyes and she said, "That sounds perfect. Do I get a honeymoon that's a little bit wicked, too?"

"Baby, our honeymoon will last the rest of our lives." He brushed his lips over hers and said, "And there's nothing *little* about *your* Wicked."

A note from Melissa

I hope you enjoyed Justin and Chloe's loves story and meeting the Wicked family. Continue reading for information on the next Wicked novel as well as more Dark Knights and Bayside Summers novels, including one for each of Chloe's Bayside friends. You'll also find details on Daphne's love story, TEMPTED BY LOVE, the first book in the Steeles on Silver Island series.

Fall in love with Tank and Leah

When the person you blame for your grief is the only one who can save you from the pain... An emotionally gripping story of love, loss, and hope, with a rich and entrancing happily ever after.

Tank Wicked lost his sister and has since vowed to save everyone else in his path. He lives by the creed of the Dark Knights motorcycle club, sworn to protect and respect his community, and he selflessly saves lives as a volunteer firefighter. He treats the men and women who work for him at his tattoo shop like family. But life isn't a balance scale where good deeds negate bad things to come, and one foggy night life guts Tank once again. When a car careens over the side of a bridge and into a river, Tank springs into action, plunging into the water to rescue the passengers. Four people go into the river, but only three come out alive.

Leah Yates is just trying to make it through each day. When the man she blames for her grief becomes the only one who can pull her from the depths of despair, she discovers that even hope comes at a price. Maybe this time she won't have to face it alone.

Ready for more Dark Knights?

The Dark Knights at Peaceful Harbor novels are waiting for you at all book retailers, starting with TRU BLUE.

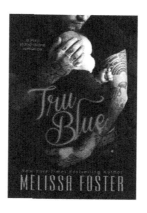

There's nothing Truman Gritt won't do to protect his family— Including spending years in jail for a crime he didn't commit. When he's finally released, the life he knew is turned upside down by his mother's overdose, and Truman steps in to raise the children she's left behind. Truman's hard, he's secretive, and he's trying to save a brother who's even more broken than he is. He's never needed help in his life, and when beautiful Gemma Wright tries to step in, he's less than accepting. But Gemma has a way of slithering into people's lives and eventually she pierces through his ironclad heart. When Truman's dark past collides with his future, his loyalties will be tested, and he'll be faced with his toughest decision yet.

Remember to download your Whiskey/Wicked family tree here:

www.MelissaFoster.com/reader-goodies

Fall in love on the sandy shores of Cape Cod Bay

Follow Chloe's sister, Serena, and each of their friends to their happily ever afters in the BAYSIDE SUMMERS series, starting with Bayside Desires.

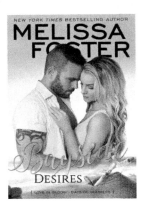

Desiree Cleary is tricked into spending the summer with her badass half sister and a misbehaving dog. What could go wrong? Did I mention the sparks flying every time she sees her hunky, pushy neighbor, Rick Savage? Yeah, there's that…

Fall in love with the Steeles on Silver Island!

Settle in on the sandy shores of Silver Island, home to coffee shops, boat races, midnight rendezvous, and the sexy, sharp-witted Steeles.

Enjoy heart-meltingly beautiful and toe-curlingly sexy romance in *Tempted by Love*, an emotionally riveting story about a man who has lost it all and carries a torturous secret, a divorced single mother who has everything to lose, and the little girl who helps them heal.

Love Melissa's Writing?

Discover more of the magic behind *New York Times* bestselling and award-winning author Melissa Foster. The Wickeds are just one of the many family series in the Love in Bloom big-family romance collection, featuring fiercely loyal heroes, sassy, sexy heroines, and stories that go above and beyond your expectations! See the collection here:
www.MelissaFoster.com/love-bloom-series

Free first-in-series ebooks, downloadable series checklists, reading orders, and more can be found on Melissa's Reader Goodies page.

More Books By Melissa Foster

LOVE IN BLOOM SERIES

SNOW SISTERS
Sisters in Love
Sisters in Bloom
Sisters in White

THE BRADENS at Weston
Lovers at Heart, Reimagined
Destined for Love
Friendship on Fire
Sea of Love
Bursting with Love
Hearts at Play

THE BRADENS at Trusty
Taken by Love
Fated for Love
Romancing My Love
Flirting with Love
Dreaming of Love
Crashing into Love

THE BRADENS at Peaceful Harbor
Healed by Love
Surrender My Love
River of Love
Crushing on Love
Whisper of Love
Thrill of Love

THE BRADENS & MONTGOMERYS at Pleasant Hill – Oak Falls
Embracing Her Heart
Anything For Love

Trails of Love
Wild, Crazy Hearts
Making You Mine
Searching For Love
Hot For Love

THE BRADEN NOVELLAS
Promise My Love
Our New Love
Daring Her Love
Story of Love
Love at Last
A Very Braden Christmas

THE REMINGTONS
Game of Love
Stroke of Love
Flames of Love
Slope of Love
Read, Write, Love
Touched by Love

SEASIDE SUMMERS
Seaside Dreams
Seaside Hearts
Seaside Sunsets
Seaside Secrets
Seaside Nights
Seaside Embrace
Seaside Lovers
Seaside Whispers
Seaside Serenade

BAYSIDE SUMMERS
Bayside Desires
Bayside Passions
Bayside Heat

Bayside Escape
Bayside Romance
Bayside Fantasies

THE STEELES AT SILVER ISLAND
Tempted by Love

THE RYDERS
Seized by Love
Claimed by Love
Chased by Love
Rescued by Love
Swept Into Love

THE WHISKEYS: DARK KNIGHTS AT PEACEFUL HARBOR
Tru Blue
Truly, Madly, Whiskey
Driving Whiskey Wild
Wicked Whiskey Love
Mad About Moon
Taming My Whiskey
The Gritty Truth

SUGAR LAKE
The Real Thing
Only for You
Love Like Ours
Finding My Girl

HARMONY POINTE
Call Her Mine
This is Love
She Loves Me

THE WICKEDS: DARK KNIGHTS AT BAYSIDE
A Little Bit Wicked
The Wicked Aftermath

WILD BOYS AFTER DARK
Logan
Heath
Jackson
Cooper

BAD BOYS AFTER DARK
Mick
Dylan
Carson
Brett

HARBORSIDE NIGHTS SERIES
Includes characters from the Love in Bloom series
Catching Cassidy
Discovering Delilah
Tempting Tristan

More Books by Melissa
Chasing Amanda (mystery/suspense)
Come Back to Me (mystery/suspense)
Have No Shame (historical fiction/romance)
Love, Lies & Mystery (3-book bundle)
Megan's Way (literary fiction)
Traces of Kara (psychological thriller)
Where Petals Fall (suspense)

Acknowledgments

I hope you enjoyed Justin and Chloe's story as much as I loved writing it. I'm looking forward to writing love stories for all of our Wicked world family and friends! In the meantime, I hope you'll read my original Dark Knights series, The Whiskeys: Dark Knights at Peaceful Harbor. If you want to know more about Justin and Chloe's friends, pick up the Bayside Summers series, and then get ready for The Steeles at Silver Island, featuring Chloe's friend Daphne.

If this is your first introduction to my work, please note that every Melissa Foster book can be read as a stand-alone novel, and characters appear in other family series, so you never miss out on an engagement, wedding, or birth. You can find information about the Love in Bloom series and my books here: www.MelissaFoster.com/melissas-books

I offer several free first-in-series ebooks. You can find them here: www.MelissaFoster.com/LIBFree

I chat with fans often in my fan club on Facebook. If you haven't joined my fan club yet, please do!
www.facebook.com/groups/MelissaFosterFans

Follow my author page on Facebook for fun giveaways and updates of what's going on in our fictional boyfriends' worlds.
www.Facebook.com/MelissaFosterAuthor

If you prefer sweet romance, with no explicit scenes or graphic language, please try the Sweet with Heat series written under my pen name, Addison Cole. You'll find the same great love stories with toned-down heat levels.

Thank you to my awesome editorial team, Kristen Weber and Penina Lopez, and my meticulous proofreaders, Elaini Caruso, Juliette Hill, Lynn Mullan, Marlene Engle, and Justinn Harrison. Last but never least, a huge thank-you to my family for their patience, support, and inspiration.

Meet Melissa

Melissa Foster is a *New York Times* and *USA Today* bestselling and award-winning author. Her books have been recommended by *USA Today's* book blog, *Hagerstown* magazine, *The Patriot*, and several other print venues. Melissa has painted and donated several murals to the Hospital for Sick Children in Washington, DC.

Visit Melissa on her website or chat with her on social media. Melissa enjoys discussing her books with book clubs and reader groups and welcomes an invitation to your event. Melissa's books are available through most online retailers in paperback and digital formats.

Melissa also writes sweet romance under the pen name Addison Cole.

www.MelissaFoster.com
Free Reader Goodies: www.MelissaFoster.com/Reader-Goodies

Printed in Great Britain
by Amazon

27217508R00280